CROWFOOT VALLEY

A Mystery Novel

BY LARRY INCOLLINGO

Reunion Books
3949 S. Knightridge Road
Bloomington, IN 47401-9747

ISBN 0-9715477-0-X

Cover by Randy Robertson

Printed by World Arts, Inc.
156 E. Franklin St.
Spencer, IN 47460

My Thanks To

MARION & LINDA

AUTHOR'S NOTE

The places and characters in this book exist only in the imagination of the author. To my knowledge there is no Moses City, Spiceland County, or Crowfoot Valley. Although I have in some cases borrowed from actual news events, those in this book could have happened anywhere. In this book, however, they come together only as fictional convenience. Any resemblance to actual happenings or to persons living or deceased is pure coincidence.

— The Author

As fish are caught in a cruel net,
Or birds are taken in a snare,
So men are caught by evil times
That fall unexpectedly on them.

—Ecc. 12:9

CAST OF FICTITIOUS CHARACTERS

Crestman Fielding, Spiceland County businessman

Winona, his wife

Roger and **James Fielding**, their sons

Mamie Verden, a Fielding neighbor

Cramer and **Craddick Fielding**, brothers to Crestman

Ira and **Irwin Brown**, Moses City undertakers and county coroners

Link Trueblood, Anthony Galiton, state troopers

Capt. Earl Martin, chief of state police crime lab

Lt. Francis Patrick (Frank) Conway, Moses City state police barracks commander

Sgt. Harley Oaks, Lt. Bradley Schultz, state police detectives

Capt. Timothy Melton, district chief of detectives, state police

William R. Carey, Colonel, state police

Dr. Hamilton Brent, pathologist, Glenview Hospital, Moses City

Dr. John Flood, state pathologist, Community Hospital, Mount Carmel

J.J. Overton, president, Bankmens Life Insurance Co.

Paragon Mutual, Unity Life, National States Underwriters, conjoining insurers

Peter J. Cayne, *The Intelligencer* police reporter

Ames Shaw, Winona's attorney

Hector Jamiel, insurance company attorney

Albert Fielding, Spiceland County prosecuting attorney

Jacob Mosco, Dogwood County judge

Harrison Alexander, Spiceland County judge

THE FIRE

1

News bulletins on the television and radio that night announcing the self-inflicted shotgun death of Crestman Fielding at his fashionable home that late autumn Thursday afternoon left Moses City and Spiceland County electric with surprise.

Until well into the night, lights shone in houses normally darkened at that late hour while their adult occupants reflected on the tragedy. Stricken as they were, they pondered the reasons a man of means and background such as Crestman Fielding might commit suicide.

Why would anyone—anyone at all—who is in her or his right mind choose to die and enter the black and uncertain unknown from which no mere mortal, other than in myth and legend, has ever returned?

Why would a visibly healthy man of respected community stature, seemingly liked by his peers—a man with a devoted wife, two loving sons, a man who generally was thought to be, at worst, comfortably situated and surely and wisely in control of his destiny—want to put a loaded shotgun to his chin and pull the trigger?

What could possibly have led such a man to destroy himself as though he were some diseased and dangerous thing that was best eradicated from this beautiful world?

And the fire! What about the mysterious fire that had reduced to ashes and twisted metal the stage for his macabre last act and in the process burned his body beyond recognition? How could it have happened? Why?

The news that the fire had been so intense that Crestman Fielding's hands and feet were burned to ashes appalled and horrified almost everyone. It was all so shocking, so strange and confusing. So...so brutal. So...so bloody. So repugnant and odious.

It was not entirely unknown that Crestman Fielding in recent months had suffered a staggering financial blow. There had been talk of a crumbled real estate venture, none of which was too clear to the public at large except that "An act of the Almighty" had befallen it.

But it was the accepted attitude of those who knew him, those who had been aware of his problem, that everyone had troubles, and sooner or later they found the means to overcome them, and Crestman Fielding— especially Crestman Fielding—considering the kind of man he was believed to have been, could have and would have eventually solved his.

It also had become increasingly obvious to a few Moses City businessmen that Fielding, known as a strictly social drinker for most of his adult life, had in recent months been imbibing regularly. The sour smell of whiskey, and later that of cheap wine, had been frequently and noticeably thick about him. Yet few believed that his financial loss would have driven a man of his respectability and integrity to take his own life. To drink? Obviously. It sometimes happened to the best of people. To blow his brains out? Some people, maybe. But Crestman Fielding? Never.

It was no secret that Fielding Mill, the limestone fabricating plant that once had kept the Fielding family modestly affluent, had been shut down for two years, ever since the recession in the building trade.

It was some months after it closed that Fielding had attempted to launch his real estate project. Judging from his and his family's lifestyle it had been, until the disastrous flash flood, an undertaking that suggested handsome rewards, much like Fielding Mill had done at its peak operation.

Then, too, on the heels of that calamity, there had been a brightening veneer of talk that Fielding Mill would reopen. The suggestion of a new building stone contract, of course all speculative, was nonetheless encouraging and stimulating. On the surface at least, where a man's public life is lived, Fielding's future seemed to the people of Moses City and Spiceland County to be well in hand. Now, suddenly, unexpectedly, he was reported dead by his own hand.

"His body," according to the news on television and radio that night, "was partially incinerated, leaving him faceless and unrecognizable."

2

Crestman Fielding and his wife Winona, and their two sons, Roger and James, were generally believed to have lived in comfort in a handsome home in Spiceland County, about five miles east of Moses City. Except for certain fraternal and business functions, Crestman and Winona—she more than he—were considered socially reserved. Yet, they appeared to occasionally enjoy being among other people and they seemed to take pleasure from the good things with which they had surrounded themselves.

There were latent rumors about Fielding having been a womanizer when as a handsome young man he had served two terms as Spiceland County sheriff. True or false, Winona had insulated herself from such talk by ignoring any and all whisperings and insinuations. Her husband's years as sheriff held no unpleasant memories for her and at this time had been put well behind her. His subsequent good fortune, especially after his acquisition of Fielding Mill, had made her life with him pleasant, satisfactory, fulfilling. And, except for the health and well-being of her children, she sought little more than that.

The Fieldings lived in a spacious well furnished home. She drove a new automobile, and ever since they had been old enough to legally drive, both sons had been provided with late model cars for their personal use. The family as a whole seemed to lack little. In the view of many city and county residents, the Fieldings were "well off."

In truth, however, in the months since the beginning of the economic recession and the subsequent closing of Fielding Mill, the family's lifestyle had become a visible departure from that of previous days. It improved somewhat when Fielding, seeking to save himself from total financial collapse, devised a real estate venture which, on paper at least, gave him the appearance of success and wealth. He invested in that enterprise what savings and assets that remained to him, including thousands of dollars borrowed against all of the Fielding properties. When disaster struck he was left without funds and teetering on the brink of total ruin. His eldest son, Roger, who worked closely with his father on that project, had suffered a similar fate.

Roger subsequently went in search of other means of earning a livelihood for himself and his beautiful wife, Penni. The elder Fielding, by then fifty-three and apparently lacking the resilience of earlier days, had been hopelessly discouraged. He went in search of relief to escape from his problems. The refuge he found was not in the application of his considerable but by then diffused ability, but in the easy availability of drink.

Crestman Fielding earlier had tried a different route, a contrived deception. In confidence he had let it become known among a few influential friends that Fielding Mill would be given new life. It would be reopened, and it would share, he boasted, with other area stone mills—larger firms than Fielding Mill that had survived the erraticisms of the recession—in the fabrication of facing limestone for a magnificent cathedral already more than fifty years under construction in the nation's capital. Participation in the construction of that structure by Fielding Mill was assured, he lied, subject to the help of certain unidentified persons in high places. His statements had a stirring, believable ring in that uncertain time and they easily found anxious ears. After all, it was known that in earlier days Fielding Mill had indeed fabricated some pieces of limestone for the cathedral. Supported by that memory the lie easily survived its unfounded beginnings.

Since Fielding was a 33rd Degree Mason—one of an esteemed few in Moses City and Spiceland County—he had little trouble selling the lie to trusting lodge brothers of financial means, at home and around the state. Ultimately, the falsehood became known for what it was, and Fielding sought to hide from his shame in extended solitude and continuing drink.

In time, depressed, dispirited and broke, he was reduced to writing worthless checks to buy himself the bottled courage needed to sustain him. As circumstances worsened, he wrote more phony checks; but these were wisely confined to amounts only large enough to purchase the cheapest bottle of wine his increasing daily need required. Of course, none of the checks were good, but they were accepted by sympathetic merchants, some of whom were lodge brothers, despite the suspicion those checks might never be made good.

In the meantime, trusting Winona was unaware of the full extent of her husband's troubles. There was an innate, secret side to Fielding that seemed to forbid him to share his innermost self with anyone, not even his wife. Being long aware of this she intuitively knew there was something wrong, and that it was serious, but she also knew that he had been through difficult times before and happily, always before he had recovered. She had an unshakable faith in his competence to do so again. However quietly and secretly he might choose to go about it, she was unquestioningly steadfast in her belief that he would survive. Fortune, she was confident, would again befriend him, perhaps to reopen Fielding Mill, or possibly to be rescued by one of his many wealthy friends. Somehow he would find some other legal, painless means of saving himself and his family. Winona believed quietly and unwaveringly that what was happening was only temporary. She believed that the good life, as her family had once known it, would one day be resumed and all of what currently was happening would be remembered only as a bad dream.

Such were the thoughts that filled Winona's mind as she made plans to drive into Moses City the Thursday afternoon of her husband's unexpected death. During the drive there she managed to put them aside. She had left her husband on a beautiful Indian summer day in the company of their eldest son in the nicely groomed expanse of front yard of the Fielding home, and she was comfortable with the sight they presented together. They looked like two old friends; her husband standing with a foot on a lower fence rail while her son, arms folded over his chest, stood facing his father as they talked. It was a warm familial sight. At the same time it also occurred to her that it was the second time that her eldest son had visited with his father that day, but she thought nothing of that. It was not the first time Roger had come to speak with his father more than once in a single day. Those two had not only been that close, they also had been a business team.

All the same, it had recently become apparent to Winona that something clouded and sinister had come between her husband and their eldest son. It was evident in what seemed to her a seething, controlled anger on Roger's part, tempered by a new and unusual silence and aversion on the part of her husband.

Innocently believing it to be a consequence of the family's worsening financial situation, Winona asked no questions, pried for no answers. Born and reared in farm life, she knew from old that men had their silent way of facing and overcoming adversity. She needed only to be patient and wait, she told herself, and all would be well again. She assured herself that as a family, theirs had been a good life—money, home, cars, comfort—and that one day it would all come back. It would be as it had been before with her husband and their eldest son close and convivial. Winona may not have been totally content with that but she remained quietly expectant and patient.

3

From the time he was a child, Roger Fielding had practically lived at his father's side. Wanting always to be near him as a boy and later as a young man, he tried to be of help to him in almost every need at almost every opportunity. The boy's love for his father bordered on worship, and the father returned that love in kind.

During summer school vacations, Roger enjoyed working with his father at Fielding Mill. After he graduated from Moses City High School his parents had hoped he would enter nearby Brackenridge University at New Washington. Despite their wishes, and ignoring the expanding war in Vietnam, which left him clearly more vulnerable to the military draft, Roger insisted that he continue at his father's side. He became his father's shadow, his father's son in almost every way and his confidant—to a point.

On that Thursday afternoon when Winona Fielding had seen them together for the last time, she could not have imagined what would happen later that day, nor could she have known that Roger then was speaking to his father in strong vibrant tones. Appearing haggard and drawn as he listened to his eldest son, Crestman Fielding, it was later alleged by Roger, at precisely the time that his mother was driving away from the Fielding home, had threatened to take his own life.

"There's no point in going on," he had sighed heavily in what Roger later described as helpless dejection and despair. "Everybody would be better off if I blew my brains out."

"That won't solve anything," Roger later told authorities he had quickly replied, and added, "Things will work out. You'll get over this. There's no need to do anything drastic. Just cool it."

In spite of those words, which were as encouraging as he could make them, Roger, at the time, could not help but wonder how the problems facing his father, and the Fielding family, would in fact be solved. A solution escaped him and had been escaping him.

"You'll find a way to make it, somehow." Roger admitted that he had tried to sound more encouraging than he really felt before he and his father had parted that day. "You'll come out of this," he said he had repeated to his father. "Don't do anything foolish."

4

Later that Thursday afternoon Mamie Verden, at her home a quarter mile from where the Fieldings lived, glanced out her kitchen window and saw puffs of smoke rising from the direction of the Fielding property. Earlier that day she had driven past there on her way to the post office and grocery store in Moses City and had seen Fielding raking leaves in the front yard. Now she assumed he was burning them.

As she continued moving about her kitchen she remembered, as she always did after having passed there, how pleasing a sight the Fielding house and yard had presented to her. Unless a passerby made it a point to look, it could easily escape attention. Like so many houses in that elegantly rustic section of Spiceland County, the Fielding house sat a considerable distance from the road. An abundance of trees gave the home an aura of charm and privacy.

Mamie Verden remembered how impressed she had been the first time she walked past there. With almost breathless interest she had stopped to study the spreading red and purple phlox-lined gravel driveway that circled in front of the handsome green-shuttered white house, and the thickly foliaged maple, poplar, oak, redbud and dogwood trees. Obvious to her then, and each time she passed afterwards, was the proud coat of arms suspended from a locust signpost at the entrance to the drive. The top of the escutcheon revealed a knight's helmet and shield and, below that, appearing vicious and threatening, a lion rampant charged a colorful but indistinguishable field. Across the lower portion of the escutcheon, black letters on a horizontal gold banner announced in Latin the motto "Dum Spiro, Spero". She had heard from someone that the strange looking words loosely translated into English meant "While I breathe, I hope." Although she could not be sure of this information, that interpretation of the motto sounded good to her, and it satisfied her, for it added a further touch of mystique to her fascination with the Fielding place.

This was November and the naked trees had done less than their usual summer effort to conceal the Fielding house or the man raking fallen leaves when she had passed there earlier that day. In the solitude of her own home now she was aware of the stillness around her. Except for the sound of the wind or that of a distant barking dog, the silence of rural Spiceland County at that time of day had always been soothing and pleasing to her. She frequently reminded herself that she loved living there, that in a very real sense it was an earthly heaven of beautiful homes in a setting of marvelous simplicity; a soundless, primitive retreat.

It was at that moment that Mamie Verden approached her kitchen window for another look at the splendor that surrounded her. She was momentarily stunned by the sight of gigantic clouds of black smoke rising from the direction of the Fielding house. This was more than a simple burning of leaves, she told herself. She immediately dialed the number for the Harrison Township Volunteer Fire Department.

"It was only some puffs of white smoke a few minutes ago," she spoke excitedly into the telephone to a Spiceland County sheriff's dispatcher. "I thought they were only burning leaves over there."

5

When fire fighters and police arrived, they found the big barn behind the Fielding home engulfed in flames roaring hopelessly out of control. Limited in what they could do, firefighters directed their efforts toward confining the inferno to the structure that had served the Fielding family as both barn and second garage.

For the longest time, it seemed, black smoke billowed upward toward the late autumn sky and was seen for miles around. A steady stream of curious spectators arrived, some parking their vehicles along the county road to watch as the fury of the raging flames consumed the large farm structure. Others allowed themselves only a frightened, inquisitive view as they inched their way through the gathering traffic passing the Fielding property.

Weakened and consumed at last, the burning building in the dusk of early evening fell in on itself with a loud whoosh. This was immediately followed by a cloud of roiling smoke and swirling sparks that belched high into the darkening sky, driving firemen back in fear for their lives. When the fiery destruction had been soaked with enough water to make it safely approachable, firefighters, some carrying high-powered lamps, some carrying pike poles, attacked the mountain of charred rubble. In the area used as a garage they found the remains of a car and a pickup truck. In what had once been a tack room at one end of the barn, they were shocked to find what was left of a human body.

It was a hideous sight. The firemen who discovered it, and those firemen drawn by morbid curiosity to see it for themselves, turned away from the dead thing, nauseated and light-headed. The hands and feet were missing, apparently burned off. The torso, bloated and split like an oversized, overcooked hot dog partially destroyed by intense heat on an outside charcoal grill, was blackened and yellowed and oozing. There was no face, only a large, gory, seared wound where it should have been. A shotgun, its wood stock burned away, lay across what remained of the chest. A sickening stench, believed to be that of burned human flesh, hung over the scene.

Quietly, soberly, firemen, their hands cupping their mouths and noses, retreated from the smoking, stinking debris that had been the Fielding barn. They stood at a distance, uncertainly in groups, speaking in subdued almost reverent sounds, awaiting the arrival of the Spiceland County coroner who by then had been summoned by radio. A few stood around a man in uniform, the sheriff of Spiceland County, Cramer Fielding. He was Crestman Fielding's brother, and he stood stoically silent in the noticeable cool of early evening.

6

The last of a huge red ball of autumn sun was sinking into the earth beyond distant Moses City when a long black station wagon, a portable revolving red bubble-light on its roof, appeared on the county road. Carrying Spiceland County Coroner Ira Brown and his son, deputy coroner Irwin Brown, it turned into the Fielding driveway.

In the gathering twilight the Browns, unhurried professional men who made up the Moses City firm of Brown & Brown Funeral Home, conferred at length with Spiceland County Sheriff Cramer Fielding. Then, accompanied by firemen carrying lamps, the trio of county officials slowly and carefully made their way through the soggy, hot, smoldering rubble to the charred, reeking thing lying in the ashes.

There appeared to be no question about the identity of the body. Firemen had already concluded it was that of Crestman Fielding. With a single horrified glance Ira Brown confirmed that conclusion, as did his son the deputy coroner. Cramer Fielding, sick with the need to turn away from what was revealed in the light of firemen's lamps, concurred. The body could be none other than that of his brother, Crestman.

Identification complete, the coroner and his son retained their professional poise as they took their time, quietly, painstakingly, working their hands into large black neoprene gauntlets. Averting their eyes as much as they could from the remains lying at their feet and still complete their unpleasant task, they lifted the loathsome, repulsive cadaver—all that was left of the body identified as that of Crestman Fielding—into a black body bag and zipped it shut.

With the ghastly thing finally out of sight the volume of firemen's voices, until then subdued and tentative, increased perceptibly. Words and sentences again becoming audible, intelligible, positive. With the dead thing in the body bag and out of sight, what had been an almost reverent yet distressing hush had turned to the sound of relieved activity. Some firemen had even hurried to assist the Browns who were carrying the body bag toward the rear of the black station wagon.

Father and son removed their soiled gauntlets and, after tossing them onto the body bag, they turned to the sheriff, by then speaking with newly arrived state trooper Link Trueblood.

"I knew he was in trouble, Cramer, but I didn't think it was this bad," Ira Brown said solicitously, speaking to the sheriff who now was standing quietly with Trueblood. "I've known Crestman all of his life. I never dreamed he'd do a thing like this."

Cramer Fielding made no reply. His state police companion also was without comment.

In the darkening silence a fireman appeared and reached a closed fist toward Trueblood.

"What is it?" Trueblood asked.

"Looks like a ring," replied the fireman. "It was where we found the body."

The state policeman extended a hand and the fireman placed the ring on the trooper's palm then lifted his lamp to illuminate it.

While shoulders hunched and heads leaned in his direction, Trueblood brushed the ring with thumb and forefinger then again placed it in his open hand. Clearly bearing a 33rd Degree Masonic emblem with diamond insets, the ring appeared unscathed.

"It's Crestman's all right," Ira Brown declared as he reached toward Trueblood's hand and with his own hand moved the trooper's upturned palm closer to himself and the fireman's lamp. "Yep," he continued, "I've seen this ring on Crestman's finger dozens of times. It was like a part of him. He was proud of it. There's an inscription inside." He raised his eyes in petition to those of the trooper's. "You've got younger eyes than mine, Link. See if you can make it out."

Trueblood raised the ring nearer to his own eyes and with the aid of the fireman's lamp read aloud the initials C. F. as they appeared to him inside the thick band.

Ira Brown then turned to the fireman who found the ring. "There ought to be a wedding band in there too," he said.

As he spoke, a car, its headlights on high beam, turned off the county blacktop and slid to a stop in the early darkness of the Fielding driveway. The driver and passenger doors swung outward. Two persons hurried up the drive. Vague and obscure in the glare of the car's headlights which had been left on, the two forms moved deliberately around parked emergency vehicles toward the group of officials gathered in ghostly illumination on the fringe of the glow cast by headlights, firemen's lamps and the whirling and flashing red and blue emergency lights. When the new arrivals were near enough that their identities could be discerned, Ira Brown recognized Winona Fielding and her youngest son, James. The coroner hurried solicitously to the woman's side.

"What's happened?" she demanded, her voice high-pitched, shaken and sharp.

"There's been an accident," the coroner said sooth-ingly as he took her arm. "Let's walk up to the house, Winona."

Gentle as he was, Winona shook off his hand as though it had seared her flesh.

"What's happened?" she shrieked at him.

"It's Crestman," Ira Brown said softly. "He's dead."

Winona collapsed.

As emergency medical technicians rushed to assist Winona, another vehicle ground to a halt in the drive-way. Roger Fielding, unaware of his mother lying on the ground, alighted and hurried to where his uncle stood with Trueblood and asked what had happened.

"He said he was going to do it," Roger exclaimed loudly when he was told. "He said he was going to do it," he repeated. Then seeing his mother where she lay still unconscious on the ground he rushed to her side.

Late that night Roger Fielding sat over coffee in the kitchen of their home with his pretty wife Penni.

"He said he was going to do it," Roger reiterated for what must have been the tenth time since being told that his father had taken his own life. He shook his head from side to side as he spoke. "He just put a shotgun to his face and pulled the trigger, Penni. My God, I just can't believe he did it, that he had the nerve to do it."

7

A father-son firm, Brown & Brown Funeral Home, occupied a spreading turn of the century two story house situated almost in the heart of Moses City. Ira Brown had inherited the firm from his father, Isaiah, who founded the mortuary there during the waning days of the horse and buggy era. Ira Brown's only son, Irwin, had later joined his father in the family enterprise.

Paired as they were as morticians, they also were similarly teamed as political office holders; Spiceland County coroner and deputy coroner. When the father held the office of county coroner, the son acted as his assistant, or deputy. When the son held the office the father became his deputy. It was an excellent arrangement, legal and reasonably profitable and, given the nature of the duties binding upon those holding such positions, quite acceptable to an unchallenging constituency.

First and last, however, the Browns earned their livelihood and reputation as morticians. One of two such concerns in Moses City, the Brown & Brown Funeral Home was the older and, according to public opinion, the more popular. Father and son were well known to be sincere, understanding men, always gracious in the extension of their services and assistance to Moses City and Spiceland County families in time of bereavement. Thus it was that in her sudden loss Winona Fielding, the widow of Crestman Fielding, was spared the sight of her dead husband. She was kindly protected from viewing his charred remains by the elder Brown who, in exercising the best of intentions, bypassed her in the identification process.

In his paternal kindness Ira Brown also excluded Winona's sons from that legally required procedure. Instead, Cramer Fielding, although for many years at odds with his late brother and family, was importuned by the coroner to act as family representative in that solemn ritual of identifying a dead body, no matter how unpleasant the task.

The sheriff's viewing of the remains in the preparation room at the funeral home late that night was therefore brief, cursory, hurried. Having already identified the body at the scene of the fatal fire earlier that evening, the sheriff was anxious to see an end to a long and disconcerting day and his role in the matter of the footless, handless, faceless thing that once had been his brother. The dead man, he advised the coroner, was indeed his brother Crestman. Obviously relieved, the sheriff then made a hasty departure from the funeral home.

The door had hardly closed behind him when Ira Brown telephoned Glenview Hospital's pathologist Hamilton Brent at his Moses City home to make arrangements for an autopsy on the body the following morning, which was Friday.

As father and son were preparing to leave the mortuary for Glenview Hospital the next day, state troopers Link Trueblood and Anthony Galiton arrived at the mortuary. "We're going out to the scene of the fire, if either of you would like to come along," Trueblood informed the morticians.

"Any particular reason?" the elder Brown asked.

"We're just going to look around," the policeman replied. "Maybe find Fielding's wedding band. You're welcome to come along."

Ira Brown shook his head negatively.

Trueblood nodded. "We'll stop back later."

After the two troopers had left, Irwin Brown asked his father why he hadn't told them that they were just then preparing to leave for the morgue at Glenview Hospital with the remains of the dead man.

"No particular reason," Ira Brown replied. "This is standard procedure for a suicide; they know that." Then as an afterthought he added, "I'll tell them later, if there's anything to tell."

At the hospital morgue father and son watched as Dr. Brent made a thorough but speedy examination of the cadaver. He concluded that while the severity of damage to the remains made identification virtually impossible, it was his opinion that the dead man did not die of a shotgun blast.

"We'll have to make some lab tests to be sure," he told the Browns. "But," he indicated with a gloved hand the extensive damage where the dead man's face should have been, "there is no doubt he was shot. Nevertheless, I'm sure the lab work will show that this man died of a lethal amount of carbon monoxide. As a matter of fact, I'd bet on it."

The Browns listened intently as Dr. Brent speculated into the small overhead microphone that carried his words to a voice recorder.

"It is possible," he continued, "that the shotgun might have been held in such a manner that the force of the blast struck the victim's face at an angle. Perhaps from the side, or from below the chin, scattering pieces of his face along with the devastating lead pellets from the shot casing. Although the shotgun blast failed to do what it is presumed to have done," he looked directly at the Browns as he spoke into the little microphone, "carbon monoxide, apparently from the inferno that had raged around the wounded man, eventually did."

Brent also believed that since the cadaver was toothless, the shotgun blast, which had demolished the chin and jaw, may have also destroyed the teeth.

"However," he advised the Browns as he continued speaking into the small microphone, and would later commit his findings to a written report, "there is too much damage to the mouth cavity to make a determination of any consequence about its prior condition."

As they listened and watched, father and son also witnessed the pathologist recover with a long tweezers a small piece of fabric from the left underarm cavity of the cadaver. Until laboratory tests could be completed Brent had declined to say more.

Meanwhile, at the scene of the disastrous fire at the Fielding home, state troopers Trueblood and Galiton made their way through the still smouldering ruins of the garage to where the body was found. Probing carefully through the ashes they found the tiny remains of what they thought was plaid fabric, perhaps, they guessed, from a plaid shirt. The little pieces of cloth, they surmised, had somehow been protected from the fire by the body that lay on them.

They also found a tiny piece of what appeared to be corded material, what might have been left of trousers, they thought, and what they believed to be a twisted belt buckle, a gnarled piece of plastic they thought might have been eyeglasses, and a blackened pencil clip. A half hour later they both expressed surprise when Galiton, who was probing with a long stick, turned up what appeared to be a piece of a jawbone—devoid of teeth.

"What do you think?" he asked Trueblood.

"Bag it," Trueblood said. "Let the lab figure it out."

The troopers carried small transparent locking plastic evidence bags, two of which already contained the fragments of cloth and their other findings. Galiton placed their newest find inside a third bag and pinched it shut.

"Let's try to find that wedding ring and some shot," he gritted as he slapped his hands one against the other in glancing blows as though to wipe from them something unclean.

"We'll have a hell of a time trying to find any shot in this mess," Trueblood growled. "That was a sixteen gauge, and unless he used buckshot, which I doubt very much, that stuff is gone."

When the troopers were unable after a brief search to find the ring or any lead pellets, Galiton suggested they bag all of the charred rubble on which the body had lain to also send to the state police laboratory at headquarters in Mount Carmel. He walked to his cruiser and returned with two medium sized white plastic kitchen-type trash bags. While Trueblood held each bag open in its turn, Galiton, his hands now protected by large, red neoprene gloves, carefully scooped into them the blackened rubble that might have been under and a couple of feet around the dead man.

It was nearing twilight when they returned to the funeral home. There they learned that the Browns had taken the victim of the fire to the hospital morgue and they listened quietly while the two morticians apprised them of Dr. Brent's autopsy. The troopers then drove to the state police barracks in Moses City where Galiton telephoned Captain Earl Martin, head of the state police crime laboratory at headquarters in Mount Carmel. Martin, a twenty-year police veteran, was preparing to leave his office for the day when his telephone rang.

Galiton informed Martin of the bags of rubble collected from the blackened, charred debris of the Fielding barn, explaining in detail how it had been gathered. "Shall we send them up to you, sir?" he asked Martin.

"Suicide, wasn't it?" Martin asked brusquely, plainly irked about something, perhaps at being delayed.

"That's what they say here, sir," Galiton responded.

"Then don't waste my time, Trooper," Martin growled into the phone. "Give it the deep six."

"But Captain Martin, sir," Galiton began a protest that was to include the curious opinion of the pathologist that the cause of Fielding's death was carbon monoxide and not a self-inflicted gunshot wound as had been presumed, but he was interrupted by his superior.

"Give it the deep six, Trooper," Martin repeated into the phone. "I don't want that crap up here."

Galiton repeated the brief exchange to Trueblood.

"Still the same old 'Captain Horsehockey', huh?" Trueblood used a reference to Martin that was becoming commonplace among line personnel in the state police department. "Well, let's not waste any more time. Let's do what the man says. Then let's eat."

Despite reservations about what he was doing, but still smarting from Martin's rebuke, Galiton went to his cruiser, backed it to the dumpster behind a lath screen at the far edge of the barracks parking lot and, with Trueblood watching, he unloaded from the trunk the two plastic bags containing debris from the fire scene into the large metal trash container.

Apparently overlooked by Galiton in his chagrin of the moment, the three small transparent plastic bags fortunately still lay on the front seat of the police cruiser.

8

Soon after the two troopers had departed that Friday evening, Ira and Irwin Brown received in their office, as previously arranged, Winona Fielding and her sons Roger and James. The five of them quietly seated themselves in the spacious, softly lighted room. Irwin Brown, of medium height and obviously overweight, wearing a gray herringbone sport coat and gray flannel slacks, businesslike in every detail of dress and movement, sat at a desk that was brightened by an overhead lamp, giving him the appearance of being center stage awaiting a cue to speak.

Then without preamble he expressed in a nasal monotone his and his father's regrets at the Fieldings' loss. He followed this with a monologue that seemed well rehearsed, in which were detailed the usual final needs and arrangements in such situations.   It was the first time Winona had ever been part of such a procedure. Her older sisters had made the funeral arrangements when their parents had died.   Now, bereaved, shaken and unsure, she sat rigidly, wept silently, and only half listened as the mortician's voice droned on.

Brown & Brown Funeral Home would attend to every need, Irwin Brown assured her and her sons, including the purchase of a two-grave plot in Moses City's new memorial park.   Without discussing the reasons why, or going into detail, it was mutually agreed that the remains of the dead man should be interred there immediately—the next day.

That Saturday dawned as the loveliest late fall day

in local memory. A summer-like sun shone in a cloudless sky and by noon the temperature hovered in the upper seventies. At precisely noon a trash packer truck backed up to the dumpster behind the lattice screen at the rear of the state police barracks parking lot and emptied it. As the truck pulled away the packer mechanism was in motion, grinding and packing its contents which included the two plastic bags tossed into the dumpster by Galiton the previous night. Before the end of the day the truck would discharge its load at the county landfill where a huge bulldozer would pulverise it, including those two bags, into oblivion.

Promptly at two o'clock that same day Brown & Brown Funeral Home, air conditioned and comfortable, became the scene of a closed casket funeral service for Crestman Fielding. Gathered to hear a short eulogy delivered by an elderly minister were Winona, Roger and James, and Roger's wife, Penni, her parents, Cramer Fielding, his wife, Mavis, the younger Fielding brother, Craddick, and several friends. As did Cramer Fielding, Craddick Fielding held himself aloof and apart from Winona and her sons before, during and after the service.

Winona, her eyes bloodshot and her face puffy from lack of sleep because she had wept almost the entire previous night, sat between her two sons. She held a tissue to a cheek but there were no tears to dry. Winona had cried herself out of her last tears sometime during the early morning. Now she sat almost in a stupor. She heard nothing the old preacher was saying until he quoted a verse from the Bible opened to John 14 on the lectern before him.

"Let not your heart be troubled," she heard the old man begin.

Let not your heart be troubled?
The words seemed to explode in Winona's brain. She thought, "What is the man saying? I am troubled. Crestman is dead, I'm left alone with many debts and a home that is not yet paid for. I am troubled. What has happened? Why is Crestman dead? What is going to happen to us, to me, to Roger, to James? Oh God," she moved her head slightly from side to side, "what will happen to us?"

The minister had finished reading the verse by this time and the voice of a woman from the choir of the church Winona had attended as a girl and as a young woman filled the funeral home viewing room with song. Although Winona was acquainted with the woman she could not recall her name. She tried and tried to remember but the woman's name eluded her. Now her voice, seeming distant and melancholy, was raised in song to the memory of Winona's husband, or was the song a prayer for Winona?

"Maybe this will be the last mile. Maybe this will be the last trial," the woman sang from the hymn 'Nearing Home.' *"Maybe this will be the last tear I shed, Maybe heaven is just a prayer away. . . ."*

The voice had the sound of mourning in it, surely intentionally put there for affect by the singer herself. The voice was not like the beautiful soprano Winona remembered from her beloved mother's funeral. That was also a sad affair for her but not quite so sad as what she was experiencing now.

Sarah McCrickland had been an elderly widow when she left this world for what she and Winona believed was a better place, to join her husband who awaited her there. In that respect it was a happy service that saw Sarah's departure.

Crestman had sat alive and warm beside Winona in

the church that day. She remembered how she had leaned against him when a sweet soprano voice sang the words to the hymn 'Nearer My God To Thee' and how after the first verse the entire congregation had joined in to repeat the words of the hymn, softly, reverently, time and again. If there was sweetness and reason to loss she had felt it then; if there was promise in death she had been aware of it then. With Crestman warm and vigorous beside her, acceptance of death then had seemed a natural part of life. She had indeed regretted her mother's passing, and she had wept then, too. But not like she was regretting the death of her husband. Not like the previous night when alone and sleepless she had wept for Crestman, for herself, for her family.

It had been easy for her to rationalize at her mother's funeral service that mothers and fathers are expected to die, no matter how much she loved her own father and mother, nor how much she preferred that they should have lived. But husbands? Husbands and wives are supposed to live happily ever after, forever and ever, or at least for a long and joyous life together, as her own parents had lived. There was no sweetness in her loss now, no reason, and she could not accept what was happening to her.

Winona was mired in these and other thoughts when she was aware of a stirring among the gathered mourners. The service had ended. A funeral home attendant had stationed himself near Winona and her sons and was now motioning them to stand. He directed them to a doorway outside of which a newly polished robin's egg blue limousine, parked behind an equally polished robin's egg blue hearse, stood waiting. Shortly thereafter the funeral cortege, preceded by a sheriff's patrol car with its emergency lights flashing, began its slow journey to the cemetery.

The brothers of Crestman Fielding declined to accompany the family there. With few more mourners there than the family and a handful of other relatives, the graveside service was brief. The earthly remains of the deceased, under the direction of the Browns, both of whom wore matching robin's egg blue blazers, white shirts, dark blue neckties and slacks, were committed to the earth.

Afterwards, Winona and her family drove to the home of Roger and Penni Fielding where Penni's mother and some friends had arranged refreshments for them. The brothers Cramer and Craddick Fielding had also absented themselves from that gathering.

Late that night Irwin Brown spent an hour or more at his desk in the funeral home. When at last he pushed back his chair to go home for the night, there lay on the desktop a white envelope which was sealed, stamped, and addressed to Winona Fielding. Inside was a bill for funeral services in the amount of $1,675.

THE SUSPICION

9

In a limestone veneered rancher on the outskirts of the town of Patterson, about twenty miles north of Moses City, Sunday morning arrived peacefully as usual. In the largest of its three bedrooms two people, a man and a woman, lay abed, he wide awake and on his back, she sound asleep, curled up with her back to him.

In his late forties, the man's normally curly red hair had begun to gray noticeably at the temples and the loose flesh at his jaws hinted at an approaching midlife sag. Though she was not young, the woman at his side clearly was not as old as he. Even in sleep her face was attractive and, judging from those parts of her body accented by the tucked-in bed covers, she was not undesirably rounded and was the possessor of pleasingly shaped legs.

For months she had worked as an employee in his presence, quietly, efficiently, as a clerk-secretary. One day she accepted his invitation to lunch. One lunch led to another and soon they had become good friends and then lovers; serious lovers, for he subsequently terminated a twenty-five year marriage so that they could be together.

The two of them had slept together numerous times before his divorce and their subsequent marriage. That part of their relationship began easily enough one summer weekend afternoon aboard his runabout. For the outing she was unusually tempting in a two-piece swim suit. He wore a white T-shirt and red swim trunks. Seated side by side as he guided the boat over the calm lake waters, ostensibly in search of a fishing hole, she had placed a hand on his thigh.

Although he had been hoping for it, and secretly expected it, her touch was pleasingly startling to him. As her hand rested there, sometimes unmoving, sometimes gently kneading, he became aware of his arousal. Steering the boat into one of several small coves among trees and undergrowth along the shore, he dropped anchor. There, with only a blue summer sky to shield them, they had yielded to an almost desperate physical need for each other.

On this Sunday morning, as the memory panned across his still awakening mind, he felt a stirring deep within himself. Raising the covers slightly and rolling to his side, he settled his body around the fleshy softness that was hers. He watched lovingly, as though for the first time, as she slowly, sleepily reacted to his touch and shifted her body so that she lay on her back. He heard her sigh his name, "Frank," saw the touch of a smile as it appeared on her face.

She turned suddenly, facing him, pressing her body into his, reaching for him, softly sighing his name again. He pushed her easily to her former position, his mouth against hers. As though from a distance at first, then nearer, from just behind him on a bedside table, he heard the unceasing ringing of the telephone. He swung an arm to one side and picked up the phone. Pressing it firmly to his ear he spoke gruffly, "Conway."

The voice that greeted him was apologetic, yet alert, direct. "Sergeant Donaldson, Lieutenant. The Colonel is on his way over here. It seems that we've got big trouble on our hands. He wants you here when he gets here."

Lieutenant Francis Patrick Conway, in charge of the Moses City State Police Barracks, forced his wife's hand away. Trouble? The Colonel on his way down? On Sunday?

Marjorie sensed in her husband the sudden transformation from lover to policeman. She raised herself on an elbow, attentive, wondering.

"What is it, Wendy?" Conway asked his barracks commander, First Sergeant Wendell "Wendy" Donaldson.

"Don't know for sure, Lieutenant," he heard Donaldson's reply. "But Colonel Carey wants us to send a couple of men to rope off the Fielding property where the fire was last Thursday. He wants it off-limits to everyone. Said he'd explain when he gets here."

10

Lieutenant Frank Conway was already in his office in the Moses City State Police Barracks when Colonel William R. Carey drove into the barracks parking lot. Unseen from where he stood looking out a window, Conway watched as Carey's shiny white late-model Thunderbird came to a stop. He watched as the tall, lanky Carey, wearing a neatly pressed brown business suit, highly polished cordovan western boots, and carrying a tan topcoat folded over his left arm, strode across the blacktop toward the barracks. On his head Carey wore the regulation wide-brimmed fawn Stetson hat of the state police, of which he'd always been so proud and which added to the handsomeness of his complete attire.

Watching him, Conway was aware of a mental image of the Carey of another time. A trooper like himself then, he used to be outfitted when on duty in oxford gray blouse with crimson shoulder boards, crimson-striped breeches, Sam Browne belt, highly polished cordovan cavalry boots and the Stetson. He was always neatly pressed then, too.

That had been a few years ago, Conway remembered. Promotions and politics had eventually taken them in separate directions and as time went by the two men had seen less and less of each other. They might have forgotten their friendship except that Carey had won appointment as superintendent of state police. A captain at the time, he was the choice of the newly elected governor to head up the state's elite police department. He was now nearing the end of his fourth year in that position.

To Conway at the moment, however, it seemed that only yesterday he and Carey had been troopers together. As he watched Carey striding across the parking lot, the memory of a stakeout they had shared one night began to take shape in his mind and to tease his mouth into the hint of a smile. Carey stood much taller than Conway, just under six-feet-six, or, as the Colonel himself in earlier days frequently responded to friendly queries about his height, "About five-feet eighteen-inches."

The tallest man on the force in or out of uniform he was impressive in bearing. Ruggedly handsome, usually smiling, he attracted the attention of both men and women wherever he went. In the years before his appointment it had become generally known around the state that Carey was ambitious. Besides a winning personality he had the sound intelligence to support his aspirations, whatever they might have been, even the governorship, which some said he coveted more now than ever before.

He was without a doubt the most articulate member of the state police department, leading some of those who served under him to remark on occasion that he could probably talk himself into, or out of, anything he desired. Whether he was the best man for the position he held was a matter of opinion. There were those in the department who believed he was, and that he was "the best thing" that had ever happened to the department. There were others who believed he was not, that he was all talk and flair. The governor, however, believed he was the best man for the job, and Carey had demonstrated many times since his appointment that he was more than capable of the kind of police leadership the governor expected. If there was any security to be had in the state police, it appeared that Carey had it, at least for the duration of the present governor's term.

Caught up as he was in the memory of the stakeout he and Carey had shared, Conway momentarily forgot about the urgency of this Sunday morning meeting between them. The smile had now begun working with increased force at the corners of his mouth as that experience spread itself in striking recollection on the canvas of his memory.

During the developing days of the 1960's drug scene in the state, Conway and Carey had been assigned to a preliminary undercover investigation. Troopers working in plainclothes late one night, they were secluded, by prearrangement with its owner, in the back room of a retail shop across the alley from the rear door of another establishment. Because of a volume of nightly traffic observed moving in and out of the latter door, the youthful owners had been suspected of dealing in drugs. Conway and Carey that night were to watch that door unseen, and were to tabulate the number and, if possible, obtain descriptions of persons who entered or exited the premises.

In the dim light of a single low-wattage night lamp, the two troopers alternated turns at a tiny window in the rear door of the shop in which they were hidden. While one stood and watched, the other rested in the only chair in the room, a wobbly, wooden folding chair. There may have been a leak, or it may have been an off night, for no one approached the door across the alley, nor did anyone leave from it. As a result, the long night became longer, boring and fatiguing, with both policemen finding it difficult, at times almost impossible, to stand and to stay awake.

About two o'clock in the morning, while standing half asleep, yet with a determined eye glued to the small window, Conway was jolted out of his weighty drowsiness by a thunderous crash behind him. The suddenness of it had not only startled him, but, as he would repeat in later recountings of the incident over coffee with other troopers, the unexpected loud noise had very nearly given him a heart attack.

"With my right hand automatically reaching for the butt of my holstered weapon," as he had been fond of saying in relating the event, Conway spun around to behold a sight he would never forget. The lanky Carey, who had finally succumbed to boredom and weariness, had unprofessionally fallen asleep in the rickety chair. Presumably trying to shift his too big body to a more comfortable position in the small seat, he had miscued and crashed to the floor, toppling with a clatter and bang in the process the wobbly wooden folding chair.

"And there he lay," Conway would later repeat through the years to the amusement of a chain of listeners, "all over the floor of that little back room, his head resting on his hands, sleeping like a baby. It sounded like the end of the world, him crashing down like that, but he didn't even bat an eye."

Conway's reverie was interrupted by the sound of heavy footsteps in the hall. He was still on his feet when Colonel Carey walked into his office. The two men shook hands.

"Frank," Carey said in greeting, using the familiar form of Conway's first name.

"Bill," Conway nodded. "Have a seat."

Before Conway could turn to offer him the swivel chair behind his desk, as was his custom when his superior visited him, one that the Colonel enjoyed immensely, Carey was speaking.

"Somebody's really screwed up in that Fielding fire, Frank," he growled angrily as he draped his topcoat across one of two chairs in front of Conway's desk, dropped heavily into the other, and crossed his long legs. "Who did we have over there, anyway?"

"Trueblood, initially. Then Trueblood and Galiton," Conway replied, a sudden curiosity at the Colonel's obvious anger now evidenced by the folds in his brow. He had been in Carey's presence before when he was angry. His crude manner at those times never ceased to ruffle Conway, and he was aware of a dislike for Carey when he was this way.

"Who the hell else was over there?" Carey demanded.

Still on his feet, Conway deliberately hesitated before answering, giving Carey time, he hoped, to get hold of himself. "The coroner, his son the deputy coroner, the sheriff," he said finally. "It's a sheriff's case, Bill."

"Not anymore," Carey exploded, his face reddening. "We're taking over, Frank. The state police are taking over. And we're not going to have any more damn mistakes, either. No more dumb tricks like throwing away evidence. What the hell, Frank!"

"What do you mean?" Conway bristled.

"Just what I said. Captain Martin called down here last night for any evidence collected at the scene of that fire and he was told it had been thrown away. What the hell, Frank! Evidence *thrown away?* Taken to the *landfill?* What kind of police work is that, Frank!"

Breathing heavily, Carey impatiently swung a booted foot in small circles as he spoke. His eyes bored aggressively into those of his lieutenant. Conway, who was about to sit down at his desk, suddenly straightened to his full height.

"Hold on, now, Colonel," he said dropping the familiar diminutive of his superior's first name with which he had earlier addressed Carey. "Let's back up a little. That stuff was disposed of on Captain Martin's orders."

Conway defensively had folded his arms across his chest fiercely gripping both elbows, the knuckles of each hand as white as the anger that had suddenly seized him and which he now sought to control. He inwardly cursed himself for allowing Carey to catch him off guard this way.

"Sergeant Galiton telephoned Captain Martin and told him what he and Trueblood had found," the lieutenant continued in measured tones. "Captain Martin told him to 'give it the deep six'." Conway released his elbows and held up his hands with the index fingers crooked to illustrate quotation marks around Captain Martin's words. "This was over Galiton's protest."

He spread the fingers of one hand and thrust it palm forward in a stop gesture to Carey when he thought his superior was going to interrupt him. "That's what Galiton reported to me, Colonel. And that's what those fellows did," he said. "They tossed the stuff into the dumpster, out back here, as they were told. And they went to eat a long-overdue supper."

With the hand he had held up to Carey, Conway had gestured roughly in the direction of the window of his office, the window from which a few minutes earlier he had watched Carey walk across the parking lot. "It was picked up sometime yesterday. That's how it got to the landfill. As much as I disagree with what they did, Colonel, these fellows were just following orders."

Conway moved to the chair behind the desk.

Making himself comfortable he leaned back, restraining himself from any further talk for the moment, he saw surprise and dismay spread over Carey's face. The Colonel appeared to be unable to speak for several moments.

"I can't believe it!" Carey spat the words at last.

He shook his head and rose to his feet, the peak of his Stetson seeming to reach nearly to the ceiling. He removed the hat, revealing black, wavy hair. He walked across the room and jammed the Stetson on the jutting prong of a wall rack. Still shaking his head in anger he turned back to Conway.

In what sounded like a groan he said, "If that's the case—"

"That's the case," snapped Conway, interrupting Carey with a rudeness unbecoming a junior officer.

"If that's the case, I apologize, Frank," Carey continued as though he had not heard. Then in a voice that sounded strained he said, "I can't believe that Martin. Damn! Damn! Damn!" He pounded the closed fist of one hand repeatedly into the palm of his other hand. "Frank, he's given me trouble for four years, ever since I took over. He had me convinced that your people messed up down here."

As he spoke Carey's face had turned gentian in hue, the color rising slowly from the white shirt collar around his neck to the line of black hair that crowded his head in thick waves and tumbled in two slightly furled lengths to the center of his forehead. Conway feared his superior was on the verge of apoplexy.

"They didn't, Colonel, believe me," Conway said, his voice now restored to its usual calm because he was sincerely more worried about Carey's well-being than he was angry about his attitude, his misinformation and his misdirected charges. "Captain Martin told them this was a suicide, a sheriff's case, and he didn't want them wasting his time."

Carey, his face still livid, stared at Conway in choked silence.

"I talked with Galiton late Saturday," Conway went on. "They shouldn't have thrown that stuff away, I agree, and I told Galiton he'd made a mistake. He would not have done it had he not been pissed, and he admitted it. But he and Trueblood found some pieces of cloth, maybe pieces from a shirt and pants, or a jacket. There was also a belt buckle, or what was left of one, a wad of plastic Galiton and Trueblood think might have been the remains of a pair of sunglasses, and a pencil clip. And they found what Galiton thought was a piece of human bone. He said a piece of jawbone. We've got that stuff, Colonel," Conway said before Carey could interrupt him. "What was thrown away," he continued, "were two plastic trash bags that Galiton and Trueblood had filled with ashes and debris they'd scooped up with their hands from where the body was found. They were brought here in the trunk of Galiton's car. The other stuff was in small bags on the car seat, and the only reason they weren't thrown away—Galiton was really ticked with the way he was treated by Captain Martin, Colonel—was because Galiton had overlooked them. When he found them later he had cooled off. We've got the stuff locked up here."

Carey's eyes widened but he said nothing. During the ensuing silence he sucked in a huge breath and expelled it slowly as his face returned to a semblance of its normal color. He sat down again, staring out the window, shaking his head from side to side.

His superior now somewhat calmed, Conway asked, "What's up, Colonel?"

"I'll tell you what's up, Frank," Carey came alive with a rush of words. "I told Captain Martin last night, that's why he made that call down here for those plastic bags. There's reason enough to believe your man Crestman Fielding didn't blow his brains out. He had a bundle of insurance on his life, well over a million dollars, and it seems that he is trying to defraud the insurance companies."

Carey paused just long enough to note his lieutenant's puzzled frown, then he continued, "I know, Frank. Everybody around here thinks it was a suicide. But we could have a well-planned homicide on our hands. And I can't begin to tell you how pleased I am that Galiton didn't throw away what sounds like the most important evidence we might have right now. We ought to have the rest of it, too. Damn that Martin! But since we don't have it, I want what's left of that barn gone over with a fine-toothed comb. I want the lab and arson people called in, and I don't want anyone except police, state police—our people—around that place."

Carey was silent again, thinking. While he waited for him to resume speaking, Conway wondered where the Colonel had obtained his information and why he was so concerned about this well-planned homicide, if that is what it was, when murder, unplanned and planned, happened frequently around the entire state. His curiosity was satisfied with Carey's next words.

"I'm not trying to run your district, Frank," Carey said almost apologetically. "I know that you are capable of handling this thing without my help. But a friend—a lodge brother—called me. J.J. Overton, the president of State Bankmens Life Insurance Company. They're holding the bag on most of that money. And he wants something done, now. Overton and the governor are good friends, Frank."

Carey's words hung briefly suspended between them while Conway repeated to himself the words *Overton and the Governor are good friends.* There it is, the governor connection, he said to himself.

"Overton has been a friend to the whole Fielding family, too, and a lodge brother of Crestman Fielding's," Carey continued. "I'm a lodge brother of his, too, but I don't know Fielding, never saw the man," Carey hurried to say the latter when it appeared Conway was about to ask a question. "Never in my life, Frank. Overton must know him pretty well, though. Said he lives somewhere near the Fielding home, too. Well, a few miles away. They entertained back and forth. He doesn't believe Fielding had the guts to kill himself, Frank. Besides that, he said that Fielding had just paid a hell of a premium to his company on that policy, and that he didn't have that kind of money. Said he was broke. Didn't have a red cent. Called him a lying sono-fabitch. The way Overton talks about the man makes this suicide business look pretty damn fishy, Frank."

Conway was impressed. "What you've said is all news to me," he told Carey. "According to the coroner and his son, and the sheriff, Fielding's own brother, Fielding killed himself, practically blew his head off. And the barn was somehow accidentally set on fire in the process."

He informed Carey of Dr. Hamilton Brent's autopsy on the dead man, as reported by Galiton. "It doesn't say much more than carbon monoxide and not the shot was the cause of death. Not at this juncture, anyway. Dr. Brent is having some tests done which could change that, or at least give us more information, and the coroner will give us a full report. No idea when, though."

It was Carey's turn to be impressed. He nodded in satisfaction.

"There was a car and a pickup in the barn," Conway continued. "There were also cans of gasoline and cans of paint and paint thinner, which contributed to the fire. Judging from Link Trueblood's report, it must have been some fire. But hell, Bill, as far as Crestman Fielding is concerned, the man's own brother, the sheriff, identified his body."

Both men were silent for a few moments, moments that seemed to Conway as he waited patiently for Carey to reply, to be of considerable length.

Carey finally spoke. "That was one hell of a way to die, Frank," he mused, nodding his head, staring straight before him. "A man's head practically blown off and he stays alive long enough to die of carbon monoxide. Hard to believe, isn't it." Then directing his full gaze at Conway he added in raised tones, "This dead man, Frank, may not be Crestman Fielding at all. He could very well be the innocent victim of Crestman Fielding. He could even have gotten that lethal dose of carbon monoxide before the fire."

Conway's eyes widened. If that possibility had occurred to anyone it was not mentioned, including the pathologist. He sat unmoving as he quietly turned the thought in his mind.

With a massive shrug that seemed to rid his entire body of what had burdened it, Carey said, "We've got to take a closer look at what's happened, Frank. I'm going to have Tim Melton and some lab people come down here to give you a hand."

Conway inwardly recoiled from the Colonel's words. With the combined assistance of the detectives assigned to his district, and troopers, he believed he was capable of handling the Fielding investigation to the satisfaction of all concerned. He didn't need Melton. Nor did he need the lab people. What the Colonel was proposing was overkill for a simple homicide investigation—if it was in fact a homicide—probably to impress the governor and their lodge brother. But Carey was top man, and he was giving the orders.

Thus it was that three days after the discovery of a body in the charred rubble of the Fielding barn, there was begun what would become the longest and most bizarre criminal investigation Spiceland County had ever known.

11

Captain Timothy Melton was district head of state police investigations, promoted from the rank of lieutenant to that position by Colonel Carey as recommended by Governor Hunter E. Wingate.

Even though he had worked but one time with the man, and then only briefly, Conway was familiar with Melton's record. He knew that Carey had made him top investigator because Wingate had insisted. Past retirement eligibility at the time of the Fielding fire, Melton was one of the department's several career policemen and was stationed at headquarters in Mount Carmel.

Except for the four years of Wingate's first term, Melton had been the designated state police chauffeur to a succession of three previous governors, two of whom had served two four-year terms. Wingate had replaced him with one of three women state troopers, all newcomers to the department.

Granted that he had little or no experience as a detective, and as a result was envied his position by many, Melton turned out to be an excellent administrator. In addition to that he also was an avuncular, easy-going sort, personality traits which undoubtedly had contributed to his success in the time he had served as an investigator, and he was generally liked in the department. After nearly four years as head of district investigations, there was little existing gossip among state police about how he was elevated to that post.

Conway wondered why Carey, aware of J.J. Overton's suspicions, as the Colonel had expressed them to him, had not already alerted Melton before he himself had left headquarters that morning. Then Conway remembered it was Sunday. Perhaps the Colonel was not at headquarters when he had earlier telephoned the Moses City State Police Barracks. He couldn't have been, he got here too quickly, Conway thought. That thought prompted another.

For several weeks Conway had been hearing echoes of department scuttlebutt which suggested Carey had a *good friend* in New Washington. Carey's white Thunderbird had been seen a number of times parked in the driveway of a certain house on Catalpa Street, on the outskirts of that community.

Once aroused, the suspicion attracted on-duty troopers and New Washington city police, who, on occasion of personal curiosity, secretly deserted their nocturnal patrols, and ventured into darkened Catalpa Street to observe for themselves the Colonel's parked car there. They snickered and snorted at the sight of it, and made lurid jokes among themselves about what they believed might be transpiring between the Colonel and "his lady," the woman who lived at that address.

Although they were friends, Conway had never mentioned such reports to Carey. Once, after declining to comment on Carey's apparent whimsy during a telephone conversation with a headquarters junior staff officer, Conway had said to his caller, "None of my business." Busybody, he had said to himself after hanging up. And he dismissed the temptation to confide the rumors to Carey. He had, however, taken the opportunity to exhort his district personnel that for their own well-being, as well as for the sake of the department itself, they should refrain from discussing Carey's purported liaison with the occupant of that house.

"Carey's off-time is his own," he had cautioned his troopers, "to do with as he pleases." He had added, "Stay away from there," an order he knew when he spoke it to be a waste of breath.

Although he kept himself above department gossip, Conway was not surprised, given the subject matter of the talk, to learn that department tongues secretly continued wagging about Carey. It seemed to add fuel to the talk that his lady friend lived a considerable distance from Carey's upstate home, which was "conveniently, if not safely" more than one hundred fifty miles from New Washington. Conway shrugged those thoughts away and turned his attention to what Carey was saying.

"I think we ought to bring Brad Schultz up here to work on this investigation," Carey kept his eyes averted as he spoke. "He and Harley Oaks would make a good team on this."

He was silent for a few moments giving an already disturbed Conway an opportunity to briefly review in his mind what he knew of the two men.

Lieutenant Bradley Schultz was one of the best sleuths in the state police department. So successful was he that early in his career as a detective someone had paid him the greatest praise ever heard in the department for one of its detectives. Conway smiled wryly as he repeated it to himself: *"Brad Schultz can sniff out a fart in a forty-acre field."* In the ensuing years Schultz's name and the compliment had become synonymous. It certainly would never be inscribed on an official departmental plaque, but it nonetheless was a well deserved compliment, for Schultz was a good detective. And except for probationary policemen who when they heard it envisioned the detective literally on his knees sniffing out an illusive fart in a meadow, veteran troopers understood the tribute for what it was. Now two years from retirement—if he wanted it, and it was even then being rumored that he did—Schultz was assigned to a barracks in the southern part of the state, where he made his home. Carey ordering him up to Moses City was unnecessary, Conway thought, and Schultz would be far from pleased.

Harley "Har-Har" Oaks was one of Conway's own detective sergeants. Four such investigators were spread thinly over the six counties that made up the Moses City state police district. Two of those detectives were also nearing retirement in terms of years of service. Oaks was a dependable fellow who through hard work and sheer doggedness was occasionally rewarded with some well deserved luck.

The nickname Har-Har, used only by his close friends, and sparingly and occasionally by a few of his superior officers, had been acquired in early life. A baby brother, finding the name Harley difficult to say, had settled for the first syllable which he pronounced twice in succession, Har-Har. Considered cute and allowed by their parents to continue in those early years, the curious diminutive stuck, only to become an embarrassment to Oaks in later years. He preferred that no one use it. During a dozen years as a state trooper Oaks had also earned himself something of an enviable reputation as an investigator. Given the opportunity, Conway thought, he would have assigned only Oaks to the Fielding investigation.

"Let's get them in here as soon as possible," Conway heard Carey's voice cutting through his thoughts. "The lab people won't mind some field work, but Tim's going to complain that he's busy at headquarters. But there's something else you and I have to do right now, Frank. Have Wendy come in here."

Conway dialed an extension.

"Come in here, please," he spoke softly into the phone.

First Sergeant Donaldson stepped into the office of his district lieutenant. A policeman who had been in service for many years, Donaldson had long ago won the respect of much of the brass at headquarters. Conway had been reminded numerous times that he was lucky to have a barracks commander of Donaldson's character and ability. The three policemen, Donaldson, Conway and Carey had been long-time co-workers and friends.

"Good morning, Colonel," Donaldson spoke respectfully, courteously as he reached a hand toward Carey.

"Good to see you again, Wendy," Carey said as he gripped the other man's hand in his. It was the Colonel's only indication of friendliness. He did not stand.

"I'd like you to make a telephone call for us, please, Wendy," he said. "Coroner Brown. Tell him we need to see him, Frank and I, and that we're on our way over to his place. We're going to stop for coffee, first. But don't tell him that. Just say that we're on our way over. I want him to think about it for a while before we get there. Thanks, Wendy."

Carey stood up then, draped his topcoat over an arm and turned to Conway who was in uniform. "Grab your bonnet, Frank," he used his favorite reference to the wide-brimmed, fawn Stetson uniform hat worn by state police. "We're going to have a little talk with Mr. Brown."

As the two policemen walked toward Conway's

51

unmarked police cruiser, Carey slipped into his topcoat and thrust his hands into the pockets. The movement seemed to hunch his shoulders, as though he
were carrying a heavy weight on them.

"You know, Frank," he said, suddenly stopping and
facing Conway. "I've got a hell of a problem with
Captain Martin. I know he was hoping to be appointed to this job, and he's sore because he wasn't. He's
been sore for almost four years now, and unforgiving;
so much so that it's impossible for me to reach him, to
get any voluntary cooperation from him. He just doesn't
want to get along. And he's carrying this thing too far,
at the expense of the whole department. I don't know
what to do about it. He's got some friends, and I don't
want to alienate them. At this time I need the support
of every man and woman in the department."

Conway realized that Carey was unburdening himself of the weight of concern placed on him by the head
of the state police crime laboratory, or at least trying
to do so, and that he did not expect an answer. When
Carey turned to resume his steps toward the car
Conway followed silently.

12 ·

Spiceland County Coroner Ira Brown had been in the business of burying the dead for as long as he could remember.

As a boy he had regularly accompanied his mortician father Isaiah Brown to homes in Moses City and Spiceland County to prepare the dead for interment. For the benefit of his grandchildren, and anyone else who would listen, he often recalled in detail how, long before county residences were equipped with electricity, he had held a lighted kerosene lamp so his father could see to do those things morticians then did to the deceased.

Being an undertaker was a calling, practically from birth, he used to say, adding that the dead were always a part of Brown family life. He frequently quoted his father whom he often heard say there was no greater service a man could render to his fellow man than to care for his dead.

Ira Brown remembered that in his father's later days Isaiah Brown had provided a Model-T Ford hearse for Moses City's burials. More precisely, only the chassis of the vehicle was a Ford product. The body itself had been manufactured by another company in the northern part of the state and had been attached to the frame by the Detroit auto maker.

Ornate in design, the sparkling black body of the vehicle was equipped with side windows through which the living could view its interior, and from which, jesters of that time had been known to say, a deceased could wave goodbye on leaving this world. In dry weather, roadways being passable, the elegant hearse was also used for rural burials. But to forestall the eventuality of inclement weather or possible mechanical breakdowns, Isaiah Brown preferred to use for that purpose the firm's horse-drawn hearse, an equally pretentious bone-black, windowed carriage.

In recollecting his beginnings as a mortician, Ira Brown, seventy three years old at the time of the Crestman Fielding incident, was inclined to refer to that early period as "the good old days." He was also quick to add that "Those were lean times," leaving a listener to wonder how they could have been both or if the good and the bad times alternated between certain days. Ira Brown never explained.

He rarely related his experiences in his father's service without some kind and proud words for the matched team of dappled mares, Iown and Myown, whose task it was to pull the ancient hearse over primitive roadways, often deep in mud or snow, to rural cemeteries.

As he had grown up on the job with his father, so had his own son, Irwin, grown up on the job with Ira. And it had been an accepted fact early in Irwin's life that when he graduated from high school he would enter embalming school. Long before that the method of preparing the dead for burial had changed, and the funeral parlor, instead of the home, had won public favor for that purpose.

Mud and snow were little match for the sleek, specially equipped, powerful machines that accompanied the change, and the horse-drawn hearse eventually was stored in a shed at the rear of the Brown & Brown Funeral Home garage. The rugged Iown and Myown,

until their demise, were lovingly retired to the secluded pastures of Ira Brown's farm in rural Spiceland
County.

The changes, so dramatic and complete over "the
good old days," left a void in Ira Brown's life. It grieved
him further of late that when he spoke of that former
period, few people knew or cared to know what he was
talking about. Still, that bygone era had provided him
with glorious memories, and in recent years he liked
more and more to talk about those old times.

Ira's son, Irwin, a short, rotund, bespectacled man
in mid-life at the time of the Fielding fire, always listened respectfully when his father spoke of the early
years. He could relate from memory any and every
story ever recounted in his presence by his father.
The younger Brown always honored his father's
advice, and, as a result, any plan, any decision concerning their partnership as morticians or as coroner
and deputy coroner seemed a foregone conclusion of
mutual acceptability. It was a seemingly perfect family and job relationship.

As individuals, as businessmen, as holders of public office, both men were regarded by the majority of
Moses City and Spiceland County residents as honest
and honorable. For as long as anyone could remember, one or the other member of the father-son firm
had held the title of Spiceland County coroner. By
virtue of their profession, each met the requirements,
as set out by state law, to hold that position. Neither
man was ever opposed at election time. The office
paid the coroner and deputy coroner an annual salary
and allowed either of them, within the jurisdiction of
Spiceland County, to legally pronounce a person dead
and to file with the county clerk a death certificate in
the name of a deceased.

Autopsies, on the other hand, were not their official duties, nor did they qualify to perform them. Upon request, post-mortems were conducted by medical examiners or pathologists, unless otherwise requested, at the Glenview Hospital morgue in Moses City, or at the Brackenridge University Hospital morgue at New Washington, in adjacent Tabor County. Yet a mortician holding the office of coroner did not lack for absolute power over such matters occurring within his sphere of authority.

At the time of the arrival that Sunday morning of state police officers Carey and Conway at the funeral home, the aging Ira Brown was approaching the last month of a second four-year term as Spiceland County coroner. Earlier that month his son had been elected to that office again, and he would become coroner again beginning at his swearing-in at one minute past midnight after the last day of the year.

As arranged by First Sergeant Donaldson, the policemen were expected, and both father and son were patiently awaiting them. After introductions were made all around, while the four men stood in the vestibule of the funeral home, Ira Brown gestured expansively toward the open door to the firm's office.

"Go on in, gentlemen," he spoke graciously. "Go on in."

Allowing them and his son to precede him, he entered the room last and occupied the large, brown leather-upholstered chair behind the broad oak desk. Ensconced there he had through the years arranged many funerals, consoled scores of bereaved and had earned for himself and his family a moderate financial independence.

"We're here about the Fielding matter," Carey spoke abruptly.

Ira Brown spread his hands palms down on the desk top.

"Yes?"

"We want to know everything you can tell us about—this death," Carey had almost said "this homicide" when he caught himself, at the same time softening his tone.

"Not to be short, but there's not much to tell," Ira Brown smiled, giving no indication that he had noticed. "Crestman shot himself. He's dead. He's buried. It's all very sad. But it's over, gentlemen."

"Maybe," Carey snapped. Then in carefully guarded tones he asked, "But wasn't that unusually fast? That is, burying a person that soon after something like this?"

"Well, we've had suicides before," the elder Brown replied. "But since we've never had anything quite like this to happen here before, we can't say if it was unusual. If you're talking about the time lapse between death and burial, I don't think so. The man killed himself on Thursday, he was buried on Saturday. Nothing unusual or fast about that."

"Can you be sure it was Crestman Fielding that you buried?" Carey suddenly shot from the hip without explanation.

Straightening in his chair with a sudden movement, Ira Brown appeared shocked and agitated by the question. "Of course," he snapped. "I'd known the man all of his life. His father before him. I know the whole family. Wife came from a fine family. He was dead, there in his garage. Who else could it have been?" He had spoken rapidly, his voice rising.

Conway, uncomfortable with the thought that Carey might have been too blunt too soon, pushed heavily backward into the upholstered chair he had chosen. The leather trappings of his uniform made strained, creaking sounds. He crossed his legs, and the toe of a smartly polished cordovan cavalry boot touched the front panel of the big oak desk. He said nothing.

"We can't say—well, we're not certain that it wasn't Crestman Fielding," Carey said as he leaned toward the older man. "But we have learned that he carried more than a million dollars in life insurance. And we just want to be positive that the right man is dead here."

Both father and son stiffened at Carey's words. When they had spoken with Winona Fielding and her two sons after the fire, in the very room where they now sat with the police officers, there had been no mention of any great amount of insurance. It flashed through Ira Brown's mind that Winona Fielding had said that there was "some" insurance. She had been uncertain as to the amount but she was sure that a policy, a small one, was in force. It was probably in the hands of the family attorney, Clare Downing, she had said, who for years had handled her husband's affairs. Winona knew absolutely nothing about it or anything else pertaining to her husband's personal matters, she had told the Browns.

"A million dollars?" Ira Brown finally gasped, surprise and what seemed to be distress evident on his face. "Winona didn't say a word about that kind of money when she was here to make the arrangements."

"More than a million," said Carey. "Was Roger here with his mother? He knew of the insurance."

Ira Brown nodded. "Not that it makes any difference, but he didn't say a word," he said, his voice now slightly higher pitched. "Not a single word about insurance."

Carey waited a few moments before asking his next question, during which time the Browns exchanged looks and the two policemen saw Irwin Brown, under his father's gaze, widen his eyes and shake his head slightly from side to side.

Carey then asked, "Have you issued a death certificate in the name of Crestman Fielding?"

With a flip of his right hand the coroner indicated at one corner of his desk a plastic basket in which were a number of papers and envelopes. "It's in there. Irwin will take it to the county clerk's office in the morning."

"Don't," Carey said gruffly. "Hold up on it. We've got some investigating to do, Mr. Brown." Deliberately softening his tone, Carey then said congenially, "We have some people coming to Spiceland County who need to look over the fire scene, Mr. Brown. We do hope that we can find something out there to prove —" here Carey paused, shifting in his chair. Then choosing his words carefully, he continued "— that you did in fact bury Crestman Fielding."

"Of course we buried Crestman," the coroner, clearly upset with the unmistakable insinuation that the dead man may not have been Fielding, smiled thinly. "It was his barn that burned. He was having problems. We all knew that. Of course, I never expected him to kill himself. But he did. He practically blew his head off. We saw him lying there, didn't we, Irwin?" He had turned to his son for confirmation and when the younger man nodded, the coroner continued. "And we picked him up and put him in a body bag. We also put him in a casket and buried him. From what we saw, I'm convinced it was Crestman. I knew the man all his life."

While he was speaking a flush of color had spread

over Ira Brown's face, and as he reached into an inside coat pocket for a handkerchief his hand shook noticeably.

"All the same, hold up on that death certificate," Carey said easily but firmly. He hesitated briefly, then looking from one to the other of the two morticians, he said softly, "Please. I know that you're under no obligation to do so without a court order. But just give us a few days. I'm not saying there is, but there could be foul play here."

At this point Carey chose to say exactly what was on his mind. "You just might have buried someone other than Crestman Fielding."

"Who?" Ira Brown asked incredulously, his palms now up on the desktop, as though he might have been expecting an answer to fall into them from above.

"I don't know," Carey's voice became sharp and he appeared to be verging on impatience, but, to the relief of the watching Conway, he was still in control, speaking slowly, cautiously. "Did you notice anything in particular about the body?" he asked.

"Nothing, except that it was all but destroyed," Ira Brown said. "In all my years in this business I've never seen anything quite like it."

Ira Brown suddenly remembered that he had yet to mention Dr. Brent's autopsy to the two police officers, and he hurried through the pathologist's tentative report.

"I don't think the cause of death is unusual," Ira Brown observed in summation. "Something like that can happen very easily. Sooner or later he'd have died from the shot. Carbon monoxide? Wel-l-l-l," he drawled almost smugly, "I suppose that's an official necessity. It doesn't say a thing to me other than Crestman is dead. But Dr. Brent will be doing some further tests tomorrow—this week, anyway—and we might know more when we hear from him."

A look that passed quickly between Carey and Conway went unnoticed by the father-son team of morticians and coroners.

"We had already heard from Sergeant Galiton about that, but thank you," Conway spoke for the first time, forcing the sound of satisfaction into his voice.

The four men continued discussing the pathologist's findings and it was agreed that Ira Brown was right in at least one respect. Until laboratory studies could be completed, Dr. Hamilton Brent's examination could shed no further light on the death. It was during this exchange that Conway found himself again wondering about Carey's active interest in the Fielding death. Thus far the Colonel had not asked a single question that Conway himself would not have asked, or any of his detectives, for that matter. The voice of Ira Brown cut into the lieutenant's thoughts.

"How long do you want us to hold up on the death certificate?" he asked Carey. "You should know that this death has to be recorded."

"I know, I know," Carey raised a hand as though to ward off any further questions about his request. "I'll be in touch with you about that. Right now just give us some time to look things over out there."

"Where?" Irwin Brown asked.

Carey explained that he and Conway planned to visit and examine the scene of the Fielding fire.

"You're kind of late for that."

Carey and Conway turned inquisitive looks in Irwin's direction.

"Roger and James—Crestman's boys—have been going over that place since late yesterday afternoon," he said. "They've been looking for whatever they can find. I was out past there myself, early this morning, taking pictures, and I talked with them."

Carey was on his feet. He seemed twice as tall to the seated Ira Brown who had to tilt his head awkwardly to look up at him.

"This is a police order," he said gruffly from under a deepening frown. "That fire site is off-limits to everyone, including the family. Everyone except the state police."

Carey began to move toward the door. "Mr. Brown, we'll get back with you," he continued. "In the meantime, we'll have to ask for your cooperation. We'll keep you informed. Now, gentlemen, we have got to leave."

There were no words spoken between the two policemen as they made their way across the funeral home parking lot. During the silence a thought began growing in Conway's mind. If the dead man proved to be someone other than Fielding, Captain Earl Martin's blunder will have placed the Colonel and the entire state police department in what could be an embarrassing light. In answer to his earlier thought about Carey's questioning of Ira Brown, Conway now wondered if Carey might also be setting the stage to save some face. Knowing Carey as he did, he assured himself that this was a possibility, and that his superior would go to almost any extreme to keep the mishandling of those plastic bags of fire debris from becoming public knowledge. Heaven help whoever gets in his way, Conway thought.

Once inside the car, Carey turned to his lieutenant. "Who've we got out at the Fielding place, Frank?"

"Trueblood and Galiton," Conway replied.

"Good!" Carey said. "Let's get out there. I want to see what the place looks like. I want to talk to those troopers. Until we can check out every detail of this fire I want that fire scene off-limits to everyone."

His mouth pulled back into a thin line, Carey shook his head from side to side as he spoke. "Take care of that, Frank. And I don't want anyone but our people digging around in those ashes. This thing has already been —," Carey paused. Then, with a softening of expression he looked directly at Conway and cautiously continued, "— fouled-up enough." After another pause he added, "Damn, Frank. Sunday morning and I'm cussing like a heathen."

The two policemen laughed dryly.

In the silence that followed it occurred to Conway that Carey was making a good-natured attempt to vent steam. But it was obvious to him that the Colonel was still angry, and he wondered how Captain Earl Martin, the man responsible for the foul-up, would fare from Carey's Sunday morning visit to Moses City and Spiceland County.

13

Troopers Link Trueblood and Anthony Galiton, both wearing winter uniform blouses because of the sudden overnight drop in temperature, stood talking with two young men when their superiors drove up. Trueblood introduced the youthful pair as brothers Roger and James Fielding.

Both brothers were tall in stature. Each was handsomely swarthy in complexion, and each wore his dark hair in the trend of the time, over the forehead in front and to almost shoulder length on the sides and in the back. Though the pair seemed pleasant enough, they exhibited a shadowed, silent curiosity at what they saw as a sudden intrusion by four policemen.

Near the debris of what had been the Fielding barn was a mass of charred and twisted rubble. To one side with a grader blade attached, a green farm tractor, its motor idling in neutral gear, sputtered and smacked while emitting from its vertical exhaust a host of heat devils that frolicked crazily in the chill autumn air.

Colonel Carey and Lieutenant Conway exchanged knowing looks, Carey, tight-lipped again and, unmistakably angry. If the sputtering tractor was any indication of what had been happening, both Carey and Conway knew that they had arrived too late. Masking his anger as best he could, Carey attempted to be casual.

"I'm sorry about your father," he had to speak loudly to be heard over the noise of the tractor. He paused to look first at Roger Fielding and then toward his brother James. "It's too bad something like this has to happen in any family," he continued in the same loud tones, and before either brother could acknowledge the condolence, he asked, "Have you fellows uncovered anything?"

"Nothing," Roger said. "We've shoved a lot of stuff around, but we haven't found a thing."

"What were you looking for?" Carey asked.

"Just anything. Anything," Roger replied. He stole a hurried glance at his brother then toward the noisy tractor.

James stood silently, his head tilted slightly as he looked up at the tall Carey. Then slowly separating himself from the group he walked to the tractor and turned the ignition switch. The ensuing quiet was acute, and dense enough, it seemed to Conway, to be stroked appreciatively. James returned to the gathering.

"We want to do the same thing." His voice now loud in the sudden silence, and firmer, Carey again moved his eyes from one to the other of the two sons of Crestman Fielding. "We want to take a closer look through this debris. We have reason to believe that your father might not have died here."

Roger and James Fielding drew themselves up sharply. After exchanging quick, puzzled glances they stared wordlessly at the director of state police. Trueblood and Galiton also had tensed at the blunt implication by their superior and turned toward Carey.

In the silence that followed Carey's announcement, Galiton thought about the plastic bags of ashes and debris he and Trueblood had collected which, on Captain Earl Martin's order, had subsequently gone to the Spiceland County landfill. Somebody, a warning sounded in Galiton's mind, is going to get burned and it's probably going to be me.

With a subdued firmness in his voice, Carey resumed speaking to the Fielding brothers, interrupting the trooper's thoughtful concern. "We're taking over here now," he said. "No one will be allowed near this place until we have sifted through this —"

"What do you mean, my father might not have died here?" James, his surprise and shock at what Carey had said plainly evident in his voice, had interrupted Carey.

"He died here," Roger's jaw was set as he spoke soothingly, reassuringly to his brother. Then facing Carey he added coldly, "We know he died here."

Both Fielding brothers looked directly into Carey's eyes. Both waited patiently for him to speak.

"You could be right, but we need to be sure," Carey spoke at last, slowly, almost uncertainly, it seemed, in the face of the brothers' reaction. "We need to be sure that your father died here."

He paused, tactfully catching himself before suggesting someone other than their father may have died there. He continued almost soothingly, "We have to be sure, that's all. But until we're finished with our investigation here, only state police will be allowed in this area."

"Can't you give us more information than that?" Roger interrupted Carey before he could say more.

"Yes, I suppose you're entitled to know," Carey's voice now sounded strangely paternal, as though he wanted to be as kind as possible. His tone was so soothing that listening to him Conway wondered, could he be thinking that Fielding did commit suicide. No. He's just being more cautious now, staying on the safe side, better to make friends than enemies. He's trying to be the old Carey now.

"It has come to our attention that your father carried a considerable amount of insurance —"

"I know that," Roger Fielding, frowning quizzically, interrupted him. "There was no secret about that. One million six-hundred thousand dollars. Dad took out that policy when he began speculating in real estate. It was a big project—apartments and condominiums—and he wanted to protect it, along with himself and his family."

"You knew," Carey said. It was a statement, not a question.

"Of course I knew," Roger's voice contained a touch of annoyance. "I knew everything about Dad. The insurance was no secret, except that it was strictly a business matter. There were three of us who knew. Dad, myself, and Dad's attorney, Mrs. Clare Downing," Roger answered. As he uttered these words he was aware of the look of surprise his brother had turned on him.

"Just the three of us," Roger repeated, speaking softly, kindly to James. "Not even Mother knew. That's the way Dad wanted it. Clare's waiting for copies of the death certificate to file the claim."

Conway studied Roger, looking for some expression that might give him a clue to the younger man's thoughts. Was he as certain as he appeared, as he sounded, that his father had died in the fire? Was there something Roger was concealing behind his dark eyes and handsome face? Conway thought so. He is a handsome young man, Conway affirmed to himself. Had he been able to see them side by side he might have been startled at the sharp resemblance of son to father. He would learn later, from examining family photographs, that Roger was almost an exact copy of a youthful Crestman Fielding. Roger cut through Conway's thoughts as the elder Fielding brother addressed the policemen.

"Look, I know my father died here last week," he said flatly. "I was the last person to see him alive, I'm sure. And before I left him he told me that he planned to kill himself. He was broke, depressed, sick. Said the best thing he could do was to end it all. Besides," he looked questioningly at each policeman in turn, "who else could it be?"

The words had come from Roger not insincerely, yet accompanied by the irony of an amused look on his face, as though he were trying to please a less than funny clown.

"We're not sure that he didn't die here," Carey said directly, gently to Roger. "We just want to be certain, that's all. And we'll have to have your cooperation. Sorry, but you'll have to wait to make the insurance claim; I've asked Mr. Brown to hold up the death certificate —"

"Wait? Hold up the death certificate?" Roger almost shouted the interruption.

In his desire to be kind Carey had committed a slip of the tongue. He had gone too far under the circumstances. He should have chosen a better time, a better place to inform the brothers of what he had done; or he should have let the Browns tell them. The sudden realization of his error angered him. He held up a hand, palm facing the angry younger men.

"It appears to be an unkind measure, we know," he spoke softly. "But as little as we like to do so, it's a step that has to be taken at this time. The hold-up could be only temporary, at least until we can ascertain what happened here." He added unctuously, "Try to understand."

"That's just it, I do understand," Roger said angrily, bitterly. His brother James had moved closer to him, saying nothing, but by his action quietly lending his support to anything Roger might say. "I understand that this is insane," Roger continued. "My father shot himself. He's dead and buried. My mother can't collect his insurance without a death certificate, and she is in desperate need of money. You," he said harshly, pointing a finger at Carey, "try to understand."

The towering Carey viewed the Fielding brothers, studying their angry, pained expressions before replying.

"I'm sorry," he said again, this time softly, sincerely but matter of factly. "That is all I can say at this time. For the moment this is temporary, as I said, at least until we can complete our investigation here. You'll be kept informed. In the meantime we must insist that you cease all activity around here. Now," Carey's voice became almost gruff, "I want you to help us to get some idea of the layout of the building, what it was like before the fire, if you please."

The Fielding brothers appeared reluctant to move or to speak. Finally, Roger sucked in a deep breath and released it slowly, noisily. Then, in clipped tones, he began explaining to the gathered policemen that the Fielding house had been built years earlier, when he and James were children.

The Fielding barn, on the other hand, he said, was of dubious vintage, already there when his parents had bought the property. At some time it had been improved and converted for various purposes. It was a deep, spacious structure whose double-door entranceway faced east, and whose center rose some fifteen feet to a loft under the main roof, then spread north and south under shed-roof extensions. It was, as were barns of rural Spiceland County, quite wide, with room enough inside at one time for farm animals, hay and other feeds, farm machinery and a vehicle or two. In recent times a section of it had become a shelter for a car and an old pickup truck.

The rear of the west shed-like extension, which originally was a stable, was used to house ponies when Roger and James were growing boys. In that section, which was also accessible through a short walkway that led to its doorway, there had been enclosed a small room in which saddles and tack had been stored. After the Fielding brothers had outgrown their ponies and showing them at 4-H fairs, it had become something of a tool room and a collection point for paints, scrap lumber and such paraphernalia that accumulates from an active rural household. Two late model cars were kept in a garage attached to the Fielding house, some distance east of the fire site.

The state policemen listened intently as the handsome Roger Fielding spoke. They were aware that his voice softened with each word of his description of the old barn. As his monologue progressed without interruption, the memory of the barn had become much like that of an old and dear friend, one with whom he might have shared many affectionate hours.

The building had indeed been an old and dear friend to Roger, one with whom he had spent many happy hours. Until the death of his father there he could recall only one unpleasant incident to occur in the old barn. Try as he might, he could not stop the instant replay of it now filling his mind.

On rainy weekends and school vacation days the barn had been a playground for Roger and James. They had gathered there with several playmates from the rural neighborhood, sometimes lounging for hours on a thick carpet of hay in the loft, sharing stories and revealing to one another their hopes and dreams of days yet to come. They often played games, utilizing all the space, all the nooks and crannies of the familiar structure for their fun.

One of their favorite games was an all-time popular boys' pastime called "Cowboys and Indians." They had fashioned with their pocket knives springy bows from new willow growths, and strung them with binder twine cut from bales of hay. They shaped long arrows from willow spikes and carved crude pistols from vagrant pieces of wood. With these seemingly harmless weapons they inflicted bloodless wounds and painless death upon one another until such time as the cowboys or the Indians stood victorious over all of their fallen enemies, or until such time as they were summoned to dinner.

It was great fun, and more often than not the shouted bang-bang-bang reports of wooden pistols and the screech of little voices in that country auditorium fell on the ears of Winona Fielding, involved in some chore at the distant house, as soothing, melodic reminders of Fielding family happiness and security. Those hours, those days were wondrous, unforgettable times. It was not unusual and certainly understandable then, that one or more of the youngsters should at times pray mightily before going to bed at night for a rainy day so that those fun times in the big barn and the pleasures they held might be further extended.

One rainy, school vacation day, when Roger and James were perhaps ten and six years old respectively, and the barn resounded with the voices of children at play, the unexpected happened. The two brothers and four neighborhood friends had evenly divided themselves into a posse in the process of stalking a band of Indians who had taken cover in the barn. A handsome, blond youngster named Peter LaChance, with wooden pistol at ready, moved stealthily on tip-toe toward the built-in wooden ladder rising to the loft, hoping to surprise another boy whom he guessed was hiding up there in the hay. Reaching the foot of the ladder, Peter cautiously placed a hand and a foot on separate rungs and stole a quick look upward.

At that very moment the boy, a youngster named Luther Kurl, seeking to vanquish his playtime enemy, chose to loose an arrow from his makeshift bow. Innocently wrought for amusement only, the plaything suddenly and irretrievably hurtled through the air to inflict incredible injury and pain upon Peter.

The missile struck the unsuspecting boy in the left eye, knocking him to the dirt floor of the barn where he lay on his back, the willow arrow sticking straight up from the gory wound like a stick protruding from a muddy hole. It lodged there, unmoving, while a thick crimson fluid oozed out from around the shaft. As it spread it stained Peter's face, seeped into his left ear and washed over his neck. It was absorbed into the collar of his white T-shirt until an excess of it matted his blond hair and puddled on the dirt floor under it.

Peter's screams of pain and fright left his throat as piercing, unearthly sounds, completely unnerving yet paralyzing his playmates. They closed their eyes to the bloody horror before them and bawled and screamed hysterically until a breathless, terrified young Winona Fielding rushed into the barn.

It took a great reserve of strength and determination to keep from fainting at the sight that greeted her, and a firm grip on her senses to bring order out of the chaos that surrounded her. Though she was able to do so, try as she often later would, she could never quite remember the sequence of that accomplishment. That she did it, she would repeat later, was a thing done without beginning or end, an achievement guided by an unseen force.

Roger and James had been a weeping, screaming part of that wild hysteria. They had also wept some more, quietly, mournfully, when the Fieldings learned later in a visit with Peter at Glenview Hospital that their little friend would never again see out of his left eye.

Luther, meanwhile, was inconsolable for days, refusing to eat or drink, or to leave his house. This was also saddening to Roger who somehow knew that while Luther had not shed blood nor felt pain that day he too had been wounded, perhaps, in a way, even as deeply and for as long as Peter.

It was the single unhappy event in the childhood of the Fielding brothers. While play in the barn did not cease, it was never quite the fun it once was. And the game that had given so much pleasure to the Fielding brothers and their neighborhood friends in those early years was never played again. Peter eventually returned there, and so did Luther, but neither they nor the Fielding brothers or any of the boys who played in the barn could ever be totally carefree again.

Now the barn was gone, or rather what was left of it lay in a heap of ashes, twisted metal and charred debris. It would never again hear the voices of small boys at play—or in pain. The memories it once sheltered and nurtured were, like the clouds of black smoke from the inferno that had destroyed it, now scattered to the winds.

However awful Peter LaChance's misfortune had been, however vividly the memory of it had remained with Roger, he was now aware that a worse incident had occurred in the barn. His father had shot and killed himself in that once happy place.

And now, at this very moment, he and James were confronted by policemen who coldly and brutally suggested that their father did not die there. What were they trying to say?

14

Roger was startled from his thoughts by the sound of his own voice as he spoke to the gathered state policemen. "There, at the entrance to the hallway that led to the tack room," he heard himself saying, pointing to a place in the burned rubble while looking directly at Colonel Carey.

Emphasizing his next words he added, "There is where my father died. I didn't see him there," he swallowed hard and noticeably. "That's what I was told. This man, here," he now pointed to trooper Link Trueblood, "was one of those who saw him there." He looked at Trueblood for confirmation and saw the trooper nod in agreement. Then Roger said, "There were others. My own uncle—my father's brother—the Browns, some firemen. Several people."

Listening to Roger as he guided them step by step through the blackened, pungent debris that had been the Fielding barn, Conway was somehow unable to escape the impression that life had once been pleasant for the Fielding brothers. A beautiful home, a small farm, a barn with a loft, ponies, cars; certainly these were the provisions of caring, loving parents. At least it might have been so until Crestman Fielding had fallen on hard times, perhaps even until the fire. Why not until the fire? Once happy families responding to hardship with the surprising resilience borne of hope and love were known to overcome almost anything. Death of a loved one, however, Conway thought, was something else. Death by suicide? He shook his head slightly. Does anyone ever recover from such a loss?

A suicide had tumbled the Fielding world. A parent, the father, dead, shockingly by his own hand. It was a staggering blow to the heart of the family. That they might be overwhelmed by it was certainly to be expected. But was Crestman Fielding dead, Conway asked himself. Maybe, according to the evidence in hand. Maybe not, according to Carey. If he was dead by his own hand he could be counted among many before him who chose that path to escape their woes. He wouldn't be the last. But did he in fact turn a shotgun on himself? Conway wondered anew.

Carey, too, was aware of a genuine sense of sorrow for Roger and James, the Fielding family as a whole. But as he listened to Roger and followed him past the reddened, scorched hulks that once were a pickup and car, where they now rested on bare, rusted rims—the tires having been burned—he cautioned himself against any emotional involvement. His only concern at this point, he told himself, must be the suspicion of his friend and lodge brother, J.J. Overton, a suspicion that was fast becoming Carey's own.

"I've seen enough," Carey told Conway on the return drive to the Moses City barracks. "I've got the whole state police department to run, so from here on this baby is yours, Frank. You handle it your way."

He did not elaborate. In no way did he indicate his reason for the sudden change, leaving Conway to wonder. Prudently Conway asked no questions. "But I'll be watching, Frank," Carey said suddenly, surprising his companion. "We don't want to overlook a thing that might lead to the dead man being someone other than Crestman Fielding, or," Carey paused, "being Crestman Fielding, for that matter."

Conway felt he should make some kind of reply.

Then he thought better of it. I'll just leave well enough alone for now, he said to himself. In his relief, uncertain though it was, that Carey was removing himself from the investigation, he was trying to make himself feel good when the Colonel did a complete about face.

"I'm going to call the Army at Camp Davidson for a tent large enough to erect over that rubble, and I'll see to it that the lab people go over everything. They just might find something that will help me put this case to rest," Carey said.

Conway, looking straight ahead through the windshield, clenched his teeth. An observer might have noticed the fine line of his lips and a tensing of muscles in his jaw. Veiling his concern and disappointment at his superior's changing attitudes, Conway said little as he and Carey continued toward Moses City. A twenty-three year member of the department, the last six as a district commander, Conway had experienced a variety of police work. There was no doubt in his mind, he told himself as he rode next to Carey, that, left entirely to him, the Fielding investigation would be open and shut, with satisfaction guaranteed to all concerned.

From where he viewed the matter, it was a routine police case. A suicide, he was almost certain, a suicide suspected of being something else. He felt sure of that. Were it not a suicide he could still handle it without Carey. He would rather do it without Carey. No problem. Not for him. He saw himself as a policeman who could get to the bottom of things in a hurry. Jump in. Do the job. Jump out. A rectangular gold pin he wore above the right breast pocket of his uniform blouse attested to his method. Bearing a bright blue star in its center, it was a tribute to the bullet he had taken in the left shoulder from the pistol of a bank robber one morning during his early trooping days in another state police district.

It was probably the quickest open and shut case of his career. Still, that day, that incident, had nearly cost him his life, and the memory of it had remained with him. Although it did not appreciably change his way of doing things, he had in the ensuing years thoughtfully reviewed it again and again.

On patrol a few minutes from the bank that morning, Conway heard his dispatcher's voice announcing an active alarm there. Reporting his location and ignoring the dispatcher's warning that he should proceed with caution, that backups were on their way, a determined young Conway sped toward the bank, a small, suburban branch office. As he guided his cruiser around a corner he saw a man, cloth bag in one hand and pistol in the other, run from the bank into the street. Conway guided his police car toward the fleeing man, almost running him down before slamming on the brakes and jumping out, magnum in hand. Before he could call out to the man the young trooper was knocked down by a powerful blow to the shoulder. Regaining his feet he was aware that his brain was reeling. He staggered and pitched facedown across the hood of the cruiser. Struggling to overcome the spinning sensation in his brain, he managed to raise himself enough to see through blurred vision what he believed was the enactment of his own execution. The bank robber had stopped in flight, turned, and was pointing a pistol in Conway's direction. Swallowing with extreme difficulty because of a sudden nausea, the young policeman was suddenly aware that his own gun was still gripped in his right hand. With a violent shake of his head to clear his failing sight, he shoved the barrel in the direction of the gunman and squeezed the trigger. The robber, his arms flailing, dropped the money bag and pitched backward as a shot from his own weapon went wildly and harmlessly overhead.

The drama had been played out in seconds. The bank robber was dead. Conway was unconscious but alive. He later underwent surgery to repair his left shoulder and was hospitalized briefly. In due time he was returned to duty and was honored by the department with a citation for bravery and awarded the gold pin with the bright blue star. Conway was not that impressed with the decoration, at least not outwardly. He would have put it away in a trunk for his grandchildren, he was known to have said, except that regulations required him to wear the pin while in uniform.

Carey, whose service time exceeded that of Conway's by three years, had once said that he considered Conway one of the finest policemen in his command. The respect was probably mutual, and mutually reserved. Still, Carey's intense personal interest and involvement in the Fielding case had come as a surprise to Conway and an intrusion on his command. Though he hadn't pursued Carey's reasons and had not asked any questions of his superior, he had listened and he was thinking. The most burdensome of his thoughts was one that concerned Carey's unusual intervention in what appeared to be a routine district matter. That thought left him more puzzled than angry.

As the two police officers continued their drive in silence, Conway reviewed some of the thoughts that had entered his mind since leaving his home that morning. Carey, he reminded himself, held an office of almost unrestricted police power in the state, a lucrative, important position as the governor's appointee. Carey and the governor had been friends long before either had attained office. As for J.J. Overton's influence, Conway could only guess that it had also reached the governor. Carey had not said, and he certainly would not strain their long friendship by asking the colonel now.

Looking back on the past four years, Conway remembered that Carey had made a lasting impression on the state, unequaled by any state police superintendent before him. He also knew that Carey's ambitions grew with every passing day. Conway would not be surprised to one day hear him announce his candidacy for governor; the man was just that ambitious and popular. It had been done before by a physician, judge and attorney. The present governor had been a small town attorney. So why not a popular head of state police. In the latter regard, Conway knew that Carey had made some enemies among his own people, yet Conway believed that Carey unquestionably was still a good policeman, interested in bettering the department, considerate of every man who served under him, and that he could easily overcome most pockets of department opposition.

Conway recalled that in his first appearance before the legislature after his appointment as supervisor of state police, Carey had stunned and pleased the entire force with demands, not requests, for additional qualified men, more money for troopers and beginning troopers, and better working conditions. Surprisingly, he had been successful, Conway remembered. Conditions had improved for the entire department, more money had indeed attracted better qualified young men, and troopers, for the first time in the history of the department, were being compensated for overtime.

The state's media had climbed on the daring Carey's bandwagon, supporting him in almost every endeavor. A well-intentioned newspaper columnist likened his concern for department personnel to a "hen with chicks." The allusion was later picked up by a droll newspaper copyreader who in a headline over a state police pension story referred to state troopers as "Mother Carey's Chickens." The reference appeared in other printed stories around the state, and early in Carey's career as the leader of the department his troopers were whimsically known by that name. He often was called "Mother Carey," even by some of his own people—the latter secretly. That is the way it had been for the past four years. Now the governor's first term would soon end, and in a matter of days he would succeed himself to serve another four years as political head of the state. Conway knew that Carey expected, and wanted, to serve four more years with Wingate. He knew, too, that, if for no other reason, Carey, like himself, would prefer to have the Fielding case settled immediately. His way if possible.

As he and Carey parted company at the state police barracks, Conway was still not convinced that he needed Carey's help with this newest investigation that had descended on his district. He felt that Carey was being unnecessarily invasive, pulling rank, and it irked him. Neither was he convinced that the body found in the fire was that of someone other than Crestman Fielding. But this was only the mere beginning of the personal differences that would surface in the Fielding investigation. Now Sunday was drawing to a close and Conway was longing to spend what was left of it with Marjorie in their home at Patterson.

15

A week had passed since Colonel Carey's unexpected visit. During that period Captain Timothy Melton, Lieutenant Bradley Schultz and Sergeant Harley Oaks, as requested, had begun pooling their efforts in the initial phase of the investigation of the Fielding fire.

As yet they had come up with nothing to indicate that the body found in the fire ruins was not that of Crestman Fielding. From his office at headquarters eighty miles away in the state capital at Mount Carmel, an undaunted Carey had been pushing them to find something to support the growing suspicion that someone other than Fielding had perished there.

In the meantime, for reasons he would never reveal, Carey had upstaged Conway. He made his and J.J. Overton's misgivings public knowledge in a surprise announcement to the Mount Carmel *Morning Sun* newspaper. During a routine weekly press conference he announced that state police were in the process of investigating a suspicious, fatal fire and possible one million six-hundred thousand dollar insurance fraud in Spiceland County. He said that although the victim's identity was not yet known, he was confident that it would soon be established by state police investigators.

The newspaper was informed that, in the interest of a complete and speedy solution to the case, he had assigned criminal investigator Captain Timothy Melton, to personally direct the probe. The paper was told that Melton was already situated at the Moses City barracks where he could be closer to the Fielding home, and, with a team of detectives, was looking into the suspicious death. Carey also revealed that a state police criminal laboratory team had been ordered to the scene to sift through fire debris in a search for clues.

Carey added that although his men had yet to determine the origin of the fire, there was a strong probability that it was arson. When questioned about this by reporters, Carey further revealed that the motive for the blaze suggested an attempt, probably by Crestman Fielding, to defraud four insurance companies of one million six-hundred thousand dollars. He went so far as to name State Bankmens Life as the prime insurance carrier, and Paragon Mutual, Unity Life and National States Underwriters as the sharing carriers of the face value of the policy issued in Fielding's name.

When he was finished talking to the *Sun*, almost everything then known by state police about the investigation was well on its way to becoming grist for the state's other newspapers and its electronic media. As might have been expected, then, it was from that metropolitan news source, and not from the commander of the Moses City State Police Barracks, that those suspicions were learned by Moses City's daily newspaper, *The Intelligencer*.

"I was as surprised as you when I heard it on television this morning," Conway told Peter J. (PJ) Cayne, the police reporter from that paper the next morning. "I haven't seen the state papers yet, but I suppose they have the whole story."

"They've got it," the reporter assured him.

"Well, I can't elaborate on what's been said," a

chagrined Conway told him. "You'll have to call Colonel Carey at headquarters. I can only tell you that we are conducting an investigation, and at this time we know very little."

Conway wished he could have added that Carey had no facts, really nothing that could positively point to foul play or to a mystery of any dimension. He secretly wished, too, that Carey had been more discreet, that he might have left well enough alone, at least for the time being.

Melton shared Conway's view. When Cayne later telephoned him, he also declined to comment on the case. His reason, he told the reporter, insisting that his words were "off the record," was that he had yet to share Carey's suspicion. Moreover, Melton said, he had no suspicions at this point.

He did confide to the reporter that he felt strongly that Carey was jumping to conclusions. He himself, he said, had already interviewed Winona Fielding and her sons and, from what they had told him, he, at this point in the probe, was leaning strongly toward the belief that there was no mystery surrounding the death.

But most apparent at the moment, he stressed to the reporter, was the fact that the investigation, for lack of evidence, had yet to get off the ground. Then because of his uncertainty about any phase of the investigation at that early time, Melton had repeated to the reporter that he preferred to remain silent and asked the man to honor his request that he should not be quoted.

Schultz, as ordered by Carey, was overseeing the work of state police crime laboratory technicians at the Fielding place. Two men and one woman worked under a huge protective tent that had been raised near the fire scene. During that same week of sifting through the rubble, in weather that had turned bitterly cold, the lab people had uncovered absolutely nothing to indicate that a person—anyone—or anything, had died there.

"We've drawn a blank, Captain," Schultz told Melton who had checked with him after a couple of days of probing the fire debris. The two policemen, in plain clothes, stood with hands outstretched for warmth toward a portable heater in which a fuel oil-fed fire blazed and roared. From where he stood Melton counted three such heating units in the large tent, but though they made much noise they did little toward keeping the interior comfortable. Schultz and the lab people, he noticed, worked bundled in winter street clothing. He had the feeling that it might be colder inside the tent than it was outside. With the palms of his hands he rubbed the warmth of the heater into his lean thighs as a shiver went through his body. He heard Schultz's voice.

"The fire marshal's people might come up with something, but they're working on their own," Schultz was saying. "They won't tell us anything until they're ready." His voice took on a harsh note. "In the meantime we're just trying to keep warm."

Blond and in his mid-forties, Schultz was a lanky, roughly handsome man. Innately quiet and easygoing, his only vice, his wife once told their good friend Melton, was an addiction to chewing tobacco. Having mastered the art at an early age while growing up on the bottomland farm of his ancestors, Schultz, Melton once observed, "Could chew all day and never spit."

Melton chuckled after such a comment to fellow officers one day and added, "He didn't dare spit. His parents were so religious they would have had him excommunicated if they knew he was committing such a terrible sin."

Another time Melton noted that, "He probably eats with that cud stuck in his jaw. But, he's one doggone fine detective."

Schultz was indeed a fine detective, one deserving more of a role in the Fielding investigation than supervising a crew of lab technicians who knew more of what they were doing than he could ever know. His expertise was in the field, digging out evidence. But in this instance he was where he was on Carey's orders, and he resented it.

It was no secret in the state police department that the two men shared little in the way of friendship. Carey did, however, respect Schultz's ability and more than once had commended him publicly. But that was all. In no way, officially or unofficially, did Carey let it be known that the two men had once trooped together and had once been close friends.

Unless he was caught in an impossible situation Schultz said little or nothing to or about Carey. Nor would he speak his name. To Schultz he was "The Colonel," nothing more, nothing less. No one knew what had come between the two policemen, and since neither of them spoke of it, it was apparent that no one would ever know. But there were those in the department who suspected Carey of having made a pass at Schultz's wife, but that was only a suspicion, and it remained that. The nearest it ever approached revelation came about one day when during a staff meeting at headquarters Carey, complimenting Schultz on a fine job, had referred to him as "Schultzie." Bristling at the familiarity, Schultz faced Carey and said loudly enough for all to hear, "Sir, my name is Bradley Schultz, in this department, Lieutenant Bradley Schultz. I will thank you to refer to me in that manner."

Obviously smarting from the censure Carey's face flushed, but he wisely said nothing. Nothing more was ever said about that confrontation. Without ever having discussed their own personal feelings about the two men, Melton and Conway had guessed months ago that given the present leadership of the department, when Schultz completed twenty years, the minimum period of service for regular retirement, he would leave. They agreed his departure would be an irreplaceable loss.

Fortunately for him but not for the Fielding investigation, Schultz, at Carey's request, returned to his own district in the northern part of the state when one week later the lab crew's fruitless search was called off. As Schultz prepared to leave he shook hands with Melton and observed, "I think we have been wasting our time, Tim. From what I've seen, I'd say this guy committed suicide."

As it turned out, Detective Sergeant Harley Oaks struck the first spark in the stalled Fielding investigation. As had often happened to Oaks in other cases in which he'd been involved, what he learned had come as the result of diligence. Since his assignment to the investigation he had been persistently asking questions of businessmen in Moses City. From them he learned the identities of some of those persons who held worthless checks written and signed by Fielding.

Sought out by the detective, the majority of them readily admitted that they had known or guessed they were contributing to Fielding's folly, his need for liquor, when they had accepted his checks. But because he had been a friend and past patron, and in some cases a lodge brother, they had felt sorry for him, and, perhaps, a bit obligated to him.

Most of them also wanted to believe, as they honestly admitted to Oaks, that Fielding would one day surely recover financially and make things right; and, in any case, the checks were for small amounts. More important, and what was not generally known, Oaks learned, was that according to one Moses City merchant, Fielding had also left a trail of bad checks in Hickory Grove, in adjacent Dogwood County.

Dogwood County was in the Moses City State Police District and Oaks knew from past experience that popular Hickory Grove was an ideal place for dumping worthless checks. With two weeks of the investigation now past, Oaks thought that a check of Hickory Grove merchants might lead to a quick conclusion to the Fielding investigation.

16

Nowhere in the southern half of the state was the enchantment of changing seasons more impressively beautiful than in remote Dogwood County, west of Moses City. Its hilly terrain, its valleys and glens, its rivers and creeks, its breathtaking overlooks and state forest and park, each year attracted tourists by the thousands; the vast majority of them arriving during the colorful autumn season.

They ultimately converged on Dogwood County's single incorporated community and county seat, Hickory Grove. A town of almost as many shops as residences, and deliberately rustic in picturesque surroundings, it was for shop owners and innkeepers alike one of the most lucrative small towns in the state.

The popularity of Hickory Grove was constant. Tourists—men, women and children—arrived daily by automobile and chartered bus from all over the state. Because of the proximity of the world renowned teaching and research center of Brackenridge University at New Washington, twenty-five miles distant, many visitors came from all over the nation and globe. They partook of the unpolished environment as though it were a curing tonic, browsed through its multitude of curio, art, antique and souvenir shops, dined and danced at inns of rustic splendor, married in its ancient limestone-brick courthouse in the center of the town square, and honeymooned in provincial lodges and tiny, chalet-like log houses both in the town and in the nearby primitive state park.

The throngs of strangers visiting the town and county provided ideal seclusion for party-goers from nearby communities such as Moses City. In the course of an evening or weekend retreat, they were able to make themselves unseen and unknown in their chosen pleasures. Also in recent years the demand for housing there by the affluent retired from the capital and other large cities in the state had turned Dogwood County into a realtor's burgeoning dream.

It was against this colorful and lucrative backdrop that Crestman Fielding's real estate venture, a beautifully landscaped colony of condominiums, had taken root, and had failed. He had borrowed heavily from bankers and lodge brothers. His primary and largest single loan was for several hundred thousand dollars from State Bankmens Life Insurance Co. The loan had been arranged by his friend and lodge brother J.J. Overton, founder and president of the insurance firm. Seeking to protect his investors and his family against loss, Fielding at that same time took out with State Bankmens Life an insurance policy for one million six hundred thousand dollars on his life. Although she was never made aware of this until after her husband's death, Winona was made his sole beneficiary. The total amount was shared by State Bankmens Life, Paragon Mutual, Unity Life and National States Underwriters. The arrangements with the latter three carriers had also been made with the influence and assistance of Overton.

Hickory Grove's popularity, its continued economic growth, and Dogwood County's increasing need for housing seemed to ensure the success of the project. It was believed to be a perceptive plan, and from its inception it had been the foregone conclusion of all parties concerned that profits and more profits and a future demand for more such housing would come of the venture.

That might have been the case had the project been completed. But midway through construction, which was rising on the outskirts of Hickory Grove in a beautiful vale in full view of Deer Park Branch, disaster had struck. For the first time in local memory a week of unyielding torrential rains had turned the narrow, charming, brownstone-floored waterway of Deer Park Branch from a normal trickle into a raging flood that had charged insanely through the glen to Big Laurel Creek miles to the south. In its path the nearly constructed condominiums were as vulnerable as matchboxes. Smashed by the maddened waters, they were swept into Big Laurel Creek—by this time itself a swirling race of turbulence and force—and from there into the Blue River and ultimately into oblivion.

It was an unprecedented calamity in the history of Hickory Grove, Dogwood County and the state. The first flood of any kind to ever strike Dogwood County, it destroyed numerous rural homes, ruined hundreds of acres of farm crops, killed countless farm and wild animals, uprooted many trees and swept away Crestman Fielding's dream of financial success and recovery.

In a complete reversal from earlier days of social reclusiveness, Fielding and his family had lived well and openly during the early construction period of the doomed condominium project. At their fashionable home, at swank restaurants, at lodge functions at Mount Carmel and other cities, and at the ever popular and heavily peopled dining and drinking halls of Hickory Grove, the Fieldings had entertained often. Fielding and his wife drove new automobiles, their sons drove late model cars. To the casual observer, as well as to the relief, if not the pleasure, of those who hoped to recoup the money they had loaned him, there was little doubt that Fielding already was wealthy.

Roger Fielding was employed by his father on the project as a construction supervisor. He knew little or nothing about construction, and while this was not generally known, it is doubtful if anyone would have cared. It was obvious to anyone who took the time to notice, however, that Roger worked long and hard, and judging from his new lifestyle, was being generously compensated by his father. What people did not know or suspect was that Fielding, to keep up appearances during the construction period, as J.J. Overton would later charge, was bilking his own project of more than two hundred thousand dollars, by cleverly altering work records and expense claims in the construction loan account of the money obtained from State Bankmens Life.

It was also during this period, prior to the Deer Park Branch misfortune, that Roger Fielding and Penni Lauderman were married.

17

As suddenly as it had forced itself into the public mind, the Fielding fire investigation was pushed aside in favor of a more joyful endeavor; preparation for the approaching four-day Thanksgiving holiday. As quickly as that had come and gone, Christmas was on the horizon, and it was even more evident that the Fielding investigation would soon be set aside again. At least temporarily.

In the meantime, while questioning tavern owners in Hickory Grove, Harley Oaks had found a few who were willing to speak out about Fielding, and to freely theorize concerning the man's alleged suicide.

In one such instance Oaks learned that in the last few days before he was reported dead, Fielding had been seen in the company of an older man, a stranger. Though the detective was able to obtain a physical description of the older man, Oaks was unable to learn the stranger's identity.

In response to his further questioning, Oaks also learned that the stranger, who reportedly was seen with Fielding a few times before the fire, had not been seen in Hickory Grove since the fire. The time of his last known appearance in the town was when he was observed in the company of Fielding the day before the fire. Though it was skimpy information, Oaks, as was his custom, made a detailed report and presented his findings to Lieutenant Conway.

"What do you make of it?" Conway asked.

Oaks shrugged. "According to everyone I talked with," he replied, "they just drank together, and they talked a lot."

"And no one has seen the guy since that day?"

"Not that I could learn. He might show up someplace though." Oaks looked hopefully at Conway.

"May not mean a thing," Conway suggested. "So for the time being we'll keep this here—between us." After a brief pause he added, "But, on second thought, I'd better tell Captain Melton. Meanwhile, you continue at Hickory Grove and learn everything you can about Fielding, and this stranger, whoever he is."

"I could use some help," Oaks said. "There are a lot of people to wade through over there, each of them with his own opinion of what happened. Another man would be a big help."

Conway seriously considered the proposal. "Let's have Sergeant Galiton give you a hand," he said at length. "He's helped before in this sort of thing. I think that will be a good arrangement."

Trooper Anthony Galiton found himself in Hickory Grove soon after the meeting between Oaks and Conway, talking to a man who claimed he also had seen Fielding in the company of a stranger. It was the morning of the day of the Fielding fire, Galiton was informed. According to the witness, the two men had been seen walking together on a Hickory Grove street.

The description of Fielding's alleged companion as given to Galiton matched that given earlier to Oaks in that he was an elderly person, but more than that he was reported as wearing a plaid shirt. Remembering the fragment of blue plaid he and Link Trueblood had gleaned with other evidence from the debris of the fire, Galiton pressed the man for a description of the plaid shirt. Other than repeating that the man wore a plaid shirt the witness was unable to remember anything more.

After Galiton had discussed this coincidence and its possible implications with Oaks, the two policemen drove to the Moses City barracks where they shared the new information with Conway. The district commander then accompanied them to the back room that had been arranged as a temporary field office for Captain Melton.

"Personally, I think the man we're looking for is Crestman Fielding, and he is dead and buried," Melton intoned as he arranged his desk top with a stuffed manila file folder, a legal pad, a couple of ballpoint pens and a box of paper clips. "I don't know what Colonel Carey expects us to find here. But in light of his interest in this case, I think we'd better let him know about this. He may think it's important. I think not. At least not right now. But, let's see what he's got to say."

"Could be important," Conway suggested.

"I've gone over this thing a dozen times," Melton continued. "I've talked with Mrs. Fielding a couple of times, with Roger and James. And I keep coming back to square one. Fielding blew his head off. The lab people couldn't find anything in that rubble out there to make me believe differently. And I, for one, would like to get on with other things."

Melton hesitated and looked at Galiton. "Sorry, Gal. That sounded pretty callous. Maybe if we had — ," he left the sentence unfinished and started a new one. "But we'll call the Colonel and let him decide our next step. He seems to want to call the shots on this thing."

By this time Christmas was little more than a week away and the New Year a week after that. At midnight on the last day of the old year those political office holders whose terms had expired and those who did not survive the November election would be replaced. It would be a time of change and upheaval in many offices in counties throughout the state. And it was a busy time for policemen everywhere whose presence on roads and highways was believed to be crucial to a safe and sane holiday season. As he dialed the telephone on his desk that knowledge weighed heavily on Melton.

"The holidays are going to be a setback to this investigation," he growled to Conway, whom he had asked to stand by in his office while he spoke with Colonel Carey. "And that means I'll just have to be around here that much longer."

In the next second he turned his attention to the telephone. As succinctly as possible he brought Carey up to date on the progress that had been made in the Fielding case. He repeated Oaks' questioning of the witness in Hickory Grove who alleged he had seen Fielding in the company of a stranger wearing a plaid shirt. In detail Melton then advised Carey of Galiton's more recent interview of a second person who said he also had seen Fielding the day of the fire with a man wearing a plaid shirt.

"Listen, Tim," Carey's voice came eagerly through the receiver. "Until we learn differently I'm going to consider this the break we've been looking for in this investigation.

"I will repeat, I want undeniable proof that Fielding is dead and buried. But in view of this development I don't think you're going to be able to find it. He's alive, Tim. This stranger is proof of that. Congratulate Galiton for me. Oaks too. And keep those fellows working on that stranger angle."

"In the meantime," he continued, "you can come back up to headquarters. Until after the holidays, at least. Conway can handle matters down there. But before you leave, Tim," he spoke somewhat more emphatically, "be sure to remind Conway that this investigation is well over a month old now and its success is in his hands. The trail to Fielding is hot and we don't want it to get cold. It's my feeling that this old man, this stranger, will lead us to what I'm hoping for—Crestman Fielding."

18

Early the next morning, as was his custom, Edward Coleman, editor of *The Intelligencer,* unfolded an exchange copy of the Mount Carmel *Morning Sun* on his desk.

From a front page story in that paper he learned that a "mysterious stranger" was now being sought for questioning in the Fielding fire. Although the Fielding home was nearer to Moses City in Spiceland County, the *Sun* writer had given its location as "Not far from the popular tourist mecca, Hickory Grove in Dogwood County."

Coleman, smiling wryly, muttered "Nuts" with vehemence, and with an elbow on the desk top, a fist clenched at his jaw, he skimmed through the account, his head all the while making slight side to side movements as he read. The information had been provided the capital city newspaper by Colonel Carey, who was liberally quoted throughout the article.

"Scooped on our front doorstep," Coleman growled as he dropped the paper on the desk of his police reporter, PJ Cayne. "Ring up your cop friend Lieutenant Conway, PJ, and find out what's going on. And bring this up to date."

When he received Cayne's telephone call about the *Sun* story Conway was simultaneously surprised and angered. "Sorry, I can't tell you a thing, PJ," Conway regretfully informed the reporter. "Not at the moment."

Cayne had always been cooperative and friendly

with police and Conway appreciated working with the man. When Cayne persisted with his questioning, Conway acquiesced, but not in any detail.

"Yes, there is a report involving a stranger who reportedly was seen with Fielding the day before the fire, but that's all. I can't tell you more than that."

After hanging up, Conway obtained from the squad room the gratis copy of the *Sun* delivered every morning to the state police barracks and read the story for himself.

"Damn!" he sucked in his breath noisily as he straightened in his chair and shoved the newspaper further onto his desk, sharply striking the heels of his hands on the desk top as he did so. "Damn!" he growled again.

Angrily he wondered why Carey had spoken prematurely about a matter still in need of substantiation. What rankled Conway more was why had the Colonel insisted on again speaking at the state capital about a local investigation.

That afternoon *The Intelligencer* carried on its own front page an update of the fire at the Fielding home. In a black-bordered sidebar that made it stand out from all other stories on the page was an elaboration of the mysterious stranger theory that had appeared in that morning's *Sun.*

Christmas being so near it was anybody's guess what impact, if any, the two stories might have had in Moses City and Spiceland and surrounding counties. Three people, however, were keenly interested. They were state policemen Conway, Oaks and Galiton. In silence Conway struggled with Carey's unaccountable interference. For the second time the Colonel had taken control of the investigation from his district commander. By his intrusiveness Conway felt that his superior was hobbling him, gagging him; he was unsure of what he himself should or should not do, what he should or should not say.

Also besieging the district commander was his superior's choice of primary news outlets for what was a purely district incident. Why should Carey take the occasion of a death in Spiceland County directly to the media in the capital city? Especially when so little was known about it, when it was not yet known if it was an accidental death, a suicide, or murder.

Was this an attempt by Carey to impress someone? J.J. Overton, perhaps, whose elaborate insurance company offices also were in Mount Carmel? Did Overton have his friend the governor's ear in this matter? Was Carey just playing ball to insure his reappointment after the first of the year? That was assured, Conway thought. Carey and the governor were the best of friends. Yet, if that were so, why was Carey meddling? Had he secretly decided to use the Fielding case for a showdown with Captain Earl Martin, to replace him as head of the state police crime lab, or simply move him—laterally, down, out? Conway shook his head and tried to wipe the disturbing thoughts from his mind, but they clung out of reach like cobwebs to a high ceiling.

Oaks and Galiton also wondered why Carey had interfered again, why he had released the report to the media. At the end of their shift late that afternoon, both policemen confided their concern to Conway. They felt the latest information about a stranger having been seen in the company of Fielding in Hickory Grove should have remained within the department, at least until they could have checked it out. They hoped that their future efforts to shed more light on the stranger angle had not been compromised by Carey's premature release of the information.

"Don't let it worry you," Conway advised his two investigators. "As policemen we have an inherent tendency to think that giving too much information too soon to the public is not in our best interest. That's argumentative. I have my own feelings about the Colonel in this matter, but in spite of that this might turn out to be a break. Let's just see what happens from here on. Right now," the lieutenant's tone became confidential, "I've got a feeling we're onto something with this stranger. I'm changing my mind, fellows. I've got a feeling our boy's alive."

Had he not heard his own voice Conway might have believed someone other than he had uttered those words. Had his life depended on it he could not have explained to Oaks and Galiton his sudden change of mind, for from the outset he had entertained the belief that Fielding was the victim in the fire. But his change of mind had happened, abruptly, and with each passing moment he was becoming more and more convinced that a stranger, and not Fielding, had died in the fire at the Fielding home.

In conjunction with that thought a plan was forming in his mind. Let Carey have his day, for whatever reason or reasons, he thought. He, Conway, knew now what he would do. He would resume control of his own district, specifically the Fielding investigation. In the last analysis he would have to answer for it. Therefore he would, in spite of Carey's tactics, oversee it and he would do so in his own way.

"We'll continue this investigation my way. Nobody else's," he spoke boldly to his sergeants, deliberately refraining at this point from mentioning Carey by name.

He was entertaining the thought that any further

information about the stranger in the Fielding file would be confined to the limits of the barracks. "We are going to keep our mouths shut, I'll see to that," he promised himself. "If anything is to be released to the public I will release it. Should Carey ask for developments he will be welcome to them. But," Conway cautioned himself, "we are just not going to volunteer anything more until we know something solid."

Aloud he explained his decision to Oaks and Galiton who nodded in satisfaction. "In the meantime," he concluded, "keep hammering away, guys. Who knows, these stories in the papers and on television could be more of a help than a hindrance. They might awaken some memories. Try talking again with Winona and Roger. See If you can turn up something Captain Melton might have overlooked. I don't know what that might be; he's a pretty thorough guy and a hard act to follow, but it won't hurt to try."

Before either sergeant could speak Conway seemed to have read their thoughts. "What a time for holidays, huh?" he said somberly, alluding to the near proximity of Christmas and the New Year and the need for traffic details.

"Well, you guys will have to work traffic," he said resignedly, "there's nothing we can do about that. We are going to be slowed down on this investigation until after the holidays, no doubt about it. Still," he suddenly smiled broadly, "I have a feeling that something good is soon going to happen. I don't have the slightest idea what, but I wouldn't be surprised if Crestman Fielding walked into my office tomorrow morning."

It was not Crestman Fielding but Ira Brown who walked into Conway's office the next morning. He carried with him a copy of pathologist Dr. Hamilton Brent's final autopsy report which he unceremoniously placed on the desk in front of Conway. After scanning the detailed paragraphs, Conway's eyes returned to two of them, the first of which amended Brent's initial finding of carbon monoxide in the body identified as that of Crestman Fielding.

"One is quite impressed," Conway read aloud from Brent's report, "with the pinkish discoloration of the tissues, suggestive of the possibility of carbon monoxide intoxication, although obvious absence of carbonaceous material within the respiratory tract is also evident."

As Conway spoke the last words his voice took on the quality of a question, and he raised his eyes to those of the Spiceland County coroner.

"Are you thinking what I'm thinking, that this guy died before the fire?" he asked.

"I probably thought of it," the coroner replied. "But I don't believe it. There's got to be some other explanation."

Conway shook his head. "If the guy was still alive and breathing during that fire, as hot as it was, there'd have been some evidence of heat, or ash residue in his throat and lungs, wouldn't there?"

Ira Brown shrugged. "Maybe. I don't know. But you'd think so." He shrugged again. "I'm not a pathologist. You'll have to take that up with Dr. Brent."

Conway nodded and returned to the report to read the second paragraph that had caught his attention, a determination of the blood sample taken from the dead man. It had been sent to Brent from the state toxicology laboratory in Mount Carmel.

"Blood of the victim," the policeman again read aloud, "was found to contain ethyl alcohol in concentration equivalent to a blood alcohol level of .137 per cent."

Conway shook his head. "This guy was more than

legally drunk when he died," he said.

Ira Brown's chin bobbed in agreement. "That would not have been unusual for Crestman Fielding. A few years ago, even several months ago, maybe, but not recently. He'd been drinking pretty heavily—morning, afternoon and night—and he could hold his liquor."

"Then what's your opinion, Mr. Brown?"

"I don't understand, but I don't think this changes a thing," Ira Brown indicated with an extended upturned palm the copy of the pathologist's report where it now lay on Conway's desk. "There's still no doubt in my mind that the dead man is Crestman. No doubt whatsoever. Not as far as I'm concerned, anyway."

19

The few days until Christmas passed tediously for Oaks and Galiton. Try as they might, in that brief yet emotionally protracted time, they could not learn more about the stranger now purportedly involved in the Fielding investigation. If Fielding had in fact been seen before the fire in the company of a stranger in a Hickory Grove tavern and on a Hickory Grove street, the two policemen were unable to learn any more than that.

It was the wrong time of the year to be asking people questions about anything except Christmas, anyway, and about those things pertaining to the holiday. Despite their discouragement the two policemen were nevertheless thankful for the break, content, when the time came, to temporarily put aside the investigation and turn their thoughts and attentions fully toward the imperative demands of increased holiday traffic.

When they were off duty and free from traffic detail, neither Oaks nor Galiton, weary with fatigue as the pre-holiday hours of constant traffic control wore on, had a moment or thought for the investigation. Despite the demands of their police duties, they, as did everyone else, had their own personal obligations and preparations to fulfill for Christmas. Each intuitively understood that he was reacting in his own personal way to the popular demands of that special holiday. Was that wrong? Was it not a time of the year to forget the real world, if at all possible, until a more convenient time, a time less personally insistent and demanding?

It was also at this time, three days before the Christmas weekend, that the new season had begun flexing its wintry muscle. The temperature dropped sharply during the afternoon, and that night a northwest wind swept three inches of freezing snow into the south central portion of the state including Moses City and Spiceland County. There were children and some adults who were delighted at the prospect of a white Christmas. For policemen, the snow and ice were tantamount to a white plague. Traffic between cities and towns, already constant with commuters and transients, became thick and hellish with skidding, crashing vehicles, last minute shoppers, homebound travelers and Christmastime revelers. Galiton and Oaks, fortunate enough to have the holiday itself off, were relieved and even happy, when the time came, to escape the madness on the highways and to give themselves completely to their families and the holiday.

On the first day of the following week Christmas was already a memory and state police thinking had automatically turned toward the inevitable approaching New Year's weekend. Again, traffic would top state police duties. The Fielding investigation was once again relegated to the back burner, with one exception. At his desk at state police headquarters in Mount Carmel on Tuesday morning after the Christmas weekend, Colonel Carey received a welcome telephone call from state fire marshal George T. Schilling. In sharply enunciated tones Schilling advised Carey that the delayed investigation conducted by his office strongly suggested that the cause of the Fielding fire was the result of arson. Carey, who had been reading a copy of that morning's Mount Carmel *Morning Sun* while reclining comfortably in his high-backed, leather upholstered swivel chair, leaned suddenly forward, the paper forgotten.

"Are you sure, George?" he almost shouted into the phone.

"As sure as we can be at this time," Schilling assured him. "We haven't been able to isolate the major catalyst, and we may never be able to, but it was either gasoline, kerosene, alcohol or paint thinner, and maybe all of them. They were all in there. Something exploded and all of that stuff burned like hell. We know for certain that the origin and the hottest part of the fire was where the body was found, and that area had been saturated with one or more inflammables."

"Anything more?" Carey's voice was tense, expectant.

"There's more here," he heard Schilling say.

"Yes, George, what is it?"

"That car and the pickup truck in the barn. They burned up and the gasoline tanks exploded. The ignition of the pickup was turned on. And the woman who reported the fire, Mrs. Verden? She told one of my inspectors that the nearest she could get to that barn was about fifty feet, it was so hot. The volunteer firemen also say that place was very hot. Something in addition to that barn was burning, you can bet on it."

"Is all of that noted in your report?"

"That last is an opinion, but yes, it is," Schilling replied.

"Have a copy of what you've got sent down to my office right away, George, will you please? That's great news. Great news. Thank you."

Schilling's office was two floors above the first floor state police headquarters in the state capital building and Carey had a copy of the report within the hour and studied it closely before reaching for the telephone. In a matter of minutes he was speaking with Lieutenant Conway in Moses City.

"Arson?" Conway seemed surprised.

"Yes. Arson," Carey repeated in metallic tones. "I had a feeling there was something more to this. Now I'm sure of it. And, Frank, the gas tanks on the car and pickup that were in the barn exploded, and the ignition of the pickup was turned on. That will have to be checked out. If the dead man died of carbon monoxide poisoning that may have some bearing on that. Have those men of yours come up with anything more?"

"Nothing new," Conway told him honestly. "But they've been spending their duty time these past several days on traffic detail, like everyone else."

"I know, I know. This is hardly a good time," Carey sighed. "And we still have one more weekend of this." Then in a friendlier mood he said, "Frank, there's got to be something that we're overlooking. When circumstances allow, get those fellows back on this. Have them go back and talk with all those people again. Somebody's got to remember something more."

On the afternoon of the next day Carey, in an unexpected, unexplained move, telephoned Spiceland County Prosecutor William Farnsworth, who had been keeping a low profile in the investigation. In a polite yet firm manner he explained his suspicions to Farnsworth. Then in measured sentences which surprisingly elicited no comment from the prosecutor, Carey asked him to obtain a disinterment permit for the exhumation of the body found in the Fielding fire. He then directed the prosecutor's attention to the fact that a death certificate in the case had not yet been issued, at his request, and that it was still in the possession of the county coroner, retained there in the name of 'John Doe', if necessary, until the completion of the investigation.

"I would appreciate your cooperation in this matter, Bill," Carey said. "I'm sure you will have to request a grand jury investigation of it before long. But for now I'll leave it up to you, sir, on how you deal with the coroner. I'd appreciate all the help you can give us on this."

Farnsworth made a few observations pertaining to the mechanics of the move. In the end he assured Carey the matter would receive his full compliance, that he would obtain a court order not only for the disinterment but also one to extend the filing time of the death certificate, if so needed.

On completion of that call Carey again telephoned the Moses City barracks and explained his newest action to Conway. Surprised to the point of speechlessness, Conway listened, saying nothing. He heard Carey quite brusquely advise him that he should put in motion the necessary arrangements for the exhumation.

"The Browns will be notified by Farnsworth, but I want you to talk to them, too, Frank. They're going to be unhappy about this. So a friendly visit from you will be good public relations. Do what you have to do to appease them," he said.

"We are going to need their full cooperation," he continued. "We want to do this no later than the first Monday after New Year's Day. Everybody should have the holidays out of their systems by then. The body is to be brought up here to Community Hospital where we'll have the state forensic pathologist Dr. John Flood examine it. It is not to be disturbed in any manner, Frank," he cautioned. "Be sure to advise the Browns of that. We want that body just the way it is right now. I'm sure you'll be there to see to that, Frank. I'm going to have Captain Melton drive down to give you a hand."

Conway winced when he heard that Melton would again be involved in the investigation. Conway repeated several times to himself that he didn't need a hand from the supervisor of the state police department, nor did he need one from the district's chief of detectives. He had his own men and they had been doing quite well without assistance. Left to themselves they'd have the investigation completed in record time. They were on their way to having it completed when they were interrupted and delayed by the holidays. But, he sighed audibly, "If Mother Carey wants it that way," he spoke aloud and derisively, "then that's just the way it'll have to be."

He knew that Melton's post holiday plans would be ruined if Carey returned him to Moses City. Melton had earlier confided to Conway that he and his wife had planned to spend a few weeks in Florida after the first of the year. He was not going to appreciate what Carey had in store for him. Considering his outspoken opinion that the investigation was a waste of time, Melton, Conway shuddered at the thought, was going to be an angry bear to work with. Worse, Conway felt that Melton's attitude, unless it had changed, would serve only to delay the probe. This latest surprise by Carey would not help matters.

Conway knew, too, that the disinterment coming so soon after the holidays, as it now must, would put a damper on his own festive spirits, and those of Oaks and Galiton. Having had Christmas off, both men were scheduled to work traffic the entire New Year's weekend. Both were looking forward to time off the following week. That's tough, Conway thought with a shake of his head. Then, picking up the telephone, he murmured sarcastically, "I might just as well make everybody happy."

He dialed the telephone number of Brown & Brown Funeral Home. Ira Brown answered and Conway informed him of the new development. Giving the coroner little opportunity to speak, he told him that the county prosecutor would also be contacting him, and that the Browns should make the necessary arrangements for the exhumation. He also asked the mortician if he would be kind enough to inform Winona Fielding. It would be better, he said, especially at this time, if Winona could be spared hearing such unpleasant news from a policeman.

Before the day was over Conway was contacted by PJ Cayne. There had been a leak. Someone had notified the newspaper of the pending disinterment. No doubt, Conway guessed, someone from the funeral home, or perhaps Winona herself.

"I can't tell you anything except that we are going to exhume the body for further examination, PJ," he told the reporter. "I don't know anything more." He explained that his orders had come directly from Carey, no questions asked, and that only Carey could provide further details.

After he replaced the phone he realized he'd been rather gruff with the reporter. "That Carey," he growled aloud. "I'm letting the guy get under my skin. Better watch myself." The story of the impending disentombment, containing extensive quotes from Carey, appeared in *The Intelligencer* the next day. With the approaching New Year's holiday weekend only a matter of hours away, Oaks and Galiton, who were expecting time off afterwards, were filled with a mixture of disappointment and curiosity. At the same time a sense of mystery and anticipation began descending on Moses City and Spiceland County.

At his stately country home in Spiceland County, about fourteen miles from Moses City, J.J. Overton that evening read with growing satisfaction the newspaper account of the planned removal from its grave in Moses City Memorial Park of the body identified as that of Crestman Fielding. He had been convinced from the outset that his lodge brother and business associate did not perish in the fire at the Fielding home. His chin bobbed as he read his own evasive words in the story, words he himself had spoken over the telephone that morning in reply to questions asked by PJ Cayne, the newspaper's police reporter.

"Do you plan to pay the beneficiary, Winona Fielding, if this proves to be the body of Crestman Fielding?" Cayne had bluntly asked him.

He read his evasive response in the paper: "Before State Bankmens Life will pay, we will have to have a body. I don't believe we have a body, nor do I believe we will have a body."

"Then you don't believe that the body buried as Crestman Fielding is that of Crestman Fielding?" Cayne had pressed for clarification of his words.

"As I told you," Overton read his answer in the newspaper story, "when we have a body we will pay. Crestman Fielding's body."

As he continued reading, Overton knew he was pleased with his answers to the reporter's questions. Now all of Moses City and Spiceland County, the whole state, would know that he believed the man who was once a prominent citizen of Spiceland County, a man who had been a friend and an active and respected lodge brother, was attempting to defraud State Bankmens Life and three other insurance companies, and Overton himself, of a fortune.

Also on the front page of the same issue of *The Intelligencer*, the president of State Bankmens Life was attracted to a separate, related article. He leaned slightly forward as he perused the account of the same reporter's interview with Winona Fielding concerning the planned exhumation.

"I don't know—I don't understand any of what is happening right now," Winona was quoted as saying. "I don't know what anyone is trying to prove. My husband is dead. He is dead and buried. I know that, and I believe it with my whole heart. My husband loved his family, and if he were alive he would not stand by and allow us to suffer this way. He was a good man. The whole county knows that if he was alive he would be right here, by my side."

Overton read on: "They say that my husband did not commit suicide, that he did not die in that fire," Winona's remarks continued. "If he didn't, then who did?" Winona's words seemed to jump off the page at Overton. "If it is not my husband who is buried in that grave, then who *is* buried there?"

Overton shook his head and murmured to himself: "Not your husband, Winona. Not your husband."

He sighed and continued reading: "Now they won't let my husband rest in peace," Winona had told the reporter. "They are going to dig his body out of the grave as though he is some kind of animal. I hate it, them doing this to him, to me, to my family. I hate them. You can't imagine how much. So much that when I think about it I feel nauseated, like I'm going to just smother and die myself.

"I can't believe this is happening to me, to my family. Who do they think they will find in that grave? I won't oppose them. I don't have the money for a lawyer. I don't have any money. Besides, I want to be legal; I want these people to satisfy themselves and everyone else that my husband is dead, and then maybe my sons and I can get on with our lives."

Overton re-folded the newspaper and tossed it to his wife who had just entered the room and seated herself in a chair opposite his.

"Read that, Margaret," he snorted. "There on the front page. Read how easily that woman can lie."

THE EXHUMATION

20

The first day of the new year brought two major changes to Spiceland County's law enforcement scene; and a week into the new year a surprising development in the Fielding investigation came to light. In the first of the two changes, in a swearing-in ceremony at one minute after midnight January 1, Irwin Brown succeeded his father as coroner. In the second change, also made during the same swearing-in ceremony, which took place in the clerk's office at the Spiceland County Courthouse in Moses City, Jefferson "Spud" Tatum officially became the new sheriff.

The surprising development in the Fielding matter a few days later concerned former sheriff Cramer Fielding, the dead man's brother. He had received in the mail a notice from the Tradesmens Trust Bank in Moses City that a six-month note he had signed in the amount of seventy-five hundred dollars was due and payable in ten days.

Shocked and confused, because he knew that he had not signed such a document and certainly had not received such a large sum of money, the former sheriff immediately called at the bank. There he was shown that an application made the previous July for the money, by his brother Crestman, bore what appeared to be Cramer's signature. Since the note would fall due in ten days and Crestman was dead, Cramer, as the apparent cosigner, which was attested to by his signed name on the note, would be expected to make full repayment.

"But I didn't cosign any note," Cramer Fielding angrily informed Charles Windom, a vice president of the bank and its chief loan officer, a man whom Cramer had known personally for many years. "I don't know anything about a loan."

"We have your signature," Windom replied indicating Cramer's name on the note.

"Not mine, Charlie," Cramer retorted. "You may have a signature, and it may be spelled like my name, but it's not my signature. Whatever that name is I didn't put it there, I'll guarantee you. What's more, Charlie, I don't want any more notices like this one sent to me, because I don't owe you a dime."

Cramer Fielding then strode out of the bank and drove directly to the state police barracks. There, after asking to see Conway, he was ushered into the lieutenant's office.

"How does it feel to be out of uniform?" Conway's greeting was friendly, cordial. On a few past occasions he had shared police work with Cramer.

"Mighty good, Frank," Cramer Fielding sighed heavily as he eased himself into the chair Conway had offered him. "I've had my fill. I wanted to be a law enforcement officer, wanted to do good as one, but I was in the wrong place for that. Contrary to popular opinion, a sheriff at this time in this state is not a policeman. He is an administrator and a victim of the political office he holds. I'm not an administrator nor a politician, Frank. Never was. That's why I refused to run for a second term. Anyway, I'm satisfied with being a private citizen again."

As he spoke Cramer Fielding leaned forward and pushed the notice he'd received from the bank onto Conway's desk.

"Take a look at that," he growled, the sound of his

voice making the request almost a demand.

Conway read the note and shrugged. "Are you trying to tell me something?" he asked with furrowed brow.

"I didn't sign that thing, Frank," Cramer said tersely.

"You mean this signature is a forgery?" Conway had leaned forward, elbows on the desk.

"I didn't sign that note, Frank," Cramer repeated.

Conway shook his head and re-read the bank notice. "Have you notified the bank?"

"Talked with Charlie Windom just before coming here. It'll be a snowy day in July before I ever pay that thing, I'll guarantee you," Cramer avowed as he pointed to the note in Conway's hand. "He got that money six months ago," Cramer said, avoiding using his brother's name, "and I didn't know a thing about it. Got it on a note payable in six months. He supposedly carried it out for my signature. I can't believe that those people at the bank could be so stupid, that they didn't at least call me. Friends and trust, Frank." Cramer's face had contorted and sarcasm coated his voice. "Friends who trust each other do these kinds of things."

Conway had a clerk make a copy of the notice for the barracks file on Crestman Fielding and another for the file at headquarters. "If you didn't sign that thing I wouldn't worry about it," he advised his visitor.

"I didn't," Cramer said again, as much for himself as for Conway. "I knew that Crestman was in trouble, and that he had been for some time. But he hadn't spoken to me for years; not me, nor to Craddick."

He started to explain that Craddick was his brother, but Conway waved a hand in acknowledgment and nodded his head to indicate that he already knew as much.

"We had some pretty harsh words with Crestman

when he took over the mill," Cramer then continued. "He'd always worked with the old man there, you know, when he was a kid. Like Roger's been working with him. Craddick and I thought we should have got more for our share of it." Cramer was thoughtful for a few moments, then he added bitterly, "It was more than words, Frank."

His mood suddenly changed and he spoke in tones more of expiation than explanation. "We had a knock-down, drag-out. We got pretty nasty with each other, and I guess each of us came out of it badly hurt, and it's been like we weren't brothers ever since, or family, or even friends. It's been a trying thing to live with, believe me, Frank. When I saw him at his place, burned up in that fire, like he was there, I couldn't even feel anything for him, or for his wife, or their boys."

Cramer was silent. Conway was also silent. He felt that the former sheriff expected him to make some comment, but he could not think of a thing to say other than to thank Cramer for telling him about the note and that he would have one of his investigators call at the bank. After a brief period of desultory conversation between the two men Cramer left the barracks.

Following his departure Conway found himself wondering about the fierce passions that sometimes divided siblings. How often had he as a policeman responded to sudden, angry family disputes that had deteriorated into physical warfare, a few of which had ended not only in injury but in broken hearts, the loss of relationships or in the annihilation of life. He thought of his sister, his parents, even his former wife. Had there ever been an unkind word among them? Arguments, yes. But an unkind, injurious word? He couldn't remember. He wondered what might further become of the Fielding family as a whole in the face of its present crisis. Could Winona and her sons survive the apparent tragedy in their family? Would brothers Cramer and Craddick eventually let bygones be bygones—whatever they may have been—and make some attempt to restore the relationship they once had with their sister-in-law and nephews?

Conway shook his head. He told himself that he could not help them in that respect, that he could not become emotionally involved. He could, however, he told himself almost angrily, get back to business and send one of his detectives to question Charlie Windom at the Tradesmens Trust Bank, as he had promised Cramer Fielding. Conway had believed Cramer when he said he had not cosigned the note for his brother, that his signature was a forgery. Was there a connection between the forgery and the fire? The former sheriff had implied as much before leaving the barracks. Conway was anxious to know.

When Captain Melton arrived unexpectedly at Conway's office later that day the lieutenant's surprise was apparent. "What the heck," Melton answered the lieutenant's unasked question. "I figured I might just as well get down here and get this thing over with now, as soon as possible, so that I can get on with my vacation."

Conway arched his brows but made no reply. He picked up the copy of the notice Cramer Fielding had received from the bank and extended it toward Melton.

"What do you make of it?" Melton asked after he read it and was taking a second look at the missive.

"Don't know," Conway answered. "Except that Cramer is mad as a wet hen and is going to see an attorney. What I'd do too, I suppose, if I were in his

shoes. But that's beside the point. From all the information we've gathered so far, we know that Fielding
didn't spend that kind of money around here in the
last six months. He'd been bouncing checks, and, as
you know, most of them were for piddling amounts."

Melton took a seat, leaned back, raised his arms
and laced his fingers behind his head. "We'll have to
look into it," he said. "We should know what it's all
about. I've got some more news for you, too, if you
think you can handle more today."

"Try me," Conway smiled.

"On the way back here I stopped in town to see
Clare Downing, Crestman Fielding's lawyer. Have
you ever met her?"

Conway shook his head negatively.

"She's quite a gal, Frank." Melton continued. "I'll
bet she's on her way to eighty. Maybe even past
eighty. Spry. Smart. Good memory. Makes me feel
like an old man. Anyway, she told me that Fielding
was in her office a few days before the fire, completely disillusioned and crying; just bawling his eyes out.
He was a big man, and she'd known him all his life,
and I guess it kind of got to her."

Melton paused to make a sympathetic face. Then
with a sharp nod of his head he added, "He started out
by saying he needed to talk to her. Then he asked her
for a loan of eight thousand dollars. Something like
that. Really shook her up, Frank. Anyway, she told
him to go to a bank. That's when he started bawling
and then he told her that there was no use in going on,
that the best thing he could do for everybody concerned
was to blow his brains out. That upset her all the more,
and she said that she kept him in her office for a long
talk, trying to settle him down. But it didn't do any
good. She said that just before he left he promised—get

this, Frank—he promised to make Winona the richest widow in Spiceland County."

Conway had been pinching his chin between thumb and forefinger as Melton spoke. "Well," he said slowly, "some people may be inclined to believe he tried. But I wonder why she didn't tell that to Oaks when he questioned her?"

Then tapping the fingers of his left hand on the desktop, he said, "Tim, I'm bugged by the seventy-five hundred dollars. Imagine shafting your own brother like that. You hear something new and different every day in this business, don't you?"

"I won't argue that," Melton agreed. "I don't have any idea what he might have done with that money, and I have no idea why he wanted to borrow so much money from Clare Downing. There's got to be a connection, Frank. We'll have to look into all of this. But I'll tell you this, after hearing Mrs. Downing, I'm more convinced than ever that Fielding is dead. He was so desperately discouraged and depressed he just blew his brains out with one messy shot."

"Any more good news?"

"Not today," Melton smiled at the insinuation. "And there won't be for a few days. At least not until the forensics people complete their examination of the body after it's been exhumed. They'll take x-rays which they want to compare to any we can locate. So you'd better have someone check Glenview Hospital in town for any of Fielding's x-rays they might have. And the Army." Melton lowered his voice. "Have Oaks and Galiton had any kind of luck?"

"Just a better description of the man Fielding is supposed to have been seen with the morning before the fire. We've put that out statewide."

"What's it amount to?"

Conway picked up Oaks' report. Rather than hand it to Melton he gave the captain a condensed version of it. One morning three days before the fire, an older man had appeared in a package store in Hickory Grove and bought a bottle of wine and a six-pack of beer. As he turned to leave he collapsed. The owner of the store hurried to his aid but the man revived as suddenly as he had fallen and was able to leave the store unassisted. Outside, he collapsed again, falling to the sidewalk. Three passersby, all men, rushed to help him. At the same time, the owner of the store telephoned the Dogwood County sheriff's office and requested an ambulance.

About that same time another man appeared at the fallen man's side. He then turned and hurried to a car parked a short distance away. He drove it to where the fallen man was being supported in a sitting position on the sidewalk. With the help of the other three men he was able to lift the stricken man into the car, and they drove away.

Oaks had learned of the incident while showing a photograph of Fielding around the popular tourist town. In questioning the package store owner and the three passersby Oaks had learned that the fallen man had thin graying hair, brown eyes, and was wearing a plaid shirt. Although he seemed to be conscious, he was unable to speak when asked his name. One of the men told Oaks the fallen man appeared to have something in his mouth and had surmised the man wore loose dentures.

"This is Oaks' report if you want to read it," Conway extended the report to Melton after briefing him on it. "There's a lot more to it, and it's about as complete as they come. Although the one man is still unidentified, after seeing the picture of Fielding that Oaks showed them, the three men who tried to help the old guy thought the driver of the car was Fielding. But the liquor store owner just shook his head when Oaks showed him the photo; said he had never seen the man before."

"How about the car?" Melton asked.

"They all thought it was a '67 Ford."

"The Fieldings didn't own one."

"I know, but listen to this," Conway pressed on. "The next day one of those men who tried to help the old man thinks he saw him with Fielding as they were going into a restaurant. Oaks spoke to a waitress there and showed her Fielding's picture, and she identified it as the picture of the younger of the two men she had seen; in other words, Fielding. The next morning the two of them had breakfast there, according to the waitress. It's all in the report."

21

In spite of recent developments, which might have suggested that he could be wrong, Captain Melton remained convinced that time and money were being wasted on the Fielding investigation.

On several occasions he had spoken at length with Winona, and each time he had come away confident that she was not trying to hide anything from police, and that her husband had indeed taken his own life and was dead and buried in the Fielding family cemetery plot.

The woman had nervously chain-smoked on those occasions during which he had questioned her, he knew, and though she had not wept or otherwise weakened in his presence, it was nevertheless obvious to Melton that she already had suffered from prolonged weeping and that she had been sleepless for some time.

He had found it difficult to view her in any manner except as a virtuous, grieving, even outraged, broken-hearted widow. He suspected her of nothing, except that she may have been drinking. And because he was sincerely touched by her condition, her openness and desire to cooperate, and her unshakable conviction that her husband was dead, Melton was oppressively resistant to any thought of questioning her again. Not anytime soon, at least. And he ordered other investigators not to disturb her.

"I just know we buried my husband," she had repeatedly told him. "As sure as I am here talking to you, I know he's dead. I don't know what they are trying to do to me. But I know that if I don't get his insurance—some money—soon, I will be out of house and home. I need help, Mr. Melton."

On each visit they had sat in the comfortable, tastefully decorated living room of the spacious, green shuttered white frame house which was situated some distance from where the charred rubble of the Fielding barn stood fixed and foreboding. Family photographs looked out from their positions of repose atop the hand-hewn wild cherry wood mantel that stretched across an open limestone hearth partially blackened apparently from much use. Among them the most recent photograph of Crestman Fielding, made not more than two years before the fire, was that of a smiling, handsome man in mid-life. There was one of Winona, too, of earlier vintage, attractive, smiling and not quite so full and round of face and body as the woman who now sat across from Melton, and one photograph each of their sons, Roger and James. On a wall across the room Melton had seen another picture, a smiling family group photo.

In quiet, studied appraisal of them, Melton saw what struck him as four persons who once had been a happy family. He received no hint from viewing the photographs, nor did he expect one, that there might have been a criminal among them. A broken man, yes. A heart-broken family, without a doubt. But nowhere among them could he see or conjure up the image of a killer.

In spite of a genuine effort on his part, he could not bring himself to fully believe that Winona's husband did not take his own life to put an end to his failures and shame. The possibility that Fielding might have killed someone else and placed the body in the barn and set fire to it was, even to Melton the policeman, ironically, unacceptable to him. Identical impressions also had followed his separate talks with Roger and James. However, in Roger's case, as Melton had confided to Lieutenant Conway at lunch one day, there was an underlying reservation about the elder Fielding son that had left their talks deficient, incomplete. Melton couldn't quite put a finger on it, he told Conway, but he was aware of an uneasiness within himself during and after both meetings with Roger, that something of importance had been withheld from him. He also had informed Conway that he would have another talk with Roger.

There was no doubt whatever in Melton's mind that Crestman Fielding had deceived his brother Cramer. He believed that with the unwitting aid of careless bankers, Fielding had forged Cramer's name to obtain money from a home town lending institution much the same as he had preyed upon the sympathies and influence of several of his lodge brothers in order to borrow other monies. After he had become hopelessly mired in treacherous financial transactions, and seeing no possible relief from his intractable situation, Fielding had turned to drink. Eventually he had found the unthinkable courage to put a loaded shotgun to his head and pull the trigger. None of which was too difficult for Melton to understand, and none of which had been disproven. But, he now asked himself over and over, what had Fielding done with the money he had obtained with the aid of his brother's forged signature? The very next morning after his meeting with Conway, Melton received his answer in a telephone call at the Moses City barracks from J.J. Overton.

"Just in case you're wondering what Crestman

Fielding did with that money he stole from Tradesmens Trust Bank, I'll tell you," Overton said loudly into the telephone. "He came here and paid the insurance premium with most of it."

"How do you know it was that money?" Melton asked lightly while at the same time wondering how Overton had learned of the forgery.

"Well, I don't. Not for sure, anyway," Overton replied. "But six months ago he walked into this office with the cash, and I know he didn't have that kind of money. At the time I just assumed he'd borrowed it. Listen," Overton had lowered his voice, as though he might have been about to impart a confidence, "I've known Crestman for years, and I'm telling you, he is not dead. Nothing in this world will make me believe that he killed himself. Take my word for it, he's definitely someplace, and I don't mean buried in a cemetery."

Melton was thoughtful for a long time. Was it possible, he thought, that Fielding hoped to borrow enough money to pay off the bank loan he had obtained by forging his brother's name? Was Clare Downing's refusal to lend him that money disappointment enough to throw him into a black pit of depression so deep that he would see his only escape in suicide? Melton nodded his head affirmatively. "That's got to be it," he said aloud to himself.

22

The short but nevertheless macabre caravan of cars and trucks that wound its way to the newest of Moses City's burial grounds began in the wet cold of a dark rainy January morning. To the nasal monotone of a meteorologist who cautioned repeatedly on the lead car radio that an expected further drop in temperature could turn travel surfaces into treacherous ice, the vehicles proceeded slowly over glistening, nearly deserted streets.

As the first gray light gave fuzzy definition to the bleakness of a soggy rural Spiceland County, the caravan crept across the eastern municipal limits of Moses City and through the attractively landscaped memorial park gateway. In the momentary brilliance of sweeping headlight beams as the vehicles moved forward, rain-soaked decorative evergreen wreaths and blankets and colorful plastic baubles, memorial sentiments of the recent Christmas holiday, flashed into incongruous being on rain-drenched graves.

The lead car, driven by the county's newly elected coroner, Irwin Brown, who now peered through his wire frame spectacles into the cold drizzle past the metronomic wavings of its windshield wipers, ground its way over the gravel drive. Although promised to early lot purchasers the cemetery's roadways had yet to be macadamized. The procession continued along the main drive, winding grim and desolate around its perimeter, until the lead car eased to a stop beyond a mounded, markerless grave. Irwin Brown's father, the former coroner Ira Brown, now his son's deputy, sat unmoving and silent in the passenger seat.

A burial vault truck behind the lead car halted opposite the mounded grave. Crouched on a lo-boy trailer attached to the rear of a second truck, a backhoe, yellow and dripping, brooded noiselessly. A couple of car lengths behind that the fourth vehicle in the procession, a white, red and gold-trimmed state police cruiser seemed gripped in a weird dance as the cold drizzle splattering on its colorful surface shimmered and sparkled in the gleaming yet shadowed headlights of the car behind it. The uniformed trooper behind the wheel of the cruiser leaned forward to switch off the car's lights. Although it was warm and comfortable inside, he shivered involuntarily.

"A helluva morning to be digging into a grave, Gal," grumbled Link Trueblood.

"Wild," his companion, also in uniform, commented somberly. Trooper Anthony Galiton then began unrolling a transparent slicker. "I hope we won't have to get out in this soup." He shook his head and repeated his single word observation. "Wild," he said. And he murmured, "I don't know of a thing we could do out there."

"Wilder than a fart in a whirlwind," Trueblood growled in agreement. "You'd think the Colonel could have at least waited for a better day. That body isn't going anywhere. But," he sighed resignedly, "I just work here, too."

In the unmarked police car behind them, which was the last car in the procession, Lieutenant Frank Conway, also in uniform, and Captain Timothy Melton, in civvies, had made the drive to the cemetery in relative silence. Now Conway spoke.

"They're going to have a time of it," he said almost

in an undertone. He too would have preferred better weather for the grim task now unfolding in the cold, early morning rain, but he kept the thought to himself. "Do you think we ought to get out?"

"No need to get wet, Frank," Melton grumbled as he gazed through the fogged passenger window at the dismal conditions outside the car. "These guys are pros, they'll have the job done in no time. All we need to do is watch; be here." He cranked the window open a few inches and shivered at the wet cold air that greeted him.

Watching should have required no more than a single trooper, one policeman to officially view the opening of the proper grave and the removal therefrom of the cumbersome concrete vault containing the casket with the remains of the dead man, the body found in the barn fire at the Crestman Fielding home. But Colonel Carey had insisted on the impressive presence there, for the record, of a multiple official police escort.

Conway kept the motor running for the benefit of the windshield wipers and the defogger. He and Melton watched in silence as workmen in glistening yellow raincoats and shining droopy-brimmed yellow rubber hats spread large sheets of plywood on the muddy ground around the mound of soggy dirt. At the same time the weighty gray stillness of the wet morning was rent by the sharp clatter of a diesel motor coming to life. They shifted their gaze to the large yellow backhoe that had begun a slow inch-by-inch pitching, loping, braking movement as it descended the lo-boy trailer in reverse gear. Like an ungainly prehistoric monster, it roared and rocked and snorted; and once on the ground it made a clumsy about face, then trundled and swayed on its tracks to a position on the rain-soaked plywood ground covering beside the grave.

In the colorful police cruiser Trueblood pursed his lips and commented to no one in particular, "One crazy way to make a living."

"I'll bet those guys make a lot more money than we do," Galiton said as he rolled down his window. He was aware that the drizzle was splattering him and that the thick, almost visible air was invigorating. "I know that guy on that backhoe," he added, cranking the window back up. "You should see the house he lives in. A castle compared to mine."

Galiton had never witnessed a disinterment. With mixed emotions he watched silently as the thick steel bucket of the backhoe, as wide as a grave, rose and fell in clanking, thudding, ripping motions while the sodden mound of dirt on the grave was slowly transferred to a new mound beside the grave. He winced slightly when he heard the huge cold steel teeth that protruded from the lower lip of the bucket at last scrape the lid of the unseen concrete vault. He tried to envision the encased casket that held the mystery begun some six weeks earlier and had on a bleak, rainy winter morning ultimately drawn this eerie assemblage to a waterlogged meadow of death. He tried to shrug off a sudden chill.

The backhoe suddenly moved away from the opened grave, and with a series of crashes and bangs it lurched up the portable metal ramps and onto its lo-boy trailer, to once again quietly crouch there. At the same time the vault truck backed slowly onto the vacated plywood panels, its boom extended over the gaping grave. In a matter of minutes workmen, standing on the muddy, domed lid of the burial vault, fitted clevises and chains to each of the steel U-bolts at its four corners. Then the rectangular mass of mud-covered concrete, making what sounded like obscene noises as it was wrenched by a winch from the grip of the red clay ooze that held it, rose reluctantly. Then, with nerve-grating squeals and clankings from the winch mechanism, it was guided into the angle iron carrier of the vault truck.

Trueblood switched his radio to three-way and spoke to Conway. "Any orders, Lieutenant?"

"Just follow them to the funeral home. We'll watch there to see the job gets done." Conway's voice was low, distant, barely audible. To Trueblood, given the early morning surroundings, it sounded ghostly.

Mud-caked tires of the cortege left multiple thick red clay tracks on the wet county blacktop as the vehicles left the cemetery. Red mud dripped from the vault to the truck bed on which it rode, dropping from there to the rain-splattered surface of the blacktop. Red mud flung backward by the rear wheels of the trailer flecked the hood and windshield of the police cruiser.

Trueblood gritted his teeth. "Will you look at that," he growled as he eased his foot back from the accelerator slowing the cruiser.

"Better your car than mine," Galiton observed.

At the rear of the funeral home, unprotected from the falling rain, workmen operating a winch on the vault truck lowered the sealed vault to the blacktopped surface of the parking lot. After several unsuccessful attempts to pry the huge lid open with a pinch bar, a hydraulic pry was inserted between vault and lid and the epoxy seal was at last broken. The lid rose grimly, almost painfully, and then, like a giant taffy-pull, the thick black sealer between the vault rim and the lid began yielding its grip in long, ropy strands.

Galiton swung open the cruiser's passenger door, donned his slicker, and moved toward the vault. He was joined there by Trueblood, also clad in his slicker, and they stood unmoving in the rain as workmen lifted out the casket. When it was free of the mud-covered vault the troopers stepped quickly to lend their assistance. At that moment Trueblood noted that a stone mason's white apron was fastened around its middle.

Together, workmen in muddy knee-high rubber boots and troopers in transparent slickers protecting neatly pressed uniforms and highly polished cordovan cavalry boots carried the coffin into the funeral home garage. Once inside they pushed it into the cavernous rear opening of a waiting black van in which it would be taken to Community Hospital Morgue at Mount Carmel, as per Colonel Carey's orders, where it would be examined by state pathologist Dr. John Flood.

As they were driving toward the state police barracks, Trueblood wondered aloud about the white mason's apron on the dead man's casket.

"That's a symbol of the Masons," Galiton said. " I arrested a guy for drunk driving one time and according to him they get one of those aprons when they join the organization and they get buried in it."

"Strange," commented Trueblood.

"Not really," rejoined Galiton. "This guy said that short white apron is supposed to be symbolic of Christ the carpenter, and they have other symbols, like a carpenter's square and compass to remind them to always be honest and moderate. It's a first rate organization made up of a fine group of men, patriotic, religious and charitable. They do a lot of good things. But like any group of men, there sometimes is a bad apple in the barrel; like this guy I arrested. He had the square and compass symbol on his license plate when I nailed him. Probably thought I should have let him go; a lot of our guys belong to the organization and probably would have."

"It's for sure I don't belong, and I would not have let the guy go," Trueblood said.

"If you did belong you'd get to wear one of those aprons up to heaven or down to hell when you die, like the poor guy in that casket back there," Galiton smiled sardonically. "But since there's so much doubt about him being Crestman Fielding I wonder what they'll do to him when he arrives at his destination with that apron if he's not a Mason."

Because of the condition of the remains of the dead man the Masonic Apron was tied around the casket

Two days later Captain Timothy Melton, at his desk at headquarters in Mount Carmel received an intra-office telephone call from Colonel Carey.

"Carey, Tim." He was informed of the caller's identity.

Melton had been expecting the call. "What's new?" he said by way of greeting.

"Judge for yourself," Carey's tone was sharp, demanding. "The forensics people at Community Hospital confirm Dr. Brent's finding that our man down at Spiceland County did not die of a gunshot, and he did not burn to death."

After a moment of thoughtful silence Melton said, "Carbon monoxide, then."

"Right," Carey assured him. "Carbon monoxide poisoning. I've got the report right here in front of me. According to it, the subject was more than likely dead from carbon monoxide poisoning before the fire. No evidence to the contrary could be found. Brent was correct in the first place. And here's something else: according to Dr. Flood the x-rays taken of the cadaver do not necessarily correspond to those made of Fielding at Glenview Hospital when he was a patient there."

Melton was silent.

"You there, Tim?"

"Yes. Yes, I'm here."

"Listen. This is beginning to sound more and more like what I suspected from the start," Carey said firmly. "We have got to identify this corpse. Let's find out who the dead man is. And don't forget, let's try to learn the whereabouts of Fielding."

"Will do," Melton replied without enthusiasm.

"One more thing."

"Yes Colonel?"

"I also want Winona and her sons watched. They've got to know something more than what they have told us. If we keep them under surveillance they may lead us to something."

There was a pause in which only the breathing of the two police officers could be heard over the phone. Then Carey spoke again.

"Got that, Tim?"

Unseen as he was by Carey, Melton shook his head negatively.

"Yes, I've got it, Colonel," he replied.

23

The state capital's media had the latest pathologist report that night and the following morning Lieutenant Conway read the account of Dr. Flood's findings in the Mount Carmel *Morning Sun* without emotion. Surprisingly he was not angered. He subsequently responded to questions put to him in a telephone call, which he fully expected, from PJ Cayne, *The Intelligencer* police reporter.

Late that afternoon he read a more complete and detailed story of the report in that paper. He then began preparing to leave his office for the ride home to Patterson when the phone rang. Barracks commander Donaldson's voice greeted him over the intercom.

"It's Cramer Fielding, Lieutenant. Are you in?"

"Yeah, Wendy. Go ahead and put him through."

Conway heard the ex-sheriff's voice and greeted him warmly. They talked briefly about the story in *The Intelligencer,* then Cramer Fielding said, "I've got something to tell you, Frank. It's for your ears alone, right now. How about if I come in sometime tomorrow?"

"Sorry, Cramer," Conway said sincerely. "Got a staff meeting at headquarters tomorrow. Be gone all day. How about Friday? Can it wait that long?"

"Be fine," Cramer Fielding agreed. "What time?"

"Well, I'm usually bright-eyed and bushy-tailed in the morning," Conway said with humor. "Nine to ten be all right? Earlier, if you like."

"Nine's okay."

Minutes later Conway eased himself behind the wheel of his police car and turned it in the direction of Patterson and home, and his wife Marjorie. He looked forward to a pleasant evening with her; he had felt this way at the end of each work day since they had been together. The feeling was mutual. Marjorie listened daily for his arrival, met him at the door. His daily departures also found her at the door. As he started out of the drive in his police car she would stand in the doorway, wave grandly and throw a farewell kiss in his direction. Making certain that he wasn't being observed by any of his neighbors, for Conway was shy about revealing his emotions in public, he would touch a hand to his mouth and then wave it in her direction. The hours they shared at home between arrivals and departures were to him unspeakably delightful and marvelously pleasant. They were for him a new and proper manner for two people to share each with the other, and he often wondered how he had managed to live before finding Marjorie.

Conway was enjoying similar thoughts about home and Marjorie while returning from Mount Carmel the following evening after the grueling day-long meeting at headquarters. He disliked the long trip to and from headquarters, but he usually enjoyed the meetings, however long and tiring they might have been. He liked being a policeman, especially being a state policeman, and he took daily pleasure from his work.

At precisely the same time as Conway was driving toward home, a Spiceland County building contractor named Mahlon L. Thompson had exchanged noisy good-byes with several drinking cronies in a Moses City tavern and had climbed into his pickup truck. Thompson had drunk too much, but, as in past instances of over-imbibing, he felt capable of making the drive to his rural home. As he guided the truck through the twilight of Moses City streets, headed for the county road that would eventually lead him there and to his waiting supper, a tranquil domestic scene was being enacted in the Cramer Fielding home.

The ex-sheriff and his wife, Mavis, had finished eating dinner and were still at the table in conversation over coffee and cigarettes. A cloud of gray smoke hung above them as they inhaled and exhaled and sipped and, with sadness and dismay, recalled the recent events that had brought the Fielding name into the news. It had become a part of their daily conversation, if not at breakfast or lunch, then at dinner. A few times they were able to delay talking about it until bedtime. But at some time each day the subject was almost certain to come up. And each time it disconcerted and grieved them.

Pushing that subject aside, finally on this evening, they shared aloud their gratitude that Cramer was no longer sheriff, an appreciation that led to the recollection of happier days. If they were not a demonstratively happy couple they were unquestionably devoted to each other. It hadn't always been that way. Years earlier Mavis had given birth to a baby girl who lived only a brief time. The cause of the infant's death was never made clear. For Mavis the loss represented the worst of disasters, and for months afterward she lived in a state of deep depression constantly on the verge of a total breakdown.

It had been a difficult time for her husband, too. There were mornings when he shrank from leaving home, fearing some unseen horrible consequence the day might bring to the brooding Mavis before he could return to her. Together they somehow managed to survive that dreadful period and, eventually, with

Cramer's care and daily thoughtfulness, Mavis had overcome the almost fatal melancholy. From then on she had committed herself to her husband. She had no more children. Not because she hadn't wanted more, she simply did not have more.

Cramer and Mavis were not strangers to Mahlon L. Thompson, his wife, Elizabeth, and their children. A scant mile separating their homes, the Thompsons were a visible part of Cramer and Mavis's lives. On more than one occasion while Cramer served as sheriff he had helped a tipsy Mahlon into a squad car after a night of drinking and taken him home, or he had ordered a deputy to do so. Cramer had helped many drivers in that manner. Rather than chance them having an accident, Cramer had made it clear to his deputies from his first day in office that they were to protect the innocent community at large by keeping drunks from driving. Most were arrested, some, such as friends and a few neighbors, were taken home. This was not an unusual arrangement among sheriffs' departments in the state.

The Thompson children, two sons and two daughters, had grown up almost within sight of Cramer and Mavis and they knew each of the siblings by name. The four were adults and married at this time, and had families of their own. They visited regularly with their parents and judging from outward appearances, the Thompson family as a whole seemed a happy family.

Were an outsider to suggest a fault in the Thompson family it would have been Mahlon Thompson's drinking. However, in his own estimation of himself he was not a drunk. As he had more than once told his wife when she expressed fears for his safety and the safety of others when he was drinking, he enjoyed the conviviality that accompanied "a drink or two." Also, a couple of drinks were not the worst thing for business, he often assured her. Despite his passive arguments and his good intentions, his drinking often went beyond a drink or two.

As early darkness began falling the evening before the morning Cramer Fielding was to meet with Conway at the state police barracks, Thompson's drinking had unfortunately taken that latter course. Although he was not aware of it as he neared the edge of Moses City, his pickup was moving briskly, its bright headlights sweeping back the descending night from the first of several curves he would need to traverse before reaching home.

Cramer Fielding and Mavis, meanwhile, had finished their coffee and cigarettes and, as was his custom after he ate dinner at home, Cramer prepared to dispose of the day's collection of household trash. He did this by incinerating it in the concrete block enclosure he had constructed several years earlier in the back yard of their home. Slipping into a heavy jacket to protect himself against the cold of evening, he moved toward the kitchen door, picking up a partially filled paper grocery sack of trash from where Mavis had earlier placed it. Then remembering something, he turned and retrieved his Zippo cigarette lighter from where they had been using it at the kitchen table.

At about this time Thompson's pickup had passed out of Moses City and was well on the county road that would lead him past the Cramer Fielding home to his own house. The beer Thompson had drunk had relaxed him enough so that he was aware of a gnawing hunger, and in his anticipation of a hot supper he anxiously increased the pressure of his booted right foot on the pickup's accelerator. He was suddenly in a hurry to get home to devour the dinner his wife

Elizabeth had prepared, the dinner he knew had been long awaiting his arrival.

While Thompson was thus engrossed, the former sheriff of Spiceland County pushed his way through the kitchen and storm doors of his home into the early dusk of the winter evening. He descended the stoop that led into the back yard and walked to the incinerator where he placed the Zippo lighter upright on the stone coping trim around the top of the incinerator. He bent over and pushed the bag of trash against its rear wall.

Thompson, meanwhile, his hunger more demanding than ever, had again increased the speed of the pickup truck. Before he realized it was happening, the right front and rear wheels of the vehicle had slipped off the blacktop and were suddenly and loudly rumbling in the gravel berm.

Startled by the suddenness of the sound and the roughness of the gravel surface, he instinctively removed his foot from the accelerator and turned the steering wheel slightly to safely regain the pavement. Although he had reacted wisely, his movements were sluggish, slower than usual. At exactly that same moment the right front fender of the pickup struck the steel standard of a large diamond-shaped, sheet-metal, traffic warning sign; one bearing a curving black arrow on its yellow face. The sound of the impact in the stillness of early evening rent the air like the report of a high-powered rifle. *Crack!* The collision was of such force that the big sign was torn from the standard and like a huge awkward Frisbee was sent spinning and zinging into space.

When he heard the sound of the sharp report, Cramer Fielding, more than a hundred and fifty feet away in his back yard, which was separated from the county road right-of-way by a high hedge, was in the act of standing erect after having placed the paper sack of trash in the incinerator. He turned curiously in the direction of the sound. As though guided by an unseen satanic hand, the road sign spinning through the twilight at precisely that moment struck Cramer Fielding just above his eyebrows, incredibly slicing off, in a single horrifying instant, the top of his head. Cramer Fielding, his spilled brain lying in mushy pieces on the ground at his feet, was dead before he collapsed.

The cigarette lighter was still upright where he had placed it, the paper sack of trash, still snug against the rear wall of the homemade incinerator, awaiting its flame.

INDECISION

24

The days of early February were marked by numbing cold winds that left Hickory Grove devoid of its usual bustle of winter visitors. Except for morning and afternoon school buses, or the occasional passing of an automobile occupied by one of the town's residents bound on or returning from an absolutely necessary errand, streets were as bare of life as those of a windswept movie ghost town. For several days the lighted thermometer at the Dogwood County State Bank had hovered around zero.

People were kept informed, often warned, by radio and television personalities, that the windchill factor posed a paralleled danger to old and young alike. A radio morning show host joked that only the dead were safe in such extreme cold. One of those, although it discreetly was not mentioned, was the exhumed cadaver in a freezer drawer in Community Hospital at Mount Carmel awaiting re-interment. The living, the radio personality went on to say that morning, should, if at all possible, remain indoors.

Such a luxury, unfortunately, was not possible for state police. Sergeant Galiton had spent half of one such morning standing in the waiting room of a gasoline service station while a mechanic tinkered with a faulty thermostat on his cruiser.

"If they're going to go bad they'll do it in this kind of weather," the man had told him, a fact Galiton had learned firsthand on the drive from the Moses City State Police Barracks to Hickory Grove, a drive that had left him cold and testy. But his discomfort soon left him when he overheard two older men who were seated side by side on a corner lounger's bench inside the station discussing the Fielding case.

No doubt his presence in uniform and that of the colorful cruiser had precipitated the topic of their conversation. It had happened before. In the presence of police, some people invariably tried to make themselves appear knowledgeable about certain cases under investigation. For that reason Galiton faked disinterest until he heard one of them say that he'd seen Fielding working in his front yard the afternoon of the fire at the Fielding home. Galiton approached the two, identified himself by name, and questioned the man.

"Nothing more than that," the man, suddenly unexplainably wary of the policeman, said. "I live out that way and pass the place about every day. That wasn't the first time I'd seen him out there."

The man turned away from Galiton to look at his friend as though for confirmation and laughed nervously. "I've passed there a hundred times before that. Saw him many times. Nothing important about that."

Galiton agreed but because the conversation had deliberately been struck up between the two oldsters he believed the speaker had wanted to tell him something. He pressed the man for more information.

Giving his name as David Collins, the man said he was retired and owned a small farm a few miles from the Fielding home. He told Galiton of having seen Fielding early in the afternoon of the day of the fire and, without being asked, stated that Fielding was wearing a bright red shirt.

Somewhat doubtful at first of the elderly man's ability to remember a day some three months earlier,

Galiton was nevertheless impressed. He recalled that the bits of fabric he himself had removed from the ashes where the body in the Fielding fire was found, and the piece of fabric discovered in the arm cavity of the corpse at the time of the first autopsy, indicated the victim may have been wearing a blue plaid shirt when he died. Captain Martin had confirmed as much after tests of his own at the state police crime lab. Galiton sensed a stir of excitement within himself, a quickening of his pulse, at the possible significance of what the man had said.

"Are you certain about the color of the shirt he was wearing?" he asked the man who had identified himself as David Collins.

"Couldn't miss it," Collins replied. "It was like a red flag on a pole. Could've seen it a mile away."

There was little more the man could tell him. After the repair on his cruiser, and he had fortified himself with a hot lunch, Galiton drove to the home of Mamie Verden, the neighbor who had reported the fire at the Fielding barn. He had never spoken to her, and to his knowledge, for some unknown reason neither had anyone else from his department. He was aware, though, that she had been interviewed by an inspector from the state fire marshal's office, and also that she had volunteered some information to Cramer Fielding while he was alive and still sheriff. Galiton had familiarized himself with the reports and had concluded there was little more she could offer to aid the investigation. Still, at this time, he felt it necessary to meet the woman.

Certain that the doorbell was out of order after he had pushed its button, Galiton knocked loudly on the front door panel. An older woman, perhaps in her late sixties, and obviously flushed of face, opened the door.

The policeman knew then that the doorbell had sounded, perhaps somewhere deep in the house, and together with his sharp knock, had unnecessarily startled the woman. He felt the color rise in his own face.

Seeing her caller's handsome uniform, his highly polished cavalry boots, his face red with embarrassment at having so rudely interrupted whatever she might have been doing, and the way Galiton had swept the fawn colored Stetson from his head in awkward greeting, Mamie Verden was suddenly pleasant and smiling. Learning the nature of her visitor's mission she invited him inside.

"Yes," the woman said after she had expressed her regrets over the death of Fielding, whom she described as having been a nice man, and her heartfelt sorrow for Winona and her sons. "I saw the smoke from here."

As she spoke she ushered Galiton from where they stood in a narrow hallway through a brightly furnished living room into a spotless kitchen where she pointed to twin windows over the sink. The windows' view opened in the direction of the Fielding house.

"And," she said, "I called the township volunteers. Then I got into my car and drove over there."

Galiton had once read in the early pages of the state police report on the fire that Mamie Verden had informed the investigator from the fire marshal's office that she not only had been the first person on the scene of the fire, but that she had tried to get close enough to the burning barn to see if anyone might be inside.

"Gutsy old girl," Galiton said admiringly to himself.

"I think I got there before anyone else," the woman continued. "I jumped out of my car and could see the fire inside. There was a lot of smoke. Both big doors were wide open. Oh, it was burning something fierce."

Mamie Verden had raised both hands and gripped them one over the other at the neckline of her dress. The knuckles became a white glaze as though, Galiton thought, she fearfully was seeing again the ferocity of the raging blaze.

"I thought I smelled kerosene, or something like that," she resumed speaking. "I couldn't see anyone inside. I thought I should try to close the doors to slow the fire, you know, like you close the damper on a wood stove. We all use them around here in the country." Seeing Galiton's questioning frown she added, "Well, many of us do, anyway."

Sensing that she may have strayed into an area of rural rusticity unfamiliar to the policeman, Mamie Verden paused, shrugged, smiled thinly in Galiton's direction, and added, "But there were several explosions, and fire just flew everywhere. And I got scared."

She looked away from her visitor and directed her gaze toward the kitchen windows from which she had first seen the rising smoke of the fire. "It was really very hot. I could feel the awful heat on my face —" she turned quickly, almost imploringly to Galiton again, "and in my mouth even. I could taste it," she said.

As she spoke both hands flew upward to cover her mouth and she was assaulted by an enormous, involuntary shrug that shook her entire body, with what appeared to the trooper to be a rebirth of her original fear apparent on her face.

Mamie Verden remained silent for a time as both of them stood motionless, looking at each other. Galiton sensed a sudden rise of pity for the woman. In that brief lapse of conversation Galiton recalled his own experience with raging fire one winter day when intense, searing heat had frozen his heart with fear. Then slowly, uncertainly, Mamie Verden moved her hands away from her mouth. Galiton waited for her to continue speaking. He wondered if this marked the only time she had spoken of the fire since giving her initial report to Cramer Fielding and the inspector from the fire marshal's office. He wondered, too, if she might now be suffering from a form of delayed shock, as he himself once did. At last he heard Mamie Verden's voice again.

"I could taste it," she repeated, panting slightly, incredulity written on the features of her face and in her blue eyes. "And I wasn't anywhere near the place yet. I went back to my car and just stood there, trembling. After what seemed an eternity I could hear the sirens. Then I was relieved to see the red lights and blue lights coming."

Marveling that a woman her age would even consider approaching the doors to the inferno that had destroyed the barn, it was several moments before Galiton spoke. "Did you see anything else, or smell or hear anything else, anything that might have aroused your suspicions?" he finally asked, admiration and kindness apparent in the sound of his voice.

Mamie Verden was thoughtfully silent for a few moments. "No," she presently answered. "Nothing. Except for the explosions. They frightened me so. I had no idea what could have been causing them."

Galiton remembered the fire marshal's report. Paint, paint thinner, several kinds of combustibles, he said to himself. "Did you see anyone?" he asked aloud.

"No. I'd seen Mr. Fielding earlier that morning, when I went to town. To the library. He was raking leaves."

Galiton tensed. "Are you sure it was him?"

"Well, yes. I saw him. I didn't study him. But it was Mr. Fielding, I'm sure," she said frowning.

"Can you remember what he was wearing?"

"For the life of me, I can't," Mamie Verden replied with a shake of her head. "I'd seen him often while driving by. I never paid attention to what he was wearing any of those times. I don't know, I must have had my mind on something else. I know only that he was there in his yard that day."

"Did you happen to see anyone when you got to the fire? Did you look around?" Galiton suddenly realized that he had unintentionally become loud, demanding, and he stopped speaking.

Mamie Verden was nervously shaking her head. Then her mouth opened slightly, and she raised a hand to her lips as though she felt a sudden embarrassment.

"Yes?" Galiton said softly.

"I can't imagine why I forgot, why I didn't think of it."

"Yes?" Galiton repeated and he stiffened perceptibly, expectantly.

"Well, there was a boy. I don't know who he was. He came around the other side of the barn. He was so white, shaking, nervous. He said he had opened the back door. Yes, I remember. He said the fire was roaring or rolling inside, or something like that. And so awfully hot. Yes, he said that the fire almost burned him, it was so hot."

"Did he say anything else? Did he give you any indication of what he might have been doing there?"

"No. At least I don't remember. I presume he was just passing by. He was just a boy."

"Do you know his name?"

"No. I didn't even think to ask."

"Can you identify him?"

"I suppose—yes, I think so. Oh, I don't know," Mamie Verden was obviously shaken. "But the

township fire chief probably can. I saw them talking, afterwards."

In Moses City late that afternoon Galiton recounted his talks with David Collins and Mamie Verden to
Irwin Brown, the Spiceland County coroner, and to
Ira Brown, who had joined his son when Galiton
called at the funeral home.

"Don't know," Irwin Brown mused, fingers and
thumb of his right hand gripping his full, round chin
just above the knot in his necktie. "That red shirt,
now, that will make you think, won't it. Maybe—" he
paused thoughtfully "— maybe this wasn't Crestman
Fielding," he finished saying barely above a murmur.

"Of course it was," his father spoke up quickly, loudly, almost plaintively. "We saw him there in the
garage, dead. Remember? We agreed it was him. We
had him here, dead. Remember? We buried Crestman
Fielding. You sent the funeral bill to his wife, remember? If it wasn't him, who in the world was it?"

"Don't know," the younger Brown now spoke in a
studied yet obviously indecisive tone. "That red
shirt—of course he could have changed after raking
leaves." He raised his eyes to those of his father who
was standing at one side of the desk. "Yes, he could
have showered and changed." Then wistfully he
added, "In a way I hope it wasn't Crestman."

Irwin Brown moved his eyes in the direction of
Galiton who was seated at the opposite side of the
desk and smiled weakly. "We went to school together,
Crestman and me," he said. "I've known him all my
life, and I liked the guy. Right now—right at this
minute—I'm not sure of what I think, or what I
believe about this case."

So that Galiton might better understand their relationship, the coroner then spent several minutes

recalling his years of friendship with Fielding. At one point, in sober tones, he dwelt on a shared experience during World War II which in ensuing years was to provide the two men with a cherished memory in their continued friendship.

"I remember that it was Election Day, 1944," Irwin Brown said. "I was a master sergeant in an infantry division and I was disembarking from a troopship in Newport News, Virginia. I'd been in North Africa, Sicily and Italy, and I was happy to be home, in the United States. As we were coming down one gangway, fresh troops bound for Europe were going up another, right alongside of us. I heard someone calling my name.

"'Hey Irwin! Hey Irwin Brown!'" His face breaking into a smile Irwin Brown mimicked the caller. "That far away from home," he shook his head from side to side, "I thought I was hearing things. Thousands of soldiers around there and I think I'm hearing my name. It was weird. I looked around and there was Crestman Fielding, big as life and waving at me. He was on his way to the war. I couldn't believe it. Who would have thought that two guys from a little place like Moses City would be meeting like that? I waved and called out to him, 'Hi Crest!' Then I hollered, 'I wondered who was going to take my place over there.' We laughed and waved and in a minute he was gone from sight. It was like something you'd see in a movie."

There ensued several moments of silence while Irwin Brown appeared deep in reverie. Galiton leaned back in his chair and crossed his legs. The movement intruded on the new coroner's thoughts.

"Crestman and I talked about that many times since the end of the war," he said looking at Galiton. "We'd laugh and say how incredible it was that we would meet like that, like in the movies, or in a storybook. I still find it hard to believe. Yes," Irwin Brown's tone suddenly became lofty. "I liked the guy. Still do. And I'm not ashamed to say it. I hope he isn't dead. But if he is I'd like to see Winona taken care of. But," he paused while he studied first Galiton's face and then his father's, "it looks like that will take more time." And for the benefit of the older man, Galiton thought, the coroner added, "At least a little more time."

"It's already been plenty of time," Ira Brown argued. "This has been an on and off thing right from the beginning. We need to dispose of it and get on with other business. Crestman is dead. He committed suicide, Irwin. Issue the death certificate and forget it."

Irwin Brown shook his head ever so slightly. "No, Dad. Not just now. Not just now."

Before either man could speak again Galiton asked, "How about that boy?" The sound of his voice suddenly thrust before the two men broke into their thoughts and they both looked at the trooper. "Do you have any idea who he might be?"

"Probably just one of the neighborhood kids, but I don't know," Ira Brown told him. "No one to worry about, I'm sure."

Ira Brown then pushed back his coat sleeve and looked at his wristwatch. "Jud might just be around the telephone." He smiled at Galiton and added facetiously, "These farmers have got the life, you know. Call him, Irwin."

Judson (Jud) Wake was chief of the Harrison Township Volunteer Fire Department. Ira Brown then set about making conversation with Galiton. He spoke of the weather, the bitter cold of February. It was uncomfortable, he admitted, but nothing at all to

155

compare with winters of his youth, when he and his father, covered with layers of protective quilts and robes, traveled by horse and buggy in sub-zero cold through deep snows to reach isolated county homes to embalm the dead, to dress and ready them for burial.

Morticians were welcome visitors in those days, his reminiscence continued, given hot coffee to warm themselves and then allowed to go to work. They usually did their work while secreted in a cold bedroom with an equally cold corpse, while the family of the deceased and relatives and neighbors passed the time nervously talking in whispers in an adjacent room warmed by a crackling-hot wood stove. When the Browns were finished they would join the gathering and, over more hot coffee, listen to repeated eulogies about the deceased. Had anyone but an undertaker been recounting the experiences, they might have been more acceptable. Galiton found the older man's recollections uninteresting, and he was relieved, if not happy, when Ira Brown was interrupted by his son.

"Jud knows the kid," he said looking directly at his father. Then addressing Galiton he said, "It's Fred Hillew's boy Dean. He told Jud he got off the school bus at a friend's house and was walking home by himself taking a shortcut when he saw the fire. I'm afraid he can't be much help."

25

The next morning Galiton reviewed with Conway, Oaks and, newly arrived from headquarters, Captain Melton his chance encounter with David Collins, his visit with Mamie Verden and his meeting with the Browns. Although his listeners exchanged thoughtful looks and frowns at the mention of Fielding having been seen wearing a red shirt the day of the fire, they did not interrupt. And, as the Browns had done, they quietly shrugged off the youth Dean Hillew's presence at the fire.

Galiton recounted to them the unusual story of the surprise wartime meeting in 1944 of Irwin Brown and Crestman Fielding. He added Irwin Brown's wish that Fielding might still be alive, and that the coroner's indecision had irritated Ira Brown who insisted Fielding was dead and that Irwin should file a death certificate to that effect.

"The old man just doesn't believe the dead man can be anyone except Fielding," Galiton said.

Melton spoke up quickly, saying that, since he himself believed the dead man to be Fielding, he could understand the older man's thinking. "It's time we come up with a live Fielding, or a new identity on the dead man, or get off this thing. We've been on it too long already," he growled.

Galiton chose to ignore Melton for the moment and returned to the matter of the red shirt. "I put those pieces of burned shirt in an evidence bag myself," he said. "I know blue plaid from red. And they weren't red. Two different lab reports support that."

Conway and Oaks remained silent. Conway thinking to himself that in view of the mounting speculation that what Galiton had said certainly appeared to
be the case, this may not have been the most favorable
time to openly disagree with Melton.

"Tell you what, Gal, I don't know what Collins
thinks he saw. People see what they want, generally,"
Melton was saying. "But why isn't it just possible that
Fielding was wearing a red shirt when Collins saw
him and then changed at a later time? Haven't you
ever changed your shirt in the middle of the day?"

Melton's tone was unmistakably condescending and
Galiton felt his face flush. He knew that Melton and
Colonel Carey were in sharp disagreement over the
identity of the dead man and that the Fielding case
was becoming something of a seething personal war
between them. He was willing to attribute Melton's
haughtiness to that. Still he couldn't help but wonder
if he himself might at some other time have said or
done something to annoy Melton and it was now man-
ifesting itself. Their relationship had been a friendly
one but they weren't friends. Yet in previous meetings
Melton had accepted Galiton's observations with
respect and prudence.

Suddenly Galiton found himself reacting defensively. He thought to himself that in as much as there
seemed to be growing disagreement in the Fielding
case between two of his superiors, he did not want to
be caught in the middle. He had the vague feeling
that something about the case was only just beginning
to tear at the state police department. The sound of
Melton's voice put a sudden end to his thoughts.

"I got a call from the Colonel late yesterday that I
want to share with you fellows," he heard Melton

saying. "He's called in Dr. Isaac Berman, a professor of anthropology at Brackenridge University, to compare the Glenview Hospital x-rays of Crestman Fielding with those taken of the cadaver after the exhumation. This guy has some impressive credentials and he's a noted authority on the identification of skeletal remains. He's helped in a number of police cases around the country and the world, in reconstructing incinerated remains. Carey is hoping he'll support Dr. Flood and Dr. Brent in this. We're bound to know something more after he takes a look.

"In the meantime, here's something else," Melton's tone had dropped an octave, as though he were participating half-heartedly in a discussion of which he disapproved. "Captain Martin has given the Colonel a report on the lining of the dead man's stomach. The cadaver is still in the deep freeze at Community, but the internal organs are at our lab now. The stomach was coated red, like maybe Fielding had been on a diet of red wine for some time. That's what Martin believes, and he knows his business in that respect."

Eyeing each of his listeners in turn, Melton continued, "I want you fellows to understand something right now, while it is on my mind," he said. "All of a sudden Martin will not listen to anything that might suggest the dead man is Fielding. He gets mean if anyone even hints that. Throws them out of his lab. And what surprises me is how he and Carey have suddenly become buddy-buddy on this thing."

Melton rose to his feet and walked to the window. Hands clasped behind his back he stood there looking out in silence for at least a full minute. At last he spoke. "For four years they've been the world's worst enemies," he said while looking into the parking lot behind the barracks. At the extreme end of the lot stood the decorative lattice that hid from view a dumpster identical to that into which Galiton had, on Captain Martin's orders, disposed of the plastic bags of evidence. "Now they eat lunch together, and they talk alike and think alike on this thing."

Melton turned again to his listeners. "I just don't understand how those two could have hated each other for so long and then become friends almost overnight. Especially after Martin ordered you to throw away those bags of evidence, Gal, and then denied it to the Colonel. Martin's still chafing over your report on that little episode. Be careful," Melton's tone was friendlier as he spoke directly to Galiton. "Cross Martin and your butt could be in a sling for a long time. As for me," he paused, then sighed, "I've got my time in and I'm tired."

Was that it, then? Galiton asked himself with new interest in Melton's mood. Was Melton less angry with him than he was about the new friendship between the Colonel and Captain Martin. He felt somewhat relieved, and yet he noted that he had assumed an attitude much like that of Melton's. At the same time he knew that he could not dispel from his mind the fact that he, himself, and Carey, Captain Martin and Conway were of the same opinion; they did not believe the dead man was Fielding. Galiton was almost certain that Oaks believed this too. He knew there was little danger of any of them arousing Martin's ire on that score. Still, he momentarily entertained the thought that life trooping the state's highways would be simpler, less complicated and with fewer personality differences than being involved in two factions of warring superiors over the Fielding case. Martin would never forgive him for honestly reporting the debacle of the plastic bags of evidence. In a flash of recollection Galiton reviewed his limited knowledge of Martin. The lab chief had taken a degree in biology and had hoped to go on to medical school when the lack of money, the need of it, or some other reason, led him to seek his future in the state police department. He was considered to be a qualified and able lab technician, but it was also accepted within the department that Martin was generally misanthropic in nature and restricted his friendship only to those persons of rank. Except in the case of Colonel Carey, that is until recently, he had been prone to lean obsequiously in the direction of his superiors. Among the large headquarters staff it was often whispered derisively that Martin sucked up to the brass.

A capital city apartment dweller in his off-duty time, Martin lived alone. He had never married, and he had no known lady friends. That was the extent of what was known about his personal life, except that in the twenty-four years he had been with the department it had been steadily rumored that he derived pleasure from sipping anesthetizing Manhattans. If the rumor was true, Martin was clever enough to restrict his pleasure to the solitude and privacy of his own quarters and to keep his drinking from interfering with his job. There were times, however, when a vitriolic outburst would escape him. Those affected by it would secretly attribute such unprofessional demeanor to "Captain Horsehockey's Problem" and go about their duties. Galiton had heard that phrase on more than one occasion. He was in the process of wondering how, or if, the lab chief's problem might affect him and his future, or if it already had, when the sound of Melton's voice again cut into his thoughts.

"We have enough problems here without worrying too much about Captain Martin," Melton said. He had resumed his seat and was saying in a dry mono-tone. "While I am not in favor of it, the Colonel wants a closer watch on Mrs. Fielding and her sons. He thinks one of them will lead us to Fielding." Looking directly at Conway, Melton shook his head. "I don't believe that will happen. And we really don't have the manpower to keep a sustained watch on them. So use your own judgment in that matter, Frank."

Melton again looked into the eyes of each of the three men who waited expectantly for his next words. "We haven't received a barracks file copy yet, but a report from Dr. Flood suggests the dead man's miss-ing feet and hands were not burned off; he thinks they may have been cut off before the fire."

26

Conclusions drawn by believers that Crestman Fielding did not die in the fire required re-examination in light of a surprising contradictory determination issued several days later by Dr. Isaac Berman. Most reluctant to do this, oddly enough since he alone was responsible for requesting the services of the scientist, was Colonel William R. Carey.

The renowned anthropologist declared that his examination of the cadaver revealed that x-rays taken of the deceased and those obtained from Glenview Hospital in Moses City were compatible. The comparisons gave substantial credence to the belief that the dead man was in fact Crestman Fielding, he said.

"I knew it," Melton exclaimed to Conway and Galiton, who were in his temporary office at the Moses City barracks when Dr. Berman's report reached him. "There was never any doubt about it in my mind that the dead man was Crestman Fielding. I hope that will satisfy everybody concerned, especially the Colonel, then maybe we can wash our hands of this thing."

Berman's report appeared in newspapers under large headlines and was given considerable play by the electronic media. In addition to its coverage of Berman's assessment of the hospital's x-rays and those of the cadaver, *The Intelligencer* carried a sidebar in which the bereaved and still angry Winona Fielding revealed her reaction to Berman's conclusions.

"I'm relieved to know that at last someone has used

good judgment in this matter," she was quoted at one point in the story. "Dr. Berman has said what I've been saying ever since my husband did that awful thing to himself—he is dead. That was his body found in our barn fire. I can't believe that someone hasn't heard me, that no one, not until Dr. Berman, had even cared."

In response to a question concerning insurance benefits, Winona said only that it was time that she received her just compensation.

"I hope," she added, "there won't be any more delay. I have waited long enough for this matter to be settled. I am in desperate need of money to settle my husband's estate so that my family and I can get on with our lives. We've waited long enough."

In reporter PJ Cayne's main story about Berman's report, there was included a solicited comment from Irwin Brown. When asked if he would issue a death certificate in the name of Crestman Fielding on the basis of Dr. Berman's evaluation of the cadaver, the Spiceland County Coroner replied, "Assuming he's right. If the dead man is Crestman Fielding, I will have no choice. But I'm not going to be in a hurry to do that until I speak with the state police. We have to be right."

Irwin Brown did not have to speak to state police. In the next day's issue of the Mount Carmel *Morning Sun,* Colonel Carey, out of hand, declared Dr. Isaac Berman's report inconclusive. In the article, the state police superintendent announced that he had called on Dr. Hamilton Brent, Glenview Hospital pathologist, to re-examine the body found in the Fielding fire. In his autopsy of the dead man Brent had determined the cause of death to be carbon monoxide poisoning. He made no effort to identify the dead man, which Carey was asking him to do now.

"What is he doing?" a distressed Melton growled to Conway in the latter's office. "This case is closed. What more does the man want?"

Within forty eight hours Melton had an answer when a statement from Dr. Brent to Carey became public. Brent had advised Carey that the identity of the dead man, based on his re-examination of the exhumed cadaver, and the discrepancies he found in the x- rays of the cadaver and the x-rays of Crestman Fielding on file at Glenview Hospital, was definitely someone other than Crestman Fielding.

When contacted the next morning by reporter PJ Cayne for his reaction to Dr. Brent's report, Dr. Berman calmly observed over the telephone that "Dr. Brent is entitled to his professional opinion."

"Do you still believe the dead man is Crestman Fielding?" the reporter asked.

"I will repeat," Berman said kindly. "The x-rays taken of the cadaver and those obtained from Glenview Hospital are compatible. The bone structure, for all practical purposes, is identical. Now, to answer your question—yes, in my opinion the body is that of Crestman Fielding."

Asked to comment further, Berman went on to say, "There is nothing so unusual about the slight discrepancies in the separate x-rays that would lead me to believe that they are not x-rays of the same body. It is my opinion that their compatibility leaves no doubt that the dead man and Crestman Fielding may be viewed as one and the same."

When asked to comment on the missing hands and feet of the dead man, Berman replied, "I am aware that it has been suggested the hands and feet of the cadaver were amputated before the fire. But it remains my opinion that the hands and the feet were incinerated.

But I do want to make one thing clear," he told the reporter. "In matters of this kind it is not unusual that there should be professional differences of opinion. You understand, don't you?"

His tone became obviously pedagogic as he added, "An identification such as this one could be argued indefinitely." He paused as though to give his listener time to absorb his words, then he said in conclusion, "But as for age, stature, racial traits and peculiarities, there has been nothing disclosed in a morphological comparison in all the reports that would be incompatible with the identification of the cadaver as being that of Crestman Fielding."

"What does all of that mean?" Harley Oaks exclaimed in Conway's office the next day.

Melton, Conway, Oaks and Galiton had once again gathered in Conway's office to read again Cayne's story and to discuss this most recent development and to decide their next move. Oaks had just heard Dr. Berman's words read aloud by Melton.

"It simply means that Crestman Fielding is dead, that he's our man in the fire," Melton chortled as he folded the paper and tossed it unto Conway's desk.

"Well, he might be right in all he says," Oaks began, "but—"

"You know doggone well he's right," Melton rudely interrupted him. "How much proof do you have to have?"

"Okay, Captain," Oaks raised both his hands, palms facing Melton. "But I picked up something yesterday, and if this case isn't closed yet, I'd like to run it past you fellows."

Melton pulled back his lips and shook his head at the sergeant's inference.

"Come on, Har-Har," he groaned, using Oaks' nickname. "Dr. Berman's an authority on this stuff, and Dr. Brent's not dry behind the ears yet. Besides that, we've had no reports of a missing person that would fit the description given us of the stranger supposedly seen with Fielding before the fire. The search has been extended nationwide, and we've come up with zip. You know that. No, this case isn't closed. Not quite. But it is well on its way. Right where it ought to be. Okay," he finally nodded resignedly toward Oaks. "Go ahead, what have you got?"

It was evident that Oaks was now reluctant to speak. Avoiding Melton's gaze, and keeping his eyes on Conway, he said softly, "Well, on the afternoon of the fire, maybe an hour or so before it was reported, a sheriff's car was seen leaving the Fielding driveway."

Conway, who had been quietly leaning back in his chair suddenly pushed himself forward, the palms of his hands striking the desktop with a bang.

"Say that again," he demanded loudly of Oaks.

Oaks was obviously startled. Melton and Galiton had also jerked upright in their chairs at the unexpected sound. Conway apologized for his sudden outburst. "Just say that again, Harley. Please."

"A man named Ulyss Hauser, an older man who has a farm out that way, says he saw a sheriff's car—"

"Damn!" Conway again brought the heel of a hand down on the desktop with a bang.

"What've I said now—" Oaks began.

"Sorry," Conway said again, cutting him off. "I'll explain later, Harley. Go ahead with what you were saying."

"Well," Oaks was almost hesitant to resume. "Well, this man, Ulyss Hauser, told me he saw a sheriff's car leave Fielding's driveway, and he thinks he recognized the man behind wheel. Said it looked like the sheriff himself, Cramer Fielding. What does it mean, Lieutenant?"

Conway struggled to assimilate the implication of his sergeant's words. *What does it mean?* he asked himself. Was it Cramer Fielding? What could Cramer Fielding have been doing at the home of his estranged brother before the fire? What would he have been doing there *at all*? On the day of the fire, brothers Cramer and Crestman Fielding were still alienated, each from the other, and had been for years. Why would Cramer have chosen that day to go to his brother's house? Was the dead man in fact Crestman Fielding and had Cramer Fielding been instrumental in his brother's death? No, that couldn't be. Crestman wasn't dead at that time. Or was he? Had Cramer Fielding been keeping secret something of importance that might have helped this case? Something he had hoped to tell Conway the morning of their planned meeting? Something that might have unscrambled the confusion now surrounding the death of his brother, or at least the death of the man found in the ashes of the fire?

Conway shook his head as though to clear his brain of the rush of questions besetting it. Then with a sweeping look at the bewildered policemen in his office, he related slowly, thoughtfully, Cramer Fielding's telephone call, and the arrangement of the morning meeting between them that had been thwarted by the wayward hand of accidental death the night before. When he was finished, Melton shook his head in disbelief.

"Here we go again," he said throwing up his hands.

BETRAYAL

27

Distressed as he was by it, Lieutenant Frank Conway was unable to even hazard a guess as to what Cramer Fielding had wanted to speak to him about before he was killed. Though he was certain now that it pertained to Cramer's visit to the Crestman Fielding property the day of the fire, Conway was convinced he would probably never know. He had a sinking feeling that too many unknowns, too many unanswered questions were confusing the Fielding investigation. Weeks had passed since the Fielding fire and the police probe had uncovered little; actually nothing of any consequence.

"All we really know is that we have a body," Conway spoke to himself. After a moment's thought he added, "I'm guessing it is not Fielding's, but whose is it?"

In defiance of the anthropological studies that revealed the dead man bore enough physical characteristics to Crestman Fielding, on the advice of Colonel Carey who insisted the investigation was still incomplete, coroner Irwin Brown filed with the county board of health and the county clerk's office, a death certificate in the name of "John Doe."

In spite of police suspicions, the cadaver was reinterred in the Fielding family plot. And to the relief of everyone concerned, the weather changed slightly for the better and the hope of a joyous spring spread smooth as velvet over Moses City and Spiceland County.

As though it might have been deliberately put out of

sight and out of mind, nothing more was spoken or written publicly about the Fielding investigation. However, on a beautiful day in May, a small rectangular granite headstone, the type made available by the federal government to all honorably discharged veterans of the armed forces, appeared on the only grave in the Fielding family cemetery plot. Contrary to the information on the death certificate, not to mention the controversy over the identity of the dead man, the grave marker bore the name "Crestman Fielding."

Arranged for through the Veterans Administration by the Brown & Brown Funeral Home at the request of Winona Fielding, the polished surface glinted in the bright sunlight, accenting the stark black letters inscribed on it. The year of Crestman Fielding's birth and the year of the Fielding barn fire, presumably the year of his death, his branch of service and rank, and a Christian cross had also been cut in perfect balance into the shiny surface.

The new installation served to underline the disturbing questions, "Was the dead man Crestman Fielding, or was he not Crestman Fielding? If he was not Crestman Fielding, *who* was he?"

The unsettling contradiction might have gone unnoticed. But the shiny granite headstone attracted someone's attention and the subsequent probing lens of a photographer from *The Intelligencer* opened a vexing phase of the Fielding matter. Predictably, after a photo of the grave and marker appeared in the newspaper, the grave was targeted by vandals. A pretentious plastic floral wreath and a vase of colorful plastic flowers, placed on the grave by Winona, unexplainably disappeared. As the days of spring continued on to summer, other plastic wreaths and more plastic flowers were covertly removed from the grave.

On one visit to the grave in which Winona believed her husband was buried, she was shocked to find a crudely fashioned wooden cross stuck in the   soft earth of the grave. In graceless, ill-balanced vertical black letters, someone had painted one below the other on the upright standard the letters J-O-H-N. On the crosspiece set at the O of that name, the same ghoulish artisan had painted from left to right respectively, flanking the O, the letters D and E.

Hurt, sickened and angry, Winona reported by telephone the desecrations to Spiceland County Sheriff Spud Tatum and to state police. Although she was assured the matter would be looked into, profanations of the grave continued. When it became evident that police could not or deliberately would not provide relief from them,   Winona, though she would have preferred to continue grieving at the graveside, reluctantly terminated her visits to the cemetery.

It was, she had confided in a telephone conversation with Captain Melton, less painful for her to vent her sorrow in the privacy of her own home than to endure the ceaseless insensitivities and contempt directed by unknown persons toward her husband's grave, and at her and her family. Peculiarly, state police and sheriff's officers who reported they were unable to find and apprehend the vandals did manage periodic watches of the comings and goings to and from the

Fielding home of Winona and her son Roger's.

"I can't even go to the drug store," Winona had written in a complaining letter to the editor of the local newspaper. "They're right behind me all the time."

This was not quite so. The surveillance was indeed a fact, but it was sporadic. Yet, in a subsequent news article inspired by that letter, Roger Fielding, who was interviewed by PJ Cayne, described the surveillance as police harassment and added acidulously, "We can't even go to the bathroom without fearing state police might be watching. They think that we are going to lead them to Dad."

While that also was an exaggeration, Roger then added pointedly, "Until she couldn't stand what was happening to his grave anymore, my mother was leading them to him every day, right there in the cemetery. And they didn't have the sense to know it. They still don't. I don't know where else they think he's going to be. My father is dead. He's in his grave."

Lieutenant Conway, who also was interviewed in conjunction with the news story, was non-committal. "We do have the family under occasional surveillance, as ordered," he told the reporter. "If you want any more information than that you'll have to get it from headquarters."

But for the first time, headquarters—specifically Colonel Carey—was silent on a matter pertaining to the investigation.

Meanwhile, on the advice of attorney Clare Downing, Winona, Roger and James visited the Moses City offices of the law firm of Peake, Ely and Farrell. There, after more than an hour of questions and answers, it was the consensus of the partners that the firm should represent Winona in her claim against State Bankmens Life Insurance Company and its companion carriers who shared the face value of her husband's life insurance policy. To that end the firm assigned to the case a junior partner and recent law school graduate named Ames Shaw.

Bespectacled, long-haired and mustached in the style of that period, the young man smiled incessantly, which worried the seriously concerned Winona, leading her to inquire of Julius Peake, the senior partner of the firm, if Shaw was not too young to handle their case. The Fieldings were assured by Peake and Morris Ely that the young man was a competent attorney, and that, on the basis of the *John Doe* death certificate, the way might probably be open for him to proceed immediately against the insurance companies in Winona's behalf. To this was added Shaw's own personal, smiling assertion that he would give her claim his full attention, beginning with a complete review of the case to date, and that he would be in touch.

Glancing into the rearview mirror on the drive home, Roger recognized a car that was following them. Having seen it on other occasions, he knew it to be an unmarked state police car. The driver was wearing dark glasses, but his identity was unmistakable. Roger jerked a thumb over his shoulder and to his mother and his brother spoke the policeman's name: "Harley Oaks," he said.

When Roger turned into the drive leading to the Fielding home, Oaks drove on past as though he were bound elsewhere, and the Fieldings went inside the house. Minutes later Roger emerged alone and began the drive to his own house, some seven or eight miles distant. In a matter of minutes he caught sight of Oaks behind him again. He tried to ignore the policeman.

"The devil with him," he said aloud to himself.

At the same time that Oaks was following Roger's

car, Melton was seated in his temporary office at the state police barracks, silently mulling Roger's earlier printed remarks to the newspaper. Somewhat ruffled at Roger's censure of state police, and moved by Roger's certainty that the body found in the ashes was that of his father, Melton was prodded by the thought that he should have another talk with Roger.

Moreover, Melton had long been aware of a visceral sense that Roger was withholding information of some kind about the fire. There was a possibility, too, Melton knew, that Roger, despite the David Collins report, might have been the last person to have seen his father alive.

Melton had been quietly thinking that Collins may or may not have seen Crestman Fielding, as he had told Galiton in Hickory Grove. Driving past the Fielding home on the county road, Collins could have seen almost anyone wearing a bright red shirt. From the sound of Galiton's report, David Collins had unquestionably seen someone wearing a bright red shirt whom he could have assumed was Fielding. That it might have been or could have been Roger Fielding, the physical characteristics of father and son were so similarly striking, was a thought that had persisted in Melton's mind.

Melton also suspected Roger might be withholding some scrap of important information. Just what that might be he did not know, could not guess. Maybe he could dig it out. Getting to his feet he removed his snap-brim hat from a rack on the opposite wall and adjusted it on his head. He then walked along a short hallway to an open door and stuck his head inside.

"Going out to the Roger Fielding place, Wendy," he said to barracks commander Donaldson. "Holler if you want me."

As he guided his unmarked police car toward Roger Fielding's home, Melton tried to sort out his thoughts, admitting to himself that he wasn't quite sure of what he was doing. He knew only that at one point during his own interrogation of Roger, the younger man had displayed a reluctance to speak, as though he was deliberately and purposely leaving something unsaid. He was aware, too, of Roger's distrust of police, and that what he was not saying could possibly pertain to the certainty that his father was indeed dead.

Melton had no argument with that. He himself had been certain from the start that Fielding was dead. Carey and Conway, along with almost everyone else connected with the investigation, had yet to be convinced of that. But if Roger had pertinent information about his father's death why should he want to withhold it? What could he possibly want to hide? Melton had no answer. He knew only that in order to put the nagging question out of his mind he must speak again with the elder son of the man he himself believed died in the fire.

A few miles from Roger's house Melton switched his radio to three-way and contacted Oaks in his car. Oaks affirmed that he had been tailing Roger and that Roger had reached home and was still there, that his car was parked in the driveway.

"Okay," Melton answered revealing nothing of his intentions. "I'll take over for a while. Take a break."

In minutes he pulled up behind Roger's parked car. Taking his time alighting from the car he strode along a concrete walk that led to the porch steps and the rear door of the house. Roger answered his knock. Of all the policemen he had encountered since the fire, Roger, perhaps because of their mutual conviction concerning the dead man, probably felt most at ease with Melton. Though his face clouded slightly when he saw the policeman, Roger retained his good manners and politely invited Melton inside. There Roger introduced Melton to his wife Penni, a diminutive, shapely blond with a sweet manner. Surprised at her beauty, Melton caught himself staring and had to tear his eyes away from her when he addressed her husband.

"If you've got nothing special to do, I'd appreciate you taking a ride with me over to your mother's place," he said. And to allay Roger's suspicions he added, "If you have something planned we can make it another time. No big rush."

Melton felt as though he'd left himself hanging, but beyond what he had said to Roger he was not quite sure of his plans, except that he knew he wanted to speak with Roger alone.

"Are you alone?" Roger asked.

Melton nodded.

"Police business, of course."

Melton shrugged. He thought he detected a note of insolence in Roger's tone. He said to himself, this guy's tired of all the snooping around. I don't blame him. This whole thing is giving me a pain, too. Aloud he said, "Yes. Since I was in the neighborhood." That sounds phony, he said to himself. Aloud he told Roger, "I thought I'd stop. But, if I'm imposing we can do this another time."

Roger shrugged. "No. Let's get it done."

He slipped into a lightweight jacket, kissed his wife, and soon he and Melton climbed into the police car. As they rode in the direction of the Crestman Fielding home they engaged in desultory conversation, saying nothing about the fire or the investigation. Roger had made up his mind that while they were in the police car he would say little or nothing to Melton; he was certain their talk was being recorded. Melton sensed his distrust and avoided any such pretensions, making it a point to refrain from even a mention of the Fielding name. As it turned out, their conversation was not being recorded.

At the Fielding place, Melton and Roger walked slowly around the ugly monument of ashes, charred beams and twisted, rusted corrugated metal that once made up the barn. As they walked, Roger explained that a homeowner's policy had lapsed long before the fire and that his mother was without the necessary funds to have the eyesore removed. It was an apology of sorts, Melton thought, but Roger might have saved himself the embarrassment since Melton had earlier heard a similar explanation from Winona Fielding herself.

With that out of the way, Roger felt more inclined to talk, and, unbidden, he began reconstructing the building with words and gestures. Melton believed Roger was being generously explicit, giving Melton the best picture of what had once stood there than any he had received from brother officers and from newspaper stories. The apparent change in the younger man's attitude gave Melton additional pause for wonder. Was this a part of Roger's attempt to hide something? The unspoken thought took the form of a lighted warning sign in Melton's head. Was he trying to steer the policeman away from something?

While he continued speaking, Roger, who turned every few moments so that his words would carry back to his listener, preceded Melton by a few steps along whatever available routes he could find through and around the clutter of debris. At one point he stopped and jabbed a finger at a mass of twisted metal roofing.

"Just this side of that pile of roofing is where they found Dad," he said.

Melton halted and faced Roger. As the eyes of the two men met, Melton asked, "You really believe that was your father, don't you?"

"I know it was him," Roger's eyes bored unwaveringly into Melton's. "He told me he was going to kill himself. I have no reason to doubt that was him."

Melton was suddenly aware of his purpose for this visit with Roger. It was so simple he should have been able to sort it from his thoughts before he had arrived, so that he might have better prepared himself. In previous interviews with police Roger had refuted implications that he was in collusion with his father to defraud the four insurance companies who shared the one million six-hundred thousand dollars coverage on the elder Fielding's life. At those times Melton had made it clear both to his colleagues and to Roger that he had accepted Roger's denials. Now, however, to his astonishment, he suddenly was not sure.

This was unlike Melton. He was usually quick to reach decisions, and once reached, unshakable in his conclusions. And now? Now he doubted Roger. All because he felt the younger man standing before him was concealing something. Could his own brother policemen be correct in their unwavering suspicion that there had been a felonious pact between father and son, husband and wife, or all three? Had something between them gone awry that had ended in the death of the elder Fielding? Melton had persistently refused to believe anything like that. Now what *did* he believe?

He still believed that Crestman Fielding was dead, that his was the body found in the ashes of the fire and buried in the Fielding family plot. No question in his mind about that. But did Fielding in fact take his own life, as Melton still wanted to believe? Or had something else happened to him? Was Roger the last person to have seen his father alive? The questions whirled in Melton's mind. It had been established that Roger was the last of the Fielding family to have seen the missing man alive. But, was he the last person— could he have been the very last person—to have seen Crestman Fielding alive? Was it Roger who reportedly was seen wearing a red shirt in the Fielding yard some time before the fire? Melton had to know. He had to ask. But that was not the question that formed itself on his lips. It was quite another. For what reason he had asked it he could not be sure. And although a thought suggested that it would be to his advantage to wait until a more appropriate time to ask it, he heard himself speaking the words.

"Roger," he asked, "did you kill your father?"

Melton was startled by the crassness and the impetuosity of his question, and his disregard for the time and place he had chosen to ask it. He was also sharply aware that he, more than anyone else in the state police department, could be painfully off base because of his original convictions in the case, convictions he had not totally abandoned. But he was further convinced now that sooner or later, if the investigation into the death of Crestman Fielding was ever going to come to an end, the question had to be asked not only of Roger but probably of his mother, Winona Fielding, and of James, the younger of the Fielding sons. He now realized he had asked it of Roger sooner, surprisingly sooner, than he should have, given the circumstances under which it was asked. But it had been asked, and now it remained to be seen if he had erred, and how badly.

Melton also realized that if Roger were to blurt out an affirmative response to his question, testimony to that fact would be one man's word against another's. Roger not having been charged as a suspect in a crime and not having been properly advised of his rights, his response would almost certainly be rendered legally useless. It was a lousy approach to good police interrogation, Melton admitted to himself, but it was too late now. He had asked the question.

Handsome, swarthy features impassive, his eyes somewhat clouded, Roger looked long and steadily at Melton. He took a deep breath, sucked in his lower lip and clenched it between his teeth. He shook his head slowly from side to side and, for what seemed an eternity to Melton who now thought the question had wounded the younger man beyond words, Roger remained silent.

While he waited for an answer, Melton shrugged more comfortably into his sport coat. Although the month of May was more than half over, he was aware of an abrupt chill in the air. Despite that he saw with some surprise that redbud and dogwood blooms, glorious in colorful life only a few weeks earlier, were waning. Struck by the fleeting passage of time, he became impatient for Roger to speak. With an effort, he calmed himself.

At last Roger spoke. Quietly, without emotion, he asked firmly, "Just between us?"

"Between us," Melton heard himself say.

Disbelieving his words, Melton, in his policeman's brain scolded himself. "Stupid," he thought. He was a cop. There could be no deals. Not between us or anyone else. He was on cop business and cop business it had to be. If Roger had killed his father, for whatever reason, Melton was bound by commitment and conscience beyond any bargain. Yet he had heard himself heedlessly utter the words of a covenant he knew he could not honor. He wondered if subconsciously he had some absolving plan—he hoped he had one—in the event that Roger would reply affirmatively to his question.

"No," Roger said earnestly, much to Melton's mixture of disappointment and relief. "No, I didn't kill my father.

"But," he continued, a chilling intensity taking command of his voice, "if anyone had a reason to kill him it was me."

Melton stood unmoving, saying nothing while he waited for Roger to resume speaking. Except that his eyes had left Melton's and were now downcast, Roger, too, stood quietly immobile. The silence between the two men lengthened. An anxiously patient Melton clenched his jaws until they ached before Roger raised his eyes to meet his.

"I wanted to kill him," he said at last, his voice now edged with unmistakable anger. "I did kill him in my heart." All of a sudden a staccato of words burst from Roger's mouth. "I shot him. I stabbed him. I strangled him. Oh God! In my mind and heart I did terrible things to him. I couldn't think of enough ways to kill him. Believe me, Captain, I wanted to kill him more than anyone will ever know."

The rush of words had been so forcefully spoken that Roger was left shaken and breathless. He gasped noisily for air, once, twice. When his lungs were filled he blurted, "He hit on my wife, Captain." Roger's face was flushed with shame and hurt. "Imagine, my own father. I idolized him. All my life. He hit on my wife."

The words were spoken with great effort as though

they had been wrenched from the depths of the younger man's being. Tears suddenly spilled from his dark eyes and ran down over his cheeks. Listening, Melton was taken aback. He'd heard some shocking stories in his career as a policeman, but he nevertheless was unprepared for Roger's outburst. He wished for a wall, anything, to lean on for support. There was nothing, and Roger had resumed speaking.

"Oh, damn his soul to hell, Captain. He was drunk, and he tried to —." Roger choked. Unable to finish the sentence he stopped speaking. For reasons known only to himself he could not bring himself to speak the word that had so easily come to his lips. Abrupt, uncontrollable sobs that twisted his handsome face into a grotesque mask and wracked his young strong body, overcame him. At length he found a way to say what he needed to say and cried out, "He tried to force himself on her! My own father, for chrissake! My own father!"

Humiliated either by his words or by his condition, or both—an astonished Melton could not tell—Roger Fielding covered his tear-streaked, distorted face with both hands and wept. Long sob-filled moments followed while the policeman, suddenly unable to swallow and almost blinded by a mist that had unexpectedly beset his own eyes, stood tall and silent, unable to move, his senses struggling in vain against what he'd heard, what he was seeing. The only thought that would come to him was that he was the dubiously privileged witness to the crushing outrage, the shattering hurt, the shame and disgrace, of a trusting soul irretrievably betrayed.

Melton had never been in the company of any man who had wept so fiercely as the young man who now stood before him was weeping. He was deeply moved to place a consoling arm around Roger's shoulders but he could not bring himself to do so. He told himself that professional propriety forbade such a show of tenderness. Yet in the policeman's deepest self, and more to the point, he believed that Roger would have been offended. So he did the only thing he dared; he stood helpless, waiting, listening to the drumbeat in his ears of his own emotions.

At last Roger produced a handkerchief and swiped at his wet face, now crimsoned by strain and embarrassment. When he was able to speak he apologized to Melton for his breakdown, saying that he was all right and that he was ashamed of himself. But it wasn't quite so easy for him. Sobs, not as deep and convulsive, and not so frequent as they had been, still attacked him without warning, still took his breath in sudden unexpected gasps. It seemed to Melton that the younger man could not stop crying.

Taking the opportunity to speak, Melton suggested in tender but firm tones that they return to the police car. After several minutes in the parked car, during which time he tried desperately to regain his poise, Roger, unbidden, related to Melton the details of his father's indiscretion as it was told to him by his wife Penni.

28

One late September morning little more than a month before the Fielding garage fire, Crestman Fielding had gone to the home of Roger and Penni Fielding, his son and daughter-in-law, ostensibly to speak with his son.

Having risen early and left for Mount Carmel, where he had an appointment for a job interview, Roger was not at home. Penni was at home alone.

Upon her father-in-law's arrival at the couple's home it was immediately obvious but not surprising to Penni that he had been drinking. His breath, as he passed her in the kitchen doorway at her invitation for him to enter, an invitation that was not uncommon for her, was heavy with the stench of what she suspected was ingested wine.

While she explained that Roger was not at home, that he was on his way to keep an appointment in Mount Carmel, she slipped easily ahead of her father-in-law and preceded him into the kitchen. As she made small talk she poured and placed a cup of coffee on the table opposite one from which she had been drinking.

"Take a load off, Dad," she said genially. "I was just having a cup myself."

As she turned to sit in her chair the lower front of the sheer morning robe she was wearing parted, exposing a naked, milky-white thigh. Embarrassed, she quickly caught the two sides of the garment in her hands as she sat and, leaning slightly forward, quickly and neatly folded them over her legs.

It became an awkward moment for the slight Penni, for as she leaned forward to cover herself the upper portion of the thin nylon garment gaped away from her body enough to expose the cleavage there. Penni felt a sudden flush of color rise to her cheeks.

The innocent unintended exposures had their affect on her father-in-law. Before she realized that he was not taking the seat she had offered him opposite hers, he had moved behind her chair and with both hands had reached under her arms. She felt the sudden pain of his large hands as they roughly gripped her round firmness. Disbelieving, appalled and frightened, Penni screamed. Instinctively she jabbed her elbows backward into her father-in-law's body and leaped out of her chair.

But once begun it seemed the big man could not stop his attack. He reached out and dug his hands into Penni's small shoulders and spun her around to face him, crushing her tiny body against his. She cringed in pain but suddenly forgot the hurt when she felt a thickness pressed hard against her and realized with terror that her assailant was fully aroused.

Frightened out of her wits, Penni screamed again and wildly pushed and punched at her father-in-law's chest and face as she struggled to free herself. She heard his panting, rasping breath and she sensed that he was shouting. In her panic and chilling fright she was unable to understand what he was saying.

To her dismay she felt herself lifted off her feet. Trapped like some animal she was carried struggling and kicking and pleading to a couch in an adjoining room. No match for the weight and strength of the man, Penni felt herself forced down on the couch. Then she felt the pain of a broad, brutish knee shoved between the folds of the morning robe, forcing her straining, trembling knees apart.

Beside herself with terror, outrage and shame, Penni could not believe that the hulk on top of her, bruising her restraining thighs, was her own husband's father. Nearly insane with fright she cried out to him, pleading with him to stop. She called his name. She shouted his wife's name. In a frenzy of begging she reminded him that he was her father-in-law, Roger's father, that he must be sick, deranged, to be treating her in such a manner, and that Roger would kill him when she told him of this. She implored him to stop, promised to forgive him if he stopped, to keep his lapse of decency their secret.

Overcome at last by fear and fatigue, and her father-in-law's powerful strength, Penni knew that she had lost her battle against him. She felt smothered, dirtied, condemned under his sweating body. It was then that she sensed a moment of sudden relief, and for an instant she believed her pleas had penetrated her father-in-law's crazed behavior.

She felt his weight lifted from her. Relieved, she thanked God. But in the next instant she knew that she had been wrong. Fielding had indeed lifted himself slightly, but not to release her. He had exposed himself, and with the aid of his right hand had begun thrusting wildly, savagely at Penni's nakedness under the morning robe.

Penni screamed again, and, with a last herculean effort, she pulled back and wrenched her small body to a partial sitting position. Caught off guard, her attacker's supporting left hand slipped off the edge of the couch, causing him to roll outward and heavily to the floor.

Before he could recover, Penni was on her feet,

dashing for the kitchen door, all the while babbling supplications to God to let her reach the safety of the out of doors. She was rational enough to know that free of her house, free of the once friendly, safe walls that now held her prisoner, she could outrun her mad assailant. Making certain that he was not in pursuit, she stopped her flight in the back yard, some distance from the house door. Breathless, she took time to readjust the morning robe around her body. She stood there, watchful, trembling violently, her heart pounding, palpitating madly, while her now grim mouth gasped the cool morning air for which her burning lungs ached.

At length her father-in-law appeared. Lumbering through the kitchen door he crossed the porch and lunged down the steps. Penni was prepared to run, for she fully expected him to resume his attack on her. But Fielding apparently did not see her. He looked neither to the right nor to the left but went directly to his car and drove away.

Penni could not bring herself to return to the house, for fear that her father-in-law might return. She sat in the lawn swing, alternately reliving and denying the nightmare of that morning until her husband returned later that day.

29

Roger's entire narration had been fraught with pain, seething anger and tears of helpless frustration.

In the face of those raw emotions Melton had himself been left unnerved and nearly impotent. He searched his mind for something to say, some kind response he could offer the young man who sat beside him in the police car.

"You understand why I wanted to kill him—why I said I had reason to kill my father, don't you?" Roger asked savagely through a deeply drawn gasping sigh. "I wanted to kill him. But I didn't kill him," he continued. "He was my father." He shook his head. Then through a sudden unexpected series of sobs which the young man tried in vain to control, he choked, "But he was a bastard. A son of a bitch." He articulated each word.

Sensing the depth of Roger's pain, anger, and embarrassment, and to hide his own emotions, Melton turned to look out the driver's side window of the car. He discreetly waited until his companion had composed himself. Then, relieved at Roger's apparent recovery, he could not keep from asking again, "And you didn't kill him?"

"No, I didn't kill him. Nobody killed him," he heard Roger reiterate evenly. "But I'll tell you the truth, Mr. Melton. I find myself thinking sometimes that if he hadn't shot himself I would have had to kill him. He was my father and I loved him, but to keep from losing my mind I think that sooner or later I would have had to kill him. You understand, don't you? Now my father's dead anyway. And I'm sorry. I'm sorry for my mother's sake that he's dead. I'm sorry for my sake, too. I've even cried for him. Especially because of the way he died. I've cried a lot. But I'm glad, too. Can you understand that? Can you? I'm sorry he's dead, but I'm glad that he's dead."

Then Roger repeated with emphasis: "But I didn't kill him. And I'll say it again, nobody killed him. He killed himself."

FORFEITURE

30

Except for an article in the *Intelligencer* calling attention to it, few people in Moses City and Spiceland County realized the first anniversary of the Fielding fire had arrived. For those few the wait for police to conclude their investigation of it had been especially long and wearying. The stress of it had taken a critical toll on Winona; long before then she had begun drinking with alarming frequency. There were days when she had imbibed to such an extent that she had moved about her home unsure of where she was and what she was doing. And when some of those nights came she was at the very brink of unconsciousness before her head touched her pillow.

Her sons had never before seen their mother under the influence of alcohol. They had been aware for years that she had taken an occasional social cocktail, but that was all. Fully cognizant that something unusual was happening to her, and why, yet unable to fully understand her emotional breakdown, they were able only to implore her to stop drinking. Too late, dipsomania had all but completely overwhelmed her, and she had reached what appeared to be an irremediable state of instability, unable to respond to their pleas or she was ignorant of them.

Having a home of his own to which he could escape, Roger saw less of this second family tragedy than did young James. In time James would find ways of his own to shut out the sight of his mother's insobriety. He took long walks and rambling drives in the old blue and white Chevy, the only automobile that had survived the Fielding calamity, and often he closeted himself in the silent privacy of his room.

The first of such escapes had come about one night while his mother, soused on cheap wine, which was all she could afford—if indeed she could afford that— sat in the still attractive Fielding living room eating large blue grapes, drooling and spitting the seeds on the floor at her feet. She had virtually stopped preparing meals and for their sustenance she and James made sandwiches as needed, or otherwise picked at snacks from what was available in the refrigerator or pantry. Often there was very little in either place. On this night, when his mother was seated in the Fielding living room eating grapes, James, overcome by a wave of disgust and a rage of contempt for her drunken condition, left the house and did not return until well past midnight.

On another occasion James had awakened late one night to find his mother staggering about the darkened rooms of the house in search of a misplaced bottle of wine. Striking matches and, in its turn, holding each tiny flame high above her head in the dark, she was mumbling barely coherently in the limited light of each match, "Where the hell did I leave that damn bottle?"

James, who until then had never heard even the mildest of expletives from the lips of his mother, was shocked and suddenly gripped in an attack of nausea and jitters. From that time on the second son of Crestman Fielding went to his bed at the end of each day fearful to the point of terror of what unspeakable horror the night might bring—another fire, the death this time of his mother, the flaming death of both of them?

Although James feared his mother's drunkenness, he still did not, could not, understand his mother's illness. Worst of all for him, when Winona was drunk, which was often, there could be no understanding, no sharing, no communication of any kind between them. If in her inebriated state his mother insisted on conversation, James refused to speak with her. He had learned that her drunken remarks were more than anything else long termagant harangues directed always at state police, of which she would later remember nothing. On the strength of his age, he also steadfastly declined to be her errand boy when she demanded from him a replacement bottle of wine, leaving her to drive herself to the nearest tavern or liquor store.

Winona usually was in no condition to drive at these times, a fact that could not have escaped state police who may have been following her. Under different circumstances she might have been apprehended and charged with driving while intoxicated. But suspicions being what they were, police, if they had been following her, balefully ignored the danger she presented to herself and to others, in the belief that she would eventually give up and lead them to a secret rendezvous with her husband.

Although James was not without filial consideration during these trials, his brother's moral support of him was limited in that Roger also was laden with his own unmerciful ordeal, the weight of which only he of Winona's two sons could carry. Simply put, the pressures from what misfortunes had overtaken the family, plus his wife's heartbreaking misadventure at the hands of his father, were by this time adversely affecting the couple's relationship. Unemployed for months as Roger had been, their lifestyle had undergone radical change. Fortunately Penni had been able to find employment as a clerk-typist, where she had worked before their marriage. Although the money she earned was enough to provide them with only the barest of essentials, to their mutual embarrassment, to make ends meet they frequently needed help from her parents.

There were greater problems; they had become estranged in ways with which Penni had eventually found it impossible to cope. Constantly withdrawn, brooding, quietly angry, Roger was ever uncommunicative. Since the repulsive episode Penni had undergone at the hands of his father, Roger had become a virtual slave to her; penitent, fawning, groveling, overtly seeking to please at the slightest opportunity. That was not what Penni wanted or expected from their life together, and she resented it to the point of becoming distraught.

She preferred—wanted, yearned for—their marriage to be as it had been before the tragedy of the Fielding fire. To her dismay and aching disappointment it was not. Roger was no longer demonstrative in his sensual affection for her, he no longer kissed her, embraced her. His usual tenderness, that part of his personality that had helped win her to him in the first place, was gone. And when she tried to interest him in her body he turned away, as though he had been stripped of his sexual potency.

In her estimation of their situation, she once had informed him, their life together had become unreal. And in the face of Roger's seeming ignorance of that fact, his continued withdrawal into himself and his growing reticence to return to the ways of earlier, happier days, she often found herself alone, in tears, and fearing their marriage was now destined to be that way forever.

Penni's relationship with her parents also seemed to be affected; she could feel it, or so she believed. Ever since the fire she had been aware of an increasing paranoia when she was in their presence. She thought she could sense from them a gradual unsociability, a feeling of mistrust in their attitude toward her, as though she might be party to some cabal the furtive intentions of which she was deliberately keeping from them. It may have been her imagination, she knew. Yet, as often as she reminded herself of that probability—for in her several discussions about the fire with her parents she had reiterated as many times her lack of knowledge about Fielding family affairs—her irritability and unhappiness with them grew. She had even reached the point where she thought she could detect similar vibrations between herself and those persons with whom she worked.

Except for the attack by her father-in-law, the details of which she had shared only with her husband, Penni kept no secrets. She was positive that her husband kept none from her, and surely none in connection with his father's death. She had never asked him if he in some way doubted his father's death was a suicide, and she had never doubted that Roger believed his father had taken his own life. But now there was a stigma attached to Roger, to the entire Fielding family, and incredibly, she often thought, to herself. State police insistence that a crime had been committed had put it there, she knew, and her hometown newspaper and the rest of the media kept the stigma alive. And these many months after the fire it seemed that it would never go away.

Penni kept reminding herself, often tearfully, that she loved Roger and, accusations or not, she would stand by him, fight for him, for herself, for them, the

Fieldings, for what they had once shared together, for what she hoped they could still share. But what could she fight? Whom could she fight? How? Unless something happened soon to resolve the plight of her husband, his mother and his brother, Penni dreaded to think of what might happen to what little remained of her own happiness. In the expanding hours of her painful solitude she was resigned to the menace of impending disaster.

"I can feel it in my heart," she often told herself through tears of bitterness.

It was at this time that Ames Shaw filed a petition with the Spiceland County Circuit Court to have Crestman Fielding declared legally dead.

Unfortunately for Winona and Penni, in the wake of media accounts of Ames Shaw's petition, the investigation, which had been inactive for so long, took a stunning new turn. A man living in Tucson, Arizona, wrote to a relative in Moses City claiming that he had seen Fielding in Tucson accompanied by a young woman with black hair.

As it later was learned, the man, a former Moses City resident and subscriber to the Moses City paper, had based his identification on a picture of Fielding which had been furnished by Winona that had appeared in *The Intelligencer* story of the legal action taken by Shaw. The newspaper account had included a complete rehash of the fire and its aftermath, including the suspicions of murder, fraud and arson, which were given prominence in the story. A sidebar to the story questioned in bold print the identity of what, by then, had become known in the media as "the mystery corpse" buried in the Fielding cemetery plot?

A copy of the letter from Tucson, the salutation and the signature deleted, enclosed in an envelope postmarked Moses City, had been mailed to "State Police" at the Moses City barracks. As was usual with such mail, the letter was opened and read by the barracks commandant, First Sergeant Donaldson. After reading it he placed the letter on the desk of the district commander.

"What do you make of this," Lieutenant Conway asked of Galiton, who had come into his office shortly after the lieutenant had read the letter.

Galiton's lips formed a fine line as he studied the letter. Handing it back to Conway, finally, he said, "I never did believe he was dead." Then he added, "Captain Melton won't be happy to see that."

"Have radio send a message to Arizona State Police and advise them on this thing. Give them a good description of Fielding, and then we'll talk with Captain Melton," Conway said while he thoughtfully tapped the fingers of his free hand on the desktop. "This could be the perfect coincidence."

As Galiton turned to leave, Conway added musingly, "Strikes me as being funny that he wasn't seen by anyone until after the report of the court hearing came out in the paper."

When another thought occurred to him he called after the trooper, "Telephone *The Intelligencer,* too, and get a list of their Tucson—their Arizona subscribers. There shouldn't be many. Maybe we can get an ID on this guy through a local relative."

"Bull," Melton predictably growled when Conway called him at headquarters in Mount Carmel. "The guy's obviously read about the hearing in the newspaper and now he's seeing things. But," he said resignedly, "we'll have to check him out."

Colonel Carey's reaction, when he was informed of the letter, was one of jubilation. "I knew Fielding would show up, Tim. Sooner or later he had to," he had chortled over the phone to Melton.

Soon afterward Conway received a phone call from PJ Cayne at the Moses City paper. The newspaper also had received a copy of the letter and Cayne was now seeking more information. Conway told the reporter there was no new information in the Fielding investigation except the copy of the letter. Before hanging up, Conway asked the reporter to aid Galiton in obtaining the names and addresses of Arizona subscribers to the paper.

That afternoon the Fielding story was again on *The Intelligencer's* front page. That same afternoon a Moses City stringer for the Mount Carmel *Morning Sun* alerted his state editor at the *Sun* about the letter. Next morning the capital city and the central portion of the state had learned from a front page story in the *Sun,* in which Carey was again liberally quoted, that Fielding had been seen in Tucson.

In a matter of days state police received additional letters at headquarters in Mount Carmel from persons in Miami, Reno, Mexico City and Toronto, who also claimed to have seen Crestman Fielding in each of those cities. In each case he was reportedly in the company of the unidentified black-haired woman.

The letters from Miami and Reno were signed by former Moses City residents living in those cities who also subscribed to the hometown paper, and who claimed that in the past they had been acquainted with Crestman Fielding. The letter from Mexico City was written by a man who said he'd found a copy of the *Sun* on an airliner he had boarded in Atlanta, and that he had recognized Crestman Fielding from a description included in a story and photo about the missing man. The letter from Toronto was from a female insomniac who told police she had recognized Fielding from a description she'd heard late one night over a radio call-in program from the United States.

"This is turning into a circus," Melton fumed in Conway's office one morning. "Either Crestman Fielding is some kind of magician or these people are nut cases. I say he's not a magician."

"Well, you've read Gal's report on the Arizona thing, Tim," Conway dispassionately reminded him of what Galiton had learned from a call to Tucson. "Gal is sure the guy saw our man. While he lived here the guy knew Fielding pretty well. Left here for his health a few years ago. But he swears he'd know Fielding any place. Gal believes him."

"Galiton's going to believe anything except Fielding is dead, that he blew his head off, Frank," Melton retorted scornfully.

Conway smiled broadly. "Me too," he said. "Don't forget me, Tim. I'm like Gal on this thing now. Even if that wasn't him in Tucson, it'll take a lot of convincing to make me believe Fielding is dead."

Both men were silent for a while, each with his own thoughts. Melton then stood up to leave Conway's office. As he turned to walk out, he hesitated in the doorway.

"You know, Frank, this sort of thing is going to play hell with the hearing," he said passively, thoughtfully. "Ames Shaw might have had this case wrapped up for trial. Now, at this moment, I'll bet there isn't anyone who takes that newspaper who believes Fielding died in that fire. And I predict they're not ever going to believe it. Not now."

31

Within a matter of days after the last of the reported sightings of Crestman Fielding had been made public, the one person who might have provided the strongest leverage to the success of Winona Fielding's claim that her husband lay buried in the Fielding family plot was dead. Dr. Isaac Berman had suffered a fatal heart attack.

In the face of the reported sightings, however spurious he thought they may have been, and Berman's unexpected demise, Ames Shaw reluctantly withdrew his petition for the hearing.

The Intelligencer ran a rather extensive feature about the life and successes of the late Brackenridge University professor of anthropology. In addition to reporting Berman's educational and professional background and an in-depth look at his years at Brackenridge University, the newspaper included in the story glowing tributes from Berman's colleagues who spoke his praises from their own domestic and foreign academic communities.

Berman's untimely death, however, was particularly distressing to Ames Shaw, and the young attorney was quoted liberally in the newspaper article. He had told PJ Cayne of *The Intelligencer:* "Dr. Berman's death at this time is an unfortunate loss to the public at large, but it is a serious loss for the Fielding family. And the loss of his personal testimony has forced me to ask for a postponement of the Fielding hearing. Although we have Dr. Berman's report, detailed and complete, it would not at this time, in the face of these perplexing reports of Crestman Fielding having been seen in various cities, carry the impact of the presence of the man himself. I spent considerable time with him on this matter and was very impressed. He held a number of degrees and was highly respected by his peers. But it was Dr. Berman's warmth of personality, his simple yet solid knowledgeable approach to this case that won me to him, and won my respect and friendship. It is all of this, and his honesty, that will be missed. All of this combined with the weight of his opinion would have had, I am sure, a positive effect on the outcome of the hearing."

In the meantime, the legal identification of the dead man found in the charred debris of the Fielding garage remained that of John Doe, a mystery corpse, a nobody. Except for continuing an occasional watch on Winona and her sons, state police had again turned their attention to other matters. The Crestman Fielding mystery again was all but forgotten. Except for Winona, no one seemed to care anymore.

So distant had the case become from the daily routine of events that even the media seemed to have fallen asleep in the matter, so much so that the editorial department of *The Intelligencer* overlooked within its own pages the news value of a legal advertisement. It read:

SUMMONS - (SERVICE BY PUBLICATION)
COUNTY OF SPICELAND
MOSES CITY TRADESMENS TRUST BANK
Plaintiffs

-V-

CRESTMAN FIELDING, WINONA FIELDING,
ROGER FIELDING, PENNI FIELDING.

NOTICE OF SUIT

You are hereby notified that you have been sued in the court above named. The nature of the suit against you is: Complaint to foreclose Real Estate Mortgages. This summons by publication is specifically directed to the following named defendants: Crestman Fielding, whose whereabouts is unknown, and to Winona Fielding, Roger Fielding and Penni Fielding, Spiceland County.

In addition to the above named defendants being served by this summons, there may be other defendants who have an interest in this lawsuit. If you have a claim for relief against the plaintiffs rising from the same transaction or occurrence, you must assert it in your written answer.

You must answer the Complaint in writing, by you or your attorney within thirty (30) days of this after the Third Notice of Suit, and if you fail to do so a judgment will be entered against you for what the plaintiff has demanded.

By Arthur B. Craig
Attorney for Plaintiff
Attest: Clerk of the Spiceland Circuit Court.

Foreclosure of Fielding real estate holdings at this time included only Roger and Penni's house, and the long vacant Fielding Mill. It was an expected blow. For weeks Winona and Roger had been receiving written demands for payment and threats of legal action. When it came, however, it was a shock nonetheless, and it plunged the family further into dejection and despondency. That the bank should name Crestman Fielding as a defendant in the suit served to exacerbate those emotions.

Public announcement of the suit could not have come at a worse time for Winona. For weeks the anniversary of the fire at the Fielding home had been heavy on her mind. Her discouragement and heartache drove her to seek with increased passion the reinforcement with cheap wine of a mental block she had thrown up to shut out any thought of the suit, and the world. She stayed drunk.

Although he didn't resort to drink, Roger, already sick at heart, was plummeted to the very depths of depression. Berman's death had left him unnerved. Upon receipt of the summons informing him of the suit he had become totally daunted. He seemed to Penni to be completely detached from reality and wholly separated in thought and deed from her. The isolation was incomprehensible to her, and she felt helplessly ineffective and friendless in the face of it. As her anguish increased it intruded upon her waking and sleeping hours to such an extent that she began fretting over the possible loss of her means of earning a livelihood for the two of them.

As another winter holiday season approached, and suddenly finding herself without a home, Penni separated herself from Roger and returned to the home of her parents "until," she had informed her husband, "we can pick up our lives where we left them when this terrible thing came about."

32

The holidays came and went and the worst of the winter eventually passed without further development in the Fielding matter. By this time Penni was living with her parents and Roger had vacated the house they once had shared as husband and wife. Although the house had yet to be sold at auction, Fielding Mill already had been auctioned at sheriff's sale. The proceeds had been applied to Crestman Fielding's indebtedness.

Early in March Captain Melton at headquarters in Mount Carmel requested a couple of extra copies of the *The Intelligencer* newspaper that contained the legal advertisement of the Tradesmens Trust Bank suit, if they were still available. He made it clear that he did not want copies but the actual papers of that date for the headquarters file of the Fielding case.

His request was made the day of the first quarterly district barracks inspection. Four times a year, beginning in March, troopers from throughout the state reported en masse to their respective district barracks. In what was felt by troopers to be harsher than military fashion, men, machines and equipment were reviewed and scrutinized by their superiors.

Beginning at eight o'clock in the morning at the Moses City barracks all personnel attired in cleaned, pressed and polished uniforms, standing at attention alongside washed and sparkling cruisers with freshly vacuumed interiors and required police equipment properly arranged in front and rear seats and in trunks, ready for use at a moment's notice were inspected. Exacting in their demands, such inspections overlooked nothing, no piece of clothing, brass, firearms or equipment, and were conducted by a ranking officer from headquarters. Accompanied by the district commander and his barracks commander who carried an inspection form attached to a clipboard, such inspections were begun not a minute before or after eight o'clock.

As district commander, Lieutenant Conway was charged with the success or failure of Moses City barracks inspections. He in turn held barracks commandant, First Sergeant Wendell Donaldson, with the primary responsibility, and Donaldson in turn shifted that responsibility to his line sergeants.

Because of their importance to a well-managed constabulary, and because the command of a district could be in jeopardy as a result of a single less than perfect outcome, such inspections, except for emergencies and some priorities given to highway patrols, overrode usual daily police routines. At the Moses City barracks no one was excused on that day. It was a sober morning for troopers and officers alike. But when it was over, relieved troopers gathered at a highway restaurant for coffee and a comparison review and bull session of the inspection.

After the better part of an hour with his co-workers at such a reunion, Galiton, still neatly pressed and polished, drove to *The Intelligencer* building in Moses City. While awaiting service at a counter there he felt a tug on his coat sleeve. He turned and was surprised to see his high school classmate and former sweetheart, Breezy Jamison, smiling up at him. His surprise at seeing her was obvious, causing her to laugh playfully, happily.

"Aren't you even going to say hello?" she asked rounding her eyes and gently placing a hand on his arm.

Galiton flushed. How many years had it been since he'd seen Breezy? How many years had it been since he had heard her voice? How long had it been since they had strolled to classes together, dreamed together, swum together in the abandoned limestone quarry hole in Crowfoot Valley? How many times had they made love in the shadows of the cast-off limestone stacks there?

His flush deepened as the memories almost overcame him. He tried to wipe his mind clean of the past and to look at her anew. Except for being somewhat heavier, rounder of face and bosom and hips, a sight he found strangely attractive and pleasing, she appeared to be the same. He noted, too, that her eyes still glistened with what he once called sweet deviltry, and that the generous fullness of her lips still smiled sensuously to frame even white teeth as they did the many times they had been together so long ago.

"Well," she struck him lightly on the arm with her hand. "The handsome trooper in his oxford gray uniform and ten gallon hat is going to remain silent, huh?"

The red of Galiton's face turned crimson. Still at a loss for something to say, he shifted his weight uncomfortably from one booted foot to the other, his leather trappings making slight straining sounds. But he managed a smile. He extended a hand, which she took and held tightly.

"Good to see you," he finally blurted. "It's been a long time."

As he spoke he remembered again how really close they'd been, physically and emotionally. Their affair had lasted through high school and beyond. He had been hopelessly in love with the girl who now stood before him as a mature woman, a woman whose warm soft hand now squeezed his in greeting.

There was a time when he considered asking her to marry him, but he was unable to bring himself to do so. She had lain with him many times and it seemed to him indecent that she, or any woman for that matter, should come to his connubial bed devoid of innocence as she was. How, he had thought, could she possibly provide a husband there with the physical and spiritual chastity he believed necessary and proper to the fulfillment of the sacrament of matrimony?

He wanted, or so he thought in those idealistic days, to share his life with a woman who had never yielded to the lustful pleasures Breezy had known, even though they were pleasures he had fostered in her and which she had shared with him and he had enjoyed. He had wanted a woman, or so he had told himself, whom he could proudly take home to his religious, widowed mother without a sense of shame and guilt. A woman worthy of his mother's often expressed hope.

It was of utmost importance to him then that the woman he should choose as his wife would have to be one who was untouched by any man. A woman pure and virtuous, free of sin. He had consciously but secretly promised himself while he and Breezy yet were lovers that the woman who was to be the mother of his children would approach the marriage altar unsullied; that her nourishing breasts should be pure and untouched.

He had chosen Jeri to fill that role. Jeri whom he believed was innocent and totally ignorant about sex. While Jeri had fit exactly within the parameters of those requirements, it still had taken him many months after their marriage to put Breezy out of his mind. With great effort he had finally succeeded.

Before he realized it, Galiton suddenly had the feeling that he and Breezy had never been apart. His mind raced backward to the time of their youth. Like starbursts, memories of the days and nights they had shared, the love, as he had never known love before or since, descended on him in a reeling shower of light. Momentarily staggered by its brilliance, Galiton, with pulse racing, found himself wondering what it would be like to again hold her, to hold this new Breezy.

"Yes," said Breezy, her voice answering his greeting seemed to be dragging him reluctantly from a distant land of enchantment into her current public presence. "It's been a long time. But it's so good to see you again, Gal, and you so handsome in your *Mountie* uniform," she teased, laughing gaily. After an extra brief squeeze, she released his hand. "But I've got to go now. Got a date with my husband. Hope to see you again. Soon. Bye."

Galiton stood immobile, watching her as she turned from him toward the deep interior of the newspaper's offices. He remembered then a news article and photograph of two, maybe three years before. Edward Coleman, the editor of the newspaper, and Breezy had married. Galiton searched his memory for an image of the face that had appeared in the paper with Breezy's. It was not there. He told himself that it did not matter; Breezy had returned briefly into his life and now she was gone again.

33

It was a painful irony that the highest bid received for Roger's and Penni's home when it did come up at sheriff's auction that summer should have been that of State Police Sergeant and Mrs. Harley Oaks.

"Well, heck, Lieutenant," Oaks later responded to department criticism by his immediate superior. "It was up for grabs. The price was right. And we'd been looking for a house with some ground. It's a nice place. Got just about everything we wanted. You've seen it."

Conway raised a hand. "I personally haven't said a word of criticism, Harley," he said. "As far as I'm concerned, if you wanted that place and you had the money, it was yours to buy. Besides that, it's none of my business."

Conway was serious and understanding. It was none of his business. He simply had passed on the complaint that had come down to him from headquarters. What was said now, if anything, would be between Oaks and the department. He put the matter out of mind.

Captain Melton, however, took a different view. "I know," he said to Conway in exasperation. "There's nothing illegal about us buying property that is legally for sale. But doggone it, the police helped to push these people into financial ruin, out of their home, and we destroyed their marriage, then one of us turns right around and buys their house. It may be all right legally, Frank; still it strikes me as being sadly unethical. Even sick. You can bet your retirement other people see it that way too. Average guys out there won't say much because we're cops, *state troopers,* and they're scared silly of us. They'll continue to lick our boots and try to please us with free coffee and meals, and smiles and under-the-counter gratuities. But deep down inside they'll see us as a bunch of bloody pirates."

Melton's anger paled beside that of Colonel Carey's. "I find it hard to believe, Tim," he raged to Melton. "What possessed Harley to do a fool thing like that?"

"The price was right, Colonel," Melton answered bluntly. "And there's no law says he didn't have a legal right to buy the place if he had the money. But I know that we're going to look like bad guys around here."

Carey's voice throbbed as he released a string of expletives.

"Agreed, agreed," Melton answered. "I know. It's a pile of manure that we could have done without, but it has been thrown against the state police wall and some of it is bound to stick. And," he added with a degree of unmistakable satisfaction that apparently escaped the angry Carey, "it is going to be pretty hard to clean up."

Surprisingly Melton's prediction seemed considerably off the mark. The visible reaction of the public to Roger and Penni's loss, if there was one at all, was one of silent acceptance. It appeared that Crestman Fielding's alleged crime had received just enough media attention to place the entire family under a widening cloud of complicity. Thus, contrary to what Melton had feared, even secretly hoped for, few people, if any, in Moses City and Spiceland County appeared sympathetically moved by the newest plight of the Fieldings.

One person did give vent to public outcry. She was Winona Fielding. Some days after the sheriff's sale her discrepant voice was heard in the sentences of a letter to the editor of *The Intelligencer.* It read as follows:

> To The Editor:
> More than a year ago my husband, Crestman Fielding, died in a fire at our home in Spiceland County and his body was buried in the Moses City Memorial Park. Because he had a large amount of insurance on his life, insurance companies and state police have been falsely claiming that my husband is not dead.
> My husband has been missing since the fire, and neither state police nor anyone else has been able to prove that he is not dead and buried. I know my husband. I know that if he were alive he would not let his family suffer as we have been suffering. He would be right here with us. He is not here with us because he is dead. His body was identified by the sheriff and the coroner. We had a funeral for him. We buried him. There is a marker furnished by the Veterans Administration on his grave. We also have the funeral bill to prove he was buried there. But the state police think we are hiding him someplace. We are being treated like criminals. We are not.
> State police are so busy watching us that they do absolutely nothing toward proving that my husband is alive, or dead, or proving who is buried in my husband's grave, if it is not him. In my opinion, and I'm sure in the opinion of a lot of other people, the state police are doing nothing in this matter.
> State police have had more than enough time to settle this. Because of them we have lost some of our property, including my son's home, which was sold by the sheriff to a state policeman. I find it hard to believe that the state police are allowed to trade on the misfortune and misery they bring to other people. I can't believe what is happening to us. If my husband is not dead, then who is buried in his grave? Who else is missing besides my husband?
> The state police have been harassing us. I don't

know which way to turn. I don't know what we are
going to do. The state police don't want me to have the
insurance money that is rightfully mine. Why?

Signed: Winona Fielding.

The next day's Mount Carmel *Morning Sun* carried
on its front page a beginning to end re-write of the
entire Crestman Fielding story, garnished with several quotes from Winona's letter to *The Intelligencer*.
Later that week the investigation took a surprisingly fresh turn. When an updated dispatch about
the missing Fielding was sent to all U.S. agencies over
Lieutenant Conway's signature, Dallas, Texas police
responded. From the meager description provided in
the dispatch of the stranger believed to have been
Fielding's companion prior to the Fielding fire, Dallas
police came up with a name. He was believed to be a
man named Felix Dombriewski. Age fifty-five,
Dombriewski was described as an itinerant house
painter who had been apprehended in that city three
times in one year on charges of public intoxication.
On one of those occasions Dombriewski had also been
charged with indecent exposure; police had witnessed
him relieving himself in an alley in downtown Dallas.

If Conway had expected that an answer might come
from the newest dispatch, he believed it would have
been from someplace nearer to Moses City. Dallas
was several hundred miles away. Nevertheless,
Dallas police apparently had the answer to the riddle
of the Fielding case, or rather he himself now had it in
their answer to his dispatch.

He immediately had a dispatcher re-enter the
information and the request for a photo into the state
police zone data and communication system, and
within hours he had his answer. Dombriewski's last

known address was 4762 Rumford Street, Cleveland, Ohio, and he was, at that time, employed by a manufacturing firm in that city.

After sixteen months it appeared that the Fielding enigma had at last been brought into the sunlight. Pieces of the aging puzzle seemed finally to be falling into place. The investigation was suddenly resurrected to active life. Conway felt a rush of sensation. Still, it was not to be that simple. Cleveland police were unable to find Dombriewski at that address. To make matters worse, Dombriewski had not left a forwarding address.

Now, armed with a photo of the man and working in plainclothes with Oaks, Galiton began rechecking Moses City and Hickory Grove taverns, hoping to find someone who might recognize Dombriewski, someone who had seen the man in the company of Fielding so many months before. With Conway daily urging them on, they showed copies of the photo to everyone and anyone. If the picture of Dombriewski could be identified as that of the man seen with Crestman Fielding the day of the fire, the odds were that it would be by someone in a tavern in one of those two communities, Conway told his investigators. The two policemen doggedly persevered, double-checking their previous efforts. Galiton was thus involved in the Hickory Grove Lounge one night when he felt a touch on his shoulder. Turning he looked full into the smiling face of Breezy Coleman.

"I've been watching you," she said smiling impishly up at him. "What have you got there?"

"Hi!" Galiton, who was genuinely surprised to see her, momentarily could say no more. Attired in a light blue shirtwaist frock that buttoned up the front to her throat, a somewhat simple attire for that period, but pleasingly attractive, she was to him breathtaking.

"Just trying to find someone who's seen this guy," he said, regaining his composure and handing her the photo of Felix Dombriewski which she took and studied briefly. She made a face and shook her head, causing her dark hair to fluff gently over her shoulders.

"Not me," she smiled again. "Never saw the man." She returned the photo to him. "Are you on the job now?"

"You might say so," Galiton replied. "What brings you here?"

"Sorority meeting and birthday party." Breezy made another face, somewhat milder than the first. "It's all over now, though. Some of us stayed over for a nightcap. We were just leaving."

Before he was aware of it he heard himself inviting her to have a drink with him.

"Are you trying to proposition me?" Breezy said with a soft laugh that sounded rich and full. "Because if you are the answer is yes, definitely."

They both laughed then, Galiton somewhat uncertainly, although he had made the offer. They moved simultaneously toward a booth deep within the dimly lit room. Seating himself opposite her, Galiton placed the photo of Dombriewski face up on the table between them. A waitress, a woman Galiton recognized as one of several persons to whom he had shown the picture the previous day appeared and they ordered drinks.

It was at once one of those unexplainably relaxed and engaging occasions for the both of them. While they sipped, Breezy spoke dispassionately of her sorority and some of her sorority sisters. Galiton answered with droll accounts of police work, the prolonged investigation into the Fielding fire and his role in it. Because of a lingering mutual uncertainty they deliberately avoided speaking about their personal lives.

Once, while they were thus caught up, they failed to hear or see the waitress when she reappeared to ask if they cared for another drink. Galiton looked questioningly at Breezy. She shrugged and smiled. When the waitress returned and had placed their drinks on the table before them, the woman casually picked up the photo and said, "Hey, this isn't the best light in the world in here but the more that I see this the more I believe I know this guy."

Galiton looked from Breezy to the waitress. Did he want to hear what the woman had to say about Felix Dombriewski just now or did he prefer that his visit with Breezy continue uninterrupted? The woman didn't give him a chance to decide.

"Wouldn't swear to it," she was saying. "But it sure looks like him. Same chin. Same bald head. No teeth. Found him, huh?"

"No. As a matter of fact, we haven't," Galiton, his interest in his prime reason for being in the public place suddenly overcoming his interest in Breezy, was quick to reply. "We're still looking for him. Are you sure you've seen this man? That picture has been in the papers and all over television."

Turning the photo first one way and then another in the dim light the waitress forced an exaggerated frown. "Who has time to read the paper and watch television?" she snapped at Galiton. "I don't know," she then mused. "It's been an awfully long time, but it sure does remind me of someone I've seen."

"Why didn't you recognize him yesterday?" Galiton said.

"Too busy, I guess," the waitress retorted. "A girl

can get that way, you know. Especially with two kids to care for and no man in the house."

"I'll let you have another look in the daytime," Galiton told her. "It's important. How about tomorrow?"

"I come in at three."

"Brought you some luck, Gal, didn't I," Breezy, aware of a sudden bristling in her companion, said as the waitress walked away. She had seen the change begin to come over Galiton when the woman first picked up the black and white police photograph and indicated she had seen the man before. He had become tense, expectant, almost forgetting her, almost forgetting everything except what the waitress was saying. Galiton studied her for a moment, then, placing his elbows on the table and leaning forward, he smiled disarmingly.

"Sorry," he said. "Once a cop, always a cop, I suppose. I hope you did bring me luck. If I hadn't run into you I'd have been long gone from here. I need all the luck I can get in this case. We're getting old together," he smiled broadly. "Maybe you and I should do this more often if you're going to bring me this kind of luck."

Galiton was joking. When he heard Breezy's rejoinder he believed that she was responding in kind.

"That's the second time you've propositioned me tonight," she smiled. "Keep it up, you just might get luckier than you think."

Forgetting the drinks before them, they began, as though on some silent, magical cue, to recall their school days, classmates and summer vacations, and it was inevitable then that they should remember Crowfoot Valley.

"When was the last time you were there, Gal?" Breezy asked.

"Long ago. Tragic time. Four kids burned to death in a shack there," he said.

"God, I remember when that happened. That was awful," she shuddered at the memory. "You were there?"

"With Henry Carter. You remember him. I was a rookie trooper then. He was with the sheriff's department. After a dozen years it still remains the worst thing I've ever seen."

"I don't want to hear any more about that," Breezy's tone was cold, firm. "The story they used to tell about old Peg-Leg and Crowfoot Valley, remember that? That was bad enough. And poor Poopy. It always made me feel so sad to hear about them. Afterwards I'd lie awake at night and worry that I might some day be like them and that someone would tell similar stories about me. It was so scary, so awfully sad."

She brightened in an instant. Placing her forearms on the tabletop and clasping her hands, she leaned forward and, with eyes cast upward toward Galiton's, rested her chin on extended thumbs and asked only enough above a whisper for him to hear, "How about the stacks? When was the last time you were there?"

Until then memories of the stacks had remained tacitly and mutually inviolate in their thoughts. Her mention of them suddenly wrought-up a delicate moment, and Galiton purposely hesitated before answering. He wondered if their conversation should continue or if he should put an end to it. But before he realized it he was saying, "With you."

The words sounded strained. After a pause he cleared his throat and added, "The last time we were there together."

Galiton tried to remember the details of that last meeting. He couldn't. He was still shaken by the audacity of what lay behind her question. But he knew that he had never been there with any other girl, not even Jeri, and that he and Breezy had made love so many times there that it would have been impossible for him to isolate any single time, except the first time, and now, after these many years, he knew that he could never forget the first time.

He hadn't intended to do so but in a sudden rush of words he told her how the memory of their first time together had come to him as he was driving into Crowfoot Valley the day the four children had perished in the fire there, how in the flash of a moment he had relived the entire experience. Now embarrassed, Galiton lowered his eyes. Still, he continued speaking. It was unbelievable, he told her, that the recollection should come to him at the moment that only a few feet away death had reached out to claim four innocent lives then beyond human help, beyond human hope, forsaken by God.

Downcast, Galiton fell silent, thinking old, unpleasant thoughts. He felt the touch of a warm hand on his and raised his eyes. "That was all a long, long time ago," Breezy was saying. To herself she wondered which of the two memories was now the stronger for him, the more indelible. The first passionate expression of the love they had shared or the tragic deaths of the four children. Reason suddenly slashed at the thought. My God, what am I thinking, the entreaty exploded in her mind. In a sudden flush of shame she forced her thoughts to form acceptable words. Aloud she said, "A long, long time ago, Gal. You mustn't look back."

As the last word left her lips she raised her drink with her free hand in a silent toast to him and drank it down. Then, with a quick squeeze of his other hand where it rested under hers on the table top, she abruptly suggested with a bright smile, "Let's take a ride over there now. To Crowfoot Valley. For old time's sake."

Galiton had also tossed off his drink, but at the sound of her suggestion he was incredulous.

"Are you kidding?" he said aloud as he leaned backward and pulled his hands from hers. To himself he was thinking, the wife of the newspaper editor and a state trooper together in Crowfoot Valley. At night? Anytime! He laughed drily. When he spoke again Breezy was stung by the sarcasm in his voice. "Would we be there on a mission of mercy, to help the ghosts of the poor derelicts who haunt the place?"

Breezy momentarily melted but regained her composure quickly. "Neither," she said as she stood up. "Don't go away," she reached down and squeezed his hand where it again rested on the table. "I've got to check out the ladies room. Be right back."

While she was gone Galiton tried to return his thoughts to the photo of Felix Dombriewski, and the waitress. It was no use. He could think only of Breezy and her suggestion. He knew he would refuse her, had to refuse her. But why, after all these years, he asked himself, was her interest in him and Crowfoot Valley suddenly renewed? There was no denying a sense of flattery that had come over him with the invitation but, he told himself, it stops there, has to stop there.

He forced his thoughts homeward, to Jeri, but the image of Breezy, fresh, vibrant, sensual, beckoning, as in the days of their youth, obscured his mind's eye. What had come over her? Him? He'd had some good times with her, he remembered. Probably should have married her. But he had married Jeri. What a lover Breezy had been back then. With that thought he was aware of a tingle of sensation. He suddenly shrugged almost violently. "What the devil is the matter with me?" he asked himself angrily. "Forget it. You're a married man. You're also a state policeman." His determination almost succeeded. But dangling at the edge of the sobering thoughts rushing into his mind was the tempting memory of Breezy and the marvelous afternoons and nights of long ago in Crowfoot Valley. Breezy at the stacks. Breezy swimming naked in the cool, blue waters of the abandoned quarry hole. And in a flash of illumination he saw her in his arms there.

"Ready?" Breezy was now suddenly at his side, a fragile wrap clinging to her shoulders and a small clutch purse clasped at her waist.

Startled out of his reverie, Galiton quickly got to his feet. "Come on," he said gruffly. "I'll walk you to your car."

As they strolled across the blacktop parking lot Galiton noted that the night had turned cool. A million stars and a slice of moon shone overhead in a clear sky, and struck by the dazzling sight, he wondered how long it had been since last he had looked toward the nighttime heavens. He stopped walking and stood unmoving, looking up at the sky. Was it recently? A month ago? A year? Was he twenty? Seventeen? He could not remember. And now as he stood there he wondered if he ever had seen such a brilliant nighttime canopy over the earth, if he ever had seen a nighttime sky before now. Unbidden the words of a Sunday school Psalm once recited in childish sing-song cadence began to piece themselves together in his mind: "When I consider Thy heavens, the work of Thy fingers, the moon and the stars —." He couldn't remember the rest of it. He was still standing there, face still upturned when he heard Breezy's voice. She had preceded him to a long, black Lincoln. With a hand on the door handle she had turned to face him.

"Get in," she called softly.

Still determined to refuse her and climb into his own car parked in the shadows and hurry home to his wife, he gently took Breezy by the upper arm to help her into the car. Feeling his hand on her flesh through the thin shawl she pressed it tightly, meaningfully against the fullness and warmth of her body. At the same moment Galiton sensed a slight but unmistakable tremor pass through her.

"Get in," she repeated.

Her words, full and sensuous, reached out to him, enveloped him. The sensation that had passed through her body at his touch had electrified and shaken him. Without a word Galiton walked around to the passenger side of the car and climbed into the sumptuously upholstered seat. At the same time his better judgment told him that he had taken leave of his senses.

Before he could think too much more the car was under way, Breezy guiding it easily out of the parking lot and in the direction of the county blacktop that led to Moses City. They rode several miles in silence. When she wheeled the big car into the gravel turnoff that opened into Crowfoot Valley the Lincoln's large tires rumbling over the loose gravel reverberated with the sound of unleashed thunder through Galiton's throbbing conscience. "We're out of our minds," he said loudly, tersely. "Turn this thing around. This is crazy."

While he was indeed worried he was not entirely serious and he knew it. Breezy, meanwhile, offered no comment and continued driving in silence. The car moved past a collection of darkened shacks.

"We both should be on our way home," Galiton growled beside her, genuine concern and worry mounting in the sound of his voice.

"I've got no problem," Breezy said. "Edward's out of town for a few days." She was silent for a moment and then without emotion she added, "There's always something that takes the editor of the newspaper out of town for a few days."

She had stopped the car and switched off the lights.

"Want to go for a swim?" she asked lightly.

"You've got to be out of your mind," he told her seriously. He voiced another concern. "Remember how the cops used to patrol this place? That's all we need right now, a cop coming in here and finding us together. Let's get out of here."

"Oh Gal, that was so long ago," she laughed as she moved across the spacious seat closer to him. "I'll bet they have better things to do now."

She had his face in her hands and was pulling it down until his mouth touched hers, smothering his reply. The kiss was tender, long and warm and moist, bearing the strongest of messages, and Galiton found himself again embracing his high school sweetheart. In another minute he was aware of her hand at his waist, fumbling with his belt buckle.

CROWFOOT VALLEY

34

Crowfoot Valley came into prominence when a rich deposit of homogenous limestone was discovered there before the turn of the 20th Century. A limestone quarry was opened on the site and although it was situated in Spiceland County, because of its proximity to Moses City it was frowned on by some residents there, especially those whose properties bordered the area. Stone quarries were noisy, dirty and did absolutely nothing to enhance the landscape. In short, they were ugly and debasing.

The deposit of limestone there was hardly a surprising discovery. Although they were situated in totally different settings, the countryside around Moses City at that time already was dotted with similar quarries. Along with several mills that fabricated limestone for use in the construction of many imposing buildings in some of the major cities of the nation, they had combined to form a "stonebelt" from which had evolved one of the state's principal early industries.

Soon after the deposit had been staked out and its shale crust had been shot away, early European immigrants moved into the valley to work in the quarry as laborers. Like many of their counterparts throughout the stonebelt, they spoke limited or no English. Their lifestyles and cultures, which at a more enlightened time might have been acceptable, even charming, were then foreign, suspicious and unwelcome to many of the native born. As a result the citizens of Moses City, in classic late 19th Century ignorance, held these strangers at a distance and disparagingly referred to them as "dagos" and "bohunks."

Despite such denigrations, these were undeniably the new Americans of that period. Many of them were artisans in their own right, and one day some of them and certainly their progeny would live to rise above those mean beginnings. In the meantime, however, they were allotted a degree of favorable regard only by their employers because as both foreigners and laborers they were impressively passive and dependable, and incredibly indefatigable.

They were also woefully underpaid, yet they made an indelible first mark on Moses City and the limestone industry. They were honest people. They were trustworthy. And they toiled ten and twelve hours a day to produce and fabricate a natural resource that yet today maintains its unshakable place and dignity as a nation's natural and majestic building material.

During their earliest days in the valley, immigrants lived in large canvas tents. In subsequent months quarry owners constructed more durable rough-sawn shelters for them from the thick stands of poplar that thrived around the new quarry. These were called "shotgun" company houses. They were composed of three small rooms: a front room, a middle room that opened behind that, and a third room behind that, a lean-to addition provided a few of them with a small kitchen on the back side of the building. The term "shotgun" was coined by an anonymous jester who upon seeing one such house observed, "Open the front door and the back door and you can fire a shotgun straight through the place and not hit a thing."

The wives of quarry workers made such dwellings surprisingly comfortable and kept them neat and clean. As they had done in their homeland, the men built stone baking ovens outside their kitchen doors. Entire families tended generous vegetable gardens in their backyards, giving much of that space to planting and growing a variety of peppers. And in the darkness of their nighttime bedrooms husbands and wives made passionate love and conceived large families of handsome, dark-skinned sons and beautiful, dark-eyed daughters.

Their appetite for peppers soon became well known. Their gardens literally glowed with green peppers, red peppers, yellow peppers, large peppers and small peppers, hot peppers and not so hot peppers. They ate them as they came out of their gardens, or they ate them in salads. They canned them and they strung them to dry for seasoning in the cramped attic crawl spaces of their shotgun houses. For as long as a season's crop lasted they ate them almost daily, the quarry workers carrying them in sandwiches in their lunch pails. Usually they pan fried them with eggs and thick slices of raw onions and while these were cooking the deliciously tantalizing aroma was carried on the wind for great distances. It was for that reason that in the early years of the limestone quarry the settlement of shotgun houses was dubbed "Peppertown."

A quarter mile distant from that settlement in a small area enclosed by a white picket fence were interred the bodies of those of their number who over the years had died of natural causes, incurable illnesses or were killed in quarry accidents there. In a variety of sizes their graves were marked with cut shapes of the same gray, blue and buff colored limestone that had provided them with the sustenance and necessities of life. Compared to the cemeteries in Moses City and surrounding Spiceland County, the valley burial ground was small. Like the homes of the settlement dwellers it also was kept neat and clean, and while it did not have a name, as such, the immigrants called it "Camposanto," which in the native language of some of them meant "field of the dead."

A decade or more into the 20th Century, after several of its ledges of limestone had been removed, widespread iron deposits were discovered in the quarry. These aberrations manifested themselves in fine-lined splashes of black and rust colorings, marring the uniform density of the limestone and, in almost every case, weakening it, rendering it worthless for use in bearing and veneered walls. In the vernacular of the industry, such spider web-like deposits were called "crow's feet," and often spelled "crowsfeet."

When they were discovered, those giant blocks containing crowsfeet were lifted from the ancient sea of natural stone from which they were cut and stacked with other discarded huge limestone blocks in towering, inelegant edifices around the deep holes. These were technically known as grout piles, but in common usage they were referred to as "stacks," or "the stacks" of a particular quarry.

The blight of crowsfeet was not new to the limestone quarries around Moses City as was attested by mountainous stacks of culled blocks piled around them. But a sudden profusion of the malformation in the valley quarry sounded its death knell and ultimately forced its abandonment. It also led to the eventual but certain exodus from the valley of the immigrant workers whose livelihood depended on quarrying flawless building stone, and who consequently moved away to more lucrative diggings.

In the ensuing years, the valley underwent a strikingly harsh change. Fewer than a dozen shotgun houses had survived the exodus. All unoccupied, they stood stark and grim, a few with their red brick chimneys tumbling down. Their corrugated metal roofs sloped under layers of rust and moss and their vertical board and batting poplar siding was bleached gray by the rays of too many suns. Ghostly windows peered in on bare, dusty living rooms, bedrooms and kitchens, and visible from them were tall stands of broom sage as high as a man's head. Over all of this there hung an ear-aching silence that added a dimension of pain to the desolation.

In spite of that the deep quarry hole, because of its remoteness, became a favorite meeting place for Moses City's young and adventurous. They swam naked in the clear, cool waters of countless rains that had fallen and been trapped there. They climbed the stacks and painted in a variety of garish hues an abundance of vulgar and suggestive graffiti on the faces of the huge blocks of discarded limestone. And by day and by night they trysted and coupled undisturbed there deep in the lush green grasses of summer, on the burnished mats of autumn, in automobiles in all seasons, and generally on the hard surfaces of the massive rejected quarry blocks.

In the years of exuberance and intemperance of these events the defilement that had precipitated that industrial failure became a designation of some distortion. In its long history of usage, the name crowsfeet underwent a misconstruction, and the abandoned quarry hole and the deserted company houses, the little cemetery and the odd shaped depression in which they lay became known as "Crowfoot Valley."

One day, one week, one month, one year, ten years after the abandonment of the the valley—the exact time is unknown—a man called Tin-Cup Dooley and a woman who was either his wife or his companion appeared in one of the forsaken tumble-down shacks there. A short, slight man with a scruff of gray beard clinging to a face shadowed by a billed winter cap that he wore in all seasons, Tin-Cup Dooley looked neither to the right nor to the left as he walked. There was nothing sinister about him, no police record of him having stolen anything or hurt anyone. Furthermore it is still noted in the hand-me-down stories about him that he was never heard to speak an unkind word to or about a soul, nor was he ever heard to use foul language.

Nearly lost in dirty, oversized bib-overalls, around the waist of which was buckled an ancient leather belt, he walked slowly. Seemingly deep in contemplation or meditation, or otherwise lost in thought, head bowed, his thumbs hooked behind the shoulder straps of his overalls, he looked neither to the right nor to the left. At almost every step, a battered tin cup, an unpretentious, unwashed vessel of some dozen ounces of capacity, attached to his belt by a piece of baling wire, tap-tap-tapped at his rump. Eyes ever downcast, he spoke to no one unless he was begging a drink of water in his tin cup.

"There's old Tin-Cup," someone was sure to call on seeing him in Moses City. Children unfailingly would shout, "There's Old Tin-Cup Dooley, ooley, ooley, OH! Give him a drink of water in his tin cup. Dooley, ooley, ooley, OH!"

Always shuffling along at some distance behind him, as though she were just emerging from a trance, was a moon-faced woman. Forever bogged down in long, flowing soiled skirts and scuffed, high-top men's shoes that clop-clopped lace-less on her feet as she walked, she was known only by the lowly and most certainly fictitious appellation "Poopy." More than likely derived from a long-forgotten, ridiculing source it nonetheless was accepted and used freely by Moses City and Spiceland County residents. "Poopy Dooley" they called her.

While their place of abode was ignored by the majority of Moses City's population, it was generally known that Tin-Cup Dooley and Poopy lived together in one of the shacks in the Crowfoot Valley village, a place that had become by then a kind of no man's land. Predictably, they were haltingly but inevitably followed into the valley by a few other outcasts who took up abject residence in some of the other abandoned structures there. Outstanding among these newcomers, because they also made regular appearances in Moses City, were two derelict characters, an old man known only as "Dink" and an old woman known as "Grass Sack Sally," dubious monikers given them by unknown persons.

Like Tin-Cup, the other few men of the valley appeared mostly old, toothless, bearded and slovenly. Most of the few women who lived there, like Poopy and Grass Sack Sally, were scraggly-haired, shabbily dressed and, by Moses City standards, unwashed. The few children seen around the hovels wore soiled, rag-tag clothing and seemed ever crusted with dirt. Except, perhaps, for the woman called Grass Sack Sally who often traipsed about Moses City carrying what was popularly believed to be a collection of mysterious treasures in a burlap sack slung over a shoulder, none of these later arrivals approached the obscure but arresting popularity of Tin-Cup Dooley and the woman called Poopy Dooley.

Generally ignored by the clean and pure of Moses City, the sorrowful inhabitants of Crowfoot Valley constituted a small degenerate community with which the heart of the stonebelt was forced to contend—if not accept. Although the valley at the time was still the property of the limestone company that had opened the quarry there, the cast-offs, for unknown and rarely questioned reasons, lived in the tumble down shelters there undisturbed. Since there were only wells in the valley and no utilities, living there required only such monies as needed to provide the barest necessities of life.

Among that inglorious group, there appeared one day a man who grew considerably in questionable reputation. He was to become known as Peg-Leg Hill. From then until his untimely and horrifying demise one night, he had, without interruption by the law, distilled moonshine in the valley. Though his still was indeed somewhere in the valley, the exact location was never publicly known. It was guessed by some Moses City residents to be within a tangle of briar-infested bushes that surrounded a thick stand of trees beyond the quarry hole. No one was ever sure. It was often repeated that Peg-Leg's illegal woodland distillery thrived in the early years by virtue of whichever Spiceland County sheriff happened to be in office.

It was also a popular rumor, one that was always sure to arouse curiosity and comment, that the moonshiner, known as Peg-Leg Hill, had a small fortune cached somewhere in the valley. There is no record of his given name, but legend recounts that he had acquired the sobriquet Peg-Leg after having lost a leg in an accident in the valley's limestone quarry. According to the story that was handed down, while being hoisted by a primitive pole derrick onto a railroad flatcar a mammoth quarry block had shattered. One of a burst of huge falling pieces had struck and pinned his lower left leg to the quarry floor, crushing it in the process. The errant chunk, estimated at fifteen tons, might have squished the life out of him, except that Peg-Leg had lunged frantically out of death's way. The severely damaged limb was surgically amputated just below the knee, and after that he walked with the aid of crutches until he appeared one day clumping around the valley on a wooden leg. It was a natural consequence then that the people of his time began calling him Peg-Leg, or by the diminutive "Peg."

Peg's face was habitually concealed behind a coarse, black stubble of beard, giving him a hostile look which was aggravated by wide, dark eyes that seemed always to glare outward. Still, except for bootlegging, no one had ever attached his name to a violent or other unlawful act.

Like Tin-Cup Dooley and Poopy, and those who later followed them into Crowfoot Valley, Peg led a quiet, peaceful existence. However, there was a rather humorous story told about him. It seems that one spring morning he was seen acting strangely in his vegetable garden. He was taking one step forward then turning around and bending over. He continued in that manner, taking one step forward and then turning around and bending over, taking one step forward and then turning around and bending over. Understanding came to the viewer with a shock. Peg-Leg Hill was setting out tomato plants. He would step forward on the freshly turned ground with his peg leg then turn around and place a tomato plant in the hole made by the wooden peg protruding from the stump of his artificial leg. All of which served to give his shocking torture-death a weird dimension. In the end it was theorized that unknown persons looking for his fabled cache killed him one night after getting drunk on Peg's own moonshine.

A hunter found Peg's body the next morning.

Hands bound, it lay where he had died, face down in the yet warm ashes of what had been a large wood fire. A prybar, whose rusted, beveled end was believed to have been used to burn to a crisp the sole of his single foot, lay nearby. Due to the extensive damage done to his face by the hot wood fire, into which he had fallen or been pushed, identification of his body might have posed a problem, except that almost anyone would have recognized Peg's stub of a leg and the attached wooden stump.

With several variations, the account of Peg's mysterious murder was told and re-told for decades in and around Moses City. The most believable version suggested that some revelers had bought whiskey from him earlier that fateful night, and after getting drunk had returned for more. There was evidence they had taken a popular route into the valley, having made their way on foot along a disused railroad spur that ran from a railroad switchyard north of Moses City through the valley, past the little cemetery, and ultimately to the distant abandoned quarry hole. It was speculated from the outset that in their abnormal state the inebriates probably refused to pay for the second jug, and when the black-bearded man with the fierce dark eyes and wooden stump for a leg insisted on the price before handing over more hootch, which was his known way of doing business, they attacked him. Their demand to know the location of his rumored cache was probably a spontaneous afterthought that probably got insanely out of hand.

Dead trees around where Peg's body was found had provided a bounty of fuel for the fire that was used to redden the torturing iron and which later destroyed his face. It was never learned where the prybar had come from. The killers were never identified, and they eventually went to their individual rewards harboring their awful secret. Whether they had succeeded in forcing Peg to disclose the hiding place of his money, if indeed such a place existed, was never known. Peg-Leg Hill was buried in the valley's little cemetery.

There were those in Moses City and Spiceland County who for many years after his murder believed that Peg's treasure was still concealed someplace in Crowfoot Valley, that it was watched over by his ghost. And in spite of such whispered warning, there were others, a brave few, who dared search for it one night and had fled the valley in terror after having heard Peg's ghost thumping around there on his wooden leg.

35

In the darkness of night, Galiton and Breezy were unable to see the differences in Crowfoot Valley over earlier days. A few remodeled shelters had changed the appearance of that storied settlement. Though signs of paint were visible on some of the other buildings, a vestige of the past, such as the streaked gray of aged, unpainted native poplar was unmistakable. At least two of the older houses had been embellished with additions, making a second bedroom in the original kitchen space of the old time shotgun-style arrangement. A few houses were now equipped with small porches. Two of those had swings.

Unlike the early days, utility meters fastened to outside walls were indicative of the greatest change; there now was electricity in the valley. Modernization had come only so far, however. There was no municipal sewer system there and where septic systems had not been installed, outhouses, like patient sentinels of mercy, still rose from some backyards.

As Breezy's Lincoln moved along the narrow roadway, it was evident even in the darkness that tall growths of poplar, sycamore and shagbark hickory had thickened along the valley's southern edge. These served to shade some of the houses from blistering afternoon suns. The single gravel road, unchanged over the years, still cut through the center of the village from west to east to end at the abandoned quarry hole. The narrow gravel ramp still inclined to the blacktop road that stretched between the outskirts of

Moses City to the west and rural Spiceland County to the east. As was the case in earlier days, the ramp was the main entrance into the valley.

Many years after the gory Peg-Leg Hill incident, two other tragedies, coming decades apart, were added to the valley's bleak history. The first of these occurred on a cold winter's afternoon when four small children, one an infant, the eldest not quite eight, perished in the blaze of one of the older shelters there. Happening when it did, at the height of the Christmas shopping season, it brought a predictable reaction from some Moses City and Spiceland County residents.

"Might the valley be cursed?" they asked furtively. "Should it not be cleaned out? Condemned? Bulldozed?"

For rookie state policeman Anthony Galiton, who was visiting the Moses City Police Station that afternoon, the memory of that tragic event would live forever. It began for him when the city police dispatcher there was notified by telephone of the fire. The caller, who was quite excited, could not be certain, but she herself—the volume of her impassioned voice spilling the sound of her words out of the dispatcher's earpiece into the police radio communications room—had been informed that a child, perhaps several children, might be trapped in the burning building.

Within seconds Galiton had dashed to his cruiser. He knew Crowfoot Valley, every inch. He also knew the shortest route there through Moses City. As he guided his machine with siren wailing and red lights flashing through city streets toward the valley, intermittent views between buildings along the route revealed clouds of black and white smoke rising in the distance. From somewhere behind him and from up ahead, he could hear other sirens over the sound of that on his cruiser. They gave him a sense of relief and hope; more help was on the way. He prayed that it would be—that he would be—in time.

As he cautiously eased the cruiser into the tight turn off the blacktop onto the narrow gravel ramp that led into the valley, the young trooper saw Spiceland County sheriff's deputy Henry Carter, who was already on the scene and out of his squad car. Galiton was also aware of the sudden, uninvited remembrance that as boys and classmates he and Henry had frequently visited the valley, curiously explored it, had hunted mushrooms there and that during summer vacations they had often skinny-dipped in the valley's abandoned quarry hole, about a half mile from where the deputy now stood.

The state trooper was appalled and ashamed that a second memory should intrude upon, if not profane, this mission of mercy. It was insistently invasive, and young Galiton had no control over it. His mind was suddenly permeated by the recollection of a warm spring afternoon when he, schoolboy Anthony Galiton, had lost his virginity near the stacks in the valley to yet another classmate. Unsolicited and unwanted, a picture of Breezy Jamison lying in the grass before him, a thin white undergarment cast carelessly aside, flashed into his mind. To the youthful Galiton, Breezy was the most beautiful of all the girls at Moses City High School, and he had been madly in love with her. For months they had been clinging to that phase of a relationship which then was popularly known as "necking," having faithfully and surprisingly gone no further.

Young and idealistic, he had always stopped at the last second, leaving himself, he knew, and Breezy, he believed, achingly disappointed and passionately wanting. But chivalrous youth that he was, he always had found a later satisfaction in telling himself that anything more would have been morally wrong, sinful, and disrespectful of Breezy; and that any further pleasures and joys they could give each other must wait until the proper time, which he then saw as marriage.

But in the shadow of the stacks on that sunny spring afternoon, something had gone wrong. Beside himself with an urgency completely beyond his control and further inflamed by a fierce eagerness and impatience he had never before seen in Breezy, Galiton was uncontrollably devoid of ideals and conscience.

They had stayed at the stacks until the chill that had accompanied an early spring sunset also brought them to a cold awareness of their fulfillment and fatigue. With arms entwined they then walked to Galiton's jalopy Ford where they embraced and kissed several more times before driving out of the valley.

Galiton had long ago lost count of the times following that memorable afternoon that he and Breezy had visited Crowfoot Valley. The recollection, though vivid and painfully sensual, had lasted but an infinitesimal portion of a second, and the young trooper's thoughts returned to the demanding scene before him.

Deputy Carter stood some distance from a smoking shack, holding his arms up as though to protect his face. Rushing to his side, Galiton became suddenly aware of the meaning of Carter's actions. The unseen blaze inside the squat building was so intense it stung the flesh of his face and seared his nostrils, making it difficult for him to breathe. Shielding his face with a forearm, Galiton called out to his friend just as the first fire truck roared into the valley.

"Henry!" he shouted grimly.

"Old woman said four kids are in there, Gal!" Carter called out.

Galiton felt his heart skip a beat. Four kids! "Dear Jesus, no!" he groaned aloud in outraged supplication. "Not kids!"

To himself he prayed the old woman was wrong. Four kids! God, please let that be a mistake, he begged inwardly. God, I'll die—he was suddenly afraid for his life. We'll die—he amended his fear to include his deputy friend—if we have to go in there. I'm not ready to die. I don't want to die. His silent prayerful overtures to God continued racing through his mind.

Despite the rampant fear that had suddenly gripped him in the face of what he knew would be certain death, Galiton had again moved instinctively, uncontrollably, unexplainably in the direction of the burning shack. He was forced to retreat when his eyes and mouth and lungs sealed themselves against the pain of searing air. In spite of his overwhelming fear, he also was angry that he could get no closer. He knew, too, that he was also relieved and pleased, that because he could get no closer, he would not have to die in the inferno. At that moment he heard Carter call out a warning. He turned away just as a deluge of cold water from the engine company sprayed past him and Carter to the hot shack, hissing and steaming loudly, frighteningly as it broke through a window.

The house literally erupted in a heart-stopping mountain of sparks and flaming debris, sending more clouds of black smoke rolling upward into the cold, late afternoon sky. The two policemen hastily withdrew to a safer place just as a second engine company thundered into the valley and yet another stream of water was soon poured into the flames.

Sometime later, the passage of an eternity for the two watching policemen and silent bystanders who had gathered, the roaring blaze was extinguished and sufficiently cooled for firemen to attempt to enter what remained of the building. They found that the door, almost untouched by the blaze, was held shut by a weight of some kind behind it and resisted their efforts. Eventually it relented and two firemen carefully gained the inside. One of them reappeared immediately, his face ashen and contorted, vomit spewing from his mouth. Galiton watched, helplessly drawn to the horror of human frailty and agony, as the man staggered into the gravel lane and collapsed, retching where he lay.

Then for the first time in his life Galiton smelled the stink of charred, human flesh. He thought he too would be ill, knew he would be. Before he could yield completely to the suffocating nausea that had suddenly attacked him, he was distracted by the demanding voice of a fireman who was standing in the open doorway, calling to him and pointing behind the door. Galiton reluctantly stepped forward and looked. The remains of three children lay in a blackened huddle there.

Emotionally gripped and sickened again, Galiton again turned away. He heard a shout and responded to the call of another fireman. He saw the man within the charred ruins of the shack, gesturing toward what was left of a bed. The yellowed, blistered and cracked body of an infant lay face up there. Unable to breathe, his brain reeling, his stomach reaching for his constricted throat, Galiton lunged blindly toward the doorway. There he was halted by the first fireman, now kneeling, who grabbed at his hand.

"Look at this!" the words heaved upward in a demanding roar from deep within the man.

Galiton looked. "What is it?" he gasped impatiently through his nausea.

"This latch! Something's wrong with it," the fireman shouted.

Deputy Carter and other firemen gathered to examine the discovery. They exchanged wide-eyed looks of disbelief.

"I don't believe it!" the fireman exclaimed. "It's a string latch and it can only be worked from the outside."

The number of spectators gathered outside had increased to a crowd of men women and children. The old woman who had spoken to Carter earlier walked amid them, holding up four long, bony, clawlike fingers, her eyes wild, her toothless mouth a gaping cavity of the horror she knew but could not articulate. She held her hand high for all to see, for all to read in those silent, extended purple digits that another gruesome event had come to Crowfoot Valley.

Galiton looked at the watch on his wrist. Evening had come and seemingly no one had noticed. It occurred to the trooper that his wife would be setting supper on the table, as were most wives of Moses City.

"Supper time," he muttered, aware that his words were more of a curse than a statement of fact. "Supper time," he repeated, "and six days until Christmas."

Galiton would later learn that the first report of the fatal blaze reached into city and county homes via the evening news over Moses City's radio station. Before the fifteen minute newscast had ended, the radio station was inundated by telephone calls from listeners seeking to be of assistance to the grieving parents of the dead children. Since the location of the blaze was given as Crowfoot Valley, listeners, without being told, intuitively knew that the parents would be in need, if not totally destitute. For the first time in its long history, Crowfoot Valley had touched deeply into the hearts of neighboring Moses City and Spiceland County. Callers pledged money, some promised clothing and food. A tavern owner and professional gambler called to guarantee payment of four caskets in which to bury the dead children. Because of the size of their tiny bodies only two were deemed necessary. A businessman appeared in person at the radio station to guarantee burial sites in the cemetery of the parents' choice. The president of a limestone fabricating company telephoned to promise that his company would provide limestone markers for the graves of the children. A single large limestone tombstone was used. Other callers promised furniture for the future home of the parents, wherever that might be. Even that night, and the next day, children from Moses City and Spiceland County arrived at the radio station with containers of money they had collected at their neighborhood doors.

Although it was possible in a single stride to step from the outskirts of Moses City into Crowfoot Valley, the latter was situated in Spiceland County. For that reason investigation of the fatal blaze fell to the sheriff's department, specifically to Henry Carter. Documented in detail in Moses City's newspaper for a few days, it revealed that the mother of the children, who was also the family breadwinner, was at her job at the time of the fire. The father, who had been unemployed for months, was filling the role of babysitter at the time. He told Carter that he had refueled the wood heating stove that afternoon, then, apparently forgetting that he had opened the damper, left the house to go to the home of a neighbor, leaving the stove unattended. It was speculated that the overheated stove had then ignited untold layers of old newspapers, which, for purposes of economy and insulation had, over the years, been pasted to the interior walls of the aged shack with an adhesive made from mixing flour and water.

"The inside of that place burned like hell itself," Moses City Fire Chief Rod Williams had told Carter. "I've seen those kinds of walls burn before. They go up like gasoline. And at one time just about every one of those shacks in the valley was papered the same way. And those kids, at least those who were piled up behind the door, might've got out, but for that damned stringlatch. I've never seen anything like that before."

Although Carter's investigation included the fire chief's report of the conditions of the interior walls of the shack, there was no inspection made of the interior walls of other such shelters in the valley. That some of them in all likelihood were still papered in the same manner, and that they too might one day contribute to a similar blaze, was either overlooked or ignored in the investigation.

Because of that awful tragedy Moses City, and, especially, a place called Crowfoot Valley, became widely known. The valley's hopeful beginnings and its inglorious later history were revived and reprinted in *The Intelligencer* and other newspapers around the state. They were detailed over radio and the still infant electronic medium of that time, television. Old stories were retold from new points of view, given new slants and shaded in popular hues. The dagos, the bohunks, Tin-Cup Dooley and the woman called Poopy, and Dink and Grass Sack Sally again walked the memorable paths of their times. And those generations who had never before heard of them warmed to and shrank from the revived tales of their days in Crowfoot Valley.

The tale of treachery and brutality that had claimed the life of Peg-Leg Hill was highlighted and enlarged upon, and re-told in such a way as to give his memory the illusion of heroic glitter. But because of the nearness of the happiest holidays of the year, Christmas and New Year's, their new existence was short-lived and all were soon dead again, re-interred in the small cemetery in Crowfoot Valley, and pushed out of mind.

But they would not remain that way. An incredible third tragedy destined to befall Crowfoot Valley in the years ahead would bring to them still another resurrection, and they would enjoy the light of day one more time.

36

In uniform when he returned to the Hickory Grove Lounge to keep his appointment with the waitress there, Galiton was informed that the woman he sought had telephoned to say that she would be late, perhaps as much as an hour. Deciding to wait there, he stood at the bar and ordered a Coke in a large glass with ice. He had been looking forward to this meeting ever since he had parted from Breezy the previous night and the unexpected delay left him both annoyed and impatiently weary.

Obviously he was tiring of the Fielding case. As far as he was concerned, Fielding was alive and most likely well. Certainly he was hiding out somewhere until his wife, who was nothing less than an accomplice in what Galiton had believed almost from the outset to be a scheme of murder and fraud, could collect his insurance and join him. He was ready to put an end to the investigation. All that was necessary now was to obtain a positive identification of the man in the photograph in his inside coat pocket, and the Fielding case would take a major step toward that end—without benefit of an insurance payoff.

It might take a little more time than that, Galiton now wisely cautioned himself. But with the identification of the man in the photo he carried, the investigation, after all this time, would at least be headed at increased speed to a conclusion. There was no doubt in his mind that since Felix Dombriewski could not be found, the man had been murdered by

Fielding and what was left of his burned and muti-
lated body was buried in the Fielding family cemetery plot at Moses City. A voice interrupted his
thoughts and he turned to face a bearded old man
wearing a faded baseball cap with a farm machinery
advertising patch above the bill.

"You're that state policeman who's been asking
about Mr. Fielding," the man said in a tone that
seemed to be telling Galiton rather than asking him.

Galiton nodded. "One of them."

"Listen, I don't want my name in the paper, 'cause I
don't want no trouble. But I recollect seeing Mr.
Fielding the day of that fire," the man said. "I seen
him right here in town, over at the Leaf. Had another feller with him."

The Leaf—the Oak Leaf Inn—was a small, neatly
maintained tavern situated at the eastern edge of
Hickory Grove. It catered year round to locals as well
as to a healthy share of the town's many tourists.
Galiton and every policeman for miles around the
tourist mecca knew it to be a popular place for what
were touted to be "the best hamburgers around."

The Leaf also was known for the privacy it afforded early morning drinkers. A rear door that opened
into an alley existed, it seemed, only to make entries
and exits discreet matters for those who craved the so-
called hair of the dog that had bitten them the previous night. Surprisingly, for the size of Hickory Grove's
small population, many were those who used it.

On two separate occasions in past months Galiton
had stopped at the Leaf in uniform and entered
through the front door to make inquiries, without success. The man now standing beside him in the
Hickory Grove Lodge may have been there at one of
those times, maybe both.

"Where have you been?" Galiton demanded of the old man. "It's been well over a year, going on two. Why didn't you say something sooner?"

The old man seemed suddenly afraid. Galiton softened his tone of voice and waved a hand, hoping the old man would understand that his tardiness was irrelevant. At the same time the trooper reached inside his coat and showed the man the photo of Dombriewski.

"Is this the man he had with him?" he asked. At the same time it belatedly occurred to Galiton that he should also have had photographs of at least two other men to show. Failing that, he should have asked the old man for a description of Fielding's alleged companion before showing him the photograph. But he decided to ignore caution and he held the photo up for the old man to see.

"That's him," the man said without hesitation. "That's the feller. I'd know that face any place. They left together and got in Mr. Fielding's car and drove off. I know, 'cause I left a couple minutes ahead of them and I was out there talking to a friend when they come out."

The old man sounded so convincing that Galiton put aside his concern at having shown a single photo and that one being of Dombriewski.

"Are you sure?" he said with restrained anxiety. "This picture has recently been in the newspapers and on television. It's been a long time since you think you saw him, too, you know. Think hard, now."

"That's him," the old man repeated. "I'd know that face anywhere."

"Tell me what you saw," Galiton's anxiety had begun to show.

"Ain't much to tell," the old man said. "They come

out of that place and walked to Mr. Fielding's car. I knowed Mr. Fielding for years. Worked as a hooker in his mill once. Worked in just about all the mills around Moses City. I started working in limestone when I was a kid, carrying water in a bucket in a quarry. Water boy, I was. Work at the Leaf now, and a little here, but only in the mornings. Cleaning up, you know—"

"How about what you saw?" Galiton interrupted him.

"Not much, 'cept that this guy fell down just as they got to the car. Mr. Fielding helped him up and they drove off."

"You mean this guy was already drunk, in the morning?" Galiton again was suddenly suspicious of the old man. Felix Dombriewski had a record of public intoxication arrests, but there was nothing in that record to suggest that he was a falling-down boozer. Not unless he'd changed for the worse.

"Nope," the man hurried to allay Galiton's fears. "It was more like he was having a fit. He shook all over like he was having one, anyway. Other people saw him too. I don't know who they were. But they just kind of looked as they passed by. Anyway, I never saw them two after that."

"Why didn't you report this sooner?" Galiton asked again but in a gentler tone.

"Didn't put no stock in it, at least not till I read in the paper that Mr. Fielding was still alive in Arizona, or someplace," the man said.

"I'll have to have your name," Galiton had a notebook and ballpoint in his hands.

"I don't care, just so it don't get in the papers," the man said. "Wilson Hackler." He watched as Galiton began to write. "I've got a little place between here and Moses City. Out in the country. Just me and the old woman. She's poorly and I don't want nobody comin' around to upset her. Y'understand, don't you?"

"Right. But I may have to come around," Galiton said. "We may need to talk to you before this thing is over. You understand that, don't you?"

The old man shook his head and raised his palms, fingers widespread. "Be happy t'talk t'the state police anytime," he said. "Got a telephone, too."

Caution, like a ringing bell, began sounding in Galiton's head. He remembered that early in the investigation of the fire at the Fielding home there had been two reports of a man having been seen with Fielding the day of the fire; however, there had been no report of the man having been ill or having had fits. Now months later an old man had placed Fielding at the side of a *fallen* man who might have been having *seizures*. In spite of his doubt and suspicion Galiton's anxiety increased.

He was concentrating on making notes under Wilson Hackler's name in his notebook when he was greeted by the tardy waitress. As she arranged a small apron around her waist she apologized for being late, then she made herself comfortable on a stool next to Galiton. Without hesitation the trooper again removed the photo of Felix Dombriewski from his inner pocket.

"That's him, all right," the woman said, a smoldering emphasis in her words. "I was sure last night and I am sure now. They were in here together late one afternoon, maybe around supper time. It's been a long time, but I remember they sat right here at the bar and ate and drank wine, both of them."

"You see a lot of people in this place," Galiton said solicitously. "Are you sure you're not confusing him with someone else? It has been a long time, as you said. And you really weren't that sure that you recognized this photo last night."

"I know, I was busy. But I never really forget a face," the woman said in injured tones despite the policeman's tactfulness. "Depend on it. I may forget a name, but never a face. When you make your living off tips you remember faces, believe me."

The woman then proceeded to tell Galiton that she had made a business of remembering faces. Especially, she pointed out, the faces of good tippers or other faces she wanted to remember. Once a face was imprinted on her memory, she said emphatically, it was there forever. Galiton waited patiently until she stopped speaking.

"Can you tell me anything more?"

"No. I was busy. Like last night. I didn't even see them leave. But that's your man, all right," she nodded her head several times.

"Why didn't you give this information to the police earlier?" Galiton was again suspicious.

"They never asked me," the waitress said coldly, her face an expressionless mask.

As he drove toward Moses City and reviewed his talks with the old man and the waitress, Galiton was conscious of his mounting excitement. Felix Dombriewski now appeared to be the most important and promising development in the Fielding investigation. He knew a rising sensation of accomplishment at last, if not one of total success. Two positive ID's that the man in the photograph was the man alleged to have been seen with Fielding the day of the fire: Wilson Hackler's account of what he'd seen outside the Oak Leaf Inn the morning of the fire, and the waitress's identification of the man in the photograph as being that of Fielding's companion the evening before the fire.

Galiton now was doubly certain the dead man was Felix Dombriewski. He thought of Captain Melton and suddenly laughed. This will be a shocker for him, he said to himself. Melton won't believe it. Not even when it's staring him in the face, he won't. He'll continue to insist that Fielding is dead and buried. Galiton admitted to himself that he really did not like Melton. Nor did he like the fact that Melton disagreed with his view of the Fielding case. He was thankful that he would not have to report to Melton and personally break the news to him. Galiton would submit his report to Lieutenant Conway, who would fill in Melton on the details. He was feeling good about his day's work. Colonel Carey would also feel good about it; of that much Galiton was certain.

So much time had passed since the fire that the theory held by state police that someone other than Fielding had died in the blaze had faltered and grown cold in the public mind. Coroner Irwin Brown had taken as much into account when in recent weeks he had informed Harley Oaks that were it not for the still lingering doubt of the dead man's identity he would not hesitate to issue a death certificate in the name of Crestman Fielding, thereby closing the aging case. With this new information in hand, Galiton was convinced that the theory that Fielding was still among the living was now on a solid foundation. He couldn't remember a time since the fire when he had felt so good, so confident. What a stroke of luck his meeting with Breezy Coleman had been.

Thoughts of Breezy suddenly flooded his mind. Long after he and Breezy had separated the previous night, while he was in the midst of a cleansing, thoughtful shower at the Moses City barracks, before going home to his wife, Galiton had steadily cursed himself for being a fool. One prowl car—he kept telling himself as the hot, needle-like spray that stung his body seemed also to enliven his conscience—one prowl car. My integrity would have been compromised. I would have lost my wife, my home, and my badge in the bargain. Integrity? My God, do I have any left? If I'd been seen in a car with the . . . with a . . . he could not bring himself to finish the thought. Instead he envisioned the consequences of what might have happened had he and Breezy been discovered together.

Right now, he thought angrily as he roughly sudsed his body with a bar of soap, somebody could be holding an axe over my head. Some cop could have me by the short hair. Of all the places to go. Go? Oh no, no, no! Of all the things to do! And in a car like some dumb kid. With the wife of the editor of the local newspaper, to boot. No. What is the matter with me? With any woman any place. Any woman but my own wife.

While viciously lathering himself, for his contempt of himself demanded some form of self-flagellation, he remembered Jeri. He tried to put himself in her position, tried to feel the sense of betrayal she surely could not escape were she aware, or if she should learn that he had broken his vow to her. To God. It could mark the end of their happy marriage.

The thought had left him shaken and nauseated. In spite of the hot water splashing on his body, he felt a chill at the magnitude of his treachery. He saw himself as a disreputable lout, fallen from grace, for since his marriage to Jeri he had never been with another woman, never desired one. He had never failed her, his promises to her and to God. He felt morally destitute, impoverished of honor. In the throes of this despair he also saw his state police badge forever tarnished and lusterless.

Galiton again had furiously worked the bar of soap over his naked body, giving rise to a coat of thick, dripping white lather. He was overcome with a need to wash, wash, wash. Working up more and more lather he saw himself hopelessly soiled forever by his brief fling with Breezy Coleman. Worse, he kept repeating to himself, he had betrayed his innocent, faithful wife and degraded her in the bargain.

He scolded himself, cursed himself, that what he had done was a base, unprincipled and unjustifiable act, unforgivable—and one he would always regret. He told himself that he was low and dishonorable. Having fallen victim to his passions—Breezy Coleman's passions, he argued the point with himself to no avail—he continued to attempt to relieve his guilt by a confusion of self-confession and self-condemnation. He repeatedly admitted to himself that, having allowed himself to be with Breezy, he had just as surely assaulted and brutalized Jeri and violated her love for him. He was so filled with genuine indignation and remorse that he actually ached and wanted to cry. In that state of mixed emotions and being alone in the barrack's shower room, he tried, in a whisper to God, to articulate his regret for his adulterous treachery and to ask God's forgiveness, his own forgiveness.

It was a grandiose effort that had failed on both accounts, for Galiton also realized with shocking abruptness that he really did not want forgiveness, God's nor his own. He *wanted* to think about Breezy, he told himself while still asking himself repeatedly if he had lost his senses. He knew he hadn't. He told himself candidly that he simply wanted to think about Breezy and her sexual aggressiveness. He found himself wanting to relive, to feel again, the unique pleasure he had derived from her during their brief visit to Crowfoot Valley in her cushiony Lincoln. He had never known anything quite like it.

Then yielding completely to the memory of Breezy, his depression and regret disappeared and were replaced by a rekindling of physical desire for her. "God," he had exclaimed irreverently to himself as he again stepped under the spray of hot water, "what a woman." Then, in the space of a single heartbeat Jeri again took over his thoughts. "She doesn't deserve to be treated this way," he had groaned inwardly. In response to his honest empathy, the image of Jeri, blonde and blue-eyed, smiled down on him, but briefly. For as if by magic it was again replaced with that of the dusky, satiny-skinned Breezy. Caught up in another attack of guilt he had been totally unprepared for her appearance. He found himself involuntarily turning away from her, trying desperately to cover himself with the bar of soap. He tried to wipe her image, her memory out of existence. Despairing anew at his fall from rectitude, again to no avail, Galiton recalled that he had made a similar move with his hands when Breezy, earlier that night in Crowfoot Valley, had begun working at his belt buckle. His had been a half-hearted move, he remembered, for he was more than mildly curious to know how far she would dare to go. By then, however, it had been too late.

With that recollection filling his mind as he showered he was again conscious of arousal. He wanted Breezy, then and there, to relive that moment. All of a sudden, in spite of the hot spray under which he stood, he again felt a cold chill. Jeri was again in his mind. He felt too ashamed to go home, did not want to go home. Unknowing, and in her innocence, she would, he knew, expect as much from him as he had shared with Breezy. He turned his face away from the splash of water, moving the bar of soap in short, quick strokes over his arms and shoulders while doubt and desperation again rose in his chest. What should he do? Fortunately, Jeri was fast asleep when he arrived home. And despite the ambivalence of his tortured conscience, he had slept soundly.

Steering the police cruiser onto the highway Galiton recalled that when morning came he had had no qualms about facing Jeri at breakfast. His mind was clear, free from the despair of the night before, and he felt good. Now, as he approached the barracks he pushed thoughts of Jeri and Breezy and the previous night from his mind. The feel of the photograph of Felix Dombriewski in his inner coat pocket, the photograph identified by Wilson Hackler and the waitress as being that of the man seen with Crestman Fielding before the fire, was comforting. He felt satisfied.

He was relieved to see the barracks when it came into view, yet he was disappointed to see that there were several cruisers, all duplicates of the one he was driving, in the parking lot. Afternoon shift change, he moaned. He recognized Link Trueblood's cruiser. He knew that if Trueblood saw him he'd want to talk. Galiton preferred not to be put into a position of having to divulge his night and day with anyone; not, he told himself, until he could sort out his good fortune and put together an impressive, meaningful written report on the identification of the photo. Deciding to delay his arrival, he turned his cruiser in the direction of a coffee stop at the opposite edge of Moses City.

37

Despite the fact that he was fully cognizant of driving, Galiton nevertheless was unmindful of the direction he had taken. Before he realized where he was, his cruiser had moved past the restaurant, past the east edge of Moses City and had turned off the county blacktop into the gravel ramp entrance to Crowfoot Valley.

"What the —," he suddenly spoke aloud to himself. "What am I doing here?"

Before he could think or say more he heard Harley Oaks calling his unit number on the car's radio. Responding, he heard Oaks asking to meet him for coffee. In the distance ahead of the moving police car Galiton could see the mountainous stacks of cast-off limestone quarry blocks. He felt drawn to them. As the car rumbled over the uneven surface of the gravel roadway, he found himself in the grip of curiosity at why, without forethought, he had compulsively turned into the valley. He pressed the key of his hand mike and gave Oaks his answer.

"Negative," he said without explanation and replaced the mike on its hanger.

The interruption by Oaks and Galiton's own fascination with the nearing stacks had diverted any attention he might have given the shelters that served as dwellings for the current denizens of Crowfoot Valley. Except for dissipating giant white tick-tack-toe squares drawn across it by a playful Air Force pilot's jet, the sky was limitlessly high and light blue.

On the ground, children, a clustered apparition of blank faces had turned and watched silently as the red and gold on white Mercury, festooned with spotlights, emergency lights and waving dual antennae, passed. Raising his eyes to the rear vision mirror Galiton belatedly glimpsed them in the retreating distance. He remembered the children he'd seen the first time he had driven into the valley in the uniform of a state trooper and shuddered at the recollection. He tried to shake from his mind the persistent memory of that December afternoon, the little fire-blackened corpses.

"That was a long time ago," he groaned aloud. "Forget it."

Yet he knew that he could never do so. Jarred suddenly by the memory of what he remembered to be the stink of burned flesh, he sawed brutally at his nose with an index finger, exhaling wildly through his nostrils as he did so. He shrugged violently and riveted his eyes on the stacks of discarded limestone quarry blocks.

"Why don't they move these people out?" he muttered angrily. "Turn a bulldozer loose in here. Bury this place."

To himself he thought, "I suppose there's nowhere for these poor devils to go. This is their place, the slums of Moses City. This is where Moses City hides its poor, its unsightly, its destitute. Buried in Crowfoot Valley. That's why the place is here. The burial ground of Moses City's castaways." He laughed bitterly then, and he said aloud, "No damn wonder there are no poor in Moses City. They're all here."

That was not entirely correct and neither was it fair, and Galiton knew it. There were a few nicer shacks with flowers blooming around them in the valley. And there were some poor in Moses City. They were scattered and not quite so obvious as were those whose destinies were imprisoned in Crowfoot Valley. The difference was in the degree of poverty. Those few who chose not to help themselves, and those who claimed the right to live in squalor and degradation, and those who could not help themselves lived in the valley.

The overall situation there was one not given to easy solution. There were those in Moses City who were happy to let the valley take care of the valley, so long as the valley stayed in the valley, out of sight. There were others who saw it as a blight and, like Galiton, wished it could be obliterated.

Unlike the days when proud immigrant quarry workers and their families made their homes there and carried drinking and wash water from wells and lived their nights by the light of kerosene lamps, now electricity, water and telephones were available to dwellers of the valley who wanted and could afford them. Although some shacks were still without telephones, bathtubs and toilets, a few had them. Those without had given rise to repeated tales of unsanitary conditions in the valley.

Arriving at the towering stacks of cast-off limestone quarry blocks Galiton got out of the police car, adjusted his Stetson, and switched on the portable radio attached to his Sam Browne belt. He stood there for a time, tall and straight, head tilted as he looked up at the agglomeration of countless inferior limestone quarry blocks rising in stacks in rough silhouette against the afternoon sky. Unmoving, he studied the crudely scrawled graffiti painted on the faces of several aging gray and buff colored stones. The dulling mark of time was evident on many of the markings. The brighter ones undoubtedly were the products of a later generation than his. These, as did the older tracings, some of which were those of his own generation and surely those of his father's, were conspicuous for the rash of obscenities among them.

Galiton found himself comparing them. He read the time-worn letters on one block and the recently painted words on another. He perused the ubiquitous "F" word in both aging and new paint on some blocks. He thought at length about a familiar name, that of a girl, drawn on one of the blocks. Had she ever visited the stacks and seen her name there? Many girls had through the years visited the stacks. Was it true, the message about this one with her name? Could it be only the revealed secret wish of the scurrilous, unknown painter? What about him? What kind of person was he to trace on a huge block of limestone for the world, at least for those of the world who came to the valley, to see the malediction?

On several occasions in earlier times he had been in the company of youths who had lettered some of the obscenities on the huge blocks of limestone. He had also joined in the laughter that accompanied those dubious accomplishments. And, as he was now, he then was smug in the knowledge that he himself had refrained from taking an active part in the actual letterings. To his belated credit was the revulsion he felt now that he had not made some effort to stop the lewd scrawlings. But he had been pretentious and timid back then, and had said nothing. He had stood back, puffed and virtuous with the knowledge that he had not wielded a brush to paint any of the defamations.

Galiton walked to the edge of the quarry and looked down at the placid blue water. He stooped and picked up a fist-sized rock, tossed it up and out and watched it plummet to the water far below where it struck with a splash. He saw in his mind his own naked body striking the water in an arching dive. How many times had he dived there? But not from this height, he shivered inwardly. Never from this height. That was certain death. There was a jumbled pile of large quarry blocks visible in the deep, clear blue water below him. They had been dropped there in random fashion from the old pole derrick that had serviced the quarry in its productive days. In falling to the quarry floor they had formed an awkward passageway among them that daring youths who frequented the swimming hole had eventually named "The Tunnel." Approaching the opening from either end of the underwater structure, swimmers who could hold their breath long enough would swim through the passageway. Galiton had done it, a few times. That was a bold enough feat. However, one day a youth was challenged to dive through that crooked corridor from a point on the quarry wall three levels below where Galiton was now standing. The youth missed the opening, dying instantly from a crushed skull. From then on the passageway was known as "The Tunnel Of Death." Although the fatal accident and the new name for the passageway put an end to any further attempts to dive through it, it did not discourage swimming at the quarry hole.

Galiton tossed another rock into the water. This time he counted the ledges as it fell past them. Including the surface on which he stood there were five. It was indeed a deep hole, a long way down. Absently he wondered how many buildings had been constructed from the faultless limestone blocks taken from the solid mass that once was buried where the hole now yawned. Considering the depth, surely many. Which buildings? Where? He'd heard of them all his life, was taught about them in high school, but he couldn't remember one. Did anyone really care?

Had they been able to speak, those who first settled

in the valley probably cared, he thought. Those immigrant men who had drilled and channeled and sledged the massive limestone blocks out of this hole must have cared. But they were gone, some of them buried in the little cemetery there, and forgotten; while their magnificent, unacclaimed memorials were proudly but mutely reaching skyward in major cities across the nation.

A sound somewhere behind him caused Galiton to turn and look over his shoulder. Two small boys stood near his cruiser, talking in hushed tones about the imposing automobile and stealing suspicious glances in his direction. How long had they been watching him? He regretted their presence, the interruption. He shook his head and walked slowly toward the car. The children retreated warily, wide-eyed.

When he reached the machine Galiton raised the trunk lid, took a boot brush from within, raised first one foot and then the other to the rear bumper and dusted his cordovan boots to their earlier shine. As he straightened to his full height he turned in the direction of the boys and waved a friendly farewell. They did not respond.

Inside the cruiser he buckled his seat belt, and through slitted eyes, made a panoramic sweep of the stacks. His eyes came to rest on the large white letters on a huge block atop the nearest stack. It read "JESUS SAVES." His mouth became pencil-line thin, and he felt as though he had been caught in the commission of a wrong.

38

On his return drive down from headquarters to the Moses City barracks that afternoon Captain Timothy Melton stopped at Tooter's, a twenty-four hour restaurant on the four-lane state highway that bypassed Moses City.

Unaware of the presence there of Harley Oaks who only by minutes had preceded him, he went in. Had he seen Oaks' car, a plain gray automobile, in the parking lot when he drove up, he might not have stopped. Events of his day at headquarters had left him with a splitting headache and uppermost in his mind at the moment was a craving for a cup of hot black coffee.

Primarily a truck stop, Tooter's was also popular with local diners for miles around for its excellent food, all-day breakfast and efficient service. The owner, Tooter, which was not his real name, had himself been a truck driver until he was forced by a severe case of hemorrhoids to find another means of earning a livelihood.

"I was so miserable all the time I was driving a truck, I used to wish I was dead," he was known to often explain to transient truckers his reason for his change in vocations. "There wasn't a single hour in my last five years of bouncing my jewels over the road that I didn't have a suppository stuck up my backside."

In the beginning, the restaurant was identified by a large sign which read simply "EAT 24 HOURS." Later, the erstwhile truck driver greeted his passing former buddies of the road with an additional sign. This one hung under the original sign with the admonition that read in smaller yet just as visible letters, "If you can't stop, TOOT YOUR HORN."

Twenty-four hours a day, truck drivers obligingly pulled lustily on the cords of their trumpeting air horns as they passed. Occasionally, when some passed in tandem, the noise from their combined salvo of horn-blowing made an ungodly eruption of sound.

Over time that practice attached to the restaurant a dimension of romance and legend that warmed the imaginations of those who had never had the dubious pleasure of bouncing over highways on eighteen big rubber wheels. Its popularity grew with each passing day. Not surprisingly, in time the horn blowers were called "tooters," and it naturally followed that the restaurant should be called "Tooter's," and its owner "Tooter."

The restaurant was also a half-price food and coffee stop for Moses City police, Spiceland County sheriff's deputies and state police. It was not unusual for a single night's entire patrols of those three departments to be eating or drinking coffee there at the same time. Traditionally, they sat together at the same table or booth when one large enough was available, or they put tables together to accommodate their need. Such gatherings rarely went unnoticed. Local diners seeing them there wondered who was protecting their town streets, county roads and state highways from the dangers of the day or night. Their concern was not so great, however, that it gave them enough courage to approach such a collection of policemen and voice their fears either angrily or reasonably. As a rule most turned their heads. Some stopped to greet one or all with a smile and offered a benign comment about the weather. Nocturnal visitors to Tooter's especially offered comments generally in the pretense of sympathy for night-shifters. Although they may have thought it and worried about it, not one of them ever dared to ask, "Who's minding the store?"

Melton was that preoccupied with his headache and his desire for hot coffee he did not see Oaks seated in a window booth until he heard Oaks call out to him. Instantly he turned in that direction and sat heavily opposite the detective sergeant. After washing down a couple of aspirin tablets with a mouthful of water, Melton deliberately kept the ensuing greeting short. The two policemen quietly sipped their coffee and accepted refills from a smiling waitress who knew that at least Oaks, of the two men in business suits, was a cop. Then, when he could stand the silence no longer, Oaks asked Melton if anything new had been turned up on Felix Dombriewski.

Because of his headache Melton preferred to avoid any discussion about Dombriewski and the Fielding case. Although Colonel Carey had long since eased his order that state police should watch the Fieldings, and troopers now watched Winona only occasionally, Melton still was of the opinion that the entire matter, prior to and including Dombriewski, had been and still was a grand waste of manpower, time and money. He shrugged in Oaks' direction and raised his cup to his lips.

"Dombriewski? New? No," he said. "But don't be surprised if he should come walking into your barracks some day."

"You still don't believe that's him over there in that cemetery?" Oaks was smiling.

Melton felt the color rise to his neck and continue up to his cheeks. "Look Harley," he said with restraint. "You've talked to that woman and you've talked to Roger. But let's just leave him out of it right now. Let's talk about Winona. Do you honestly believe after all these months that she could be part of any kind of criminal scheme? Do you really believe she is lying when she tells us repeatedly that her husband would be at her side right now if he were alive?"

"Well, she may not be lying," Oaks said, "but there's no way I'm going to believe that her husband is dead."

"I wanted Lieutenant Conway to listen to her side of this business," Melton went on as though he hadn't heard. "If he would just listen with an open mind, listen to her and Roger, and weigh all the evidence. You too, Harley, and Galiton—I know, I know." Melton raised a hand when Oaks appeared startled and attempted to interrupt him. "A lot of people believe that someone other than Fielding died in that fire—but the most sophisticated and convincing evidence in my opinion came from Dr. Berman. There was no question in his mind about the identity of the man."

"Everybody—," Oaks began.

"I know what *everybody* believes," Melton cut him off. "But not me." Melton tried to smile. "I've heard it over and over, and yet nobody has been able to come up with Fielding—alive, that is."

"No disrespect, Captain," Oaks said defensively pulling in his jaw much as a boxer would, "but that's my opinion and not anyone else's. We've just got too much evidence."

"What evidence?" Melton turned up his palms. "More than a million and a half bucks in insurance? Boil it all down, Harley. Dr. Flood's report, which isn't conclusive? Dr. Brent's? Guesswork. There's proof enough right there that Fielding died in that fire.

"No Harley," Melton's tone became almost paternal

as he addressed the younger detective. "As far as I'm concerned we've a lot of people—the Colonel and Captain Martin leading the pack—who want the dead man to be someone other than Fielding. They've come too far and they can't turn back. Face-saving, it's called, Harley. And frankly, it might be more than just saving face."

Melton paused and sipped from his cup, aware that Oaks was studying him questioningly.

"What do you mean?" the sergeant asked at length.

"I'm not sure," Melton answered. Then thoughtfully he repeated more slowly, "I'm not sure. There has been no progress on this case for months. We're too damn busy with other problems. And this case is still open, still supposed to be active. But there is no proof of anything to substantiate the claim—now, now, Harley." Oaks had again started to interrupt and Melton held him off with a raised hand "I'm talking about proof, not speculation," Melton pushed on. "Not playing to the insurance companies—one in particular—as the Colonel has been doing since day one of this case. There's been really no evidence to build a foolproof case on, anyway, just circumstantial evidence. No more. And yet the state police won't admit we could be wrong, and we won't let that poor woman collect her life together, let alone her husband's insurance."

"Captain," Oaks obviously had recoiled from Melton's bald insinuation concerning Carey and insurance companies. "I think you're wrong there. And besides that, aren't you forgetting Felix Dombriewski?"

"Who is Dombriewski?" Melton growled through gritted teeth. "Hell, Harley. You can't just pull a name, an identity, out of nowhere and tag it on a corpse. What proof do we have that's Dombriewski buried out there? None. Not a damn thing. But we've got considerably more proof, and a lot more reason to believe that Crestman Fielding is in that grave. I've tried to get the Colonel to see that, but he won't listen. Think about it, Harley."

"You mean to say that you've told the Colonel this? And Lieutenant Conway?" Oaks was both curious and suspicious.

"Of course. And Captain Martin," Melton shook his head. "I think there are others who could be made to see things differently. But they're going to go along with the Colonel. Hell, that's the safest way, I suppose. But it isn't necessarily the right way. Not in my opinion."

"Got a date with Link Trueblood," Oaks had heard enough. And he really did have a scheduled meeting. Melton could try, but he was not going to change his mind. For effect, Oaks had looked at his watch.

"Listen, Harley," Melton ignored the act while his tone became authoritative and at the same time confidential. "We've already been too long on this thing and all we do is play cat and mouse with Winona and Roger. And if James was not in the Navy we'd be doing the same with him. I've said before that we've made paupers of that family."

Melton took a noisy breath, then continued, "Let's just say for the sake of argument that Fielding is alive, that he did kill someone. Withhold the insurance, sure, but do we have the right to destroy his innocent family? Are we God? That's what we've done, you know. And, if we're wrong about Fielding, are we prepared to restore Winona and her sons to their previous stature as a family, as human beings, as vital members of the community? Would we want to? Like hell, Harley. I know cops. I've known cops for almost all of my life. We are never wrong, or at least we will never admit to being wrong. No two ways about it, Harley, too often too many of us think we are God."

"What are you saying, Captain?" Oaks flicked a hand as though he were shooing away a fly. "Winona's been killing herself. With booze. You know that."

"She's not killing herself," Melton shook his head. "Sure, she's doing the drinking. She's self-destructing. No doubt about it. But do you believe that if she were concealing something she would be doing this to herself? Not in my opinion. She'd be as sober as a judge. But now she's a woman without a husband, without a friend, without hope. Not even a son, Harley, and she has two; Roger lives away from her and James is in the service. She doesn't have the proverbial pot and when they kick her out of her house she won't even have a decent window to throw it out of. And we haven't helped her." Melton shook his head from side to side.

"Hell, Captain, we're police officers, not our brothers' keepers," Oaks said defensively.

"Yes, we're policemen," Melton agreed. "And I think I'm a pretty good one, too. At least I have tried my best to be. And I'm a tough one. But I wonder if, as police officers, each of us doesn't bear a responsibility greater than we have been willing to accept, Harley. Doesn't that sort of thing worry you?"

Melton's voice had fallen to just above a whisper, as though he were speaking to himself. He pushed his coffee cup toward the center of the table and, placing his forearms on the surface, he leaned toward Oaks. The detective sergeant instinctively pushed back on his side of the booth, as though to put more space between himself and his superior. At the same time he almost spat his answer to Melton's query.

"Not a damn bit, Captain. Not me. Why should I? It's enough that I put my life on the line every day for people like the Fieldings."

Melton's eyes suddenly widened and seemed to drill right through Oaks. His voice, when he spoke now sounded brittle.

"As one policeman to another, Harley, that just doesn't wash," he said. "If you'll just step out into the real world for a minute, my friend, instead of seeing yourself as some kind of Blue Knight riding across a television screen and waving goodbye to your wife in the background as you leave home for work each day, you'll have to admit as much."

He waved a hand at Oaks, who had opened his mouth as though to speak. "I have to wonder every time I hear a policeman say what you just said, Harley," Melton's voice rose slightly. "I've been a cop for years and you can take it from me; I have never felt I put my life on the line any more than the fireman who responds to a call for help, or the ambulance driver who goes out on a mercy run, or the farmer who climbs up on his tractor, or the truck driver, or the factory worker who drives to his job, or the kid who gets into a school bus every day and hopes he's going to be safe in the classroom, or his mother who drives to the grocery store. We all live on the edge of life. Or death. Take it either way you like."

Melton leaned backward, expelling his breath in a long sigh. He was aware of a sense of embarrassment. Had he thought before he had spoken, he knew he would have bitten his tongue before subjecting Oaks to what he had just said. He felt that he at least might have said it better.

Aloud he said, "Sorry, Harley. I guess I got carried away. What I really should have said, I suppose, is

271

that the potential for accidentally ending up six feet under ground is a daily part of life. This is not true only for a policeman, it is true for every person. Always has been. Where there's life there's death. As far as we're concerned, cops like you and me, Harley, no one is after us because we are cops. It's what we are supposed to stand for, what all decent people stand for. That is what is on the line. That is what is in danger and what is being attacked, not us as police officers. But even in that respect we are responsible for our brothers. We may not fully understand it, but we are one with them, each of them. And if we as cops try to ignore that obligation, if for any reason we bring pain and suffering to the innocent, or allow it, we really are not worthy of the oath we've taken, or the badge we wear. Winona Fielding may be a drunk right now, Harley, but suppose she's an innocent drunk wracked with heartbreak and pain. Are you ready and willing to repair the damage?"

Melton waited quietly for Oaks to respond. The detective sergeant appeared thoughtful for several moments.

"I can't say about any of that, Captain, but I don't know how else we would have handled this thing," Oaks muttered at last.

"For my money Fielding is dead," Melton said as he tried to hide his disappointment with Oaks' reply. "We should have backed off from Winona and her family long ago and we might have had this thing behind us now. But no. State police managed to turn this case into a carnival—the Colonel, really," Melton shook his head. "This thing has been turned into a joke, an unsolvable one at that, Harley."

That Harley Oaks had become more and more uncomfortable was obvious. He could not hide his anxiety to get away. He had six years of service left to be eligible for retirement and he wanted nothing to stand in the way of that. Listening to Melton made him nervous, made him fear for his future. He spoke again of Trueblood waiting for him, but he was no more interested in Trueblood than he was a passing trucker who at that moment jerked on the cord of his air horns, sending a blast of sound into the waning afternoon. In his fourteen years as a state policeman Oaks had never been in the company of a superior who spoke so freely, so mutinously, as did Melton. He had never seen this side of Melton, or any other policeman, for that matter, and now that he was seeing it, he wanted only to get away from it, to leave. But Melton had more to say.

"I'll tell you something else, Harley," Melton pushed himself to the back side of the booth. "That woman will go to her grave still wishing and hoping for that money; begging, too."

The corners of Melton's mouth had become moist with saliva. He dug out a handkerchief from a hip pocket and swiped his lips dry. His handsome face, now flushed under a coverlet of neatly combed graying straight hair parted on one side, glowed with passionate sincerity.

Oaks suddenly took a deep breath. "That's the difference in us, Captain," he said with what might have passed for a smile. "I believe Winona will lead us to her husband one day, if we are patient. But right now I've got to be moving along." He pushed his closed fists into the padded seat to lift himself out of the booth they occupied.

Melton snorted. "Wait a minute." He lifted his cup toward a passing waitress, indicating a refill. "Have another cup of coffee while I tell you something, Harley."

Oaks frowned and made a face. "Hell, Captain," he complained, "if I drink any more coffee I won't be able to get anything done for going to the bathroom the rest of my shift."

"One more cup, Harley," Melton insisted, and he smiled warmly for the first time. "It won't take any longer than that."

As suddenly as it had appeared, Melton's smile disappeared.

"I've never told anyone else this, but you are free to talk about this any time and any place," Melton had leaned forward slightly and lowered his voice to a confidential pitch. "In the beginning, I may have doubted Winona, but something happened that changed my opinion of her, and I haven't been able to get it out of my mind. It supports my belief that Winona is not a party to any kind of conspiracy.

"This happened when we had that big snow a couple of months after the fire. I was on the way to see Winona at her house to speak to her when I saw her in the old Chevy going in the opposite direction. I turned around and followed her. No one, not even I, knew what I was doing.

"She drove directly to the cemetery. The roads had been plowed and they were in fairly good shape. Even the cemetery drives had been plowed. For funerals, I suppose. Anyway, when she turned into the cemetery I drove on past and just took a ride, to give her some privacy. And I wasn't worried about her. I don't know how long I was gone, half hour, maybe. Maybe more. When I got back her car was gone. I started to drive to her house when something urged me to go back to the cemetery. You know where the grave is located, Harley. Well, I drove in that direction, and when I got to where she'd parked I stopped. I could see her tracks where she had walked through the deep snow."

Melton paused to allow the waitress to top off their cups. He smiled up at her when she said playfully to Oaks who reddened visibly, "Want me to saucer and blow it for you, Harley?"

Making no comment about the familiarity, to Oaks' relief, Melton continued, "I sat there for a while, alone, looking at those tracks in the deep snow around that grave, and wondering why anyone would drive to the cemetery in the dead of winter with a snow on like that one. A person would either have to be crazy, I thought, or hurting. Hurting like hell, Harley.

"I don't know what made me do it, Harley, but I got out of my car and followed that woman's tracks. They were the only ones around, and I stepped in each one of them to keep from getting snow down in the tops of my shoes. I followed them right to the grave. The temporary marker couldn't be seen with that deep snow, but she knew exactly where the grave was.

"Well, when I got to the grave I couldn't believe what I was seeing. Listen to this, Harley." Melton's voice had become slightly constricted and he paused to sip from his cup. "Winona had knelt in the snow," he said as he put the cup down. "I could see the imprint of her knees and the imprint of her left hand where she put it down and leaned on it for balance. You wouldn't believe—you won't believe—what she did there."

There followed a weighty silence as Melton again pushed his cup toward the center of the table and again leaned his forearms heavily on the table top and inclined his head and shoulders toward Oaks. Then as though he were admonishing the man across the table from him, Melton held up the index finger of his right hand.

"With her finger, man," he uttered the words slowly, almost painfully. "It had to be her finger. I can't imagine how else she might have done it. But with her finger," Melton now shook the finger at Oaks for emphasis, "she had written her husband a message in the snow. She had written the words, 'I love you,' and she signed her name, 'Winona,' in the snow on that grave."

There was another silence, a long one, as though neither policeman dared to speak, dared to break the spell of the moment. Finally Melton, who again had leaned back on his side of the booth, resumed speaking.

"In the snow, Harley," he repeated with a shake of his head. "On her knees in the snow. That woman had driven to the cemetery on a cold winter's day to write a sentiment in the snow to her dead husband."

Melton paused, studying the face of the policeman who sat opposite him. When he spoke again it was through a half smile. "Now," he said with a long sigh, "do I believe that Winona will someday lead us to Fielding?" he asked. "She already has, Harley."

Oaks drained his cup in two noisy swallows and in a single movement he slid out of the booth and got to his feet.

"I've got to make a trip to the john, Captain," he said with eyes averted. "Too damn much coffee. And Link Trueblood is surely wondering where I am."

39

The media had given long and sensational play to the introduction of Felix Dombriewski into the Crestman Fielding case. For his role in learning the identity of the alleged mystery man, Galiton received high praise from Colonel Carey. Then, probably because Dombriewski could not immediately be found, and almost certain anyway that the mystery of the partially incinerated corpse had been solved, it seemed that state police again allowed their active probe into the Fielding matter to come to a virtual halt.

As did almost everyone else, they believed that a man named Felix Dombriewski was dead and buried in the Fielding family cemetery plot. Despite this thinking, no effort was made by authorities to disinter the body from the Fielding cemetery plot and bury it elsewhere. There was not even a suggestion that this might be done. Unbelievably, from the time that police perceived the dead man to be Dombriewski, the investigation remained relatively stagnant.

For attorney Ames Shaw, meanwhile, the materialization of Felix Dombriewski had raised several new questions. He had believed that Crestman Fielding had died in the fire. He had also believed in Winona's honesty and integrity, and he still wanted to believe in his client. But now in his most candid moments with himself he was tormented by doubt; if not concerning the living Winona, at least about the disturbing new identity of the dead man whom he had tenaciously believed was Crestman Fielding.

Shaw had slowly been putting together what he thought was a simple but sound argument to support Winona's claim that it was her husband's body that had been discovered after the fire. With so little evidence in the hands of police to prove foul play, Shaw by this late date in the fruitless police investigation had begun taking success for granted.

The evidence held by state police suggesting the dead man might have been someone other than Fielding had been of little concern to him. There was just as much hard evidence to support the claim that the dead man was the missing Fielding. The findings of the late Dr. Isaac Berman and the careless handling by state police of what might have been vital evidence found at the fire scene would have overcome, or at least easily balanced, the speculations of pathologists, those of the state fire marshal, and the suspicions of state police investigators.

Shaw's hole card, he had hoped, was Fielding's erratic behavior before and leading up to the fire. In particular, Fielding's threats on his own life made in the presence of his attorney, Clare Downing, and his son, Roger, would be difficult to overcome. The failure of state police after so many months to produce a live Fielding had favored Shaw's planned argument.

Now, however, the incarnation of Felix Dombriewski as the mystery man in the case had dramatically changed Shaw's somewhat comfortable stance. Unless he could provide unquestionable proof of Fielding's death, or even a calculable rebuttal to the police claim that the dead man was the man identified as Felix Dombriewski, he knew he would now have little chance before a hearing judge. Although there had been no recent reported sightings of Fielding, the prevailing weight of official and public suspicion still loomed solidly against him. Shaw could only hope that in time the situation might somehow improve in his favor.

In mid-October the Fielding home was sold at sheriff's auction. A share of the proceeds went to satisfy the mortgage against it, which was held by the Tradesmens Trust Bank of Moses City. The remainder went to pay as many of the loudly insistent Fielding creditors as was possible. Winona Fielding was dispossessed. She had never felt more disillusioned, abandoned and alone. Her eldest son, Roger, was living in obscurity someplace in remote northern Dogwood County. Winona didn't know where. She was certain that police knew. Her younger son, James, according to his last letter to his mother, was still in the war in Vietnam. Her parents had gone to their reward long before the fire. Winona's sister Frona had by this time died of cancer, and her husband had remarried and moved away from Moses City. Her sister Leona had not spoken to her for months. Winona's aloneness seemed to envelop her like a suffocating shroud.

Crestman Fielding's parents were also dead. His brothers Cramer and Craddick Fielding had broken with their brother after Crestman had purchased from them their shares of the Fielding Mill the three brothers had equally inherited upon the death of their father. After Crestman became sole owner of the mill, the early post-war years began showing evidence of a building boom. Taking advantage of the growing demand for building materials, Crestman, who by then had reopened the mill, began fabricating limestone home siding in direct competition with brick and other masonry products for a share of the home building market. The venture was a success, and Crestman Fielding and his family, much to the chagrin of his two brothers who had sold out so easily and so cheaply, had begun living the good life. There were words of recrimination against Crestman, but it had been an honest, legal transaction. His brothers had wanted to sell, Crestman had wanted to buy. It was as simple as that. But Cramer and Craddick, angry at themselves for selling and envious of their brother's subsequent success, had severed relations with him and his family. Now Cramer was dead anyway and Winona knew she could not turn to Craddick for help.

There was only Leona to whom Winona could turn. A widow for some years by this time, Leona lived alone. As Cramer and Craddick Fielding had disavowed their brother and his family, Leona too had forsworn her sister, brother-in-law and nephews, but purely on religious grounds. A devout born-again Christian, as was her husband until his death, Leona, a stern pinch-faced woman, had unsuccessfully attempted to "save" her relatives. On a number of occasions convenient to her purpose, she had tried to coax, cajole, frighten or otherwise force her youngest sister and her family into submitting mind and soul to the God in which Leona believed, at the altar of the church in which Leona worshiped, before the congregation to whom Leona gave devoted kindred allegiance. Failing that, Leona disassociated herself from Winona.

Few humans at this time could have felt more unwanted and desolate than Winona. No one came to console her, to extend solace, to offer her succor, to befriend her in any way; not the zealously religious Leona, not a member of her church, nor a member of any church. Not anyone. Addicted to alcohol as she was it followed that liquor was Winona's only companion, her only comforter, and she had indulged in it the more. Because of that and the increased suspicions overshadowing her husband's death, she had become an anathema not only to what family was left to her, but also to the community in which she lived. With no place to live and no relative or friend to whom she could turn, and with virtually no money and no possessions, except for a few pieces of furniture she had arranged to store in the barn of a neighbor, and some few personal things she could carry in her old Chevrolet car, Winona was hopelessly desperate. Haggard in mind, shrinking in soul and faltering in body, two weeks before Christmas that year she retreated unwillingly and tearfully to the only affordable accommodation she could find—a vacant shelter in Crowfoot Valley.

While it was not the most comfortable arrangement for her, the rent was cheap and the dwelling was at least equipped with electricity, a propane space heater and plumbing. And there she lived amid the valley's few inhabitants and the aging ghosts of old Tin Cup Dooley, the woman known as Poopy, Peg-Leg Hill and others, and those of the four innocent children who perished in the disastrous Christmastime blaze that had destroyed their childhood home.

In addition to this crisis in the series of crises in her life, Winona already had been virtually shattered at the introduction of Felix Dombriewski into the Fielding investigation, and the implication by police and the media that his body and not her husband's was buried in the Fielding cemetery plot. Who was this Dombriewski? She had never before heard the name. Certainly she had never heard it spoken by her husband. She had never heard it spoken by anyone until it roared out at her from the six o'clock news. She had never seen it in print until she saw it in the columns of *The Intelligencer*.

On the strength of reports by two pathologists, whom she had never heard of, a stranger had been murdered by her husband and now, these many months later, was identified as Felix Dombriewski. That's what the television, the papers and the police were saying, too, wasn't it? They left little doubt. It was as though the occupant of the grave, in which she'd witnessed her husband's body in its coffin placed to rest so long ago, had been summoned forth and arbitrarily given the unfamiliar appellation Felix Dombriewki. It was ridiculously and helplessly maddening.

In her consternation and anger she had leafed through the telephone directory in search of such a name, or similar name. There was none. Yet it became a name that she could not separate from her waking and sleeping hours. Paraded across newspaper front pages and television screens as it had been until the media had tired of it, along with the photograph said to be that of Dombriewski, the strange name was indelibly fixed in her mind: *Felix Dombriewski*. An itinerant house painter from Cleveland?

It was insane, outrageous trickery, that police should discover him at such a late time. It had to be a continuation of the vengeful game they had been playing with her ever since her husband had taken his own life. Police said they had learned that Felix Dombriewski had no family, no friends, that he came and went to and from the many places in which he had lived, arriving unannounced and staying only for short periods, disappearing for longer periods. He was a nobody, the perfect nobody, Winona thought, to place between her and her rightful claim against the insurance companies that were unlawfully withholding settlement from her.

So convinced of the suicide and burial of her husband was she that Winona knew only a brief moment of doubt. Yet she had read in a newspaper and heard on television that Felix Dombriewski had served in the Army during World War II. Could he possibly have served with her husband? Might they have been wartime friends? Acquaintances? Could he have been invited to come to Spiceland County to visit Crestman? Could this terrible insinuation by state police and the media really have happened? Could fate be playing some kind of trick on her? Had it played one—a fatal one—on the man called Felix Dombriewski? Had he trustingly sought a reunion with a friend of old only to have it end at the cost of his own life? Was he now buried under the government marker bearing the name Crestman Fielding?

No, no, no, a bemused Winona shook that doubt from her mind. The dead man was none other than her husband, Crestman Fielding. She saw his casket lowered into the grave right in front of her. She had not seen his body. She had been protected from that horror by sympathetic morticians Ira and Irwin Brown, friends of her late husband. She had expressed a desire to view his body, but they had convinced her that there had been no need, that her husband's brother Cramer Fielding, then sheriff and now dead himself, had already identified the body as that of his brother, Crestman, her husband, and that had been sufficient for official needs.

The Browns had also kindly protected Winona's sons from viewing the pitifully ravaged remains of the man believed to be their father. The dead man was Crestman Fielding. Winona knew that. She knew her husband had killed himself. She knew he was dead. Were he alive he would be at her side this very moment.

Winona Fielding fought back the only way she knew how; she increased her daily intake of cheap wine. Yet despite a constant alcoholic haze, she knew that state police had made a strong enough case of Felix Dombriewski that people in general had long been scoffing at the mention of her husband's name and accusing him of felonious crimes. She feared and was unnerved by the possibility that her attorney, Ames Shaw, in the face of the turn of events, might withdraw from the case. If she could see the almost hopelessness of her position, he certainly could too; and her despondency deepened.

In one respect, time seemed to stand still. In truth, it was more fleeting than ever. Except for an occasional unmarked police car she thought was following her, with a driver hoping she would lead him to her husband, her days were empty. At night, if she was sober enough, she thought she heard a police car, or cars, she could never be sure. The sound passed by her Crowfoot Valley house slowly while its driver, she believed, satisfied himself that her old Chevy was still in the driveway. It seemed that the passing car was always passing. She thought she heard it in her sleep. Passing. Passing.

Adamantly certain that her husband had taken his own life, she could never quite understand what state police expected to learn from her. Did they really think that she was meeting secretly with her husband, that she was a partner with him in a plot of murder to defraud insurance companies? Nothing could have been more preposterous to Winona.

Despite her certainty, there was no police car following her, no policeman watching her house. For all intents and purposes, Winona Fielding no longer existed in police minds.

It was at this time that Winona took an incredible, courageous, yet desperately necessary step toward providing for herself. Having learned cooking and baking from her mother, Sarah McCrickland, she applied for a position as pie baker at a Hickory Grove restaurant.

Sarah McCrickland's pies had won their share of blue ribbon awards at Spiceland County fairs and, long before her death, they had become something of local legend, especially her gooseberry and rhubarb pies. As a boy, John Harking, owner of the popular Grist Mill Restaurant, had heard his father speak of the McCricklands, that Thrasher McCrickland was a fine upstanding man, and that the McCricklands were a remarkably good family. His mother would then boast of Sister Sarah McCrickland's delicious pies and that she was a respected church-going soul who was rearing her three daughters, Leona, Frona and Winona, "right."

Relatively young, but a shrewd, perceptive businessman nevertheless, Harking was more concerned with his successes as a restaurateur and realtor than he was with neighborhood happenings and gossip. He had, however, followed the Fielding case in its sporadic appearances in the columns of *The Intelligencer* and from its outset he was one of those few persons who believed that Crestman Fielding had taken his own life. But whether he had or had not was of little moment to Harking or to his business schemes. The only Fielding of importance to him, he told an associate, was Winona and how she might benefit his popular restaurant. Moreover, Harking characteristically had been moved by Winona's deprivations and, during an interview with her, had told himself that "If anyone needed a job it is this woman."

Winona had taken the position with some trepidation. Haunted by her addiction and her continued craving for alcohol, any attempt to control herself would not be easy. She had the shakes and she suffered sudden and uncontrollable attacks of vertigo and acute nausea. She had crying fits. Without warning she was seized with dizziness, weakness and rage. Fear of going public filled her with panic and threatened to strip her of her courage. But because she would arrive and leave the Grist Mill Restaurant through an alley door, and the pastry kitchen was in an alcove at one end of the restaurant's main kitchen, she would rarely be seen by the public or by most of the restaurant's other employees, she would try. In time she was able, to a point, to lose herself in her work, and she was able to take some limited relief and pleasure from it. Though she made no friends and most other restaurant employees shunned her, she did become acquainted with a few of her elderly co-workers.

Like the majority of workers in the tourist town, Winona received the minimum wage. Her earnings were such that she could provide herself only with such personal items as she needed and the gasoline and maintenance required by her old Chevy to make the daily trips to and from her job. Skillfully managing her income, despite her weakened condition, she was able each week to buy enough food for herself and for a protective long-haired, black and white cur that had come to her Crowfoot Valley door one night and stayed, and enough cheap wine and cigarettes to satisfy her cravings.

In this manner she passed several months, during which time the Crestman Fielding investigation still lay dormant in state police files and attorney Ames Shaw had turned his attention and talents to other unrelated legal matters.

WINONA

40

Of the three daughters of Spiceland County farmer Thrasher McCrickland and his wife Sarah, Winona was the youngest. As a consequence of that she was never, as a child, too far from her mother's side. Yet Winona McCrickland was reared as a typical farmer's daughter. She learned early on how in pleasure, pain and sometimes sorrow, life produced life. She learned, too, that when properly sown, tiny seeds placed in the soil flourished into new life, a life of green sprouts that grew into stores of foods, and that of such processes came important and necessary contributions to farm family livelihood.

As did her older sisters, Frona and Leona, Winona also learned that she bore an inescapable yet laudable responsibility toward that fulfillment. She learned almost from the time she learned to walk that her contribution to that end included a share in such everyday yet gratifying tasks as washing, sewing, ironing, tending the vegetable garden, canning, cooking, baking, gathering eggs, milking cows, churning butter and others.

During one of the earlier interviews with Captain Melton one day when she was more inclined to talk with policemen in her home, Winona had become nostalgic about the past and she revealed to him some of what farm life had meant to a girl of her time. She had begun her sentimental account quite unexpectedly while she and Melton were seated in front of the glowing embers in the fireplace in the comfortable

Fielding living room. Although she was far from young, Winona's cheeks had nonetheless reddened with the flush of revived youth as the memories of early family life flooded her mind. For those few minutes that she spoke, her thoughts were far from the Fielding tragedy.

"We were three girls, no brothers," she began. "And we did the work that needed to be done on the farm. While I was still a little girl Dad turned the earth with a horse-drawn plow. And every spring before plowing we'd have to follow the wagon and pick up stones, all the stones we could see, and put them into the wagon. That was hard work, let me tell you.

"I'll never forget having to get up in the morning to milk the cows before we went to school. We'd have to go out to the barn, wash those sacks—that's what we called udders then: sacks—and milk by hand. Dad had several cows, and that was before he got a milking machine."

Melton had looked at her hands where they were folded in her lap. They did not appear to be the hands of one who had spent a childhood milking cows. Winona saw his look and read his thoughts. She laughed and held up her hands, fingers widespread.

"I've milked many a cow with these," she said. "Ugh," an unhappy thought which she did not express had occurred to her. "We'd milk," she continued speaking, "and when we were finished we'd come back to the house and wash with what hot water was in the kettle on the stove, eat our breakfast, and then go off to school."

She explained to Melton how she would put a shoulder against a cow's side and pressure a leg to a cow's leg to keep from being kicked or having the milk bucket toppled by the animal. She laughed when she told him of the aggravation of swishing cow tails, and the plop-plop and splash of droppings behind the milking process. And wordlessly pinching her nose, she indicated the offensive smell.

Of the three sisters she was the fastest milker, or so she claimed, having been able to milk more than either of her sisters in one morning, or one evening. "If you have milk cows," she added informatively, "they have to be milked every morning and every evening, seven days a week. We'd come home from school, get off the bus, and make right for the barn."

While she spoke there was just enough heat coming from the fireplace to make the room feel cozy. To Melton, the woman's memories of her childhood and days of adolescence on the farm were relaxing, the sound of her voice soothing. He pushed himself back in his chair and made himself more comfortable.

"Sometimes the younger cows would get so full," he heard her saying, "you'd have to work with just two fingers, like this," she had put the tips of her thumbs and forefingers together and moved them in an up and down motion. "Older cows were big, and you could really take hold of them," she clenched her fists and again moved her hands in an up and down motion. "It didn't take long to milk one of them."

Quietly Winona reminisced aloud about the McCrickland family's church attendance, how every Sunday morning and Wednesday evening they were present in the Walnut Grove Church for Sunday School and services. "And as a family we believed in making a joyful noise, too, and we would sing hymns together at home. Mother would play the piano and we would gather around and harmonize. And sometimes we'd sing hymns on the ride to church."

Winona paused briefly and then she resumed the

recollection. "It was reverent but it was fun, too. It made you feel good, and it made you feel safe." Her face had flushed with a warm radiance as she spoke the memory. Then just as suddenly she sobered and said, "That was a long time ago. As we got older and got married we sort of grew apart. I suppose that happens in all families. But every so often I think about those song fests we had around the old piano and I could cry, I miss them so. There was something about them that I have never felt in anything else I have ever done. Those joyful noises were very special."

Melton was moved deeply by her words. Although he had grown up in a happy home, as an only child he had never known the pleasures of sibling society. All his life he had considered this an unfortunate deprivation of life and, as Winona spoke, he again was aware of the aching it brought him. "You're just being sentimental," his wife, Mary, would comment after he had repeated such feelings to her. Melton would shrug and fall into a thoughtful silence, and no more would be said on the subject until the feeling of loss would again overcome his reticence to give vent to it.

Winona did not reveal to Melton all that was on her mind that morning. She had withheld much of her past. After he had gone she remembered that one of her best and lasting impressions of those early years had begun one early September morning during her sixth year. And now, for the umpteenth time, she thought, it glided past on the stage of her memory. Although it was a lengthy walk, the McCricklands lived too close to the Amity Jane School for the McCrickland children to be eligible for school bus service. Winona saw herself happily walking hand in hand between Frona and Leona, escorted along a cross-country path to the one-room country school, a half mile or more from the McCrickland home, where she was enrolled in the first grade. She could never forget that first day of school.

In a sudden rush of recollection, Winona recalled a winter morning that year when, despite her woolen mittens, her little fingers had got so cold she had wept from the pain. In an act of sisterly love, Frona had swept her up into her arms and carried her to a log by the roadside and there had sat her down. Then Frona had done an unforgettable thing. She squatted down beside Winona and grasping a handful of the hem of her own long skirt she wrapped the thick, warm fabric around her little sister's cold hands and held the wrapped digits tightly. Winona had never forgotten the warmth that had suddenly flowed from the loving Frona into her little fingers. She had never forgotten how that sudden warmth had flowed from her fingers to her heart that had pounded almost out of her little chest with appreciation and love for Frona. There were times in later life when Frona's simple act of sisterly love would come unbidden to her and Winona would weep. Such tears, she remembered, seemed not to come from her eyes but from somewhere deep within herself, and she would yearn for a return to those days long past.

Dear old Amity Jane, she remembered. It was there she spent what she in later years would frequently refer to as some of the happiest days of her childhood. After completing the eighth grade at age fourteen, she received a diploma of graduation. When the next fall arrived she found herself aboard an aging yellow school bus, thrilled, yet somewhat apprehensive, bound for the recently consolidated Moses City High School. There, early in her freshman year, she found herself nervously attracted to a senior boy named Crestman Fielding.

Swarthy, handsome, and the possessor of a disarming smile, Crestman Fielding appeared to her, from a distance—for she shyly averted her eyes when he came near—to be grown-up and assuring; more so than any of the other boys she had observed in the school. For the entire school year she quietly watched for him every day, always from afar. Almost every day she felt blessed with the good fortune of having had him in her sight or having passed near him in a corridor during the rush of changing classrooms. Other boys at the school attempted to make her acquaintance, for Winona, by then fifteen, already was beginning to show promise. An attractive brunette with large, soft, brown eyes and a burgeoning bosom over a trim waist, she not unsociably but modestly declined their own sheepish advances.

Though she may not have wholly understood why at the time, she believed that she was in love with this older boy, this handsome Crestman Fielding. In borrowed moments during classes and study hall at school and while doing homework at the kitchen table in her home at night, she secretly wrote tender notes to him. Dreamily she recounted in simple prose her feelings for him, that she could think only of him, and that he was the only boy she would ever love. She would then read the notes to herself with warm satisfaction, sometimes with the wisp of a smile touching her lips. Usually one reading would suffice the growing feeling for him within her, but there were some notes that she would read and re-read before tearing them into tiny pieces and discarding them.

Winona and Crestman had not yet been formally introduced. Their eyes sometimes met as Winona, with the passage of weeks, became bolder, at least bold enough to raise her eyes to his when they passed in corridors, and they had on occasion smiled silent, sly greetings. But they had yet to speak to each other. It was not until a few weeks after his graduation, an event that had left her morose and saddened, that they became friends and took their first steps toward what would become a lifelong relationship.

In what had grown to be a family tradition, Thrasher McCrickland that summer had brought his wife and daughters to Moses City to join in the annual Fourth of July festivities. The three girls, in typical farm-family style and dressed in holiday finery, rode to town seated on a makeshift couch in the bed of their father's pickup truck. Whether it was to go visiting, to town, to church, to funerals or just for a Sunday afternoon ride, the pickup truck was the McCricklands' mode of travel. They were not poor by the standards of that period, but they had no automobile.

With their backs pressed against the rear of the cab for support, the girls viewed the countryside after the vehicle had passed through it, as opposed to how Thrasher and Sarah McCrickland saw it riding inside the cab of the truck and facing forward. The difference always gave the sisters cause for laughter. One of them would occasionally twist around to peer through the rear window, through the cab between their parents, and through the windshield, to herald the approach of some familiar sight, or a walker at whom they would call and wave as they passed.

As a family in Moses City that day the McCricklands added their attention and applause to that of other city and county families and visitors, who watched the colorful, booming, trumpeting Fourth of July parade. They politely, if disinterestedly, listened to the usual patriotic Independence Day speeches from the bandstand at Garrison Common, and, after a picnic lunch, Winona and her sisters were encouraged by their parents to stroll about and join other young people in the carnival midway on the west side of Courthouse Square.

On this special day Moses City was teeming with colorfully clad people, among whom were many brightly attired young men and young women. These latter were familiarly and happily engaged in various activities, or were clustered in talking, laughing animated groups. The day was sunny and clear and the air was filled with the festival sound of the hooting-tooting calliope in the center of the kaleidoscopic charging wooden horses of the whirling merry-go-round. The mouthwatering aroma of cooking hamburgers and hot dogs and other good things to eat wafted temptingly from the food concession stands. It was a time for hearty appetites, a happy time for everyone, especially the young, and in their eagerness to become a part of the fun, the McCrickland sisters rushed to join them.

Eyes wide with the curiosity and excitement of youth on holiday and heads turning impetuously in first one direction and then another while they chattered and laughed, in their enthusiasm they accidentally collided with a group of young men and young women who were similarly involved and equally oblivious to those around them. It was a desperate moment for Winona when she realized how reckless she and her sisters had been, how embarrassing it was to simply smash into people as they had so carelessly done. And it was while she was faltering through a gasping, crimson-faced apology that she discovered the person she had blundered into was her high school idol, Crestman Fielding.

She was acutely aware, too, that at the moment of collision, he had instinctively raised a protective hand, which had inadvertently come to rest on Winona's bare forearm. For the attractive farm girl who had never been so close to a boy, let alone the boy of her dreams, it was a rapturous moment and a touch so intimate she thought she would remember it for the rest of her life. As she slowly recovered her composure, for she had deliberately tried to make the thrill of the experience of as long duration as possible, Winona heard Crestman's voice assuring her that all was well, that there had been no harm done. And then she heard him saying that if she and her companions were not otherwise committed they were welcome to join him and his friends. Winona and her sisters were pleased to do so.

It seemed that within minutes of that breathtaking arrival into the group, Crestman had invited Winona to join him for a ride on the Ferris wheel. Desperately wanting to be with him, she almost accepted, but then she suddenly thought better of it and declined. Seconds later she was sorry for having done so. She wanted so to be alone with him, close to him, but what would her father and mother think? The youngest of the McCrickland girls in the company of a boy on the Ferris wheel? Not only riding on the Ferris wheel with a boy, but doing so without their permission, which Winona wasn't too sure she would get anyway. It was out of the question.

But when he almost pleadingly asked her again, her resolve weakened and she was tempted to accept his offer. Still, discretion and doubt ruled and she was on the verge of again declining his offer when her sisters and almost the entire group of friends urged her to acquiesce. Bursting with desire then, and shrugging helplessly, she began laughing nervously and, with Crestman following closely behind, she darted toward the Ferris wheel.

Minutes later, smiling happily and seated side by side, they were lofted on high and around and around. Once, when the huge turning wheel was brought to a halt they were at the very top of the arc, suspended and swaying slightly in the bright sunlight just below a clear blue sky, far from the world below. Crestman had chosen that moment to lift an arm to the back of the swaying carriage in which they sat, inadvertently allowing part of his forearm to lightly rest on the back of Winona's neck and shoulders. At his touch Winona felt her heart skip a beat; she was nearly overwhelmed with a dreamlike warm feeling for the boy at her side. Eyes wide, lips trembling, she turned her head in his direction. Reaching slowly so that he would not frighten her, he placed the palm of his other hand flat on her cheek and leaned slightly in her direction. Eyes locked with his, she gently pressed her face into his hand, raising her shoulder to hold his hand there in affectionate embrace. She smiled lovingly at him.

It was the most sensual emotion she had ever allowed herself or displayed toward anyone, and at that moment she thought she would melt with feeling for him. She felt herself floating in time on the enchanting notes of the distant calliope. Could she ever forget that sound? Her first ride ever on the Ferris wheel? This Fourth of July? All too soon the ride was over, and Winona, now suddenly poised and in control of her emotions, with Crestman at her side, rejoined their friends. Except for a continuation of the shouts and laughter that seemed to be a necessary part of youth on holiday, the rest of the day passed without further·incident between the two.

The following Sunday, however, brought the surprise of a lifetime to Winona. It came after the

McCrickland family had returned home from church service and Sunday School, and mother and daughters were preparing the noonday meal. They were attracted to the sound of an automobile moving slowly up the long, tree-lined, gravel lane from the county blacktop. Sarah McCrickland, her daughters trailing curiously behind, walked out to the front porch and, with a hand shading her eyes from a brilliant July sun, peered inquiringly at the approaching car.

The girls who, like their mother, wore aprons over their Sunday frocks, watched and waited expectantly. Company in the country was never an intrusion upon the monotony of long and, at times, lonely Sunday afternoons. The car stopped where the drive circled in front of the porch. When the driver alighted from it Winona very nearly panicked, for it was Crestman Fielding. Tall, dark, handsome, he flashed a smile and waved as he approached, and called out that he had been just passing and decided to stop. Sarah smiled knowingly but said nothing.

Thrasher and Sarah McCrickland had long been acquainted with the Fielding name. One of a number of successful fabricators of building stone, Fielding Mill was a respected industry that was then making an important and needed contribution to the city-county economy, and the Fielding family was counted among the elite of the municipal and rural communities. Thus, when Winona, red-faced and haltingly introduced a son and heir of that family to her mother, Sarah, although she arched her brows slightly, was not surprised. For the past week she had been hearing bits of whispered conversation among her three daughters about the good time they had in Moses City on the Fourth of July and the "handsome wealthy" boy who had shown an interest in Winona.

It was a memorable occasion for Winona. Her mother invited Crestman to stay for dinner and went into the house to set another plate. Left to themselves the four young people stood together on the porch in whispered but pleased conversation. From where she lifted lids and stirred and seasoned food cooking on the propane range in the hot kitchen, Sarah soon heard a mixture of enthusiastic voices and tinkling laughter coming from the group.

At dinner, however, with Thrasher McCrickland seated silently and unsmiling at the head of the table, and Sarah, who respectfully and just as silently occupied a chair across the table from him, little more than formal remarks were heard from the four young people. There were knowing looks and smiles, however, and uppermost in the mind of each of them was a single thought: escape, as quickly as possible, to the freedom of their own circle in the privacy of the sunny July day outside.

After that Sunday, young Crestman Fielding became a frequent weekend visitor to the McCrickland home, and each visit was happily noted in Winona's diary. On a Sunday when he did not come, Winona recorded in painful prose the sadness of his absence. Thankfully, those Sundays were few the rest of that summer and fall. Although Crestman was allowed to visit the McCrickland home, Winona, who was not allowed to date, did not leave the farm in his company. They were, nevertheless, free to stroll about the widespread acreage. Typical of young people, they took advantage of this freedom and would wander as far from the McCrickland house as possible. Through the small orchard that provided the McCricklands with fruit for their own use and for market, around the dairy and horse barns and other outbuildings, and down to Little

Salt Creek that cut through the McCrickland place they went.

There was much for the young man to see, for Thrasher McCrickland, while not an affluent man, was a reasonably successful farmer and horse breeder and, unlike earlier days when he could afford no more than a plow horse, he now was the possessor of considerable stock and farming equipment. And much of what Crestman saw on his Sunday visits was interesting and fascinating enough at times to almost completely distract him, a town boy, from the pretty young girl at his side.

On one or perhaps two occasions they were accompanied by one or both of Winona's sisters, Frona and Leona, but as a rule they were left to themselves. At those times they would hold hands as they walked. More than once, when they were sure they could not be seen, Crestman had stood close to Winona and kissed her on the mouth. It was at these times while she was in his embrace that she was fully aware of him, the smell of him, his maleness, his strength. But even though she had hungrily accepted and returned his kisses, for to her they were the sweetest of sensations and she welcomed even encouraged his embrace, and felt the need of his closeness, as she had on the Ferris wheel on the Fourth of July, Winona was aware of no other physical reaction in herself.

41

As the sun moved on its inexorable seasonal path, the days in Spiceland County and environs became shorter. The autumnal equinox had already passed and the sunshine and warmth of the shorter days had begun yielding to cooler and cooler nights. No question, the things of summer were fading surely and sadly into the past. It was truly a slow change, for at the McCrickland farm Thrasher McCrickland had yet to bring in the late summer harvest.

It was a subtle time between summer and fall given to reflection on pleasures enjoyed, when one is filled with nostalgia combined with a sense of introspection and a determination to live fully every precious second of the future. It was that time, also, for Mother Nature to begin the autumnal ritual of presenting, at no cost to those who cared to look, spectacular extravaganzas of gold and crimson and russet.

For Sarah McCrickland the approach of autumn had always been a most precious gift. It was one of foreboding, too, and waxing poetically one sunlit morning she said to her daughters, "This is a time that nurtures the soul. Enjoy it, for just beyond the fun of Halloween and Thanksgiving Day the long cold winter awaits."

On an unusually warm, sunshiny Sunday afternoon after that, Winona and young Crestman Fielding had strolled hand in hand to the banks of Little Salt Creek where it made its serpentine way through the property some distance behind the McCrickland house. There they laughingly slipped out of their shoes and socks and waded in the cold, shallow water, Winona daintily holding her skirt well above the water's surface.

The garment normally came to just below her knees, but more to be able to better see the creek bottom under her bare feet rather than from fear of getting wet, Winona had gathered up one side of the full skirt in one hand. When she did so she innocently and unwittingly exposed her knees and lower thighs. Seeing her companion staring at her bared white flesh she quickly released her grip on the skirt, letting it fall in place, her face scarlet.

"You have beautiful legs," he smiled boldly. "Don't hide them."

Winona's flush deepened. She was unused to the word beautiful being used in reference to herself. Aware now that he might be embarrassing her, Crestman waded gingerly in the cold water until he was closer and took her hand in his. Gently, kindly, for he was always fearful of frightening her, he brought her to him, held her tightly and kissed her on the mouth.

It was a long kiss, warm and moist, absorbing all of Winona's distress over her bared knees and lower thighs until her only thought was of the charm of the moment. When her companion released her they joined hands again and waded silently back to the grassy bank where they had so hastily removed their shoes.

Except for these playful forays around the McCrickland property, the two rarely had been alone with each other. Between attending classes during college years and spending his summers working in his father's stone mill, Crestman had little time to be with Winona. When they were together, however, he made the most of those moments, but he had refrained from being presumptuous. Pleased with himself now, yet uncertain about his boldness in mentioning her thighs and its ultimate effect on Winona, he quickly sat down and began fumbling with his socks. Winona, who could easily have slipped into her sandals while standing, opted to sit beside him while she put them on. She said nothing. Pushing her hands downward into the front of her skirt between her legs, she leaned back and kicked first one bare foot and then the other in front of her to shake them free of moisture and grains of creek bottom sand. She pulled up each knee in turn as she dabbed her feet with the hem of her skirt.

The movements again revealed her knees and considerably more of her white thighs. Unable to resist, Crestman cautiously reached out and placed a hand on her thigh nearest him. Although his touch was a welcome sensation to Winona, she nevertheless stiffened involuntarily. Fearing it might further worry her, a cautious Crestman quickly took his hand away.

"That's all right," she hurriedly whispered, and she leaned toward him, pressing her lips firmly to his cheek. They kissed again, and again it was a long, moist kiss. Crestman's hand returned to her thigh and rested there. He jerked it away when suddenly a long piercing shriek rent the quiet afternoon.

"Mygod, what was that?" Crestman had jumped to his feet, splashing creek water as he stood.

Winona had also risen, but more slowly. She laughed, shaking out her skirt with both hands. "That's only Soldier. Don't be afraid."

"Soldier?" Crestman gasped, his brow furrowing as with obvious questioning concern he turned to look over first one shoulder and then the other.

Seeing that he was shaken, Winona laughed again,

a soothing, happy laugh. "Come," she said taking his hand. "I'll show you."

She led him along the creek to where a barbed wire fence stretched from bank to bank and up a rise and out of sight. Crestman hesitated there as the shrill sound again reached them. And again Winona laughed disarmingly.

"It's only Soldier, I told you." She squeezed his hand. "Don't be afraid."

Then warning him to be careful, she released his hand and preceded him in crossing the stream on time-worn stepping stones that rose slightly above the surface of the shallow clear water. Following the fence, they made their way through a density of still verdant willows that flourished on the opposite bank and, leaving the creek behind, continued up the rise. At its top they stopped, breathless, and looked down on a gently rolling sweep of summer's last growth of luxuriant pasture grass.

From that vantage Little Salt Creek was again visible in the distance below them where it wound its way through the grassland, a live thing reaching a single curling tentacle into the sweeping expanse of McCrickland farmland. All of a sudden, between them and the creek, some thirty to forty feet beyond a barbed wire fence, the couple faced an enormous dapple-gray draft mare, her head held high, her ears erect and slightly inclined in their direction, standing motionless, intently watching them.

"Is that Soldier?" Crestman asked, breathing deeply from the climb, yet obviously relieved at the sight of nothing more than a horse.

Winona's response came in light musical tones of laughter that carried over the meadow. "No," she trilled into the autumn sunlight. "That's Mr. Hobbs' mare. He brought her over yesterday."

Before she could say more and before Crestman could form a reply, they heard again the piercing shriek. It was followed by a thunder of hooves and they turned together to their left to see a huge, gray-black horse, much larger than Mr. Hobbs' mare, if that were possible, charging at the gallop the barbed wire fence between them. As it reached the fence it veered suddenly and raced along the wire in their direction. Crestman instinctively stepped backward. Stopping immediately in front of the pair at the fence, the animal reared threateningly, its great height dwarfing the youth and the girl, and leaving Crestman mute and frightened. Fearfully he took another step backward, two. At the same time the horse, bloodshot eyes glaring fiercely, its nostrils flaring widely, slashed wildly with flailing hooves the air between them.

With lips curled back to expose enormous yellowed teeth, the largest teeth Crestman had ever seen, and a prodigious pink and black tongue that alternately unfurled from and furled back into its gaping mouth, the big horse again released an ear-splitting, whistling scream. Awed by the sight and the sound, the young man from Moses City fully expected to see jets of flame and puffs of smoke shooting from its open mouth and flared nostrils.

The animal was so close that the afternoon air was at once choked with the pungent odor of horse. To Crestman it was an offensive stench. Nauseated, shocked and frightened, and despite the protective strands of barbed wire fencing between them and the animal, he involuntarily took another step back. At the same time his eyes beheld an astonishing spectacle. Still upright, the animal had become between him and the rest of the world an insurmountable colossal wall of mottled gray and white, smelly horse flesh.

Buffered as she was by life on a farm, Winona was unmoved. Crestman, however, could not have been less prepared for such a sight. He thought he should not look, but he could not turn away; he could not avert his eyes, he could only gape, gripped in a sudden perspiring incredulity. It had happened so quickly that understanding what was taking place on the other side of the fence had barely registered on Crestman's consciousness before the stallion suddenly dropped to all four hooves. To Winona's delight, for she clapped her hands and cheered him on, the huge horse, wild-eyed, tossing its head into the air and shattering the afternoon with its shrieking, began racing wildly along the barbed wire fence, up and down, up and down, rearing on its hind legs and whistling its awful scream each time it neared the two humans.

Veering suddenly in the course of one of its charges, the stallion had suddenly dashed toward the mare. Unmoved by the fierceness of the exhibition, the mare grazed placidly. The stallion stretched out its long neck, bared its huge yellow teeth in a hideous grin and nipped at her forelegs. She whirled and lashed out, rear hooves kicking high. The big stallion stretched out its neck again and, with lips twisted and curled over its exposed large teeth, bit at the mare's flanks. She turned, reared and charged toward him, front hooves pawing dangerously.

The stallion lunged to one side and just as suddenly sat down on its massive haunches, hind legs spread wide. As Crestman and Winona watched, the animal remained there for several seconds, immobile, silent, preposterously ludicrous in that position. Then, with head thrown back and mane on end, its shrill whistling again disintegrating the afternoon calm, the beast, by the strength of its long muscular forelegs, began pulling itself forward, dragging its ponderous buttocks across the tall green grass.

"That's Soldier," Crestman heard Winona laughingly exclaim. "Isn't he beautiful? He's gentle as a kitten, too. But you mustn't go near him right now."

If Crestman heard, he gave no indication, for he felt flushed and sweaty, and he felt himself yielding uncontrollably to a gathering, quiet excitement. He wanted to run away from there, to hide. Instead, with eyes glued to the unfolding exhibition, he moved nearer to Winona and placed an impulsive, trembling arm around her waist. Winona turned her head and momentarily studied her companion inquiringly. Then she knew. She sought to reassure him. She pressed against him and placed a comforting arm around his waist.

When she returned her attention to the shrieking horse, she saw that the stallion had moved behind Mr. Hobbs' mare and had again reared on its hind legs. With its mouth set in a fiendish grin, the horse called Soldier had stretched its long neck and barrel chest across the mare's back. With forelegs gripped on either side of the mare, he already was lunging and thrusting wildly and forcefully behind her. At the same time Winona was aware that Crestman was holding her more tightly.

When it was over, and a subdued Soldier had moved some distance away from Mr. Hobbs' mare, Crestman, now more in awe than in fear of what he had witnessed, was left weak and shaken. Bending his knees, he sank slowly to the deep grass at his feet, pulling Winona down beside him. Stretched full length, he raised a forearm to cover his eyes and replayed in his mind the wonder of what he had just seen. It had been for him an overpowering display of might and potency, and he was glad he had witnessed it, yet he felt that for Winona's sake he probably should have been embarrassed by it. He also was still keenly aware that Soldier's show of unrepressed virility and power had done something more to him, and he should have been embarrassed by that, too.

Winona was unmoved. For as long as she could remember she had observed the farm animals in unveiled and uninhibited mating rituals. Always she had been unimpressed by them, like now. But, intuitively she knew that this time, this mating that had occurred between Soldier and Mr. Hobbs' mare, had had a profound effect on Crestman. She sensed a growing sympathy for him and a desire to be closer to him.

To her diary that night Winona confided that the event of that afternoon was inscribed on her heart where she knew it would remain for the rest of her life. At the top left corner of the page her pen traced a tiny five-pointed star, a symbol that would occur again in those private, delicate pages.

42

While Winona was finishing her senior year of high school, Crestman was employed with his father at Fielding Mill. There was such a demand for cut limestone at the time the mill had extended its work week from five to six days. The couple saw so little of each other at this time that Winona's diary grew to be a succession of forlorn and desolate entries which sometimes reflected a deep and resentful anger at those forces that kept them apart.

Time passed excruciatingly slowly for her. Saturdays found Crestman hard at work in Fielding Mill. There he and his younger brothers, Cramer and Craddick, were constantly under the watchful, helpful supervision of a kindly yet demanding father. Cramer and Craddick disliked working for their father, but their brother Crestman loved the mill.

Although Winona and Crestman's times together were fewer, there were compensations for Winona. Crestman received a wage for his work. The eldest of the three Fielding sons a second family car was convenient to him, and Crestman usually had some money to spend.

However, Fielding Mill then suffered a serious setback, as had the stone industry in general. Europe was under the black cloud of war and the United States was gearing for the mass production of the greatest U. S. military fighting machine the world had ever known. Under the circumstances, building stone was not to be a part of it. Those stone fabricating mills in and around Moses City that were able retooled as rapidly as possible to participate in the building and maintenance of that fighting machine.

It seemed that the world had changed overnight, and the future, once steadfast and predictable, had become fearfully uncertain. Yet, in spite of that precarious outlook, or perhaps because of it, on a sun-filled summer Saturday afternoon soon after her graduation from high school, Winona McCrickland and Crestman Fielding were married in the Walnut Grove Church.

They had several blissful months together before Crestman, like scores of thousands of young American men then being called upon to serve in World War II, was drafted into the Army. Six months after he had arrived in Europe with his infantry division, Winona gave birth to the first of their two sons, Roger Thrasher Fielding.

Until her husband returned to the U.S. after Victory in Europe Day, Winona and her baby lived at the home of her parents. Although her sisters had also married, they both were without children. Consequently, infant Roger enjoyed the attentions of four loving mothers—Winona, her mother, and her sisters, Frona and Leona. To these attentions were added those of a proud and loving grandfather, Thrasher McCrickland.

Winona was happy there, happy to be still at home with her parents, happy to have and to hold a part of Crestman in their child, to feel the child warm and cuddly beside her in bed at night. Yet she ached for the company of her husband. Some nights her loneliness could be dispelled only through a re-reading in her diaries of the intimacies they had shared and by the shedding of copious tears on her pillow.

She wept quietly, secretly, confiding her misery to no one except to her current diary. It did not occur to her that she might seek relief in the touch, the embrace, the comfort of another person, another man. Winona yearned only for her husband's presence. To fill some of her lonely hours she became active in the church of her childhood, the church where she and Crestman had been married.

With Sarah's help she was able to take time away from her child and thus become an interested, eager church worker. She was pleasant and cooperative, yet she maintained a reserve that limited her to few friends. Among those who felt excluded from friendship with her was the young assistant pastor who had made several attempts to be friendly. She was not interested, didn't care. She did not want to be friends with any man. Besides that, the assistant pastor had more than once stood very close to her and tried to take her hand in his and that had frightened her. She insisted to herself that except for the company of her own family she preferred to be alone. She terminated her volunteer work at the church.

Ever since she had first seen him at Moses City High School and throughout the time of their courtship and marriage, Winona was happiest when Crestman was near enough to touch, to have him touch her. And though she loved him dearly and loved to receive his long, often sensual letters from overseas, from the very first time he had made love to her he had awakened no sexual emotion in her. Nor could she, for his or her own sake, arouse herself in that manner. She had sought desperately to do so with his help, and by herself in the pages of romance novels, in the fantasy of her imagination. The futility of her efforts served only to increase her frustration, and in the end she was content to take satisfaction only from Crestman's nearness, his touch, and his love.

Winona had never experienced the ultimate thrill of their most intimate moments, nor would she in the ensuing years of their marriage. Her passion for Crestman was one of pure love and companionship in whatever forms they might take, and she resigned herself to wishing for no more than that, but she wished for that passionately.

After his return from the war, Winona's husband, as did his father before him, became a member of the Order of Free and Accepted Masons. He also proudly took memberships in the Veterans of Foreign Wars and the American Legion. It was in connection with those organizations that he began traveling to other cities on social occasions. Winona knew that he was making new friends, and she was happy for him. It never crossed her mind that some of those friends might be women, attracted to her tall, handsome husband. Nor was she aware that on occasion he had gone to bed with some of them, for in Paris during the war he had learned to his surprise and delight that, unlike Winona, some women were more than a match for his own sexual prowess.

At Crestman's urging, after the birth of their second son, James Crestman Fielding, Winona sometimes accompanied him at certain functions. It was at one of these that Winona, unsuspecting that dormant in the recesses of her brain lay corrupt and obsessive cells, accepted her first alcoholic drink. Unaware of the ingredients or the name of that which had been passed to her, she knew only that in spite of a burning as she swallowed the fiery mixture, she was pleasured and excited mentally and physically by the strange liquid. She had taken but a single cocktail that day. But in the weeks that followed, before she was able to attend another social event, she covertly pined, even ached, for another. More than once she was tempted to slip off during the day to some distant place where she might secretly quench her new and undying thirst.

It had never entered her mind that something unusual, a strange passion, one that was even stronger than the sexual passion that she had hoped for and had been denied her, was taking hold of her, that a satanic need was beginning to possess her. She was cognizant only of having become a new and different Winona, that she had undergone a mysteriously ambiguous transformation that had left her wanting and quietly, yet deliciously, disturbed.

THE STOLEN GUN

43

With the approach of the second anniversary of the Fielding fire it had become readily visible that the months of her ordeal had been unkind to Winona. Whether it was a result of her habitual drinking or for some other reason, she had gained weight. Anyone who had known her before tragedy struck her family probably would not have recognized her at this time. Although her hair had grayed considerably she had attempted to cover the change with a tint. Whatever the shade, the final effect was an unnatural hue of shocking reddish orange.

With the passage of time her habit of smoking cigarettes, like her drinking, had worsened. Except when she was working in the pastry kitchen where smoking was forbidden, she seemed constantly to have a cigarette dangling from a corner of her mouth. She smoked so much that a yellowing nicotine mustache was usually evident on her upper lip, and the index and middle fingers of her left hand bore the telltale ingrained umber stain of heavy smokers.

A telephone request from PJ Cayne of *The Intelligencer* to interview her on the second anniversary of the fire was met with her stern refusal to talk with the reporter. Because he could find no telephone listed in her name he had called her on her job. She insisted she wanted no publicity. Until a death certificate was issued in her husband's name, the less publicity about her and her family the better, she told the reporter. And she asked that he refrain from calling her at her place of employment.

Undaunted, Cayne wrote a token anniversary piece that was carried on the newspaper's front page. If it was read by anyone, it failed to generate noticeable public comment from any source. If it was read by anyone connected to the Moses City State Police Barracks, it prompted no discussion there. State police, Moses City and Spiceland County apparently were too busy with other matters of greater interest.

A similar attempt by Cayne on the third anniversary of that blaze had suffered the same fate. At that time Winona again requested he stop calling her at the restaurant. When Cayne, thinking she might have an unlisted telephone, asked for her home telephone number she denied having one, adding that she could not afford such a luxury. When he offered to call on her in person at her home, she angrily declined, adding that she would not be responsible for any injury caused by her dog. She also asked the reporter to forgo another anniversary story and to let well enough alone.

But well enough would not last. Another election, one that would adversely affect the Fielding case, was less than a year away, and on the very day that she had refused Cayne his most recent request, a twist of fortune involving a man named Walter Hill, a man she had never met, was to bring her a breath of hope and a great deal of personal pleasure.

That day began for Walter Hill like all weekdays that were not holidays; awake at five, a splash of cold water on his face, a cup of coffee and a long drive from the town of Lincoln in Tabor County to the Woodville Army Weapons Supply Center twenty-eight miles southwest of Moses City. As chief inspector in the small-weapons section of the supply center he was expected to be on the job by seven, a half hour sooner than the start of the day shift. But Walter Hill liked to arrive earlier than that, early enough to breakfast on donuts or a cinnamon roll and drink a second cup of coffee in the center's cafeteria before occupying the chair at his desk.

Hill was usually absorbed during the automobile ride to and from his job with his good fortune. After having ended what he described as a bad marriage to a woman whom he claimed did not understand him, he had found a young widow with two small children who agreed to share his bed. Actually it was her bed, for Hill's first wife and their child had left him with few possessions.

A year later, when they were wed, except for his salary minus taxes and child support, Hill brought little more to the marriage than himself. It was of little concern to him. His new family had been well provided for by his deceased predecessor, a blessed bonanza beyond his fondest expectations. Hill had never been so lucky and he knew it, and he took pleasure from thinking about how he so cleverly had improved his circumstances.

But Walter Hill was not in love, at least not with his new wife. He was in love with money, or rather with those things that money could buy. His or hers, it mattered not to him so long as it was available to him. Although he at times found it in himself to be sympathetic to certain family needs or problems that arose, he not only did not love his new pretty wife, he did not particularly like her.

He could suffer her and would suffer her. Why not, he thought on this particular morning while riding to Woodville. They lived in a spacious, comfortable new home. A hunter and fisherman since his early youth, Hill now owned an enviable collection of fine guns, excellent fishing gear, a boat and a four-wheel drive vehicle for his own personal enjoyment. And he had hopes of obtaining more possessions as time went by. For being little more than an average worker he had it good, he thought, and he took satisfaction from the knowledge.

Through church attendance, the Hills made several friends, and on the surface at least they seemed to be happy. But a little more than a year into their marriage the new Mrs. Hill began to sense a problem. She was giving one hundred per cent to the marriage while her husband gave little, yet took much. Except for the time they spent together at church, her weekends were lonely, heartbreaking periods, her husband being away, hunting and fishing with friends. She was also concerned about his growing collection of expensive guns, hi-tech fish detecting devices, and a new boat. Somehow he was not being honest with her, and she brooded.

When he suggested Lincoln needed a sporting goods store and that her savings would earn more were they wisely invested in a thriving business she thought she saw an opportunity to keep him nearer to her and her children. It turned out to be an excellent suggestion, for the business upon which they embarked served sportsmen within a wide radius of Lincoln and was an overnight success. Since he had retained his job at the army supply center, while she and a helper operated the sporting goods store on weekdays, their income rose appreciably and they were certain they were on their way to greater affluence.

A year later a national retail chain which sold at cut rate almost everything imaginable, including sporting goods, opened on the outskirts of Lincoln with an adjacent parking lot of immense size. Offering sporting goods at prices often for less than the Hills could purchase their supplies at wholesale, the huge chain store dealt a knockout blow to the family operated store.

The nest egg inheritance of the second Mrs. Hill was soon dangerously depleted. The Hills managed to retain their home and Walter Hill managed to keep his collection of guns, fishing equipment and boat. The couple's financial security had certainly suffered a setback, yet Hill still had his job which, by this time, was paying him a higher salary since he had attained a higher position, and Mrs. Hill, still a comparatively young and ambitious woman, had taken employment.

Thus it was that on this particular morning as he was driving to Woodville, Hill was enjoying a comfortable degree of complacency. He was content, too, in the knowledge that numerous of his church friends had been pained at the loss of the Hills' store and still extended kind words and overt acts of sympathy toward the family.

Walter Hill took sustenance from this, and, one could say, he was pleased, if not happy with the attention. Life at home, however, his relationship with his wife, with her two children, had steadily deteriorated. It had reached a point that saw Hill continuously grumpy, often angry, while at home, and leaving there after weeknight dinners and on weekends to seek the company of friends who better understood him.

He was an entirely different person on the job. Friendly, sociable, understanding in his relationships with workers in his section, Hill was regarded as an all-right fellow. His superiors also found him likeable, cooperative and competent. On more than one occasion he had been recommended to do classified work both at the weapons supply center and at Army bases around the U.S., and in at least two foreign countries.

For these reasons Hill was held in high regard by many of his fellow workers.

In the fourteen years he had been employed by the government, Hill's job classification might have been much higher had he not terminated his education after graduation from Lincoln High School. Hill knew his job, but he was not bookish. He easily interpreted and defined technical data pertaining to his work, but his off the job reading was limited to an occasional scanning of Lincoln's small daily newspaper and a monthly hunting and fishing magazine. Away from the job, outside his circle of hunting and fishing and church friends, he seemed a man of no interests. If someone were to take the time to apprise him of the state of the war in Vietnam he might listen. But even though a younger cousin was serving in the Marines there, he would never seek out information about the progress of the war for himself. His political views were inherently, blindly Republican, yet he never voted.

It was unlikely that Walter Hill had ever read a word about the Crestman Fielding case. In the first place it is doubtful that the small Lincoln paper had ever carried a story about it. Whether he knew of it or whether he didn't, Hill could not have known that on this day, many months after the fire at the Crestman Fielding home, he would play a significant role in the investigative process of the case.

While busily engaged in his work on this morning, he was interrupted two hours before noon by a telephone page. Answering it, he heard a voice instructing him to report immediately to the supply center's commanding officer's quarters. Thinking that he might again be slated for another classified assignment, Hill stopped in a men's room on the way to check his appearance.

Once in Colonel Harper Ericson's office he was introduced to Gerard Thibideau and Harold Chelsea, special
agents of the Federal Bureau of Investigation. Hill was
dumbfounded. His lower lip quivered, his hands shook
as though he was suddenly stricken with a palsy and
his face reddened perceptibly.

"These gentlemen would like to speak with you,"
Colonel Ericson informed Hill. "I suggest you give
them your fullest cooperation."

Indeed they did want to talk with Hill. For several months Thibideau and Chelsea had been secretly
investigating the disappearance from the weapons
supply center of numerous small arms, including the
Army's popular 45 caliber automatic sidearm. The
two agents had uncovered evidence that led to a ring
of employees who had been smuggling gun parts out
of the supply center. Smugglers had taped them to
their legs, hidden them under their arms, in lunch
buckets, boot tops and by other means, and had
reassembled them outside the center to be sold to the
highest bidder. Thousands of dollars worth of guns
had been stolen in that manner and, Walter Hill was
informed by Thibideau, "We know that you are a
member of that ring."

Hill attempted to deny any complicity. However,
under a little pressure exerted by first one and then
the other of the two special agents he soon admitted
his part in the thefts. He told them approximately
how much money it had netted him and how he had
spent it. He wept violently during his confession, so
much so that much of it was lost in a profusion of sobs,
wails and pleas for the retention of his job.

Though the agents recoiled in displeasure from his
sudden, emotional outburst, they were not averse to
taping it and taking opportunity from it. They offered

Hill a deal: the names and addresses of all the members of the ring, the names and addresses of all the purchasers of the stolen guns, the number of guns involved, the amount of money received, everything he could tell them, his full cooperation for leniency and perhaps the keeping of his job.

In the meantime Hill was to continue with his job as though nothing had happened. He was to speak to no one about the investigation, not even his wife. Hill grabbed the deal, with two exceptions. Through another flood of tears that night he broke his promise to the government agents by divulging the entire story and his part in it to his wife. Together, late the next afternoon, they kept an appointment with an attorney, a member of their church, and apprised him of Hill's predicament.

During the next two weeks the two agents met almost daily with Hill. Arrests eventually were made and stolen small arms were confiscated. In following one lead given them, Thibideau and Chelsea drove to New Washington and rang the doorbell at a certain house on Catalpa Street. They were greeted by an attractive lady in her late thirties who, after seeing their ID's, invited them inside. When the agents learned that she had been a widow for more than three years and that they therefore could not speak with her husband, they asked her if he had owned a 45 caliber automatic pistol. He had owned a gun, she told them. She knew nothing about guns and could not be sure what kind it was. It was big and black, and so heavy she could hardly hold it, a frightening looking thing, and it made her nervous to know that it was in the house. The agents understood. If she would just hand over the weapon to them they would take it away.

"I can't give it to you," she told them. "I don't have it. I gave it to a friend."

"We'll have to have his name," Chelsea informed her. "It's very important that we know who has that weapon."

The woman was hesitant. "I don't know," she said. "I don't want to get anyone in trouble. He's such a good friend."

"Do you see him often?" Thibideau asked kindly.

"Oh yes," she replied. "We spend quite a lot of time together."

"Good," the agent got to his feet. Then with a side-long glance at Chelsea he added, "We'll just park in front of your house until he gets here. Of course your neighbors will see us, and they might ask questions."

"Oh my," the woman took the bait with a long sigh. "I don't know what I should do. Will he get in trouble? What is this all about?"

"We can't tell you a thing," Chelsea said firmly. "Really, you don't have much choice in this matter. We —"

"All right, all right," the woman held one hand at her mouth and pressed the open palm of the other against her abdomen as though she were in pain. "I'll tell you. His name is Bill — William Carey."

The federal agents exchanged surprised looks.

"You mean William Carey. Colonel William Carey of the state police?" Thibideau asked.

"Yes," the woman groaned.

HOPE

44

The breath of late October wound softly, inevitably along the hilly twisting blacktop that led to the Walnut Grove Church and its adjacent small cemetery. There it probed deeply to reveal where nature unveiled in unreserved generosity an intensity and magnificence of its exotically tinted and portentously multi-shaded soul. The inexorable change there from one season to the next was a grand thing to witness; it was a grand time to be alive.

Sluggish, dulled and lifeless from the effects of the wine she had consumed the night before, Winona Fielding, sitting behind the wheel of her old Chevrolet, was unmoved by the beauty around her or by the thrill of being alive. As she guided the car into a gravel drive that led to a gravel parking lot behind the old log church, she saw nothing of her vivid surroundings. Furthermore, she knew of no reason that had impelled her to come to this place this morning. She knew only that the bodies of her parents, Thrasher and Sarah McCrickland, lay buried here in this remote cemetery, but she also knew that had not been a consideration of her visit.

It was Tuesday, her day off from baking pies at the restaurant. She had spent the past few nights at her sister Leona's house. Illness had forced Leona to appeal to Winona to spend some care time with her and Winona had reluctantly agreed. Even though the sick Leona had slept soundly through the night, Winona had spent miserable hours wide awake.

When daylight came she was anxious to get away and to be alone. When she had left her sister's home Leona was still asleep.

Having drunk heavily during the long, lonely hours, Winona did not want to be near her sister this morning. The stink of stale wine seemed to ooze from her pores until even she was sure she could smell herself. Her tongue felt twice its usual size, and her insides were painfully ablaze. When she had looked into the bathroom mirror her face was pale and puffy and her eyes stared back at her as dully and empty as the hollow, lifeless openings of the deserted old Fielding Mill. She knew that had the religiously strict Leona seen her, as sick as Leona was, there would have been a reproachful confrontation; so she had left a note on the kitchen table and quietly slipped out.

Now, at the old country church, Winona ached for a glass of ice-cold water. She slowly and heavily got out of the car and moved toward the burial ground. At the McCrickland plot she stopped to survey the weather-stained gray limestone marker which bore the chiseled names of her father and mother. Cold, lifeless stone, the thought dragged through her dulled mind, passed as a poor memorial to lives that once were warm and soft and loving, lives which once had been reachable, touchable, responsive. Ever since their demise she had missed her parents and she had often yearned for their presence, their counsel and understanding and, in recent years, especially their solace. Slowly their images took some kind of form in Winona's still drugged and sleep-heavy thoughts. She began to see them as they had been when she was a girl.

At the sound of a distant farm tractor on the early morning air, she wondered how much of her father's life had been spent bumping along in the perforated

metal seat of his old green tractor. He had loved horses and had always kept them and taken much pride
and pleasure from buying and selling them, working
them, working with them, but they had been no match
for the faster, indefatigable machine. For the comfort
of his bottom-side Sarah had made him a thick, quilt-
ed pad, for which he had often expressed his gratitude, especially during planting and harvest times.
Winona now saw him astride the padded tractor seat
as she remembered him, slightly hunched over the
wheel, his always pleasant face shaded by a wide-
brimmed straw hat.

He had ridden the big green machine by the hour,
by the day; first in one direction, then in the opposite,
plowing, disking, cutting hay, threshing. He was a
man of great patience, durable, dependable and, in
his quiet unruffled way, loving. How could such a
man be vanquished by death, she wondered. When as
a child she had watched from the front porch of the
house or from the back yard swing while he plied the
surrounding fields she never dreamed that death
would ever overtake him. But in those days the
thought of death rarely entered Winona's mind. When
a farm animal died, yes, or a neighbor, or a member of
the church. But death held little or no intimate meaning for her then. Whatever it was it could never come
between her and her father. The Thrasher
McCrickland of her early years was as certain and as
indestructible as the earth itself.

Again she saw him on the big green tractor, the
pad so thoughtfully, so lovingly made by Sarah,
between him and the perforated metal seat. She
watched idolistically fascinated as his protruding
Adam's apple moved up and down in cadence to the
long, thirsty draughts he took from a Mason jar filled

with cool lemonade, prepared for him by Sarah on hot summer afternoons and brought to him by Winona and her sisters. Like no one she had known before or since, her father had enjoyed the replenishment of liquid in his tall, angular body, and the brief respite from the interminable bouncing of the brutal, confining power plant under him. It was such a pleasure to watch him that she could almost feel in her own body his relief, his appreciation. And for a moment she forgot the fire in her belly.

They seemed to be one then, her father and the tractor and hard work and his family. She suddenly heard his voice as he spoke one day with no little amount of dignity to an itinerant stove salesman: "I like farming and what it does for me and my family. Besides that, somebody has got to feed the people." Thrasher had pointed to a saffron field and Winona again heard him addressing the salesman, "Wheat'll be ready this year about the Fourth of July."

The Fourth of July. It was on a Fourth of July that she and Crestman Fielding had been together for the first time. She tried to recapture the thrill of that meeting, his accidental touch of her arm that day, the subsequent unforgettable ride on the Ferris wheel. Instead there came to her ears the sound of visceral growling, rumbling from deep within herself. She heard it as an obscene sound and felt a sense of shame at being responsible for it happening at the graves of her parents. She had often heard that same sound unwittingly rising from among the elderly in the quiet of church services. But that was an affliction of aging. She knew quite well the cause of that grumbling complaint coming from her own insides. How Thrasher and Sarah would have objected to her drinking, her current lifestyle.

Sarah. Thoughts of childhood days Winona had

spent with her mother filled her mind. If she had idolized her father she also had worshiped her mother. She had learned so much from Sarah, but at the moment a single childhood recollection came to mind. While seated in a circle in the back yard with her sisters and Sarah snapping beans one lovely summer afternoon, Winona had become intrigued by the varied antics and breathless trilling of a catbird on a nearby clothesline. Leaning back in her chair she had inquired of Sarah, "Mother, why does the catbird sing so many different songs?" Sarah paused in her work and looked kindly at her youngest daughter.

"I don't know, Winona," she smiled honestly. "And I don't worry myself about why. I'm just thankful that I can hear him."

Winona had never forgotten those words, and in many respects they had been a guide in her later years. There were many things she did not presume to understand, but she had absorbed fully and innocently, without question or complaint, what pleasures life had sent her way, especially those that had come from marriage and childbearing and family life.

All of a sudden, Thrasher and Sarah McCrickland were forgotten. Winona now thought of her children. She wondered where they were. She had not seen Roger in months. She had not heard from James since long before the U.S. troop withdrawal from Vietnam. Where were her sons now? She felt a rise of anger. She had given unselfishly of herself to her children.   Where were they now that she needed them? Why hadn't they kept in touch? Winona again remembered the varied songs of the catbird and Sarah's response to her question that summer afternoon so long ago, and her anger subsided.

"I don't know where they are, or why they are not

here. I do miss them," she spoke aloud to Sarah's chiseled name on the gray stone. "But I suppose I can enjoy what I remember of them. The good times. The fun times."

As much as she would have liked, however, she could not get overly sentimental about her sons. As much as she would have liked, she could not shed a tear over their unexplained estrangement from her. Not this morning. Angry and disappointed in them as she was, she told herself, "I'll probably never see them again." She tried to concentrate on their early years, but the only memory that would stay with her now was one of a runt pig that her father had given her when she was in the third grade.

"You do everything for this runt pig that I do for the other pigs and what money he brings at market time will be yours to do with whatever you like," she could hear the sound of Thrasher's voice, the words of his promise to her.

Winona had never been quite so proud of any child-hood possession. She daily prepared feed for the little pig, she washed it and babied it. She dressed it and played with it as she might have played with a doll. And, although it was a male pig and it frequently squealed unnervingly, she named it "Melody." When she became impatient with the little animal she scold-ed it, addressing it as "You runty pig." But she never expressed real anger toward it.

Around the farm, around the McCrickland home, Melody had become Winona's constant companion. She soon realized that she loved the little pig and hoped they would spend the rest of their lives together, that nothing should ever come between them. On more than one occasion, however, she had been confronted by a vigorously kind Sarah who had made it unquestionably clear to her that the house was no place for a pig, even if it was a runt and had been bathed and rinsed under the garden hose and had a pretty name and was dressed in clean cast-off child's clothing.

Ultimately the time came that a fattened hog named Melody should go to market, and Winona was overcome with grief. The prospect of her pet being led to slaughter left her plaintive and inconsolable. Sleepless and without appetite for days, she had begged Thrasher and Sarah that Melody be spared, that he be allowed to spend the rest of his days on the farm with her. Thrasher was understanding and kind to the point of heartache himself, yet with a gentle firmness he spoke to her patiently and unyieldingly on the facts of farm life.

Early one morning Winona was allowed to accompany her parents to the livestock market at Mount Carmel where she tearfully kissed Melody goodbye. Later that day her broken heart began slowly to mend when on the return trip to the farm, Winona hugged to her breast a colorfully wrapped package. Inside were shiny black patent leather slippers, purchased with some of the money the man at the hog market had paid her for Melody. It was as though Melody himself had reimbursed her for the love and attention she had lavished on him. And for as long as they lasted she never wore the glistening black slippers without entertaining fond memories of her runty pig.

A sudden cascade of squirrel cuttings rustling down from a nearby beech tree startled Winona from her thoughts.

"What am I doing here?" she angrily asked herself aloud as she regained her composure and surveyed her surroundings.

She had made no plan for such a visit; she was not

aware of having had a desire to come here to dwell on a time eternally apart and far from this one. At once she knew that she did not care to think about the present time, either. Not any more. Just as she could never go back to the carefree happy days of childhood, the days of comfort and security in Thrasher and Sarah's house, she knew that she could no longer face her present condition.

It was for her an excruciating trial to live in Crowfoot Valley. But with no more than she was earning baking pies for hungry tourists at the restaurant in Hickory Grove, she knew of no other place she could afford to live. Live? The thought washed over her with chilled suddenness. Crestman was dead. It would soon be four years since he took his own life. Thrasher and Sarah were dead. Roger and James had abandoned her. And she was a hopeless drunk. She could not stop drinking. That's not true, she suddenly argued with herself. I can stop. But why should I? Despite her excuses, deep within herself she knew that she could never stop drinking.

Another fall of cuttings rattled down through the leaves of the beech. Winona tilted her head and searched the mass of limbs and branches for the tiny culprit that was interrupting her thoughts. Having no sons, Thrasher McCrickland had taught his three daughters the safe use of a small caliber rifle and the art of hunting squirrels with such a weapon. Each season Sarah had canned squirrel meat in Mason jars for cooking an off-season family favorite of squirrel meat and dumplings. Unlike her older sisters who became skilled squirrel hunters and enjoyed hunting, Winona, although she savored squirrel meat and dumplings, had refused to kill the little animals.

Now, as her eyes probed the leafy mass of the tall

tree, she saw herself one day aiming a rifle, and there it was, a twitching gray tail in her sights. But even in this momentary mental replay of that day she refused to pull the trigger. She again heard the voice of her father urging her to shoot, to "Git the little varmint." She could not then, even as now, pull the trigger. Thrasher McCrickland was almost beside himself at her refusal to kill a squirrel until he was moved by what he saw in his youngest daughter's face. Lowering himself to one knee he carefully removed the rifle from Winona's hands and tenderly wrapped his free arm around her waist.

"It's all right, Nona," she heard him say close to her ear. "It's all right."

Winona could no longer see the small gray squirrel in the tree of that memory for the tears suddenly filling her eyes. They felt warm and soothing as they coursed down her cheeks, down her neck, and into the top of her blouse. She lowered her head and suddenly dropped to her knees. With one hand loosely holding the long strap of her purse and the other hand gripping a corner of the gravestone, she leaned forward over the graves of her father and mother. The flow of her tears was unstoppable, and it spilled onto the blanket of green grass that covered Thrasher and Sarah.

Her father's words raced through her mind again. "It's all right Nona. It's all right Nona." She shook her head violently. "No Dad," she sobbed to the ground under her knees. "It's not all right. Not anymore. Nothing is right. Crestman is dead. The state police say he isn't, that he has killed someone. He would never. They have taken away my home, my life."

A loud moan escaped her, momentarily interrupting her words. "They have taken away everything, everything," she continued through choking sobs. "There is nothing left. I want to die. I want to be with Crestman. With you. With mother. But I'm afraid. I'm afraid to die. I'm afraid to live. Oh God, I'm so afraid."

Winona's words and sobs had increased in volume, shattering the tranquility that had followed the last noisy rain of squirrel cuttings. She snuffed and gasped uncontrollably. Saliva slavering from her gaping mouth reached in long strings to the grass and the purse at her knees. From the pressure of her grip on the gravestone the knuckles of her hand stood out stark and white.

"Oh Dad! Oh Mother! Oh God!" she cried. "Crestman is dead! Dead! Dead! Dead!"

With each repetition she pounded the saddle of the gravestone with her fist until a sharp hurting brought her out of her blind despair. She was shocked to see through her tears red stains from her scraped knuckles on the weathered headstone.

She began apologizing to Thrasher and Sarah. "I'm sorry, I'm sorry," she shuddered with senseless remorse as she looked at the bloodstains. "I didn't mean to hurt you. I'm sorry. I'm sorry."

Winona remained on her knees, doubled over, sobbing for a long time. Finally she was quiet. With the support of the gravestone again under one hand she rose to her feet. She took some tissues from her purse and dabbed at her eyes and mouth and blew her nose loudly. With another tissue she wiped her face and her bloody knuckles. Her legs were sore from kneeling and she tottered to her old Chevrolet and pulled more tissues from a box on the front seat. She turned, then, looking first in one direction and then another. Satisfied that she was still alone, she lumbered to the back of the old log church to one of two privies separated by a vine-covered lattice screen.

45

Winona spent the rest of that morning and afternoon staying away from Leona's house. She had made it a point to do so after having looked at herself in the rear vision mirror of her old car before she left the Walnut Grove Church parking lot.

"My God," she had exclaimed to as much of her image as she could see in the rectangular slice of mirror, "I look horrible. I can't go anywhere near Leona, or she'll know."

Late that afternoon, however, after several cups of black coffee at her house in Crowfoot Valley, and, at last, a sandwich, the first food she'd had in almost twenty-four hours, she gave up trying to hide. Fearing the sick Leona might be in need of her, she drove toward her sister's house.

Arriving there Winona stopped at *The Intelligencer* newspaper tube by the side of the road in front of Leona's house for the day's newspaper and dropped it on the seat by her side without looking at the front page. She already knew that it would be filled with news of the approaching November election. Ever since the day after Labor Day the newspaper had daily been steeped in boring political news and political advertisements, and Winona had no interest in politics and less in politicians. She was tired of seeing the unchanging headlines and reading the wearisome issue-burdened stories which grew in intensity from one day to the next and were forgotten soon after an election.

Inside the house she was pleased to see Leona seated

on the couch in the living room. She must be feeling much better, Winona thought. Perhaps she could return to the privacy of her own dwelling place soon. She greeted her sister perfunctorily and let the folded paper fall on the couch by the silent Leona's side as she went through a short hallway to a back room that for the past few days had served as her bedroom. Seconds later she heard Leona call loudly.

"Winona!"

Believing something was wrong with the ailing Leona, Winona hastily retraced her steps through the hallway and into the sitting room. There was nothing wrong, not that she could see. Leona still sat there in the corner of the couch, but now she was holding out the newspaper to her. Taking it from her, Winona looked down at the front page. Then she let herself fall into the other corner of the couch, the paper lying in her lap.

Winona looked again at the bold-faced headline. She tried to say something to her sister but her throat was constricted. She tried to think but could not. All she could do was stare, her eyes glued on the big black two-line headline which read

'DEAD MAN' IN FIELDING CASE
FOUND ALIVE.

She tried to read the columns of words below the bold type but for the second time that day she was blinded by a cataract of tears. But she needed no explanation; Felix Dombriewski was alive.

For the first time in almost four years Winona felt a surge of hope. She thought she felt her heart swell almost to bursting the next day when she learned that Ames Shaw was preparing a motion to file in Spiceland Circuit Court for a hearing to have Crestman Fielding declared legally dead. Her heart dropped one week later when Ames Shaw informed her that attorneys acting in behalf of the four insurance companies contesting her claim for one million six-hundred thousand dollars in her husband's death had requested a stay in the proceedings.

Because of the daily publicity given by *The Intelligencer* to the impending general election, newspaper accounts about the Crestman Fielding case went virtually unnoticed by Moses City and Spiceland County residents. Circuit Judge Harrison Alexander, a candidate himself for re-election, seemed grateful for the respite a delay would afford him. And now that the action had been taken, he secretly hoped he would be given enough reason to grant a stay long enough that would continue the proceedings well past the election, if not through the year-end holidays recess of the court. He would need the rest.

As of that moment he was concerned with winning another six-year term. For the first time in his illustrious career Alexander faced the threat of opposition in his bid for yet another term, his fourth as judge of the circuit court. A young upstart attorney of the opposite political faith had been making worrisome sounds since long before the younger man's unopposed success in the earlier May primary election.

Ames Shaw, meanwhile, had shielded his disappointment by filing with Alexander's court another motion. This one asked to overturn the newest action on the grounds that too much time had already elapsed in the case, and that his client, after four years, was in desperate need of relief.

Alexander was prepared to deny that request out of hand, but he was spared the effort. In a sudden flurry of activity, insurance company attorneys filed a pleading for more time to prepare a rebuttal to the argument that Crestman Fielding was dead. After hearing brief arguments from both sides, Alexander agreed with counsel for the insurance companies. Surprisingly then, at least to Ames Shaw, Alexander, claiming a choked calendar, granted the insurance company attorneys a delay. Because of the nature of the case, and yielding to the pleading of the insurance company attorneys for enough time to collect more evidence to support their argument that Crestman Fielding was alive, and to give Alexander himself time to further study the Fielding matter, the stay would be of indeterminate duration. Alexander's unexpected decision could not have bound Shaw's hands more securely.

In addition to Judge Alexander, Spiceland County that year also re-elected mortician Irwin Brown to the post of coroner. As expected, Irwin Brown named his father, Ira Brown, his deputy. This was hardly a surprise. And it was no surprise that voters should have returned Sheriff Jefferson "Spud" Tatum to office for another four years.

The election brought a new face into Spiceland County government, that of another young attorney who was elected prosecutor. Because he was unopposed for the office, his election also came as no surprise to city and county residents. But in a matter of days he would have a big surprise for them.

REPRIEVE

45

Meanwhile Galiton and Breezy's relationship, which they managed very carefully, was still their secret, and theirs alone. Although Breezy on occasion had suggested a return to the stacks in Crowfoot Valley, Galiton had been leery of being together so close to Moses City. The chance meeting at the Hickory Grove Lounge and what followed was one thing, but repeated meetings so close to their respective homes spelled trouble, he cautioned.

By pre-arrangement they had been meeting in first one and then the other of two different cities separated by many miles from Moses City. Leaving one or the other of their cars in an inconspicuous city parking lot they registered in one of a collection of nearby lodging places. It was chancy, Galiton knew, but to further discourage curiosity and the likelihood of familiarity, they had dined in a different restaurant each time they were together. They had no problems, except one: they sincerely believed that they had fallen in love again.

Though Galiton could not speak for Breezy, he had long been aware that he was not only in love with Breezy, he was still in love with Jeri, his wife. Try as he would he could not separate himself from either woman. While he was with Jeri he was dutifully in love with her. While he was with Breezy he was hopelessly in love with her. While he was with Jeri his innermost thoughts were of Breezy. When he was with Breezy his conscience wrestled with thoughts of Jeri.

He knew that he and Jeri were bound together by love and marriage. He told himself that he and Breezy were joined by a love of old, a first love that should never have been denied, that had he not played the fool, Breezy, not Jeri, would now be his wife.

His dilemma was complete. Jeri was his wife, and he was bound to her legally, and emotionally. He felt compelled to stay with her. Yet, he was convinced that he could no more turn from Breezy than he could from Jeri. She meant as much to him now as she did when they were in high school, despite a challenging conscience that would not let him or his clandestine entanglement rest. On the one hand he could not believe that he had allowed this renewed relationship to come between him and what had been a happy marriage for him and Jeri. On the other hand he in some twisted way was happy that he had.

It was wrong, and he knew it, believed it. And there were times when conscience bit deeply into his very soul. Still, he persisted with Breezy, wanted Breezy, needed Breezy. She wasn't the willowy girl of earlier days. She was older. She was also heavier. Not much, but enough to have made an unusual and powerful sexual impact on him. He had always been pleased with Jeri, the slender suppleness of her body, her breasts neither too small nor large, her stomach flat even now. But, he repeated to himself, there was something different, a rising joy, a fulfilling satisfaction that came to him each time he took the fullness of Breezy's body into his arms. Fleshy, cushiony, enveloping, devouring, it gave him a totality of sensation and luxury he had never known with Jeri, nor, for that matter, with Breezy in previous days. In her embrace he knew a sense of peace, of completeness, of security. To hold her close, to lower himself in the abundance and maturity that was now her, to feel and breathe into himself her matronliness, was like nothing he had ever known or dreamed. There was beyond all of that the essence of sensual individuality, a triumphant headiness of flesh and fragrances that in themselves were entirely Breezy, entirely captivating.

It had come over him slowly and it wasn't until after their third or fourth surreptitious meeting that he realized she had become a commanding desire from which he thought he did not want to be separated, no more than he cared to be separated from life itself. If he were made to choose between her and Jeri, he told himself, while hoping desperately that he would never have to face such a decision, he would choose Breezy. She was his life, he told himself.

Furthermore, Galiton believed that Breezy needed him as much as he believed he needed her. She had made the point each time they were together, beginning with their night together in a city motel at Mount Carmel. She had poured out her deepest feelings to him. She had wanted him for her very own from the beginning. He was the first to make love with her. There had been only one other, her husband. She avowed that she loved Edward and would rather die than hurt him. But she found herself in the same dilemma in which Galiton found himself. Unlike Galiton, however, she claimed that she was ready to take whatever steps necessary to be his and his alone.

She had confessed tearfully to him one night that were the choice hers to make she would never again go to bed with her husband. Not because she didn't love him. She did. And, in a manner of speaking, she did enjoy that part of their marriage. But even on her wedding night she had been filled with memories of her first love, and now that she had rediscovered it she preferred to save herself only for Galiton.

Galiton believed her, believed she was doing so, for when they were together she was insatiable. She sighed time and again that she yearned daily for him, and waited in pain until they could be together and she could cradle him to herself.

He observed that she had always taken considerable pleasure from their physical unions, and that it was, in fact, precisely that, her passion, that initially had come between them. Had it not been for the pleasure she had derived from their love-making in the beginning he—in his innocence, or ignorance— might have married her, but her passion had turned him against her. And the deeply ingrained social and religious mores of his youth had kept him from taking such a corrupted, defiled woman home to his mother. How stupid, he now thought reproachfully.

Still, his and Jeri's had been a happy marriage. Ever since they had been together Jeri periodically seemed to enjoy the physical intimacy they shared. Their relationship had otherwise been satisfactory. Except for the Breezy of earlier years, Jeri, had been the only woman in his life. In their time together he had adjusted so well to their sex life that he was content to make only occasional demands of her. Now his needs were different. He now found himself wanting Jeri at incredible times, and often greedily satisfying his need for Breezy with her, much to Jeri's consternation. Still he was kind to Jeri and understanding, for as time went on he was unable to forget that he still loved her, that he still wanted her, even if he did love Breezy more and wanted Breezy more.

Cruising in the vicinity of Crowfoot Valley one day with such thoughts in mind he turned into the gravel roadway and drove to the abandoned quarry hole. Parking the cruiser he strolled about with no apparent intent. He looked down into the blue waters of the quarry hole and saw Breezy. He turned and looked up at the stacks of discarded limestone blocks. Again he saw Breezy. Wherever he looked it was impossible to repress from his sight a picture of Breezy. He remembered their meeting at the Hickory Grove Lounge, their subsequent drive to Crowfoot Valley. The touch of a smile played at his lips as he reminded himself that he had been seduced.

In the beginning, as he remembered, he had fretted over his fall from virtue before he finally came around to accepting it. His betrayal of Jeri having been almost more than he could accept, he at first was consumed by conscience. He had considered telling her of his meeting with Breezy that same night, and all that had transpired. A confession. He had almost convinced himself that would be the honest and honorable thing to do. She would forgive him and they would continue their life happily together. But when he got home that night Jeri was asleep.

Telling himself he would make his confession to her in the morning, he slept soundly the entire night. In the morning Jeri seemed so bright and happy he decided to delay it another day, then another, until enough tomorrows had elapsed to bring him once more into Breezy's company, once again into her embrace, and then it was too late. And he realized that he was glad that he had not disclosed his infidelity. Instead, he found himself each day looking forward to the next time he could be with Breezy, and the next, until they had become lovers again, not as freely as they had been in high school, but whose meetings were limited by the normal and expected restraints of their separate lives and to carefully spaced and arranged meeting times and places.

In an unexpected rush of tears one night in a motel near Mount Carmel Breezy surprised Galiton of the end of their relationship. Dabbing at her eyes with a tissue she explained they would have to part, not next month or next week but right then. Edward, she told an incredulous Galiton, had accepted a lucrative position with a daily newspaper in a city on the West Coast, something he had always dreamed of and hoped for, and she was obligated to accompany him there.

Taken by surprise as he was, Galiton at first was speechless. Then, incredibly, he heard himself assuring her that there was no need for tears, that such things happen, that her departure from Moses City, from him, was just one of those unfortunate twists of fate. As these heartening, encouraging words left his lips Galiton could not help but wonder who was speaking them. Surely not he. Some unidentified person deep inside him was speaking.

"Who is this cavalier stranger?" he asked himself. "Whoever he is he is not speaking for me."

At once he was overcome with a desire to appeal to Breezy for forgiveness for speaking such drivel to her at such a critical, heartbreaking time in her life. He wanted to say he didn't mean what she had just heard from his lips, that he would not let her go, that he would rather die than to see her leave him.

Then, as he held her close, he suddenly was aware of an enormous sense of relief. By his acceptance of a new position in a distant city Edward Coleman unintentionally had solved Galiton's dilemma; he had lifted the burden of confusion from his heart. And Galiton realized that the sobbing woman he now held in his arms, his Crowfoot Valley lover, meant absolutely nothing to him.

Breezy sobbed at length, dabbing at her eyes repeatedly with a series of fresh tissues. At last she apologized for the disaster that had befallen them, for breaking Galiton's heart. Weeping almost uncontrollably she asked Galiton's forgiveness, and again she apologized because she was too emotionally upset to make love. He patted her shoulder consolingly and said he understood. In the end they parted. No embrace, no kiss goodbye, just goodbye. Galiton was aware of a strange excitement—he was going home to Jeri.

ALBERT

46

Albert Fielding, the son of a stone mill worker, was born and reared in Moses City. There was nothing outstanding about him as he was growing up. He played neither basketball nor baseball in high school, but because he played on the school's football team he had achieved a degree of popularity there.

Still, Albert had grown up in the shadow of another Fielding boy, his cousin Roger, son of Crestman and Winona Fielding. The boys were distant cousins, a relationship that neither boy claimed or attempted to develop, nor was it one that was acknowledged by their parents.

While Albert Fielding's father labored in a limestone fabricating mill, Roger's father had owned one. While Albert rode a school bus to classes every day, Roger rode in a car with his mother. Beginning in their junior year in high school, Roger drove a late model used car while Albert continued riding the bus. Physically they seemed evenly proportioned, just under six feet, perhaps a few pounds overweight. They differed in that Albert, although a roughly handsome young man, was nonetheless tacit and unsmiling, while Roger was a handsome, outgoing, laughing youth who was popular with the girls in their class.

One Penni Laughton, an attractive girl with blue eyes and blond hair, was especially fond of Roger. That she should have been interested in Roger mattered little to Albert whose interest in girls did not blossom until later. Yet, Penni's obvious infatuation with Roger added to Albert's guarded dislike of his distant cousin and his envy of Roger's good fortune. Except for averted eyes and a clouded countenance on his part when he was in the close presence of Roger, it was unlikely that anyone ever guessed Albert was jealous of his cousin. He was adept at keeping his mouth shut and his feelings to himself, and it was an easy matter for him to mask his emotions by applying himself to his studies. Albert did like to study. And it was therefore not surprising when Roger had declined an opportunity to go to college, that Albert should have won a scholarship to Brackenridge University at New Washington. Roger was college material, without a doubt, but he preferred working with his father in Fielding Mill to going to college.

Albert was in his junior year at the university when he received from his mother a letter that included a clipping from *The Intelligencer* that Roger and Penni had married. By this time Albert had discovered Helen Mathers, an education major whom he would much later marry, and he put the clipping aside without further thought, confident that the paths of cousins Albert and Roger Fielding would never have to cross.

Albert earned his undergraduate degree in political science, with a minor in history. It had not been easy. Andrew and Millie Fielding, Albert's devoted and proud parents, had helped him in every possible way, but they were of limited financial means. As a result Albert was forced to seek out grants and to take off-campus jobs to supplement their help and the money provided by the scholarship. Uncomplaining and undeterred by the struggle to educate himself, Albert went on to work himself through law school and later passed the bar exam on the first attempt.

When he returned to Moses City he launched, with the help of his parents who had co-signed a bank loan for the needed money for the venture, a private practice in a small second floor suite on Moses City's Courthouse Square. He was in practice there at the time of the mysterious barn fire at the Crestman Fielding home.

Being registered as a Republican, he was tagged that fall for appointment as Moses City solicitor. For more than three years he was moderately successful. He and Helen Mathers had married, and although they had no children they did have two bouncing Irish Setters that lived with them in their suburban Moses City home. They seemed to be a happily married couple.

With an eye to a future political career, Albert, when filing time came around for the first primary election after the Fielding fire, dared to file his candidacy for the office of Spiceland County Prosecutor. Fortune had smiled down upon him. For reasons unknown, incumbent prosecutor William Farnsworth had declined to run for a second term and Albert found himself unopposed in his bid to run for that public office.

Nevertheless, beginning a few weeks before the primary election he did arrange for a series of small advertisements in *The Intelligencer* because, he smilingly informed friends, "They make it look like my hat really is in the ring." Despite being opposed in the general election of the following November he was elected prosecutor. With Irwin Brown, who had been reelected coroner, and Spud Tatum who had won a second term as Spiceland County sheriff, he was sworn in to this post one minute after midnight on the first day of January.

Albert was certain he was on his way politically and

financially. For the next four years, if not eight, he would not only enjoy a guaranteed living wage as prosecutor, he would have an opportunity to plant the political seeds of loyal public service and goodwill toward a future goal which, he had confided to Helen, was a seat in the state legislature. "And," he added, "there is no telling where that may lead." Smiling then he said facetiously, "Even to the governor's mansion."

Falling short of that, he then seriously assured her, he would not be totally disappointed. Having earlier availed himself of the long history of the county's past prosecutors and the numerous future benefits the office had afforded them, he explained to Helen that he was fully cognizant of an oft-proved fact that the financial future of past Spiceland County prosecutors was in many ways practically guaranteed.

Given the long term benefits that had accrued to previous holders of that office, he could depend on at least a modicum of lasting success. This was much to Albert's liking. A usually intense person in the matter of his future, he now needed simply to do his job diligently and exercise patience.

47

Although he gave no public explanation for his action, soon after occupying his office in the Spiceland County Courthouse, Albert Fielding, the new prosecutor, assumed a personal role in the four-year-old Crestman Fielding investigation.

He notified by registered mail, John V. McKnight, named interim superintendent of state police after William R. Carey's resignation, as well as Spiceland County Coroner Irwin Brown, Sheriff "Spud" Tatum and Lt. Frank Conway, that all matters pertaining to the Fielding investigation were to be reported to and/or cleared with his office.

In addition to that notice, he ordered that a copy of the entire state police investigation report be sent to his office as soon as possible and that any further publicity concerning the case was to be released by his office, and his office only.

As county prosecutor, Albert Fielding, in these matters, was fully aware of his authority. Unlike his predecessor William Farnsworth, who had left the investigation totally in the hands of state police, Albert, as he subsequently did explain in a public statement in *The Intelligencer,* was conducting his own investigation of the Crestman Fielding alleged suicide.

Since taking office he had spent every free moment familiarizing himself with all aspects of the mysterious case because, as he told his deputy, Stanley "Stash" Pinkala, he did not believe that Crestman Fielding had perished in the fire that destroyed the barn at the Fielding home.

From the creaky swivel chair in his first floor office Albert interviewed at different times Irwin Brown, Sheriff Tatum, former state police colonel William R. Carey; and state policemen Captain Timothy Melton, Lieutenant Frank Conway, troopers Link Trueblood, Harley Oaks and Anthony Galiton, and Winona and Roger Fielding.

He had ordered and studied the reports of state fire marshal George Schilling, Dr. Hamilton Brent, Dr. John Flood and the report of the late Professor Isaac Berman. He had spent almost a half hour on the telephone with Captain Earl Martin at state police headquarters in Mount Carmel. On two separate nights curious Spiceland County sheriff's deputies on patrol had witnessed an automobile licensed to J.J. Overton, in which Albert was recognized as the only passenger, parked on the public square near Albert's own downtown office, and had reported the incidents to state police.

It was considered unusual by state police that the Spiceland County prosecutor should be conferring in what appeared to be surreptitious meetings with the president of Bankmens Life Insurance Company. Unprivileged as he was to the topics of those two meetings, Lieutenant Conway, in a discussion about them with Galiton, could only surmise that Albert Fielding, in his quiet secretive manner, planned to leave no stone unturned in his own investigation of the senescent Fielding case.

During this time and for some days before Albert's election, the media, after having sensationalized the resurrection of Felix Dombriewski, had been almost devoid of any mention of the case. The few exceptions concerned renewed reports of Crestman Fielding having again been seen in cities in other states; one of which was Los Angeles, and another, Atlanta. Neither report was ever substantiated.

It was anyone's guess what effect these reports may have had on Albert Fielding. However, in a belated and expected request by him to Judge Harrison Alexander to convene a grand jury to inspect the Spiceland County Jail, which was normal first-of-a-new-year procedure, Albert had a surprise for Alexander. He also informed the court that he would have the grand jury evaluate all the available evidence pertaining to the Crestman Fielding case.

Although it was the duty of the county prosecutor to request a grand jury soon after the first of the year to inspect the jail, its accounts, and to examine any of the several county offices and or properties, such plans usually were announced in the newspaper before the request for a grand jury was made to the court. It followed, then, that the reason or reasons for the request were publicized in the newspaper. This was not a rule cut in stone. It was, nevertheless, common practice. But Albert's plans were kept secret from everyone, including his closest confidant, his wife Helen. And even after he had made his intent public, he was callously reticent to explain the reasons to anyone for his actions or what he expected from them.

On the morning of the seating of the grand jury, Albert, appearing stern and foreboding behind a black rope mustache and under a massive black hairdo that came down over his forehead, seemingly to rest on his thick, black eyebrows, paraded four men and two women into the circuit court room. There they were sworn by an unsmiling Judge Alexander who also cautioned them that while their findings in their inspection of the county jail would be a matter of public record, the testimony they were to hear in other matters was not, at least not until such times as it was released at the discretion of the county prosecutor.

Still stern of face, Albert then ushered the six persons to the jury room, leaving instructions with a bailiff at the door to allow no one in or out of the room except witnesses, as he himself should request and dismiss them. He then ordered the bailiff to close the door.

After reiterating the cautions expressed by Judge Alexander the first witness Albert called was Winona Fielding. As she made her way along the corridor from the courtroom where other waiting witnesses reclined in scattered seats, she appeared heavier of body than she had when last seen in public. Her face seemed swollen, and her eyes were obscured by dark glasses. She walked slowly, heavily, looking neither to the right nor to the left. After more than an hour, and reminded that she was sworn to secrecy and should speak to no one about her testimony, she reappeared from the jury room and left the courthouse. The second witness to be called was Roger Fielding, Winona's elder son. It was already nearing lunchtime when he left the jury room.

The first witness after lunch was Ira Brown, who was coroner at the time of the Fielding fire. He was followed by his son, Irwin, current coroner serving his second consecutive term. He was the last witness on the first day. For three more days after that, a long procession of witnesses moved in and out of the jury room. It came to a halt only because it was Friday evening. After the jurors were admonished to speak to no one about what had transpired in the jury room, they were excused for the weekend and ordered to be ready to resume their investigation at nine o'clock the following Monday morning.

That weekend Albert and Helen were nowhere to be found. That weekend, too, newspaper reporters and television and radio newscasters rehashed accounts of the Fielding fire and its subsequent investigation and played guessing games with what they speculated had come to light in the presence of the grand jury.

On Monday morning a smiling Albert Fielding, swinging a black attache case in one hand and carrying a stuffed, large manila envelope in the other, returned to his office in the courthouse. After conversing briefly with his deputy "Stash" Pinkala, a recent law school graduate, he made his way still smiling, but otherwise without ceremony, to the jury room where the four men and two women jurors had preceded him. The rest of that day and all day Tuesday and Wednesday, each new witness remained before the panel longer than those of the preceding week. Among them were state policemen Conway, Melton, Trueblood, Galiton and Oaks and former state police colonel William R. Carey, all of whom but Trueblood had been recalled a second time.

It was dinner time on Wednesday before Albert finished with the last witness of the long afternoon. Begging the indulgence of the grand jurors, Albert requested the bailiff to take the group to a dinner restaurant and to return them to the jury room at no later than half-past seven o'clock. Again he cautioned the men and women against discussing what had taken place in the jury room.

At ten o'clock that night, after questioning the last witness, the prosecutor warned the jurors to maintain their silence. He thanked them for performing their civic duty, and then he dismissed the four men and two women. Albert then asked the court reporter to telephone Judge Alexander at his home. However, Alexander was not expected for another hour, and did he want to leave a message? The prosecutor said he would await Judge Alexander's call in his office.

As he walked along the courthouse corridor to his office, Albert knew a sense of exhilaration. His deputy was speaking to someone on the office phone. "It's your wife," he said looking up at Albert.

"I'll take it in here, Stash," Albert said motioning to his own private office. He walked in and fell heavily into the spacious swivel chair and picked up the phone.

"Hi there," Pinkala heard him jovially greet his wife. The greeting was followed by a series of affirmative replies.

The telephone rang and as Pinkala reached for the second line button he heard Albert say to his wife, "That must be him on the other line now."

Pinkala spoke into the telephone and a man replied. The young attorney recognized the sharp metallic tones of the caller's voice.

"One second," Pinkala spoke into the phone, and he turned and called to Albert, "J. J. Overton on line two."

Albert said goodbye to his wife, promising to be home soon, and switched to the second line. "Yes sir," he spoke enthusiastically.

After a pause Albert spoke into the phone again. "Yes sir," Pinkala was later to divulge the side of the conversation he could hear. "They did it. Kidnap, murder, arson, unlawful flight to avoid prosecution."

In the stillness of the outer office in which he sat behind his own desk, Pinkala thought he could hear the sounds of jubilant responses come through

Albert's receiver. Then he heard Albert's voice. "I've got him where we want him, J.J.," Albert spoke emphatically into the phone. He hesitated. "Just one minute, hold on," he said as he put the phone down on his desk. Albert then got up and closed his office door.

Pinkala heard no more. Tempted though he was to pick up the extension and secretly listen to the continuing conversation between Albert and Overton, he didn't dare. Given the opportunity, he had learned early on as deputy prosecutor, his boss had a hair-trigger temper that once aroused turned him into a wrathful despot.

He satisfied himself with the knowledge that a telephone call from J.J. Overton to the prosecutor at that hour of the night, immediately after the dismissal of the grand jury investigating the Fielding case, might be considered by some as being highly irregular. It also occurred to the young Pinkala that Albert's action perhaps had even constituted a breach of ethics on the part of the prosecutor; more so since the judge of record had yet to be apprised of the grand jury's findings.

The next morning Judge Alexander was in his chambers in high spirits. His thoughts were of the belated election victory party of the previous night at which he had been the guest of honor. Because he had retired late after that affair and had risen early, he was aware of a nagging fatigue. But his re-election, coupled with the brief vacation afforded him by the year-end holidays and the back-slapping of friends and well-wishers the night before, had somewhat refreshed and invigorated him.

Besides that, in just a matter of a few weeks circuit court would shut down for the winter recess, and Alexander had plans to enjoy a long-awaited vacation in Florida. The judge's world at that moment, and his immediate future, could not have been more appealing.

His thoughts were suddenly interrupted by the buzzer on the intercom on his desk. Answering it he heard the voice of his court reporter announce that the county prosecutor was waiting to see him. Judge Alexander, for the first time since the grand jury had been dismissed, was about to learn from Albert Fielding of a surprising development. Crestman Fielding had been indicted by the grand jury on four separate counts. When the prosecutor made that announcement to Alexander it was so unexpected that the judge remained unusually silent, at the same time keeping Albert on his feet.

Albert either hadn't noticed the unintentional discourtesy, or didn't care, for he continued talking. Except for the report of the inspection of the jail, he requested that Alexander seal the entire grand jury proceedings. Although Alexander knew the request was unusual, he was bound by law to grant it. Albert further requested the court issue two warrants for the arrest of Crestman Fielding. In one warrant he asked that Fielding be charged with kidnap, and in the other, murder.

Albert also informed the judge that he additionally wanted two other warrants, one of them charging Fielding with arson, the other charging him with unlawful flight to avoid prosecution.

Alexander was surprised at the extent of the charges. But he said nothing to Albert except that he would have his court reporter prepare the warrants immediately.

Albert would later have his deputy inform the media only that indictments against Crestman Fielding had been returned by the grand jury, and define their explicit charges. Pinkala explained he could say nothing more, except that the proceedings were under court seal.

In connection with the charges, Pinkala was to also inform reporters that the assistance of the Federal Bureau of Investigation would be requested in the search for Crestman Fielding. It would mark the first time the FBI had been asked to participate in the case.

Subsequent print and electronic news stories had their effect. At the end of one week a report from Jefferson City, Missouri, placed Crestman Fielding in a tavern there with a black-haired woman. Another report the next day had the missing man in Miami. Similar reports arrived from two other cities in two separate other states. Commenting to his deputy on the conflicting reports, Albert smiled broadly.

"Sooner or later somebody is going to come up with the bastard, Stash," he said vehemently. "I don't know who, or where, or how, but sooner or later we're going to find him. I'm sure he didn't die in that fire."

Albert waved a hand in the direction of the single office window and added, "He's out there, someplace. We just need to be patient and we'll get him."

Pinkala said nothing.

ENIGMA

48

It was inconceivable to interim State Police Colonel John V. McKnight that the headquarters' working file of the Crestman Fielding investigation should vanish seemingly into thin air. The disappearance was not learned until Spiceland County Prosecutor Albert Fielding had requested a complete copy of the file. Among the first of several official steps taken by McKnight after the loss was discovered was to set in motion an all-out intra-department probe into the mystery.

Every detail, every scrap of printed and annotated written evidence kept on file at headquarters had disappeared. Unless it had walked away from its usual place in a four-drawer gray metal filing cabinet in a regiment of four-drawer gray filing cabinets, or flown away, neither of which McKnight knew was possible, the missing file undoubtedly had been mislaid or stolen.

Exactly how news of the loss was leaked to the media was as frustrating to McKnight as was the disappearance of the case report itself. Only after it had become public knowledge did a very red-faced Major Chester Vale, head of the state police headquarters clerical section, officially announce that the working file, including pertinent newspaper clippings and official written commentaries and elucidations which had been made part of the file, was missing. He added that it was his hope that it carelessly, even innocently, had been misplaced. He did not suggest that it might deliberately have been removed from its usual file space, nor did he utter the word "stolen" in connection with the disappearance. However, that word was readily supplied by a helpfully suggestive media. It was a week after that announcement before a harried Major Vale himself gently but bitterly implied publicly that the report may have been stolen. He speculated, but did not really want to believe, that someone within the department was certainly guilty. To add to his embarrassment and chagrin, someone within the department, "God only knows who at this time," he said, had also revealed to the media privileged investigational data relative to the Fielding case. He declined to explain this.

There had always been a leak of some kind in the state police department. McKnight knew that. He had always excused it by telling himself that state policemen were appointed from the ranks of men and women who were human. Had he been forthright in that respect, he might have allowed Vale to express that same degree of honesty to the public. But having been given command of state police in the wake of former superintendent William R. Carey's stolen gun scandal, McKnight now felt personally attacked, and, truth be known, he was incensed. In the short time since his appointment someone had leaked not one but two stories to the press, most recently the missing Fielding file, and the earlier FBI investigation of his predecessor which ultimately had brought about Carey's resignation.

Unlike previous major developments in the Fielding case, which regularly and deliberately had been released by Carey to the Mount Carmel *Morning Sun,* both stories, unrelated yet certainly inseparable, first appeared in *The Intelligencer* at Moses City before they were received by wire services for distribution to statewide subscribers. And McKnight, a cop for more than thirty years, found himself suspecting—although he was unable to prove it—a pipeline from somewhere in his department to the latter newspaper.

While serving as a lieutenant colonel in charge of personnel under Carey, McKnight had been aware of increased whisperings along the department grapevine that the handsome Carey with weekly regularity had been visiting a female resident of Catalpa Street in New Washington. When the story of the FBI investigation of the former colonel broke in Moses City's newspaper, before the appearance of the initial story of the missing file, McKnight was certain that someone at the newspaper had also known of Carey's secret relationship with the woman at New Washington. That someone had been patiently sitting on it, like a nesting hen on an egg, waiting for a tell-tale crack through which that clandestine liaison might be brought to light.

What had puzzled McKnight was how anyone on the paper in Moses City was able to learn that Carey was secretly being investigated by the FBI for possession of stolen government property. It was not the function of agents Gerard Thibideau and Harold Chelsea to give out such information. Nor was that information released by the bureau's Mount Carmel office. McKnight also knew that his own department had made every effort to keep the entire episode under wraps. Yet he was certain that a trusted member of his own department had snitched. But who? Why?

If it was someone with a grudge against Carey, he or she had more than evened the score, for after days of newspaper front page and six o'clock television stories the entire state knew that the esteemed Carey was not only found to be in possession of a government owned 45 caliber automatic pistol stolen from the Army Weapons Supply Center at Woodville, but that it had been a gift to him from an attractive New Washington widow reported by *The Intelligencer* to be his paramour.

Not in his wildest imaginings could McNight have suspected at this time, nor was he ever aware, as was the entire state police department never aware, that a married trooper in his command had been covertly involved with the wife of the editor of *The Intelligencer*. Whether that was the leak was never learned.

Carey's secret lover was identified as Martha Tilbertson, widow of the late George Tilbertson who until his retirement had been employed at the Army supply center. Tilbertson, before his untimely passing, either was a member of a ring of gun thieves on the Army payroll there, or was one of a number of unwitting victims of that group. Martha Tilbertson was quick to confess to a reporter from *The Intelligencer* that she was unaware that the weapon she had given to Carey was stolen. She gave it to Carey, she said, because it was huge and ugly and threatening in appearance and she was frightened of it and wanted it out of the house.

Unsavory publicity continually directed at Carey led the governor to suggest his resignation might be in order. In the end, however, the choice was not up to Carey. When he left the department he seemed satisfied to take with him his pension and retirement benefits, and a guarantee that he would not be prosecuted. There was nothing McKnight or anyone else could do for Carey. The popular colonel was out. Gone.

McKnight had publicly regretted Carey's loss. He

had been quoted as saying that, in his opinion, Carey had been a good friend, an exemplary policeman, an excellent administrator, and that his resignation was a painful and costly loss. He added that Carey, obviously, was the victim of unfortunate circumstances. He also had wished aloud that both Carey and the department might have been spared the unpleasant state of affairs, but they had not, and there was nothing he could do to change what had happened.

But there was something McKnight could do about the stolen Fielding case report. The primary computer file stored at headquarters was intact and safe. What was taken was the printed headquarters working file. Copies of printed working files of state police investigations were also kept at the barracks of origin. Therefore, from the outset, a printed file of the Fielding investigation was at the Moses City State Police Barracks. Except that a crime had been committed, the theft of the working file from headquarters had little or no effect on the investigation. It was, then, a matter of only a few minutes until a printout of the computer file was ready for delivery to Albert Fielding. In spite of that McKnight forthwith ordered Lieutenant Conway to place the working file at the Moses City barracks under lock and key.

49

At the truck stop called Tooter's one night, state troopers Anthony Galiton and Link Trueblood met for coffee. As soon as a waitress had served the two men, Trueblood demanded bluntly while a broad smile broke over his face, "Where's the Crestman Fielding case report?"

Feigning shock and fear Galiton pushed himself back from the table and raised his hands to his shoulders, palms facing Trueblood. "Don't ask me," his voice was pitched at least an octave higher than normal. "Ask Captain Martin."

Both troopers laughed.

"You really believe he took it?" Trueblood asked seriously, the smile gone.

"Do you?" retorted Galiton stirring sugar in his coffee.

"It was a damnfool thing to do, whoever did it," Trueblood mused. "Everything's also on file at the barracks. A guy would have to be crazy."

"Drunk, too," Galiton said meaningfully. "Desperate drunk. I'll bet there's nothing a certain someone would like more than to see my report of us dumping those bags of ashes destroyed."

"Yeah," agreed Trueblood. Then he added, "Doesn't make sense."

Galiton was silent.

"Even a rookie cop fresh out of the academy knows that every barracks has its own complete working file," Trueblood said.

"I'll tell you something," Galiton said placing his

elbows on the table and bringing his hands together in tent fashion, fingertips to fingertips. "And if you say I told you, I'll swear you're a liar."

When he hesitated the touch of a smile played at Trueblood's lips as he asked, "What?"

"Ever since this thing happened with Captain Martin, I've been keeping my own duplicate case report on everything I have done in this investigation," Galiton said returning the smile. "Neither Martin nor anyone else is going to catch me with my pants down."

Trueblood now smiled broadly. "You're not the only one, Gal," he said understandably. "This case has really messed things up at the barracks. Our people just don't trust one another anymore. Not like they used to. Ever since he got roasted by the department for buying Roger Fielding's house, Harley Oaks has been keeping his own file on this case, too. Newspaper stories and all. Told me so himself one night when he and his wife came over to play cards."

Despite their concern and caution, Galiton and Oaks would make few more if any entries in their secret files. In the wake of the grand jury investigation the Fielding probe had again come to a virtual stop. Weeks had passed and even the media had been silent about the matter. As it turned out those weeks were to mark the beginning of a long dormancy in the investigation that would evolve into months and years.

During the long silence little if anything was done by police agencies to find the missing Fielding and bring him to justice. During that quiet period the man wanted on four warrants for murder, arson, kidnap and being a fugitive from justice clearly had been forgotten. If in fact he was a fugitive from justice, no one but Winona seemed to care as to his whereabouts.

However, during this time she made no further public outburst, no public lament.

Meanwhile, despite some mildly surprising twists and turns, life in Moses City and Spiceland County had gone on. Since the departure of the Edward Colemans from Moses City months earlier—namely Breezy Coleman—a relieved Galiton was again happily married to Jeri. Free to think more clearly about their future together, he was seriously considering resigning from the state police department. On the eve of the seventh anniversary of the Fielding fire, he confided his plan to Trueblood.

"I'm thinking about running for sheriff of Spiceland County," he told him. "There's going to be another primary election before too long, and I'd like to be a part of it. If I can get elected I think I'll have as good a shot at the sheriff's office as anyone next election."

Sheriff's pay was of itself attractive, he explained to Trueblood. It was much more than he was earning as a state policeman. Fringe benefits, which included living quarters for the sheriff and his family and a salary for Jeri, who would serve in the capacity as jail matron, gave the position a tempting attraction that was difficult to ignore.

Additionally, he pointed out, he had nothing to lose; and he detailed how he could remain a state policeman during his campaign for the office and, should he win it, he could retire and take his state police retirement benefits with him. Should he lose his bid for that office, he could continue serving as a state policeman. It was such a lucrative, no-risk challenge that in recent years state policemen all around the state who were eligible for retirement had begun seeking sheriff posts.

Galiton had served the required minimum amount of time to be eligible for retirement from the state police department. Moreover, he was weary of and ready to separate himself from the long hours of traffic patrol and the many hours away from home. As a county sheriff he would be free from state police department restrictions and limitations, free to stay at home at night, if he so chose. He would be in charge. His work hours would be reduced. County sheriff was an enviable position. Considering the perks that accrued to the job, he would more than double his state police salary;   and being sheriff was, to a greater degree than ever before, still being a policeman.

Granted, he was not a politician, but in the years since Cramer Fielding had complained to Lieutenant Conway that the position of county sheriff reeked of politics, sheriffing in the state had undergone sophisticated changes. With more and more counties around the state converting sheriffs' departments to county police departments, that position required professional law enforcement experience, know-how and intelligence than was incumbent upon those who had held that position in previous years.

Trueblood congratulated Galiton. "Go to it. If I had my twenty years in I'd be tempted to do the same thing," he said.

By this time, Lieutenant Frank Conway had been promoted to the rank of major and was attached to headquarters in Mount Carmel. Timothy Melton had attained the rank of lieutenant colonel and was no longer district chief of state police investigations but had replaced McKnight as head of the department's personnel division after the governor had named McKnight interim superintendent of state police. Melton had more than enough years on the state police force to retire, but as he was to tell his wife, Mary, "Why should I? There are no more headaches around here."

Sadly in that time too, some life had come to an end. Wilson Hackler, the old man who claimed he had seen Crestman Fielding and a mystery man at the Dew Drop Inn at Hickory Grove before the Fielding fire, had passed away. Also dead was Ulys Hauser, the senior gentleman who said he had seen a Spiccland County sheriff's car near the Fielding home prior to the barn fire there. The Fielding neighbor who reported the fire to the Harrison Township Volunteer Fire Department, Mamie Verden, had also gone to her reward. And the esteemed Clare Downing, long-time Moses City attorney and attorney for Crestman Fielding before the fire, now suffering from a debilitating condition, was a resident in a Moses City nursing home.

Ineluctably time moved on and suddenly it was November again and Moses City and Spiceland County were caught up in another general election. As expected, Albert Fielding, who was unopposed for the post, was returned to the office of county prosecutor. Ira Brown succeeded his son, Irwin, who had served two terms as county coroner and, as was the practice of the father son team, named his son deputy coroner. Although a number of other persons were reelected, or elected to office for the first time, only one of these stood out. That was state trooper Anthony Galiton who was elected to the office of county sheriff. At 12:01 a.m. on the first day of January the following year, more than eight years after the mysterious fire at the Fielding home, Galiton, along with other election victors, stood before judge Harrison Alexander to be duly sworn to uphold his new duties.

THE ARENA

50

Although it was late February, Christmas decorations and strings of colorful lights still clung to the roof and eaves of the Dogwood County Courthouse in the center of the Hickory Grove public square.

It had been an unseasonably cold December and January, and it was still quite cold. For that reason county workers responsible for installing the holiday adornments were awaiting warmer weather to remove them.

Though the decorations did appear out of place in late February, no one was heard to complain. Courthouse visitors intent on personal and government business arrived and left without concern or comment about them. Winter tourists, most of whom were there to enjoy skiing on the surrounding snow covered hills and on the popular man-made slides paid them no mind.

Constructed at the turn of the century, the courthouse itself was of an unusual early architectural design. To a first-time visitor, the presence of medieval knights in armor guarding the entrances to the building would not have appeared incongruous. Some seven decades after its construction it probably seemed as out of place in the center of Hickory Grove as did its Christmas decorations in the month of February.

A masonry structure of limestone and red brick, it rose three stories from a solid limestone foundation. Huge, bronze double doors, were set one in the east facade of the building and one at the west. Each of these opened at street level onto wide expanses of limestone slab public square walkways. Built of split faced limestone, a bell tower—with no bell—had vertical slot apertures under four gaping circular openings for clock faces near its top—but no clocks. It rose from ground level at one front corner of the building to several feet above a carved limestone balustrade that enclosed a terrace roof. Gray limestone quoins set in random sizes at the four corners of the building and around tall, narrow windows with limestone keystone insets at their arched tops added to the castle-like appearance of the building.

On a limestone ledge above the east doorway, which was the main means of accessing the building, there stood a five-foot high gray limestone carving of a stately gowned female. In one limestone hand she held a limestone torch, and in the other a balanced scale also carved from gray limestone. Depicting justice, the word "Justice" had been carved into the statue's limestone base. Over the years the statue was often referred to as "Lady Justice."

At one time in its long life, the arm holding the scales was mysteriously broken and for several years while that member was missing, the statue became the butt of local wiseacres who when the opportunity afforded quipped, "There is no longer any justice in Dogwood County."

The statue was eventually repaired, but, much to the disappointment of many, the replaced hand was devoid of the scales. This led to jeers by some that, "There still ain't no justice in Dogwood County."

Inside the building, against the west wall on the top floor, in plain view at the revered seat of justice was the name plate of the circuit court judge of record:

Jacob M. Mosco a native New Yorker. Having lived in Hickory Grove for many years he was well-liked there, and on the golf links and at the Hickory Grove Country Club he was familiarly known as "Jake."

A gallery at the east side of the room, facing the bench, had a seating capacity for about eighty spectators. Immediately in front of the gallery, with their backs to it, stood the twelve juror and two alternate seats. They were comparatively modern juror chairs; padded, swivelled, fastened to the floor, obviously recent replacements of older chairs. Though seven of them were on a higher level than the other seven, there was no rail separating the chairs from the rest of the courtroom. Almost directly in front of the jury seats were the long, oak tables of the prosecuting and defense attorneys. And at some distance in front of them were the bench and witness stand, the latter rising two steps above the courtroom floor.

Large squares of discolored green and brown tiles in a garish marble swirl pattern covered the floor. The fluorescent light-lined ceiling had at one time been lowered, and though it was bright and attractive it struck the high narrow windows unbecomingly at about two-thirds of their height, giving them the awkward appearance of having been only partially completed.

Courthouse employees down through the years made a joke of responding to inquiries about the architectural style of the building as being "Early Dogwood County." Such derision was usually followed by, "And they put holes in the bell tower for four clock faces but they forgot to put in the clocks."

During warm weather it was not unusual to see on the northwest corner of the courthouse square a huckster, his harvest of vegetables and fruits for sale spread over the flat bed of his parked farm truck.

Weather permitting, nearby benches ideally situated on the courthouse lawn in the shade of some tall maple trees there held the usual collection of courthouse loungers. Often referred to as "liars' benches," on this day they were abandoned by their liars to the February cold.

Because of the biting cold people moved with brisk motions on the limestone slab pedestrian sidewalks flanking the municipal streets around the courthouse. One of them was a figure unfamiliar to the courthouse. He was Moses City attorney Ames Shaw. Bundled against the cold in a heavy overcoat and wearing on his head, pulled down over his ears, a long, maroon and cream colored woolen toque, such as those worn by members of a toboggan club, he walked toward the east entrance to the courthouse.

In the crook of one arm Shaw carried pressed to his chest, a soft, pliable brown leather brief case. Now more than eight years after the faceless, charred, dismembered corpse was discovered in the barn fire at the Crestman Fielding home, a decisive, but not yet quite final act of that mystery was soon to be played out in the Dogwood County Courthouse.

51

The winter—what was left of it—seemed to pass at a snail's pace. Eventually spring did arrive and one day soon afterward there appeared on the front page of *The Intelligencer* a news story about the Crestman Fielding hearing scheduled to begin the first Monday in May. In part the story read:

> Crestman Fielding's wife, Winona, is asking Dogwood County Circuit Court Judge Jacob M. Mosco to declare her husband legally dead so that she may claim the one million six-hundred thousand dollars in benefits, plus interest, from four insurance companies that had insured his life.
>
> The insurance companies claim Fielding is not dead but has been eluding police for more than eight years. The insurance companies are being represented by Moses City attorney Hector Jamiel.
>
> The hearing was moved from Spiceland County to Dogwood County after Jamiel filed a motion for a change of venue. Supporting the motion he cited possible prejudice because of years of local newspaper publicity and Spiceland Circuit Judge Harrison Alexander's past friendship with Crestman Fielding.
>
> The hearing is the outgrowth of a fire at the Fielding home more than eight years ago in which Fielding is alleged to have been burned beyond recognition after taking his own life . . .

Awaiting the bailiff's call to order while seated in the courtroom before the bench at the plaintiff's table that Monday morning, Ames Shaw was reviewing his notes. Heading the list was the name of Felix Dombriewski.

He had clipped and read *The Intelligencer* articles concerning Dombriewski's return from the dead. Most of them were long and detailed, but the message for Shaw was a simple one. Dombriewski was alive and well and certainly not buried in the Fielding cemetery plot as authorities had believed.

Under police interrogation Dombriewski not only denied ever having been acquainted with Crestman Fielding or ever before having been in Hickory Grove, Moses City or Spiceland County, the man insisted he was not aware of the existence of Fielding, his family, or of such places. At the request of police he willingly submitted to a polygraph test and was found to be telling the truth.

Despite this victory, for which Shaw was grateful, a live Dombriewski constituted only half the legal battle awaiting him, and he knew it. He knew he would still have to produce enough evidence that the dead man in the Fielding cemetery plot in Moses City's Memorial Park was Crestman Fielding. Moreover, he would have to show beyond a reasonable doubt that Fielding had died by his own hand, and that his body had been disfigured beyond recognition by an ensuing accidental barn fire at the Fielding home.

That, Shaw knew, could be difficult, especially since a preponderance of evidence against such a conclusion would surely be presented by state police and attorneys for the insurance companies involved. Yet, Shaw also knew that no one but the Fielding family had claimed the body of the dead man, that no other person had been reported missing. And it was a fact that Crestman Fielding was indeed missing. On those grounds alone he should, at this late date, be declared legally dead. And Shaw was determined that the hearing judge should agree.

Shaw was not unmindful of the fact that a dead man buried in the Fielding cemetery plot more than eight years earlier was believed by state police and others to be someone other than Fielding, a dead man identified only as "John Doe." In possession of the late Dr. Isaac Berman's examination report of that body in the grave, in which the renowned anthropologist concluded that it was the body of the missing Crestman Fielding, Shaw was prepared to pull out all possible legal stops to win for Winona Fielding the right to her husband's insurance benefits.

Although he felt moderately comfortable with that, Shaw also took additional assurance from the highly publicized bungling by state police surrounding their initial investigation of the fire; and from the knowledge that the county coroner and his deputy had made some procedural errors. He was determined to argue that their decisions had been strongly—if not too strongly—influenced by state police. He was similarly cognizant of the past questionable friendship between the former head of state police and the president of the primary insurance company that shared the face value of the insurance policy on Fielding's life.

Shaw certainly was not unaware that there had been and still were indications of serious contention among state police concerning the Fielding case. It might be interesting, he had told himself, to see what effect this internal strife with all of its ramifications might have on Judge Mosco. Still, Shaw knew that while state police in-fighting might make interesting reading and listening, in the end a decision would be based solely on the facts of the case and their legal interpretation. That is all he could expect from Judge Mosco. Nonetheless he felt that he was in possession of a hole card and when the time was right he would reveal it. It was on that hole card that he believed the hearing could turn in his favor.

Shaw looked toward the defense table. He was acquainted with Hector Jamiel, an attorney of some repute in Moses City. Jamiel at the moment seemed intent on poring over notes scrawled on a legal pad. He was a big man, well over six feet, blond hair and red of face.

Shaw's gaze swept the courtroom and came to rest on the gallery. With seating room for eighty persons, there were perhaps one fourth that number of people in attendance. Not like the old days, Shaw thought. Not that he had experienced such times. He'd been in practice less than ten years and, in the view of some of his older colleagues, was still damp behind the ears. However, he had heard stories from his senior law partners, each of whom was old enough to be his father, speak of the "good old days" when courtrooms were also places of public interest and entertainment. People would come from miles around the county to hear cases argued. On rainy days when farmers were unable to work in their fields the gallery was always crowded.

Courtrooms no longer held that degree of interest for people. There was too much else to do, too many other demands on people's time. If they desired court-room drama they turned on their televisions at night from the comfort of easy chairs in their homes. In view of the change, county courtrooms in larger cir-cuits around the state had been renovated, making them smaller, in many cases arranging two or three separate modern courtrooms from one large ancient one. These had been supplied with new names and

younger judges. Shaw had seen a few of such courtrooms, and he secretly envied the attorneys who regularly practiced in them. Similar courtrooms would
one day come to rural jurisdictions such as Dogwood
and Spiceland counties. But from his present seat
Shaw felt as though he was peering out of a distant
time frame.

THE ACTION

52

Among the first witnesses called to testify on Monday was Ira Brown who was coroner at the time of the fire at the Fielding home.

Now eighty, he was slow and somewhat confused in his answers to attorney Hector Jamiel who represented the insurance companies. As he spoke it was learned for the first time that late on that afternoon in mid-November Irwin had entered the funeral home and announced to his father, "I was just up at Crestman Fielding's and his barn is on fire."

Ira said he had studied his son for a moment and then asked, "Did you see Crestman?" According to the father, Irwin had shaken his head and said, "No I didn't." Ira said that his son might have continued speaking if the ringing of the telephone hadn't interrupted him.

It had taken Jamiel so much time to get this much out of the elderly man that he asked Ira Brown to relate his recollections to the hearing judge as he best remembered them.

"Well, they'd called to tell us that they had found a body up there," he began recounting. "And Irwin and I went up there. I was the county coroner then, too, and Irwin was my deputy, like now. There was a body up there all right. We found him in the ashes with a burned-up shotgun across his chest. We took it for granted that it was Crestman Fielding and that he had committed suicide. I knew he was in some kind of trouble, but I didn't think it was that bad."

The witness reached for a small plastic cup of water

on a stand at his elbow and took a sip. Replacing the cup he continued, "I picked up what was left of the gun from the body. It was lying across the body like this"—he drew an imaginary line from his right hip to his left shoulder—"and I picked it up and handed it to Link Trueblood, the state policeman.

"Well, now wait." Doubt had crept into Ira Brown's voice. "There were two policemen there. Link, and also Cramer—Sheriff Cramer Fielding—Crestman's brother. Well, I gave the gun to one of them and he broke it down and there was one shell in it and it had been shot. I said to Cramer, 'What would cause Crestman to do a thing like that?' And Cramer said, 'I don't know.'"

Ira Brown interrupted his recollections to say, "I liked Crestman. He treated me nice all the years I knew him, and I knew him all his life." He cleared his throat and went on, "After Cramer said what he did, we put the body in a body bag. We took it for granted it was Crestman Fielding. I never thought of him as a man who would ever shoot himself. I figured he had serious problems that I never knew anything about, and that he might have killed himself.

"The body was in good shape from here to there—" Ira Brown placed his hands at his thighs and moved them to his neck. "He didn't have a face; it was blown away. He didn't have any hands or feet, they were burned off at the elbows and the knees. It wasn't a very nice thing to see. We looked for shot pellets from the shotgun shell, but we couldn't find any. We began to get worried. We wondered what had happened up there. After we got the body to the mortuary we took a blood sample out of his heart and gave it to his brother, Cramer. Next morning we took the body in for an autopsy and we were told that Crestman didn't die of a gunshot but of carbon monoxide poisoning."

Again Ira Brown hesitated to sip from the cup of water. Apologizing then, he said, "I didn't mean Crestman. I meant the dead man, whoever he was. Anyway, this man didn't have any teeth. I knew Crestman had teeth. I looked in the sheet we had him wrapped in, and I ran my finger all around inside the dead man's mouth."

At this juncture in Ira Brown's testimony audible sighs were heard followed by a shifting of feet in the gallery. Judge Mosco raised his eyes peeringly to the spectators in the balcony.

Clearing his throat, Ira Brown continued: "There were no teeth in either place. I had my doubts then, but I thought maybe the shot blew out all his teeth, too; I don't know. I still believe that could have been Crestman. They've been saying for eight years that he is still alive, that he has been seen in Mexico and other places. I don't know whether to believe that stuff. There's not much proof. But if he's alive you'd think the insurance companies would either have to produce him or pay off."

Hector Jamiel was seen to lower his head and shake it from side to side at Ira Brown's last words. There was little the defense attorney could do about them; they had been spoken. But he tried. "Your honor," he addressed Judge Mosco. "We ask that the witness's last statement be stricken from the record."

Judge Mosco thought for a few moments and then said, "I think I'll let them stand. Call your next witness, Mr. Jamiel."

The defense attorney for the insurance companies called Irwin Brown to the witness stand. His testimony differed little from that given by his father, except that Irwin made it clear that he still believed the dead man was someone other than Crestman Fielding.

"There's been nothing new that would make me change my mind," he said under cross examination by Ames Shaw. "I hate that, too. Crestman was a close friend of mine." Before Shaw could ask another question Irwin continued, "But he still was not the kind of guy who would desert his family. He wasn't the kind of guy to do anything crazy. He was a big, slow, easy-going guy. You could say a dozen words while he was saying one. He always did for his family. Always thought his family was better than anyone else's. I liked him."

"When did you begin to doubt the dead man was Crestman Fielding?" Shaw asked.

"When the state police said it wasn't."

"Now Mr. Brown," Shaw raised his voice slightly, "if you doubted the dead man was Crestman Fielding, why did your firm continue to send Fielding's wife Winona a bill for the funeral services for a man you believed to be someone other than her husband?"

For long moments Irwin Brown remained silent, his face impassive. When he spoke his words were barely audible.

"Well," he cleared his throat, "we did think it was Crestman who died there in that fire. And I guess I thought that it would be proven some day that it was. But I felt like I had to wait for the state police to say it was."

"Have you always been on good terms with state police?"

"Yes. I always tried to cooperate with them."

"Did you ever want to be a state policeman, Mr. Brown?"

Jamiel was on his feet. "Your Honor," he addressed Judge Mosco while glaring at Shaw, "I object to that question. It has no relevance to the purpose of this hearing."

"Sustained," Mosco murmured. "Mr. Shaw—," he began.

"No more questions for this witness, Your Honor," Shaw said nodding toward the bench and resuming his seat at the plaintiff's table.

After Irwin had spoken those conflicting emotions one witness after another was methodically questioned in detail by attorneys for both sides, and the first day of the hearing passed.

The second day began quietly. So near boring was the droning course of due process that by mid-afternoon Judge Mosco appeared to be reclining in the swivel chair in which he was seated behind the bench. He rested his right elbow on the bench top and supported his inclined head by holding his right palm to his face. His mood underwent a surprising change when Spiceland County's new sheriff, former state trooper Anthony Galiton was called to testify.

"There were too many discrepancies in the evidence I was able to find," Galiton said loudly and clearly in answer to Jamiel's first question. "My opinion is based on what I was able to learn from my own investigation, from the scientific evidence made available to me, and from what I was told. I don't believe it was Crestman Fielding's body that was found in that fire."

Under cross examination by Shaw, a red-faced Galiton explained how the evidence he and trooper Link Trueblood had collected after the Fielding fire had ended up in the Spiceland County landfill, and why.

"And in spite of that lost evidence you still disagree with the opinion of the man who was your superior, now Lieutenant Colonel Melton?" Shaw asked pointedly.

Taking pains to avoid the use of Melton's name, Galiton replied, "I can't speak of what someone else believes; I believe someone other than Crestman Fielding was dead in that fire."

"Then who is the dead man buried in the Fielding family plot in the Moses City Memorial Park?" Shaw demanded, raising his voice.

"I don't know."

"Did you ever try to learn the identity of the dead man?"

"No. Not really. Not after the Dombriewski thing."

"Did state police ever try to learn the identity of the dead man?"

"Yes."

"Were they able to learn his identity?"

"We thought so with Dombriewski. But we were wrong."

Shaw stood up and moved closer to the witness stand. Stopping within a few feet of Galiton he pointed a finger at the former trooper and demanded in forceful tones, "Then how can you be so sure that the dead man is not Crestman Fielding?"

Galiton was silent for a few moments before he said quietly, "I can only believe what I believe."

As though he was surprised and dumbfounded by that answer, Shaw stood rooted, shaking his head from side to side as he studied Galiton. Then he took a different tack.

"Isn't it true," he began, "that instead of immediately trying to learn the identity of the dead man, state police spent several weeks of their time watching the home of Mrs. Fielding, hoping she would lead them to her missing husband?"

"As far as watching Mrs. Fielding is concerned, we were following orders—"

"You mean," Shaw interrupted him, "that you were told to ignore the importance of the identity of the dead man because state police suspected an innocent, penniless widow of fraud and deceit?"

"We did try to identify the dead man," Galiton answered in a raised voice. "For a good while we were pretty sure the dead man was Felix Dombriewski."

"Yes, we know all about that," Shaw said scornfully. "Just how many months of your investigation were wasted on that presumption?"

Just as Galiton opened his mouth to reply, Shaw turned from the witness and waving a hand said loudly, "That is all."

As Galiton stood up to leave the witness stand Shaw suddenly whirled on him and called out, "One moment please," and he again approached Galiton who had resumed his seat.

"Remember, you are still under oath, Sheriff Galiton," Shaw began. "Had you ever made the remark at any time that you believed Lieutenant Colonel Melton was in collusion with Mrs. Fielding to share in the insurance money if she was ever to be awarded that money?"

The question was what Shaw believed to be half of his hole card. It was completely unexpected and had the effect of a bombshell in the courtroom. Jamiel was on his feet but before he could speak Galiton straightened in the witness chair with a sudden motion and blurted out, "Hell no! I never said anything like that."

"Had you heard anyone else say that?"

"Well there was always a lot of talk about this case," Galiton replied.

"Among state policemen?"

"Yes, but—"

"Was there also talk about Colonel Carey to the effect that if it could be proven that Fielding was alive—," Shaw had chosen this moment to submit the other half of the hole card, "—he stood to collect a handsome reward from his good friend J.J. Overton, president of the primary insurance company in this case?"

"Well . . . , you . . . ," Galiton stammered.

"Was there or wasn't there?"

"There's always some kind of talk going on some-place—," Galiton began.

"That is all."

Raising a hand in the direction of the witness at that moment as though he were waving farewell, Shaw spun around and returned to his seat, leaving Galiton open-mouthed.

"You may step down," Judge Mosco said softly to him.

It was past lunchtime and Judge Mosco called a halt to the hearing until two o'clock in the afternoon. At that time Lieutenant Colonel Timothy Melton took the stand. Defense attorney Jamiel raised a hand in Mosco's direction and said, "We have no questions for this witness at this time,"

Shaw bounded up from his seat and strode to the witness stand. "Colonel," he began loudly, "why is it that you seem to be the only state police investigator in this case to believe that Crestman Fielding died in that fire at his home?"

Before Melton could answer, Shaw raised a hand to stop him. "Let me rephrase that, Colonel. I'll ask you this: are you conspiring with Winona Fielding to defraud the insurance companies of one million six-hundred thousand dollars?"

Melton had straightened as though from a blow to his back. "That's preposterous," he snorted.

"Answer the question, please, Colonel. Yes or no?"

"No," Melton replied with a shake of his head.

"Has Captain Martin of the state police laboratory made some kind of deal with the insurance companies?"

Jamiel was on his feet shouting objections.

"I'm going to allow the question," Mosco nodded in his direction. He leaned slightly in Melton's direction and said, "You may answer."

"You'll have to ask him," Melton shrugged his shoulders.

"Do you believe he would do a thing like that?" Shaw asked.

Jamiel again objected. Mosco again allowed the question.

Melton's eyes bored into Shaw for a few moments before answering. Then he said, "Sorry. I can speak only for myself."

"Is it true that Captain Martin is secretly looked upon in the state police department as a heavy drinker? An alcoholic?"

Jamiel had raised a hand. "Objection," he called out to Judge Mosco.

"I withdraw the question." Shaw raised his palms in the direction of the bench. And turning again to Melton he asked, "Your former superintendent? William Carey. Do you believe he is being paid by the insurance companies for saying the dead man is someone other than Fielding?"

Jamiel again objected.

"Sustained," said Mosco.

"Galiton, then?" Shaw pushed on.

"Galiton has a mind of his own," Melton said as he took hold of the arms of the witness chair and pushed himself into its back. "I've tried to get Galiton and a few others to see the light of day in this case, but I think they are prejudiced. I think they were so inclined from the start. In my opinion they allowed their prejudice to destroy an innocent family. I have told them as much."

"And you? Are you not also prejudiced in your own opinion?" Shaw had wisely asked.

"Definitely not," said Melton. "Just take a look at what has happened to that family in the past eight years. They have lost everything, their homes, their friends, their community, their dignity, and each other. How could anyone believe they'd be playing such a charade for this many years? How could they want to live through a nightmare such as this one has been for them? Policemen, good policemen do not decimate families as has been done to this family. Just look back, and think how they have been treated. Look back at the Dombriewski thing. My God, they went to great lengths to dig up somebody to fit their needs. And you see what happened there."

For the moment Shaw seemed satisfied and returned to the plaintiff's table. It was then that Jamiel stood up and addressed the bench.

"I have some questions for the witness before he is excused, Your Honor."

Melton was then asked by Jamiel if he believed an attempt was being made by Winona Fielding to defraud the insurance companies.

"No, I don't believe that, and never did," Melton quickly responded, his voice loud enough to carry throughout the courtroom. "I had taken part in the investigation from the very beginning and I found no reason to suspect a conspiracy."

Before Jamiel could ask another question Melton continued, "And I was unable to find any evidence that Mr. Fielding escaped the fire. My opinion is that Mr. Fielding died in the fire."

It was nearing four o'clock and Judge Mosco adjourned the hearing until nine o'clock the following morning, cautioning Melton that he was still under oath and that he could be asked to resume the witness stand the next day. When the hearing resumed the next morning it was Shaw and not Jamiel who faced Melton again.

"I'll be brief," Shaw said matter-of-factly. "One question, maybe two. Were you aware during this entire investigation that personal differences were hampering state police efforts to bring this matter to a satisfactory close?"

"Absolutely," Melton replied. "No question about it."

"How did that manifest itself?"

"It is hard to put your finger on something like that," Melton said, leaning forward in his chair. "You just know that the cooperation is not there, mainly. And there was interference from above."

"Interference from whom?"

"Well, there were at least two supervisors of the investigation. Maybe three. One in Moses City and the others in Mount Carmel."

"Namely?"

"It was Major Conway's case, in his district. But he was often upstaged by Colonel Carey and Captain Martin."

"And you?"

"No. Major Conway's and my opinion of this case were—and still are—miles apart, but I tried to cooperate with him in every other instance. I think we had a good relationship."

"But there was strife and personal differences in the state police department over this matter," Shaw insisted.

"Well," Melton was thoughtful for a moment before he answered, "if you mean there was a difference of opinion concerning this case, the answer is yes."

"Do you think it had a negative effect on the outcome? Do you think we would be where we are now had there been no discord among investigating state policemen?"

Jamiel was striking a palm on the table in front of him shouting an objection before Shaw had finished asking the last question.

In the ensuing silence Judge Mosco looked directly at Shaw then at Jamiel before shifting his gaze to the witness.

"You may answer," he said.

"Well, speaking from my own experience, any time you have conflict in a matter such as this one, you are going to have serious problems," Melton said.

The next witness called was retired state policeman Brad Schultz. When Jamiel had finished with him he was approached by Shaw who asked if he too was of the opinion that the dead man found in the fire was Crestman Fielding.

"I was called to take part in the investigation after the body was removed from the fire scene," Schultz said. "I at first had no opinion who the dead man was. But from what I was able to learn, and from my brief investigation and from reading Dr. Berman's report, I concluded the dead man had to be Fielding."

Shaw thanked the witness and nodded toward the defense table.

Speaking from where he was seated, Jamiel began unctuously. "Now Mr. Schultz, I'd like to believe that is your honest opinion. But is it possible that your opinion may be somewhat prejudiced?"

"No," Schultz said flatly, sitting up a little straighter.

"Is this what your superior at the time of the fire, Superintendent Carey, believed? Did he believe Crestman Fielding's body was found in the ashes of that fire?"

"No, he did not."

"Weren't you and Mr. Carey estranged from each other at that time, Mr. Schultz? Didn't you and Mr. Carey have personal differences unrelated to your work as state policemen? And didn't this affect your working relationship with Mr. Carey? "

"I don't know what you mean."

At some point during the early weeks of the investigation into the Fielding fire, Shaw had been apprised of state police department scuttlebutt that Carey had at one time made a pass at Schultz's attractive wife. Perceiving where Jamiel's questioning was leading, Shaw stood up and offered an objection. But the damage had been done. Jamiel need not have gone any further. The seed of personal differences and disunity among state police involved in the Fielding investigation by this time had been well planted. But Jamiel was not quite finished.

"Now Mr. Schultz," he continued. "Did you not take this stance just to oppose Colonel Carey's belief, at that time?"

"No. I reached this opinion independently, honestly, from my own investigation."

"Did you reach a conclusion as to how the man you believe was Crestman Fielding died, then, Mr. Schultz?"

"Nobody but God will ever know the circumstances surrounding Fielding's death," Schultz calmly uncrossed his legs and then recrossed them and leaned further back in his seat, outwardly assured of what he was about to say. "He may have set the fire and then shot himself or been murdered and his killer put him in there. In my investigation I was trying to ascertain if it was Fielding's body found in that fire. I eventually assured myself that it was. From the very beginning it was believed that this was not a homicide."

Former state police superintendent William Carey, now past fifty, but as impressive in bearing and handsome as ever, was then called to testify. Upright on the stand taking the oath, his six-foot-six height dwarfed the medium-sized bailiff.

"I was not convinced that Mr. Fielding was the victim of suicide or that he died in that fire," he answered Jamiel's first question. "Furthermore, I am still not convinced."

Apparently that was all Jamiel cared to have entered into the record from Carey and after a few ineffective questions he turned and nodded to Shaw.

"Mr. Carey," Shaw began, "were you not a lodge brother and a good friend of J.J. Overton, president of State Bankmens Life Insurance Company?"

"I still am."

"Mr. Carey, was it not at Mr. Overton's insistence that you played a leading role in the Fielding investigation?"

"My role was that of an involved police official," Carey asserted.

"Of course," Shaw agreed. "Mr. Carey, are you and Mr. Overton still good friends?"

"Yes."

Still lodge brothers?"

"Yes."

"Were not the two of you also friends with the governor?"

"Yes," he answered.

"Mr. Carey," Shaw had moved nearer to the witness stand and in a low voice he asked sharply, very nearly sneeringly, "Is it true that the governor had telephoned you regarding the Fielding matter?"

"It is."

"Wasn't this unusual?"

Before Carey could reply, Shaw employed a tactic he had used on Galiton. He spun away from the witness and, waving a hand, said loudly, "That is all."

Then as Judge Mosco leaned in Carey's direction to tell him that he could step down, Shaw turned and called, "I'm sorry, Your Honor. I have one more question for the witness."

"Very well," the judge addressed Shaw. Then nodding to Carey he said, "You may answer, Mr. Carey."

"Mr. Carey," Shaw began. "Detective Schultz disagreed with you on the identity of the dead man, is that right?"

"Yes it is."

"Is that not the reason you took him off the investigation, Mr. Carey?"

"No."

"Come now, Mr. Carey," Shaw had become friendly. "Did you not believe that Detective Schultz disagreed with your opinion because of personal differences between the two of you? Something unrelated to police work? And you relieved him?"

"No, that is not true," Carey's face had reddened at the insinuation and he had leaned forward.

"Come now, Mr. Carey," Shaw continued soothingly. "Wasn't he about the best detective in the state police department at that time? Why didn't you keep him on the investigation?"

Carey didn't hesitate. "We had plenty of capable people down here already."

"Not because you didn't like him?"

Jamiel got to his feet. "Objection Your Honor. Where is counsel supposed to be going with his questions?"

Shaw raised a hand in the judge's direction and said, "No more questions Your Honor. I am finished with this witness."

After the testimony of the state policemen, it was apparent to everyone in the courtroom that there had been suspicion and distrust among them concerning the Fielding case. Was Melton guilty of scheming with Winona? Was there a payoff for Carey should it be proven that Fielding was alive? With the implications of those questions still ringing in the courtroom, Mosco called a recess until nine o'clock the next morning.

By mid-afternoon of the following day the hearing had settled into the humdrum of legal technicalities and defense and plaintiff speculations. Boredom seemed to enshroud the courtroom. It was at that time that PJ Cayne, *The Intelligencer's* police reporter, began wondering if Judge Mosco had become weary, if he was giving his full attention to every word that was being spoken, for he seemed, to the newspaper reporter, to be dozing. The judge's right leg crossed over his extended left leg appeared to accentuate that impression.

Cayne also had noticed that the bailiff, at a desk to one side of the bench, his right elbow on the desktop, his chin in his right hand, also sat unmoving. The afternoon wore on and the gallery had dwindled down to only a few spectators who made their presence known by twisting and shifting on the creaky wooden benches. Occasionally one of them would carefully tiptoe to the heavy double oaken doors and silently leave the room, the massive bronze hinges on the large door signaling the exit by grating and groaning loudly as it closed.

It was during this lull that Dr. Hamilton Brent had been called to the stand. He was being questioned by Jamiel, who appeared assured and comfortable while seated at the defense table. When he was finished with his witness Jamiel turned and nodded toward Shaw.

"Your witness," he said softly.

It was getting on toward late afternoon. Jamiel was quietly gathering up a collection of papers from the table and slipping them into his briefcase in preparation for his departure as soon as Shaw had finished with his cross examination of the witness. On the surface it seemed that no one was paying any attention to Shaw and Brent. That is, until Brent's voice suddenly filled the courtroom.

"I am now totally and completely convinced," he was saying, "that the dead man is Crestman Fielding."

What was Shaw's question? It no longer mattered. Before Shaw could ask another question, the courtroom had come alive with the alerted sounds and motions of what few persons remained in the gallery; the motions of people waking up, sitting up, straightening up, and standing up. Judge Mosco had also sat up with a noticeable squeal from his swivel chair. The court bailiff dropped his hand from his chin to the desk top in front of him with an unintentional loud thump. The court reporter, yielding to an obvious surge of renewed energy, in one quick motion threw her shoulders back and her bosom forward. Attorney Jamiel was on his feet.

Ever since he had examined the dead man after the fire and the body had been exhumed from the grave in the Fielding family cemetery, Brent had been unshakable in his opinion that the victim found in the Fielding fire was someone other than Crestman Fielding.

Now, more than eight years later, Brent had chosen the witness stand from which to announce what seemed to be an earth-shaking about-face. It was the most stunning development in the eight year old case. Why Brent had not spoken those words while under direct questioning by defense attorney Jamiel was not known. Perhaps it was because the question had not been put to him. Jamiel had asked him point-blank if certain statements about the identity of the dead man made early in the investigation and attributed to him were true, to which he had answered affirmatively and honestly each time; but Jamiel apparently had not considered the direct question necessary since it was well known that Brent had from the early days of the investigation believed the dead man was someone other than Crestman Fielding.

Why Brent had reserved the timing of the bombshell until under cross examination by Shaw was never explained. Had the rules of discovery been suspended for the hearing? Were there any? Was it a failure on the part of defense attorney? Was it simply because of the way Shaw had phrased the question: "And in your professional opinion the dead man was Crestman Fielding?"

It was the first time that either of the pathologists in the case had even so much as hinted that the dead man might have been Crestman Fielding. Of the three professionals originally involved, the late Dr. Isaac Berman was the only one on record to believe the dead man in the fire was Fielding.

"Yes," Brent replied. "Yes, that is my belief now."

There was more stirring and shuffling noise in the courtroom. Particularly affected by Brent's disclosure was Winona Fielding. She was seen to suddenly straighten up in her chair where she sat alone at the plaintiff's table, to uncross and recross her legs, and to cough noisily. To anyone in the courtroom who cared to notice, her fleshy face had become ripe tomato red. Had Shaw been seated by her side at that moment, instead of standing before the witness chair as he was, she might have leaned in his direction for support for she seemed to be unbalanced in her chair.

Quickly recovering from his surprise, Jamiel, already on his feet in reaction to Brent's avowal, charged toward the witness stand as though he would attack Brent. Stopping midway there he turned toward Judge Mosco and shouted an objection.

"Your Honor," he continued, "this witness is already on record as saying that he believed from his initial examination of the body that the dead man was someone other than Crestman Fielding!"

Before the judge could reply, Brent spoke up. "Yes," he said quietly. "That is true."

Ignoring the judge, Jamiel raised his voice sharply and demanded of Brent, "Isn't it unusual, then, that you should change your mind at this time?"

"I don't think so," Brent answered calmly. "I put a lot of thought into my decision."

"Such as what?"

Brent had taken the stand with a large manila folder in one hand. He proceeded to open it, saying, "I have some slides—"

If anyone had failed to come to life after that, they certainly did so when Hector Jamiel, who had resumed his chair at the defense table, bounded to his feet shouting, "Permission to approach the bench, Your Honor?"

"I should think so," Judge Mosco said quietly, at the same time firmly rapping for quiet in the courtroom with a single warning bang with his gavel on the bench before him. "We are on the brink of disorder here."

Judge Mosco had leaned forward as the two attorneys stood at the bench. There ensued an anxious buzz of sound from the huddled group. When the attorneys returned to their respective counsel tables Judge Mosco addressed the court.

"I want everybody to have the opportunity to present whatever evidence they think is pertinent to this case," he said decisively. "If I am to resolve this issue, I want to have every piece of evidence possible."

Jamiel stood and objected to the photos being admitted as evidence, saying the defense had not had a pre-hearing opportunity to view whatever material Brent had in the manila folder.

Although Judge Mosco overruled Jamiel, he continued the trial until nine o'clock the following Tuesday morning so that the defense could have Brent's slides viewed by expert witnesses being called on behalf of the insurance companies.

Shaw was then on his feet objecting forcefully. "Your Honor," he flared, "the defense has had ample time in the past eight years since the fire to prepare its case."

"It would seem so, Mr. Shaw," Judge Mosco said soothingly. "But I am going to allow the delay. As I said, I want everybody to have the opportunity to present whatever evidence or argument they think is necessary."

53

At her house in Crowfoot Valley that Saturday morning Winona sat at her kitchen table pampering a cup of coffee and smoking king-sized cigarettes. Fighting an almost overwhelming desire to bolt the liquid down, for her system was responding slowly to an early morning sluggishness, she nervously cradled the cup in both hands. She thought food might be beneficial, but she was not hungry. Although she had gained weight in the years since the fire at the Fielding home, even in that long time she had eaten little. She had lost her desire for food. As she sipped coffee and inhaled deeply the smoke from her fourth or fifth cigarette already that morning, Winona's eyes repeatedly darted toward a bottle of wine sitting on a cabinet top. She had purchased it the previous day on her way home from the hearing. She had yearned to drink some of it that night but she hadn't dared, thinking she wanted to stay sober at least until after the hearing was completed. Between her burning desire for a drink and smoking almost a pack of cigarettes through a fitful night, she was now exhausted and agitated, and she wanted a drink more than ever.

In spite of her craving, Winona knew that she might not be able to stop at one drink. By this time in her life she knew better than anyone that she was an alcoholic. She knew it from her image in her bathroom mirror. "A drunk is a drunk," she would say aloud with each look at her reflection, "and you're a drunk." There was one time after such candor with herself that she had wept violently. But then as soon as she recovered from that emotional outburst, Winona sought out her bottle of wine. One drink would bring appeasement, two drinks assurance. Or so she thought. But from past experience she knew that in time a second drink often needed to be supported by a third, and later a fourth, until drink by drink she eventually would consume the contents of that bottle on the cabinet and then she would go out and buy another. When Tuesday morning came she would be so drunk she might not be able to leave her home. And at the moment she somehow had the presence of mind to believe the hearing was of greater importance to her than her desire for a drink. Could she convince her deep craving of that? Could she survive the entire weekend, the entire recess of the hearing until Tuesday morning, without a drink? She would try. And gulping the last of the coffee she lit another cigarette and refilled her cup. When that was gone she stood up on bare feet and with one eye closed against the smoke curling upwards from a cigarette drooping from a corner of her mouth, she waddled into the bathroom.

At some point in its long life the ancient limestone company quarry shack that had become her home had been renovated and enlarged by one room. All the rooms were sparsely furnished, containing only such pieces of furniture that might be deemed absolutely necessary to assure a modicum of comfort. A brown, cabinet type, propane space heater stood in the living room and was the sole source of heat for the entire house. A small propane cook range in the kitchen doubled as a cook stove and—foolishly, for it was a dangerous practice—on especially cold winter days, as a supplemental heater.

During the renovation process the bathroom, which

replaced the primitive outhouse in the back yard, had been installed in a corner between the third and fourth rooms. It was a small cubicle, just large enough for a shower stall, wash basin, toilet and a thirty-gallon automatic propane water heater.

Disrobing, Winona moved to the small basin. She soaped a washcloth and sponged her face. She was angered and saddened by its puffy appearance. She remembered that not long ago she had been an attractive woman, even pretty in a matronly kind of way. She looked away from her face in the mirror and scrubbed her underarms. While doing so she could not help but notice the expansiveness of her bosom over that earlier time. Fat, she thought. I'm fat. Drying herself on a towel, she then vigorously brushed her teeth. Despite her age and her years of drinking and smoking, plus an insufficient diet, she surprisingly still had her own slightly nicotine-stained teeth. After attending to them, Winona clenched her teeth and parted her lips in what might have passed for a smile. Apparently satisfied with what she saw, she turned away from the mirror and went into her bedroom. There she slipped into a dress, returned to the bathroom mirror and made up her face, and then she set about cleaning house.

She washed floors, she dusted, she re-arranged what few pieces of furniture she owned, she washed the two living room windows. She removed the sheets from her bed and put them into the washing machine in the kitchen. She cleaned the bathroom and scrubbed the toilet. She moved deliberately, quickly, and when she was finished she stepped through the front door and swept the ground-level concrete floor of the small porch. She swept the short concrete walkway that led to the valley's gravel roadway that bordered her tiny yard.

When she was finished she sat down in an old hickory rocking chair in the small living room. She lit another cigarette and thoughtfully puffed on that. Thinking at last that it might be lunchtime she reluctantly began contemplating food. Looking at her wristwatch she was shocked to note that less than two hours had passed. She sighed heavily. She wanted to cry. The weekend would never pass, she told herself. She wanted a drink. She knew that before much more time passed she would be mad with craving. Somehow, in the midst of that irrupting fear, a face appeared in her mind: the face of George Schilling, former state fire marshal, as it had appeared to her on the witness stand on Tuesday, the second day of the hearing.

She saw Schilling, middle-aged, portly, jowly and bald as he answered questions put to him by attorney Hector Jamiel.

"It was a vapor fire," Winona recalled Schilling's words. "We found traces of a flammable liquid at the scene where the body was found."

Under further questioning, Schilling had told the court that before his recent retirement he had spent his entire work life as a firefighter and fire investigator.

"In your opinion, was the fire set?" Jamiel had asked.

"In my opinion, yes," Schilling had replied without hesitation. "There were cans of paint and other inflammables stored near where the body was found, but it is my opinion, based on tests that we performed, the body was saturated with gasoline."

"Was this the only evidence from which you reached your conclusion?"

"No," said Schilling. "There was a ring, presumably found under where the body lay. It was undamaged."

"What kind of ring?"

"A 33rd Degree Masonic ring."

"Should it have been damaged?" asked Jamiel.

"Again, in my opinion, yes," Schilling nodded his head to reinforce his words. "Yes. If it had survived the fire it should have sustained some damage, but it did not. It is also my opinion that had it survived the fire a part of the victim's finger would also have been found attached to it."

As she replayed in her mind those moments of the hearing Winona, seated as she was in the old hickory rocking chair, rocked thoughtfully to and fro. She hadn't liked Schilling's looks. She didn't trust him.

Ames Shaw had tried to discredit Schilling's testimony that the blaze had been set and that the body had been saturated with gasoline, Winona remembered. He had called Schilling's attention to other inflammables stored in the barn and that their containers had exploded due to the excessive heat from the fire.

"One of these containers was a five-gallon gasoline can, and when that accidentally exploded could not the body have been sprayed with gasoline?" Ames asked.

Schilling had attempted a reply. "Yes," he began, "but—"

He got no further than that when Shaw suddenly spun away from the witness and walking toward his seat, shouted, "That will be all!"

Winona wondered why Ames Shaw had not tried to refute the earlier testimony given by state pathologist Dr. John Flood. But she was to learn that Shaw had his reasons.

In an instant replay, Flood's testimony whirled through Winona's mind. As he spoke Winona was aware that Flood was of average height, with black wavy hair, a lock of which curled over his forehead. He was a handsome man, too handsome to be trusted,

Winona thought. In a cloud of cigarette smoke above her head she could see Dr. Flood seated in the witness chair. She could see him open his mouth to speak.

"No," he had affirmed to Hector Jamiel. "It is my opinion that the feet and hands of the victim did not go through the fire. They had been removed from the body before the fire. There were marks on the arms and legs that led me to believe that the hands and feet were cut off—perhaps chopped off."

Jamiel then walked to the defense table and picked up a legal size sheet of paper. Approaching the witness, he held out the paper and said, "This is a deposition signed by Dr. Marie Copeland-Smith. Are you familiar with Dr. Copeland-Smith?"

"I know her only professionally," Flood replied. "She is a professor of anthropology at Southern Union University. She is well known for her work in her field."

"It says here in this deposition that she examined the humerus and femur bones from the dead man and found that some unevenly spaced marks near the charred ends indicated some type of implement had been used to cut the hands and feet from the body. Do you agree with that?"

"I do," Flood answered.

"Then you do not believe that the hands and feet of the victim found in the fire at the Fielding residence were destroyed by the fire?"

"They are missing, but I don't believe they were incinerated," replied Flood.

Ames Shaw had waved a hand indicating he had no questions for the witness, an act on his part that had surprised Winona, she remembered. But Judge Mosco had called a recess for lunch at that moment and, weary and impatient, she had given the matter no more thought. She also had desperately needed to relieve her bladder at that time and had quickly left the courtroom in search of the public restroom.

Winona's rocking came to a stop. She placed her feet squarely on the floor and rose from the chair and made her way back to the kitchen. There she pushed the bottle of wine to a position further back on the cabinet top, out of her way, hopefully out of sight and mind. She then picked up a small jar of instant coffee and put a heaping teaspoonful into her cup. On second thought she added another half-teaspoonful. Turning on the hot water tap at the sink, she allowed the water to get as hot as possible and filled her cup, stirring noisily all the while. There was too much at stake. She would drink coffee until Tuesday, she told herself.

She returned to the small living room and sat once more in the rocking chair, balancing the cup of coffee in her right hand. From her seat she was able to see through the parted curtains of one of the newly washed windows the valley's main gravel road. With hardly any deviation at all it ran straight through Crowfoot Valley. Her eyes followed it almost without interest until they came to rest on the distant mountainous stacks of culled limestone quarry blocks. Winona shuddered at the thought of climbing those huge piles of rubble as so many young people past and present dared. Because she had no desire to see them up close, she had never ventured that far into the valley. She had been told of the graffiti that decorated many of the cast-off blocks. Some of it, she had been told, was quite interesting. But Winona had seen graffiti in much more accessible places than that, and none of it had ever been appealing to her. How could the graffiti painted on the cast-off limestone blocks in the stacks be of more interest?

She also had heard that beyond the stacks, not visible to her from her seat in the rocking chair, was the abandoned quarry hole with its deep blue waters.

Many were the tales she had heard about the secret meetings of couples at that swimming hole, how they swam naked there, and how they coupled shamelessly high above the blue waters in the shadow of the tall stacks. She was never tempted to go and see for herself. Typically she was not titillated by thoughts of sex and what may have been transpiring there. Without having to go and see, she was certain that something furtive was taking place. How many times in the years that she had been living there had she noticed automobiles and pickup trucks passing her home on their way there? How many times had she been awakened by noisy nocturnal trysters on their anxious way to the stacks and the quarry hole?

Remembering the nighttime disruptions reminded her of the peaceful, restful nights at her former home, the home she had shared for so many happy years with Crestman and their two sons, Roger and James. She looked around at the small living room. Surely this was a happy little home at one time for someone, she thought. There once was life here, and joy and loving voices. But no more. There was nothing here now but four walls. For a moment she thought she could actually hear the resonance of vacancy, of abandonment, of disconsolateness. Suddenly her thoughts were of the warm, soft, intimate living room of memory. Winona raised a hand to her chest and placed the flat of it above her ample bosom. There was an ache deep inside her, an emptiness she could feel when she had such thoughts. My home, she thought, my beautiful home. Her eyes suddenly welled with tears and with the heel of her free hand she dabbed and swiped at them.

Suddenly her thoughts were only of her husband. She missed him desperately. From the first day she had seen him at Moses City High School she had been in love with him. From that moment she had been

415

happy with life, with him, with everything he stood for, with everything they had together. Although she had never known the ultimate joy of coition she derived untold pleasure and satisfaction from his nearness. Simply having him warm and snug in his most amorous moments was ecstacy and gratification enough for her. He was her husband and he was a good man and she loved him. How could they have said such things about him at the hearing? Where did they find the witnesses who dared call him a thief and a murderer? How could anyone testify that he was an adulterer, and that he spoke contemptuously of his family? Where did they find these people who said such terrible things about her husband, and that he murdered an old man, dismembered his body, burned it and fled the country? They were wrong. All of them. How could they have uttered such damaging testimony? They were so wrong. She knew Crestman better than anyone. She had shared the same bed with him for more than a quarter of a century. No one knew him as she had known him.

For a long time Winona was without thought and during this period she puffed quietly on her cigarette and urged the rocking chair into faster back and forth movements. At last the undulating motions came to a stop. A low moan escaped Winona's lips accompanied by a mental vision of her husband as she had last seen him with their son Roger the day of the fateful fire. My beautiful Crestman, she thought. It is so unfair. A series of questions ran through her mind. What happened? Why did anything have to happen? Why to me—us? Why?

With those agonizing thoughts came the words of her testimony early in the hearing. "It was a staggering blow when they told me that they had found Crestman dead in the fire," she had told Ames Shaw.

"I didn't know what was going on. The whole world was spinning and I think I fainted. Later, I wanted to cry, but for a while I couldn't cry. It was all so crazy. It's always been on my mind, for all these years. Why me? Why my family? Why can't things be like before? We were a happy family. I wake up nights thinking about it. I used to visit my husband's grave and put flowers on it. I put a flag on it, too. He was a veteran of World War II. But when I'd go back to the cemetery they'd be gone. I don't know who was taking them off. So I just stopped putting flowers out there. I have never put another flag on his grave."

The reminiscence reminded Winona of her two sons from whom she had heard absolutely nothing for a number of years. Then as large as life there appeared in her mind the bottle of wine she had so carelessly pushed out of her sight on the kitchen cabinet top. It would be so easy, she thought, to take one small drink, it would make her feel so much better, and she could then face her situation with courage. Wasn't that what she needed now more than ever, courage? Could she settle for one drink? Would the craving deep inside her be quenched by one small drink? Next Tuesday is such a long time away. Winona's hand trembled as she raised the coffee cup to her parted lips.

54

While that weekend lingered long and fretfully for Winona Fielding, it conversely had brought hours of appreciated rest and relaxation to attorney Ames Shaw. Not because he was totally free of the hearing for that period. On the contrary. There had been times during that weekend when he was completely absorbed with it. Like Winona, he was, in his way, desirous to get on with the hearing. His eagerness, unlike Winona's, however, was not born of fear and trepidation, but more from a readiness to conclude the work at hand.

Where he had begun the proceedings somewhat uncertain of success, given the weight of the unfolding evidence against such an outcome, Shaw now felt much more optimistic. He had replayed in memory almost every detail of the past week a number of times, determining where he might have served his client's cause better, how his arguments had stacked up against those of the defense attorney; his success at bringing to light the depth of dissension among state police investigators, so important to Winona's case.

Shaw felt so good about the progress of the hearing that on Sunday he had played eighteen holes of golf with three attorney friends at the Moses City Country Club. Over drinks in the clubhouse later with one of them, he felt confident enough to answer the man's questions about the hearing. Not only did Shaw feel good enough to do so, the opportunity to talk to someone else about the past week was a relief, and he spoke freely.

Shaw soon was recalling for his friend how he had succeeded in eliminating beyond a reasonable doubt any question about the blood sample taken from the dead man's body found in the Fielding barn fire. That had come in the early hours of the hearing. State police testimony had revealed that a typing of the blood sample done at the state police crime laboratory in Mount Carmel had determined it to be Type AB. This suggested that the blood had been taken from the body of someone other than Fielding. Early in the investigation it was learned by state police from Fielding's records at Glenview Hospital where he had undergone two separate surgeries long before the fire at the Fielding home, that his blood was Type B.

The sample in question had been drawn only hours after the fire by Ira Brown. He had testified that in his estimation the only undamaged place from which a sample could be taken was the dead man's heart. He further testified that he had given it to then Spiceland County Sheriff Cramer Fielding, Crestman Fielding's brother. He said he later learned from Cramer Fielding that the vial containing the blood sample had inadvertently been placed on the sheet metal box cover of a heat radiator at the jail, and had remained there for several days before it was mailed to the state police lab.

To refute that testimony Shaw recounted to his attorney friend that he had called to the stand a forensic expert named Bernie Craton, director of a regional police laboratory in St. Louis, Missouri. Craton was well known all over the country for his work in determining blood samples in police cases.

Shaw remembered his testimony and quoted it verbatim to his friend: "I have found in independent tests on blood taken from victims who were deceased that in two-thirds of the cases results were wrong when tests were conducted after the samples were heated. Very likely tests would result in a finding of Type AB blood in a sample of blood which was actually Type B, which had been subjected to heat of at least 140 degrees for one hour."

"Then," Shaw paraphrased the remainder of the witness's words, "he was not certain how long the sample had been exposed to heat in the sheriff's office, nor could he say how hot they kept that office. But he was sure that the heat of the fire itself was enough to cause a chemical change in that sample while it was still in the victim."

"What did the defense do with that?" Shaw's friend asked.

"It boiled down to the unreliability of a blood sample taken under those circumstances and subjected to possible contamination from exposure to heat as that one was," Shaw replied.

Driving away from the country club Shaw later was well aware of his exhilaration. Talking with his friend had apparently been good for him. Not because he had previously entertained doubts about the direction of the hearing. He had not. The talk with his friend had not been a purgation, either. Shaw didn't feel that he needed any such thing. No. Expressing himself as he had to his friend served more as a reinforcement of his earlier feelings of success.

Shaw was aware that Dr. Brent's testimony on Friday had provided him with the beginnings of that burgeoning sensation of success. Now, he told himself, he was more than anxious for the hearing to resume. At the conclusion of the hearing on Tuesday, perhaps Wednesday at the latest, he thought, he would triumph. How could he not, he asked himself. Obvious police prejudices in the case and the blood sample were strong medicine, he smiled to himself at his choice of euphemism. But, he reassured himself, if they are not enough then Brent's testimony, his slides and photographs will surely prove to be the pivotal point of the hearing.

Shaw slept soundly that night. When morning came he was eager to get to his office. After a week away from his desk he knew he was needed there. He would spend the day there, catching up. He also had some important dictation for the stenographer he shared with his law partners. And they would expect a complete briefing on the events of the hearing. Then he would review his notes for the resumption of testimony on Tuesday.

55

To the untraveled, the name Moses City was deceiv-
ing. It was not a city in the sense that Mount Carmel
was a city. The population of Mount Carmel exceeded a quarter million people. Moses City, on the other
hand, was an oversized town with a population of less
than eight thousand people. Why it was ever designated a city was not known at the time of the Fielding
fire. But it was an old town, founded early in the
state's history surely with the expectation that it
would someday grow into a metropolis.

The Intelligencer, for its size, was a successful news-
paper with a circulation in Moses City, Spiceland and
adjacent counties. Compared to Mount Carmel's
Morning Sun's circulation, which also reached into
Spiceland and surrounding counties, though sparingly,
The Intelligencer was indeed a small-town newspaper.

As police reporter for Moses City's newspaper,
Peter J. Cayne, also covered the courthouse beat.
Because of the size of the town, neither beat, the
police beat nor the courthouse beat, would support a
full-time reporter. Cayne liked it that way. If a
police beat story was of any value he could follow it
from the police blotter through the court to its ultimate conclusion. In a manner of speaking he held a
position of envy on the newspaper, and at the same
time it was a position of respect. If you wanted to
know anything about such stories you went to
Cayne. He kept two files on all of them, one in a file
cabinet alongside his desk, the other in his head. PJ

Cayne, it was said around the newsroom, had all the answers.

On the Saturday morning that Winona was struggling against her craving to take a drink from the bottle of wine on her kitchen cabinet top, Cayne had risen a couple hours before noon and, while seated at the breakfast table, was procrastinating over a second cup of coffee. He had awakened late because he had allowed himself to become involved in a television movie the previous night and had retired well after midnight. He also had drunk two cans of beer. He didn't particularly care for beer, but he thought it helped him sleep better. Sleep was a problem for him. As quickly as his head would touch his pillow it was certain that the events of the day would begin parading through his mind in technicolor. Before long he would be up and seated at the kitchen table puffing on a cigarette, perusing a magazine or a portion of the daily paper he had overlooked. Even the classified ads. That is what had happened the previous night. No sooner had he made himself comfortable in bed than the happenings of the day had crushed down on him, leading him into fitful sleep.

From the very beginning of the Fielding matter, Cayne believed he had the answer to the mystery that would for years surround the identity of the dead man found in the Fielding fire. According to Cayne, the dead man was none other than Crestman Fielding. It was just that simple for him. Fielding had committed suicide. He either deliberately had started the blaze that subsequently destroyed the barn and most of his body, or the fire was accidentally ignited by the self-inflicted shotgun blast that very nearly blew Fielding's head off.

In past conversations with Lieutenant—now Major—Conway, and with troopers Anthony Galiton, Link Trueblood and Harley Oaks, with whom over the years he had become friendly, Cayne had argued from the outset that the dead man could have been none other than Fielding. During the early years of the mystery he also had written features and opinions on the Fielding fire, drawing more on the views of the late Dr. Isaac Berman than on those of police. His sympathy for Winona was obvious in each of the articles. And, ultimately, his employers, colleagues, the paper's subscribers, and almost everyone in Moses City and Spiceland County were aware of Cayne's prejudices in the Fielding matter.

Probably because no one could be sure of the truth, whatever that may have been, Cayne was more or less respected for his honesty and outspoken opinion. However, Conway once had told him that he was insane, and Oaks had suggested that Cayne should have his eyes examined. But there were others who were of the same opinion as Cayne, one of whom was Timothy Melton.

If there had been an inkling of doubt in Cayne's thinking, it was erased early on after he had interviewed Dr. Berman. His opinion was reinforced after reading Dr. Berman's obituary published two months after his death in the *Journal of Anthropology.*

Cayne couldn't remember the entire obituary, but some of it came to mind. "Dr. Berman's interest in human variation led him to collect over 2,000 lantern and 35 mm slides of physical types . . . he traveled to many of the major museums in Europe and the Americas for purposes of studying skeletal series there . . . and he found time to serve as consultant to police departments around the United States in successfully identifying incinerated human remains."

The recollection brought a wry smile to Cayne's lips as he sat at the kitchen table in his home that Saturday morning. This had all been brought out early in the hearing by Ames Shaw. In Cayne's opinion it was evidence enough to decide the case in favor of Winona Fielding, but he immediately found himself wondering on whose side Judge Mosco's decision would come down. There could be no doubt that Dr. Hamilton Brent's testimony when the hearing resumed on Tuesday would make a stronger case for Winona—for her attorney Ames Shaw. Still, Brent was a strange duck, Cayne reminded himself. From the very beginning of the Fielding case, there was no one more convinced nor more convincing than Brent that the dead man was someone other than Fielding. Cayne remembered questioning him about his examination of the dead man early in the investigation.

"Then it is your opinion that the dead man is someone other than Crestman Fielding?"

"Yes."

"Who?"

"I have no idea, but from my examination, and from the scientific tests made on the body, it is my opinion that it has to be someone other than Fielding."

"You're sure?"

"No, I am not."

"Are you familiar with Dr. Isaac Berman's report about the dead man?"

"Yes."

"Are you familiar with his profession, his life's work in successfully identifying skeletal remains, and that he believes the dead man to be Crestman Fielding?"

"Yes."

"Then will you explain why you disagree with Dr. Berman?"

Cayne had tilted his head back and swallowed in a single gulp the coffee remaining in his cup. Placing the cup on the table in front of him, he leaned forward and forced his chair back. As he stood up he shook his head unbelievably at the memory of Brent's answer to that question.

"Well," Cayne remembered Brent's voice coming over the telephone, "it is not unusual for a young professional to disagree with an older professional. It makes the younger professional look good, you know?"

Cayne was perplexed by that answer. Had he heard it right? Yet, when the quote appeared in the story he subsequently had written for *The Intelligencer*, it evoked no comment from readers. And Cayne tucked Brent's words into a corner of his memory. Now, still standing at the kitchen table, he recalled how startled he was on Friday when Brent announced to Judge Mosco and the courtroom at large that he had changed his mind about the identity of the corpse found in the fire of the Fielding barn.

Cayne shrugged as he walked out of the kitchen. "I know what his decision ought to be," he said to himself. "But I sense a premonition—something. I have a bad feeling that this hearing will solve nothing. Nothing, that is, for Winona Fielding."

56

Although Tuesday morning's sunrise was bright with the promise of a beautiful spring day, the air was crisp enough for warm outer clothing. By nine o'clock, however, it became obvious that the sun, unhampered by clouds in an immense blue sky, was intent on heating up the rest of the day. Yet, on opening the main entrance door to the Dogwood County Courthouse, visitors were greeted with the comforting feel and smell of heat from the furnace. It was at this time that the scheduled hearing into the Crestman Fielding matter being conducted in the second floor courtroom was reconvened by Judge Jacob Mosco. Three hours later the hearing was recessed until two o'clock for lunch.

Begging the use of a courthouse telephone line in the county clerk's office, *The Intelligencer* reporter PJ Cayne dialed his newspaper in Moses City. Within thirty minutes, with a re-write person at the other end of the line taking his dictation, he had filed his account of what had transpired at the hearing that morning.

The newspaper's deadline was met soon after lunchtime that afternoon and *The Intelligencer* city and motor route carriers were able to deliver the newspaper to homes in Moses City and Spiceland County on time. Below the break on the paper's front page Cayne's story of the morning's proceedings appeared under a four column headline:

Theory: Fielding Bones
Warped In Fire

HICKORY GROVE—Pathologist Hamilton Brent said today that Crestman Fielding's left clavicle (collar bone) may have been warped by intense heat during the fire that swept the barn at the Fielding home more than eight years ago. Brent reiterated his claim of last Friday that the victim in that fire was Crestman Fielding.

Brent testified before Judge Jacob Mosco that a clavicle bone found at the scene of the fire matches that of x-rays taken of Fielding at Glenview Hospital before he disappeared. Proceedings are being conducted without a jury.

Brent was the first witness called today in the one million six-hundred thousand dollar insurance suit brought by Fielding's wife, Winona. She is asking Judge Mosco to declare her husband legally dead so that she may collect the insurance money plus interest.

Brent testified that he was initially unable to match the clavicle to the Glenview Hospital x-rays of Fielding. But, he added, he later realized the bone would have been altered by a shrinking and contraction of body muscles characteristic of fire victims. The Glenview Hospital pathologist said arms and legs of fire victims contract and assume a pugilistic posture.

Testimony was cut short last Friday when under questioning by plaintiff's attorney Ames Shaw he surprised the hearing by saying he had slides and photographs that he said indicate Fielding was the victim of the fire in the barn at the Fielding home.

Produced at the hearing this morning, the slides included several pictures of x-rays taken of the clavicle of the victim of the fire. Brent said he had made several slides of the clavicle rotated in a number of different positions. The single picture which most closely matched that of Fielding's x-rays taken at Glenview Hospital, Brent said, show at least ten points of similarity when superimposed on a slide screen. On a large screen set up for that purpose in the courtroom, Brent, using a long pointer, indicated each of these similarities.

At the close of his demonstration, Brent startled the hearing and brought shouted objections from Hector Jamiel attorney for the insurance companies when he announced, "If I had been the coroner in this case at the time of the fire at the Fielding place and had been provided with this identical evidence, I would have issued a death certificate in the name of Crestman Fielding and avoided this prolonged investigation and trial."

Judge Mosco banged his gavel several times before the courtroom was restored to order. He overruled the objections and again overruled attorney Jamiel when he repeated an objection he made last Friday, that the defense had not been given an opportunity to review the slides before the hearing and that they should not be admitted as evidence in the case.

A death certificate in Fielding's name had never been issued since no positive identification was ever made of the victim in the fire. An early identification made by Fielding's brother, Cramer Fielding, then sheriff of Spiceland County, now deceased, and by Ira Brown, coroner of Spiceland County, was challenged by state police.

Since then the dead man has been identified only as John Doe.

Testimony produced by the defense last Friday that the missing hands and feet of the dead man were severed from the body by cutting or chopping before the fire was disputed by Brent.

"No, there was no indication of cutting or chopping marks," he told the court. "Those marks on the bones were made when they were boiled, then scraped as part of the cleaning process after the fire. None of the marks on any of the bones are associated with dismemberment."

Fielding, meanwhile, has been indicted by a Spiceland County grand jury on counts of kidnap, murder, arson, forgery, and being a fugitive from justice. At the request of Spiceland Prosecutor Albert Fielding, the grand jury deliberations were immediately sealed by Judge Harrison Alexander of the Spiceland Circuit Court. They remain sealed to this date.

Prosecutor Fielding, a distant relative of Crestman Fielding, has repeatedly declined to explain his action, saying that he was not at liberty to discuss the grand jury investigation nor its revelations. He explained that it is against state law for any officer of the court, judge, clerk, or juror to discuss the deliberations of a grand jury until the defendant has been arrested or otherwise brought within the custody of the court.

If Crestman Fielding is alive, he has been at large for more than eight years. Reports that he has been seen in various cities in other states have not produced positive results. Although state law allows for a presumption of death after a person is missing for more than seven years, the burden of proof of Fielding's death in this case rests with Winona Fielding and her attorney, Judge Mosco said.

Meanwhile, the victim of the fire, whose remains are buried in a grave in the Fielding family plot in the Moses City Memorial Park, has never been identified.

Recessed at noon today for lunch, the hearing was to resume at two o'clock. Thus far, several pieces of evidence on behalf of Winona Fielding's claim against the insurance companies have been presented to Judge Mosco. Although there has been no formal announcement, court observers speculate Mosco would urge attorneys to wrap up remaining testimony this afternoon.

If Judge Mosco had presumed to make such a request, he refrained from doing so that afternoon. Before he decided to do so, the hearing had consumed another week. When it was finally over, a total of twenty different exhibits had been authenticated by the court for Mosco to study. The trial ended on a Thursday. A front page story in the next day's edition of *The Intelligencer* wrapped up the hearing for readers.

HICKORY GROVE— Another page was turned in the unsolved mystery of missing businessman Crestman Fielding at four o'clock Thursday when two weeks of testimony came to a close in Dogwood Circuit Court. Attorneys arguing both sides of a suit brought by Fielding's wife, Winona, against four defendant insurance companies that shared a policy on his life, rested their cases before Judge Jacob Mosco, special judge in the case.

More than eight years of speculation, conjecture, puzzlement and doubt resurfaced during the hearing as attorney Ames Shaw, representing Winona Fielding, attempted to prove her husband died in a barn fire at their home north of Moses City. Mrs. Fielding hopes to claim one million six-hundred thousand dollars plus interest from the insurance firms.

The insurance companies, represented by attorney Hector Jamiel, hold that Mrs. Fielding has no actual proof of her husband's death since only a "John Doe" death certificate was issued in the wake of the fire.

Rather than allow attorneys to make closing arguments, Mosco asked that they immediately file final briefs with his court. He said he hoped to enter a verdict in the case within thirty days after those briefs are filed.

57

At his desk in Moses City on a Friday afternoon three weeks later, Ames Shaw received a telephone call from the Dogwood County Circuit Court reporter. He was requested to appear in the courtroom there at nine o'clock the following Monday morning. Judge Jacob Mosco had reached his decision in the Fielding matter.

After an anxious weekend during which time he rested and slept little, Ames Shaw that Monday morning sat uneasily at the plaintiff's counsel table in the courtroom awaiting the appearance of Judge Mosco. Seated beside him was an obviously nervous and fidgety Winona Fielding. At the defense table, Hector Jamiel sat alone.

Seated with legs crossed in a chair in the front row of the vacant jury box PJ Cayne leafed through a notebook while he also waited. The gallery was empty. After several long minutes, black-robed Judge Mosco climbed the two steps leading up to the bench and seated himself in the squeaky swivel chair.

"Gentlemen," he addressed the two attorneys, "good morning." Then without preamble he got right to the purpose of their meeting. "Mr. Ames, Mr. Jamiel, even though you do not normally practice in my jurisdiction, I have known both of you for some time. I have respected your work, and for two weeks I have been impressed with your professional demeanor in my courtroom. Believe me when I say, I did not relish hearing this case. I would rather have been doing almost anything else. But there are times in our profession when we have no choice in what we must do."

Ames Shaw sensed that Judge Mosco was speaking directly to him. Although he maintained his outward poise, Shaw began involuntarily to shrink within himself. He swallowed nervously, and somewhat noisily, he thought, and he hoped the sound went unnoticed. He concentrated on Judge Mosco's next words.

"I would have been the wrong man for this hearing had I not focused my undivided attention on all the evidence brought before me. And because I did focus my undivided attention on the facts in this matter, I had almost reached a conclusion by the end of the hearing. However, gentlemen, I wanted to be certain, and I thoroughly reviewed several hundred pages of transcripts of the hearing. I have done that. And I find that Winona Fielding's claim that her husband, Crestman Fielding, died in the barn fire at their home has not been proven."

At that moment Winona took in a noisy deep breath and seemed to collapse in her chair. Judge Mosco hesitated long enough for her to compose herself and then looked sharply at Ames Shaw. With a satisfied nod of his head he continued reading.

"And it must be noted, especially in this matter," he looked first at one attorney and then the other, "that when a reasonable hypothesis other than death can be provided for an absence, presumption of death is not raised after seven years."

Directing his next words to Shaw and Winona, he said, "Court costs will be borne by the plaintiff."

Judge Mosco looked up from his reading, and glancing at Jamiel and then at Shaw he said,

"Gentlemen, that is my decision." And rapping his gavel a single time on the bench, he announced, "This hearing is adjourned."

Adjourned. The word rang in Winona's ears like the pealing of a bell. Over and over. Adjourned. Adjourned. It was over. Life was over. The world had come to an end. She tried to stand up but could not move from her chair. Suddenly she did not want to move from it. From a distance she heard someone calling her name. "Winona. Winona. Winona." Could it be Crestman? Crestman calling from his grave? She looked up. It was Ames Shaw. "Winona, it's over," he was saying soothingly yet forcefully. "Winona, it's over."

In PJ Cayne's story that afternoon, those readers of *The Intelligencer* who were interested in the aged case learned of Judge Mosco's decision. They read Ames Shaw's words that he would appeal the decision.

"This lawsuit could continue forever, the way it is going," Shaw was quoted as saying. " I intend to get some justice for Winona Fielding. Maybe not money, but at least getting Crestman Fielding declared dead so she can have some peace of mind."

Shaw confirmed to Cayne that his financial arrangement with Winona called for him to be paid only if she received the insurance monies.

"That's absolutely true," he told the reporter. "But that doesn't have anything to do with my feelings about this case or Winona Fielding. If it did, then I shouldn't be on it. I feel very sorry for her. She hasn't done anything wrong. I want to get her some peace of mind and get her out of this. She obviously is disappointed, particularly the hypothetical part—about her husband not being dead."

Shaw went on to say that the Crestman Fielding hearing had been a prolonged and difficult case to argue. He said he believed he had done as well as anyone might have done in trying to prove that Crestman Fielding was dead.

"But," Cayne quoted him again, "although I respect Judge Mosco and feel no animosity toward him, I disagree with his decision on the proof. However, I will save that argument for the appeal."

In the same article, Cayne quoted Hector Jamiel, the other attorney, as saying, "We felt fairly confident throughout the entire hearing. All the evidence we had at our disposal indicated it was not Crestman Fielding who died in that fire. We were not surprised by the verdict at all."

That night Winona Fielding sat in the rocking chair in the meagerly furnished living room of her house in Crowfoot Valley. She had been sitting in the chair ever since she had returned home that forenoon from the Dogwood County courtroom. Her disappointment had been acute. After hearing Judge Mosco's judgment her mind seemed to close and she was unable to remember anything else. She could not remember leaving the courthouse, nor could she remember the drive back from Hickory Grove to Crowfoot Valley. And for the remainder of that evening she had moved about numbly, mechanically, as in a daze.

On an end table within easy reach was a bottle of wine and a partially filled glass. Although she had been drinking ever since she had arrived home, she could not remember having started. She looked neither to the right nor to the left but stared straight ahead. If she saw anything at all she gave no indication of it. Except for a generally dull countenance, there was no expression on her face.

Living without a telephone since being dispossessed of her own home, she was unable to telephone anyone to share her disappointment or to seek comfort. There was no one to call anyway. Ostracized almost from the beginning of the Fielding family ordeal, she had no friends. There was no one who cared about her or what became of her. By their own choice even her two sons were no longer available to her.

But in this hour of disillusionment, she gave no clue as to what may have been transpiring in her mind. The only suggestion that she may have been thinking at all was the forward and backward motions of the rocking chair, but she may have been unaware even of that. She rocked. Forward and back. Not fast. Not slow. Just a regular, almost floundering dip and rise, her two feet solidly on the floor. Rock, rock, rock. As she rocked the words of Ames Shaw hammered at her dulled brain: "Winona, it's over. Winona, it's over, Winona, it's over." And every so often she reached zombie-like for the glass of wine and took a sip.

The next morning Winona failed to report for work at the Grist Mill Restaurant in Hickory Grove. Having read of Judge Mosco's decision in the previous evening's issue of *The Intelligencer,* owner John Harking, when informed of her absence, was not surprised. Still sympathetic toward her and guessing her intense disappointment, he decided to overlook her failure to report for work. He further told himself that Winona might require a few days to overcome her disappointment. She was an excellent pie baker and a loyal and trusted worker, and worth his consideration. He even weighed the value of visiting her at her home to encourage her to take a few days to work through her pain and bitter frustration, but for some reason he thought better of it. She would return in her own time, he was certain.

Winona did not return to the restaurant. She went

into seclusion in the little house in Crowfoot Valley. She was seldom seen by her neighbors except for the few times she passed in her old Chevy. But because no one cared about her, because she had no friends, no acquaintances, she was unnoticed, inconspicuous.

She remained in seclusion for the remainder of that spring. Toward the end of that summer Ames Shaw learned with disappointment that the appeal was denied. Deciding to inform her in person, rather than by mail, Shaw drove to Crowfoot Valley one sunny afternoon. Arriving at her dwelling, he saw that Winona's old blue and white Chevy was parked almost at the small front porch. He was pleased that she was home. There was no answer to his knock. However, from inside the house there came to him the sounds of what he interpreted to be the loud barking and growling of a large, vicious dog. Guessing that Winona was probably indisposed, while at the same time fearing that the raging animal inside would surely crash through the door and devour him, Shaw thought it best to notify Winona by mail after all, and he left.

A few days after Shaw's experience at her house, the reporter Cayne, hoping to obtain an interview with Winona about the denial of her appeal, was also met with the frightening sounds of barking and snarling coming from behind Winona's door. Determined, to a point, Cayne knocked a second time and called Winona's name. He was to later tell his editor, "I was sure that dog was going to come through the door, and I didn't wait around to see if it would."

Although he was unable to speak with Winona about it, Cayne did write a story about the denied appeal. In it he also speculated that Winona undoubtedly must have saved some of the money she had earned while working at the Grist Mill Restaurant to support herself at this time. Unless the confined dog had eaten her, Winona was alive. To remain so, she had to eat. Her dog had to eat. Crowfoot Valley residents reported to an investigating sheriff's deputy that she had been seen several times driving out of the valley and back to her shack. She looked at no one, spoke to no one, and consequently she was ignored.

In the ensuing weeks Winona was forgotten. The rest of the summer passed. As the days of still another autumn slipped by, Crowfoot Valley slowly changed its appearance. The stands of maple, oak, sassafras, dogwood, redbud, poplar and sumac trees that rimmed the area began changing their dulled verdant colors to hues of red and gold and crimson and russet. Because of the bright colors, the valley became a thing of splendor.

It is doubtful that those who visited the valley for whatever reason ever saw the wonder of fall there. Certainly no one in Moses City ever went there to see that miracle. Many were those who drove past the entrance to the valley on their way to see nature's brilliance of autumn colors in popular Dogwood County.

Except for its early inhabitants, those immigrants who arrived in Crowfoot Valley to a new way of life in a new country, it is debatable if anyone else ever really noticed the valley's autumnal magnificence.

FIRE

58

After watching a college basketball game on television a few nights before Christmas, Sheriff Anthony Galiton and his wife, Jeri, were casually making preparations to retire. Another two months and they were to begin marking their first full winter in the residence attached to the county jail and with a measure of curious expectancy they looked forward to that time. During the game time-outs and at half-time, they had ignored commercials and touched lightly on the subject, coming to no conclusions but just mulling some random thoughts about heat, insulation and the general winter comfort of the quarters.

After taking office the previous January 1, Galiton was in no hurry to move Jeri into the county jail's attached residence. In late February, however, the Galitons had leased their own house, and except for some things they had put in storage, they had moved into the county-owned property.

For a while this late December night, as they took their time moving from the family room and the now silent television set toward their bedroom, the Galitons talked about that. There was no question in Jeri's mind about the winter comforts that their own house afforded. She had lived in it for almost the entire time that her husband had been a state trooper, and now she was telling him that she at least knew that their renters would be comfortable during the approaching winter months. She also was aware that the short time of the current winter they had spent in the jail residence it also had been relatively comfortable. It wasn't home, she was remarking to her husband, but it would be good enough. She was about to add, "For no longer than we plan to live here," but before she could say that the telephone rang. As he moved to answer it Galiton happened to look at a wall clock. It was a half hour from midnight. In the process of picking up the receiver he noted that the call had come through on the jail extension.

"Yes," he spoke into the telephone. He was greeted by the voice of the department's second shift dispatcher. "We have a report of an explosion and fire in Crowfoot Valley, Sheriff," the woman informed him. "Fire trucks have been dispatched and we have dispatched one of our units. Thought you should know."

As she was speaking Galiton already could hear the wail of sirens. "Of course," he told the dispatcher. "Thank you." He was about to hang up the receiver when a thought struck him and he had a sudden change of mind. "Have another unit pick me up in front of the jail," he said sharply, "I'll be right over there."

With a brief explanation to Jeri while he was shrugging into his uniform mackinaw, Galiton grabbed his uniform winter hat and bolted for the connecting door between the sheriff's residence and the sheriff's office and jail area. Minutes later he was riding as a passenger in a sheriff's department car, red lights flashing, siren piercing the night.

"This is not my first fire in Crowfoot Valley," he remarked to the deputy driving the car. "I hope this is not a repeat of that other one."

The deputy, a young man, apparently had no knowledge of the fatal fire of nearly two decades earlier that had taken the lives of four children that Galiton was talking about. So he made no reply. As the deputy quietly continued giving his attention to his driving, Galiton's mind whirled back over the years to that other fire in Crowfoot Valley. It was nearing Christmas then, too. He saw himself, a rookie state policeman, racing toward the valley in a state police car. He saw again the black smoke rising on the suppertime horizon. Spiceland County Deputy Sheriff Henry Carter came into his mind's view, waving his arms. The flaming shack filled Galiton's memory. He felt the heat from it, saw again the blackened bodies of the little children. The recollection caused Galiton to cough nervously and strain at the seat belt to improve his sitting position; his breathing seemed suddenly to be impaired.

He tried to wipe that picture from his mind. But there were others. Some of the most unforgettable experiences of his life were Crowfoot Valley–related. Now they fulminated in a jumble of trepidation and conscience. He didn't need them, he thought. He could live without them. But they persisted. He saw again the bodies of the dead children, burned and roasted. He again felt the intense heat that had driven him back in cold fear for his life, the hot, choking heat that had seared his throat and kept him from breathing. Suddenly the blaze in his mind was thankfully extinguished. In its place lay Breezy, on the ground in the shadow of the stacks.

Galiton tried to push that picture out of his mind. This was not the first time Breezy had appeared there as he approached the valley. His effort was in vain. Breezy stayed in his mind. He growled at himself; he didn't need to be thinking of her. And for the briefest of moments his mind was clear of her. But then she appeared again, this time on the posh front seat of her big Lincoln automobile parked in Crowfoot Valley near the stacks one night, her trembling hands working at his belt buckle.

"My God," he groaned to himself. "Why—?"

Whatever his silent question might have been, it did not materialize, for his thoughts were interrupted by the voice of his deputy.

"God!"

Galiton looked through the windshield. In the headlights of the car and the flashing lights of fire trucks and other emergency vehicles, he saw what was left of a valley dwelling. It apparently had been burning so fiercely before firemen had arrived that it had crumbled in on itself and was now a large pile of burning, smoking debris. The heat from it was so intense even in the cold of a December night it was impossible to approach, and wisely from a safe distance firemen poured untold gallons of water on it. The sheriff of Spiceland County remained seated in the warm patrol car while his deputy went to learn what he could about the fire. When the man returned he approached the car on the passenger side. Galiton rolled down the window.

"Our guys checked at a couple of houses and were told about a big explosion," the man began. "People said when they went out to look the house was a big ball of fire. Said they couldn't do anything about it."

"Anybody inside?" Galiton asked hesitantly.

"Don't know," the deputy replied. "But an old car parked near the house was destroyed."

At that moment a figure in a yellow fire coat and white helmet appeared in the glare of the patrol car's headlights and Galiton recognized Moses City Fire Chief Ott Caswell.

"Hi Sheriff," he touched the brim of his helmet.

"Anyone in there?" Galiton asked.

"Afraid so, Sheriff," Caswell's voice sounded hoarse

and he was breathing noisily as though he had been under some physical strain. "It's still too hot to be sure." The fire chief had both hands on the car's window frame and was leaning toward the seated Galiton. "From what we have been able to see, it looks like there may be a body in what was a bed. We should know more before too much longer."

As though he was finished speaking and would return to his duties, Caswell had straightened and turned away from Galiton. Then he suddenly whirled around and bent down again.

"One other thing, Sheriff," he growled. "There's an awful stench of gasoline coming from that mess. The people around here say they heard a big bang before they saw the flames."

Another sheriff's deputy appeared.

"Checked at a couple houses and learned that an old woman lived there by herself with her dog," he told Galiton. "I have a name, a possible ID on the person who lived there. The neighbors are not very talkative, but they think it was an old woman by the name of Fielding."

Galiton was incredulous. Winona Fielding? The name whirled around in his brain. Is this the way it was to end? Winona dead in yet another fire? Was it possible then that the burning, smoking pile of debris had been her home? What kind of final trick had fate played on her? Galiton was unable to think further. He didn't want to think further.

59

In what probably was its best read story of the year, the next day's edition of *The Intelligencer* carried a complete account of the previous night's fire in Crowfoot Valley. Beginning with a page-wide, large bold-faced double headline, most of the newspaper's front page was devoted to a report of the blaze.

Readers were shocked to read in the headline that not only was Winona Fielding believed to be a victim of a conflagration that had destroyed her Crowfoot Valley home, but that a second body found that morning in the charred ruins was believed to be that of her missing husband Crestman Fielding. Under the byline of PJ Cayne, the lead story began:

> An explosion and raging blaze in Crowfoot Valley last night destroyed the home of Winona Fielding and is believed to have taken her life.
>
> Authorities said that a second body found in the debris this morning may be that of her husband, long-missing Crestman Fielding.
>
> Spiceland County Sheriff Anthony Galiton said this morning that he is almost certain the bodies are those of the Fieldings. Both bodies were burned beyond recognition, he said. An autopsy of the remains was scheduled for some time today by pathologist Hamilton Brent at Glenview Hospital.
>
> A report of the fire was received at the Moses City Fire Department headquarters at about 11:30 p.m. According to fire chief Ott Caswell, the small shelter that was Winona Fielding's home for several years was engulfed in flames when firefighters arrived on the scene.

"It was burning fiercely," Caswell told investigators from the sheriff's office and state police. "We couldn't do anything but pour water on it."

Caswell told Sheriff Galiton that he believed the destructive blaze was aided by some kind of accelerant, probably gasoline. He said the odor of gasoline was very strong during the blaze. Although a blackened and ruptured five gallon gasoline can was found in the rubble of the blaze this morning, Caswell said he could not be sure if that particular container had any bearing on the fire. The can has been sent to the state police crime lab at Mount Carmel for examination, he said.

Sifting through the rubble this morning firemen collected several empty bottles believed to have once contained wine and, it was presumed, vodka. Several empty large plastic bottles, twisted and melted by the blaze, were also found. These were believed to have contained a soft drink.

State and county police officials at the scene early this morning declined to speculate on the cause of the fire and if it had been deliberately set. Neither would they comment on the possibility that both victims had been under the influence when they were overcome by smoke and died. Fire department investigators plan a complete probe into the blackened and charred rubble as soon as it cools enough, Caswell said.

Although both bodies were burned beyond recognition, police said one body was that of a female, leading investigators to speculate it was the body of Winona Fielding. The other body was that of a male.

Meanwhile, a state police spokesman said he planned to confer with Sheriff Galiton about the possibility of the second body being that of Crestman Fielding. He has been missing ever since a late autumn fire about nine years ago destroyed a barn at the former Fielding home. A badly burned body was also found in that blaze and it also was initially identified as being that of the missing Crestman Fielding.

Firemen were still pouring water on the fire at two o'clock this morning. It was not until after daybreak that they could recover what was believed to be

Winona Fielding's body. It was found lying face up on the remains of a bed in a middle room of the house, in an area believed to have been a bedroom next to the living room.

Discovery of the second body was unexpected. It was not found until later in the morning when firefighters were directing a stream of water toward a secondary blaze that had erupted in the back bedroom of the small house. According to Chief Caswell, the body was lying face down in debris and had been almost totally incinerated by the blaze. Caswell added that the odor of gasoline this morning was still strong amid the fire rubble.

Until the second body was found it was believed that Winona Fielding lived alone in the house. She was known to have had a large black and white long-haired dog living with her but firemen were unable to locate the animal's body.

Cayne's story continued with a full recounting of the fire more than nine years earlier that had destroyed the barn at the Fielding home and the long police investigation into the disappearance of Crestman Fielding. In a sidebar story, Cayne reviewed the hearing requested by Winona the previous May in which she sought to have Fielding declared legally dead.

Readers of *The Intelligencer*, having lost interest in the Fielding case, apparently were caught up in the new mystery, and every available copy of that day's edition of the paper was sold out by supper time that evening. Much like the fire that had reduced to ashes the barn at the Fielding home, this one had also proved of great interest to the residents of Moses City and Spiceland County.

Uppermost in the minds of readers that evening was the question of the identity of the man who had died with Winona. Was it her husband? A companion? A lover? Those who had known Winona in earlier days were quick to discount the lover theory. Some stranger? The empty wine and vodka bottles and the empty soft drink bottles found in the ashes suggested that the victims had been drinking heavily before the fire. Could they have been drunk, and later accidentally been overcome by smoke and subsequently perished?

Could they have been murdered? What else would the thick odor of gasoline and the blackened empty gasoline can and the raging blaze suggest?

Arson?

Murder?

Had a third person spent the evening drinking with the pair and when the two were sufficiently inebriated had poured gasoline over them and the shack and ignited the raging blaze?

Perhaps.

But who could that third person have been?

And why?

There had been a rumor, but it was thought by authorities to be of no consequence. Or was it? A state conservation officer making a routine check of the wild goose population at the abandoned quarry hole in Crowfoot Valley two months earlier had reported seeing a strange man entering what he thought was Winona Fielding's house. In response to that report state police for a time watched Winona's house hoping to identify the man. Except for Winona they reported seeing no one enter or leave the place.

Was it an itinerant stranger, then, who had unintentionally died or was murdered with Winona? Another Felix Dombriewski?

Was it her missing husband, Crestman Fielding?

Or was he already dead?

There were those readers of the day's newspaper

who believed Crestman Fielding was indeed a fugitive from justice and after having been missing for years had come back to visit his wife only to become   an unwitting victim of the mysterious blaze that destroyed her and her home.

There also were those few people who believed just as strongly that Crestman Fielding was dead and had been dead ever since the fire at the Fielding home more than nine years prior to this latest mysterious blaze.

Only the previous spring, pathologist Dr. Hamilton Brent had presented, at the hearing to have Fielding declared legally dead, evidence of bone structure sufficient to lead him to believe that Fielding was dead and was buried in a grave in the Fielding plot in Moses City Memorial Park.

As happened nine years earlier, Moses City and Spiceland County on this night had much to puzzle over.

EPILOGUE

60

Could it be that still another fatal fire was to write the last chapter of the Fielding enigma? What strange twist of fate could have led to such an incredible ending? By some unthinkable irony did Winona and her missing husband die together? Two days after this latest blaze these official disclosures appeared in the columns of *The Intelligencer's* front page.

Under another glaring bold-faced headline, the newspaper carried the autopsy results on the two bodies as reported by pathologist Dr. Hamilton Brent. He announced that blood samples taken from the hearts of the two victims had revealed exceptionally high alcohol content. Both probably had drunk enough intoxicants to have rendered themselves unconscious before the fire, he said.

He further stated that without the slightest doubt the two had died of smoke inhalation and that the bodily remains and the jewelry found on the dead female, including a wedding ring with her first name inscribed on its inner surface, unquestionably were those of Winona Fielding. He also asserted that it was his opinion that the man who died in the fire with Winona could have been no one else but her missing husband, Crestman Fielding.

Brent added that although there was no jewelry on the male victim, he had made his determination on the basis of x-rays taken of Crestman Fielding at Glenview Hospital during the man's illness of a previous time. He also said that he could find no evidence on the remains or in the bone structure of the victims that would have indicated foul play, and that it was his opinion that both the man and the woman were so overcome with drink at the time of the fire they were unable to help themselves.

"Their blood alcohol content was so high they probably had drunk themselves into unconsciousness and more than likely were unaware that they were being overcome by smoke," he was quoted as saying.

While those findings may have been acceptable to most people, what left some other readers of the newspaper story wondering was Brent's identity of the male victim. Only a few months earlier, while testifying under oath at the hearing to have Crestman Fielding declared legally dead, Brent had attested that Fielding already was dead. He had declared the body found in the barn fire at the fashionable Fielding home was, in his opinion, that of the missing Fielding. Brent had also testified that, had he been the coroner in the case at that time, he would have issued a death certificate in the name of Crestman Fielding.

Brent's change of mind, his second such in the Fielding investigation, surprised and dismayed some readers. Eager to close the Fielding investigation police authorities were satisfied with his newest decision.

But for those who found Brent's change of mind ambiguous, a state of uncertainty and an aura of mystery, if not evil, still surrounded the Fielding case. If Brent's decision was to be considered conclusive, they wondered, who, then, was the dead man found in the initial fire, the dead man who at first was identified as Crestman Fielding?

Those most outspokenly perturbed and angered at Brent's latest reversal were the two sons of Crestman and Winona Fielding. Roger and James Fielding arrived in Moses City together to claim the remains of their mother. But only their mother's. They were adamant in their refusal to accept those of the dead man identified by Brent as those of their father.

"Our father has been dead for more than nine years," Roger Fielding informed Sheriff Galiton. "He's buried in our family's cemetery plot here in Moses City. There is a government plaque on his grave with his name on it. We refuse to accept the remains of this other man. He is not our father."

Roger and James had then arranged with Brown & Brown Funeral Home for their mother's body to be cremated and her ashes buried at the foot of the same grave with the dead man whom Winona had always believed to be her husband, the dead man her sons believed to be their father; the same dead man officially identified as "John Doe."

This left authorities wrestling with the question of what to do with the small pasteboard box that contained the cremated remains identified as being those of Crestman Fielding. Unclaimed, it stayed on a tool shelf in the funeral home garage until after the deaths of both Browns some years later. In the end the small box with its pitiful contents of powdered and fragmented white bones was taken to Crowfoot Valley where the man had perished, and buried in a small hole in the ground in the little cemetery there. Although county records identify the occupant of that grave to be Crestman Fielding, no marker bearing his name was ever installed at the site.

For the record, the Crestman Fielding matter was officially closed. However, almost a half century later it is not unusual to hear in Moses City or Spiceland County a lingering sour note about the on again–off again police investigation of the case, and about Dr.

Brent's changing decisions. There are still those who also express disbelief at the Fielding investigation's hurried, last-minute pre-Christmas final outcome.

Down through the years no one seemed interested in re-opening the investigation to at least determine the identity of the so-called "mystery man," the dead man once believed to be Crestman Fielding and later said to be the itinerant house painter Felix Dombriewski. He officially is a nobody and, sadly, under the name "John Doe", will apparently continue so throughout eternity.

Legally and ironically the ashes of Winona Fielding share a grave in Moses City Memorial Park with this mysterious stranger. What was left of her officially pronounced husband's incinerated body lies in an unmarked grave in the little abandoned cemetery in Crowfoot Valley in the company of other outcasts. Among them the long-forgotten Tin Cup Dooley, the woman called Poopy, Dink and Grass Sack Sally, and Peg Leg Hill. Unmarked by tombstones, untended and ignored by the living, their graves these many years later are grown over and lost forever.

The valley as it once was is no more; in its place grows a wilderness of broom sage. The gravel road, now weed infested, still leads to the abandoned limestone quarry hole. And still today its clear blue water challenges the unmindful, adventurous youth of Moses City and Spiceland County. The stacks of cast-off limestone quarry blocks still tower there as foreboding memorials to the all but forgotten events of a place once known as Crowfoot Valley.

Other books by Larry Incollingo:

Merry-Go-Round
Festival
The Cottonwood Tree
The Wind Chime Tales
The Tin Can Man
ECHOES of Journeys Past
Ol' Sam Payton
Precious Rascal
G'bye My Honey
Laughing All The Way

For more information write Larry Incollingo at
3949 S. Knightridge Road
Bloomington, IN 47   9747

Telephone 812-336-8403
Fax 812-336-8599
E-mail larryi@kiva.net

SEND A GIFT COPY TO A LOVED ONE OR FRIEND